The Elementals

The Elementals

Abby Lattanzio

CURIOUS CURLS PUBLISHING

Curious Curls Publishing
CuriousCurlsPublishing.com
@CuriousCurlsPub

Lattanzio, Abby.
The Elementals / Abby Lattanzio.
ISBN 978-1-958373-04-0 (paperback)
Print: May 2023

Cover Illustrations by Grace Toscano
Map Illustration by Teresa Wiles

For Mom. I know you would be proud.

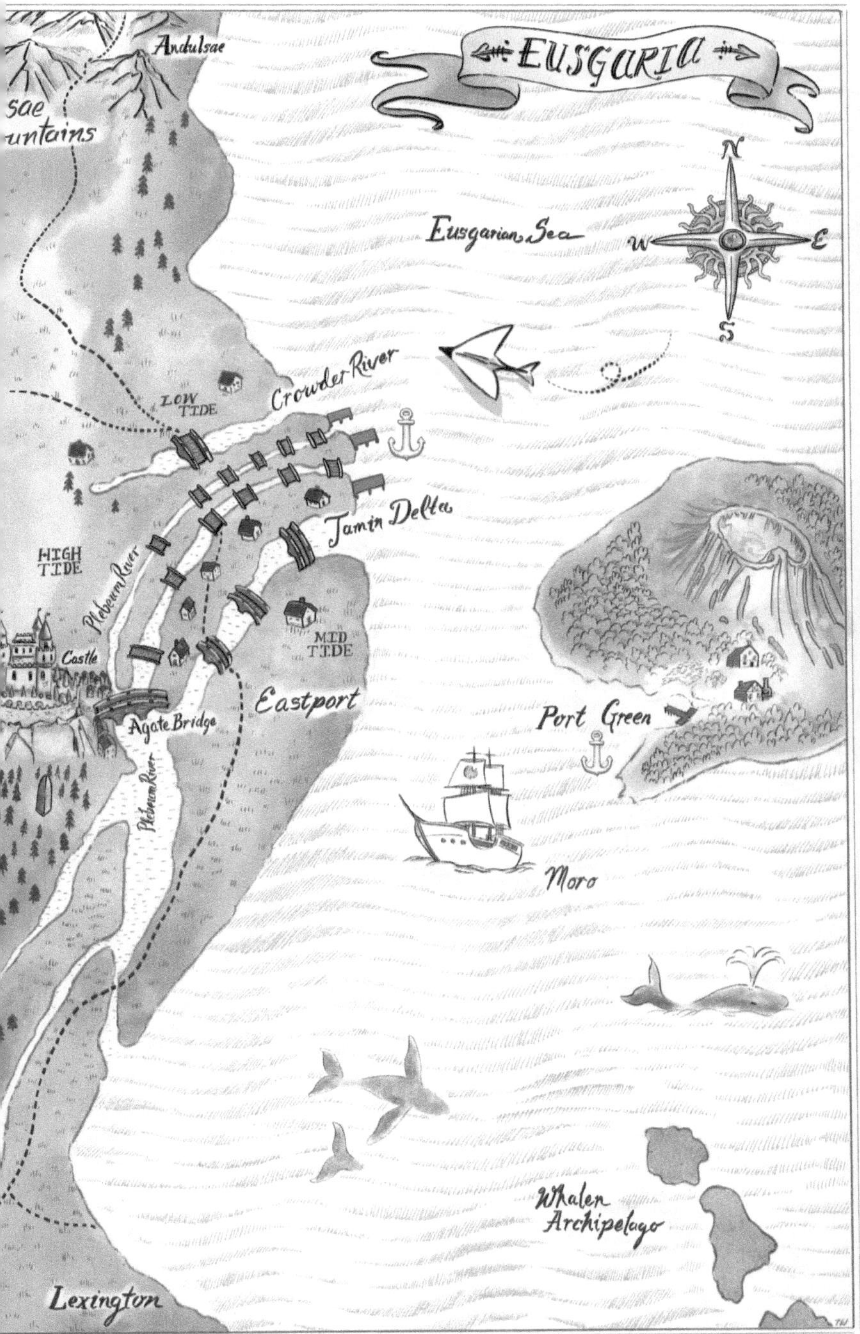

EUSGARIA
Andulsae
sae untains
Eusgarian Sea
N
W
E
S
Crowder River
LOW TIDE
Tamin Delta
HIGH TIDE
Plebeum River
Castle
MID TIDE
Eastport
Agate Bridge
Plebeum River
Port Green
Moro
Lexington
Whalen Archipelago

1

n the east, out over the harbor, the night slowly began to release its hold on the sky. The black curtain that enveloped the kingdom of Eastport sleepily lightened to gray, allowing the sun to reclaim the land. The awakening rays of light stretched out, brushing their long fingers over the city. Beginning at the docks, the rays tickled the waves lapping gently against pillars and wharves, continuing up to the warehouses and whorehouses lining the shore. A few late-night revelers shielded their eyes from the bright intrusion as they scurried home before their wives and husbands awoke to empty beds.

The sun wandered up dark alleys, illuminating all the sordid corners of the business district, surrounded as it was by the fingers of the Jamin Delta, severing this part of Eastport into several crowded islands. The business district was separated from the shanties and diminutive huts, in which most of the city's hardworking men and women lived, by the River Yessop, accessible only by the Crowder's Bridge. On this bridge, the castle guard, known to the public as the Wardens, were stationed night and day to prevent lower class intrusion into the upper echelons a mere mile away. The sun started her day here, for she believed rays of happiness could be found in even the most desolate of places if one only looked.

She danced over the business district, alighting on the square, grazing the taverns, tailors, cobblers, and other various merchants that crowded the narrow probe of land nearest the castle. She passed bakers kneading the day's dough and lamplighters snuffing out the now useless streetlamps with long poles. She almost reveled in the square, excited for the prospect of mingling bodies exchanging ideas and goods. But alas, she must continue her rise. Climbing the Agate Bridge, the longest bridge in Eastport, the sun resumed her waking probe. She caressed several massive obelisks made of pure eusgare ore, mined from the Mersae Mountains to the north, the forbidding facades quickly absorbing her brilliance in their murky obsidian depths. These silent sentinels dotted the street corners of the nobles' estates, clustering closer as they marched toward the castle. She shivered as she moved up to the roofs of noblemen's sturdy mansions, twinkling along copper weathervanes, rising higher with each one as the mansions grew bigger and grander closer to the castle. Try as she might, though, she could not penetrate the woods near the castle, where a stone monument with odd symbols stood waiting, a reminder of those who once owned this land.

Finally, the sun alighted the castle's three towers, showering each one in gold, like radiant lighthouses declaring for all to see the might of Eastport. Creeping through the east wing's windows, she dappled along the face of young Prince Jonathon Montavalo, crowning his blond hair in an ethereal light.

With an eager smile, Prince Jonathon bounded out of his overly large bed as quietly as he could, so as to not wake his little brother, Prince Joseph, in the bed opposite. Running to the tall, narrow window, he pushed aside the heavy forest green curtain with two hands, released the window lock to open it a crack, and pressed his face out to greet the day. Closing his eyes, Jonathon sighed in the sun's warmth then ran across the room to his door, wincing as it squeaked open. Turning quickly, he saw that his brother did not stir from slumber. Prince Jonathon smiled and raced down the hall, bare feet making no noise on the green-and-blue-patterned rug lining the hallway. Tiptoeing past his older brothers' room, he put on a burst of speed and turned right at the end of the hall. He flew down the servant stairs to the main entrance hall and took the final right off the entrance hall to the library where he knew his mother would be waiting for him. It was their tradition once a week to greet the sunrise together. Having three brothers, he found the early mornings were the only times he could have his mother all to himself.

And today he was excited to tell her all about the game he and Prince Joseph invented. They started playing it yesterday in the gardens, a game of skill in which one brother must create and maintain a disc of his element while the other tried to destroy it. Prince Jonathon was far superior at the game than Joseph was, as he had more practice with using his powers, but he let Joseph win every now and then because he loved to see the excitement on his little brother's face when he smashed Jonathon's rock disc. They had spent hours terrorizing the gardeners with the game, earning both good-natured annoyance and downright hostility from various staff as they tried to avoid the two small blond princes.

Prince Jonathon slowed as he approached the library, hearing voices inside. Silently, he crept to the slightly open mahogany door and poked his head around, something urging him not to be seen. The owners of the voices were not in sight. Crouching, Jonathon slithered inside along the left wall, running his hand atop the old tomes that resided on the shelves. He followed the wall until it ended, then ducked to the right, slinking from chair to chair that lined the floor-to-ceiling windows, the castle gardens just on the other side. Soon, he came to the free-standing shelves containing the histories of the kingdom of Eastport. He shimmied his back against his favorite shelf, housing fairytales of the old elementals that lived in Eastport hundreds of years ago before humans came, back when Eastport was still called Esdaria.

The voices were louder here, one gruff and deep. The other he recognized as the high, nasal pitch of his uncle, Magistrate Rufus Montavalo. Prince Jonathon peered around the end of the shelf and saw his uncle in quiet discussion with the Head Chemist, Gregor Stephane. They were huddled against the back wall beside a painting of Jonathon's grandfather, King Rupert, Eastport's previous king. Head Chemist Gregor always unnerved Jonathon. The man was tall and imposing, with a completely bald head and muscles more natural on the Wardens than a chemist. Gregor towered over Prince Jonathon's uncle, a diminutive man with ear-length gray hair even though he was not yet forty years old. Magistrate Rufus was thin, much like Jonathon himself, and had a long, straight nose, a contrast to the prince's small, rounded one.

Prince Jonathon strained to hear their discussion, but instead, the shuffling of slippers on carpet caused him to turn toward the library door where his mother, Queen Valencia Montavalo, had just entered. He noticed his uncle and Gregor fall immediately silent as he quickly turned back to them. Magistrate Rufus pressed a finger to his lips and pulled on the frame of King Rupert's painting, swinging it soundlessly outward. Gregor slipped away down the passage unseen by Queen Valencia. Rufus closed the painting and stepped out to approach the sunlit chairs by the windows, pretending to gaze out over the gardens at the new day dawning.

Queen Valencia smiled wearily at her brother as she sat in her favorite chair. Rufus, his face like granite, came and sat beside her. He upturned two cups from a small table laid out between them for morning tea.

"It's getting worse every day, Rufus," Queen Valencia sighed. "More fights are breaking out between citizens and the Wardens because of your obelisks. Those things create more trouble than not. We should have never installed them. We should get rid of them," Valencia looked sharply at her brother, "as a sign of good faith." She fussily pushed straggling strands of chestnut hair behind her ears. Her brother had asked her to tea this morning, a rare gesture from him, and she had left her chambers before the maids had a chance to come in and dress her. They would be appalled at the state of her bedhead, but Queen Valencia had felt the distance between her and her brother Rufus grow wider each year, so when she received his invitation to morning tea, she jumped at the request. She was hoping to meet with him early enough that they could repair some of the strain that had developed after she took over as ruler of Eastport once their father, King Rupert, had passed. Queen Valencia knew that Rufus had coveted the throne, but, as she was older, it was rightfully hers.

"The obelisks are a necessary evil," Magistrate Rufus replied, his face emotionless as he poured a cup of tea out of an ornate midnight blue and silver-dappled teapot.

"A necessary evil? What purpose do they serve? They send the wrong message, that elementals aren't welcome here in Eastport." Queen Valencia gratefully accepted the cup Rufus held out to her. While she was happy to meet with her brother, she could already feel a headache pinching the sides of her temples as she realized that this meeting would be more of Rufus complaining about elementals. Ever since Chief Andulssan and his son, Nils, came to discuss peace fifteen years ago, all Rufus would talk about was how elementals would be Eastport's downfall. Queen Valencia never saw the reasoning behind her brother's sentiments, sometimes catching Rufus staring enviously at Nils as the king demonstrated his powers to Valencia.

"I think we need to rethink our policy on welcoming elementals," stated the Magistrate bluntly, snapping Queen Valencia back to the present.

"Rufus!" Queen Valencia exclaimed. "Elementals have lived here for years! This was originally their land! The peace treaty was signed fifteen years ago. And yet, it is still only in these past few years that elementals have actually been accepted in Eastport instead of spat upon. Your own nephews are elementals. How can you be that callous?" She shook her head and looked out at the shining new day. In the gardens, she could see patches of earth dug up and broken rocks strewn about the flower beds. Smiling to herself, she remembered the gardeners grumbling to her yesterday about the mess her two youngest sons had made. Queen Valencia assured the gardeners that she would speak with the small princes, but she actually wanted to speak with their father, King Consort Nils. While she was supportive of him teaching their two older boys about their elemental roots, she felt Nils was neglecting Jonathon and Joseph. Stepping out into the garden to play with his youngest sons, instead of being cooped up indoors discussing history and politics, would do him some good.

"I don't know where we went wrong," Queen Valencia lamented. "Ever since Father died, the peace we had achieved with the elementals has been chipped away."

"Marrying an elemental and bearing his children is not peace," Magistrate Rufus glared pointedly at her over the cup he brought up to his mouth. "Especially marrying *that* elemental."

Queen Valencia frowned at her brother. "The treaty between our peoples was already in place. I married him for love. Something which you will never know." Her face softened as she saw her brother's confused look. "We will make arrangements to meet up with my father-in-law, Chief Markas of Andulsae. Ensure that the treaty between our two kingdoms is in no danger of being broken. That humans and elementals have nothing to fear from one another, and that the strife among the citizens and the Wardens will resolve. And we will remove those obelisks at once." She looked sternly at Rufus.

His jaw clenched and a look of pure loathing flitted quickly across his face before dissolving into something more placating.

"You know I don't always agree with your decisions, but alas, you are queen, and I am simply the Magistrate." Queen Valencia opened her mouth to retort, but her brother held up a hand.

"Dear Sister, I wish not to fight with you about this anymore. Your word is rule, so it will be as you say. Perhaps you can put all this negativity aside and join me for a cup of tea? I had it brought with the intention of sharing breakfast with you today."

"How very unlike you," she teased. "But I'm glad that we are reconnecting. It's been lonely without you. I mean, we both live here in the castle, but ever since your nephews were born, it's like you've been avoiding me. I can't even remember the last time we truly sat down and talked together."

"The court keeps me busy. What seems to you as avoidance is simply me performing my duties." Her brother grimaced as he raised his cup to his mouth once more. "But I'm here now." Queen Valencia rolled her eyes but accepted his offering with a grateful smile, raised her own cup, and took an invigorating drink.

Sighing with contentment, she leaned back in her chair a moment before her brows furrowed in confusion. Suddenly, the cup toppled from her grasp as she clutched at her throat. Falling to her knees, she clawed at her brother's crimson robe, silently imploring him to help. Rufus stared down at her, flicking her hands off his robe with disgust. Her mouth opened in utter surprise as she struggled for air. Finally, she dropped to the floor and moved no more. In a matter of mere minutes, Queen Valencia was dead.

Behind the shelf, Jonathon gasped, staring into his mother's glassy eyes, trying to comprehend what he had just witnessed. Surely it was a mistake. His mother would get up and run to him, saying it was all a joke. Perhaps she just fainted, and his uncle would soon call out for a servant to get the physician.

Hearing Prince Jonathon's gasp, Magistrate Rufus whirled around, searching for the source of the sound. His eyes roved the room, going from wooden shelf to wooden shelf before he noticed a slight movement behind the row of fairytales. Seeing his nephew, he took a step forward, hand out as if he could grab the boy. Quickly, Jonathon jumped up from his crouch and sprinted past his uncle out the library door. He raced as fast as he could, hoping against hope that his uncle wasn't following, that his mother would get up, that maybe this was all a terribly bad dream.

Magistrate Rufus stopped at the entrance to the library, torn, his knuckles turning white as he gripped the mahogany door. There wasn't supposed to be anyone around. That's why he requested such an early meeting. How dare his nephew interrupt his plans? But the boy was young, susceptible. A devilish grin spread from cheek to cheek. No, the boy wouldn't tell anyone. Rufus would make sure of that. He strode from the library and down the hall, crimson robes trailing behind, a new plan already forming of how to break the terrible news of Queen Valencia's untimely passing.

Back in the library, the risen sun shone cautiously through the immense windows and onto the dead queen's face, offering what little warmth it could to her now cold form.

*	*	*	*

Sprinting back to the entrance hall, Prince Jonathon pushed past servants who were going about their daily routines, causing more than one to almost drop fresh linens or breakfast trays. He rushed up the center stairs toward the throne room, looking for his father. Accidentally stepping on the foot of a valet exiting the throne room, he burst inside. Jonathon frantically searched for his father, King Consort Nils, but did not find him among the colorful tapestries depicting Eastport's history. Nor did he find King Nils among the prim noblemen and noblewomen waiting for an audience with Queen Valencia. Several nobles scoffed at his sudden arrival and disheveled appearance, but Jonathon didn't care. He needed to find his father, fast.

Backing into the upstairs hall, he ran in the direction of the council room, knocking into his older brother, Prince Jordan, who was coming up the servant stairs from the kitchens below with a pastry in his mouth. Jordan began to say something, but Jonathon didn't have time to stop. He burst past two Wardens guarding the door and into the council room to find his father and oldest brother, Prince Jacob, bent over the large council table made of deep red wood, intently studying a map of the kingdom. Several of the queen's councilors were mingling about the room, placing books and scrolls on the table and offering pointers to Prince Jacob as he studied.

King Consort Nils brought a small, round object out from his vest pocket and placed it on the table in front of Jacob.

"Jacob, now that you are twelve years of age, it's time that I showed you a cherished object from my homeland." Nils pointed to the opalescent orb before them. No bigger than a marble, it pulsed with a spectral blue light. Jacob carefully reached out to touch the orb, but Nils snatched it away, moving it to rest on the northern most part of the map.

"What part of Eusgaria is this orb sitting on?" King Consort Nils asked his son.

Jacob rolled his eyes. "Challenge me a little, Father. That is Andulsae, the largest village in the Mersae Mountains, where Chief Markas Andulssan rules over all the elemental tribes of the Mersae. He's also my grandfather," Jacob dutifully replied.

"Very good!" Nils beamed at his eldest son. Jacob absorbed everything Nils taught him like a sponge. "And how many tribes live in the Mersae Mountains?"

"There are twelve tribes scattered throughout the mountains. After Andulsae, the second largest village is Srandule, followed by Kraska. The remaining tribes live in small, nomadic villages that travel with the mammoth migrations." Jacob rattled off these facts with ease.

Nils ruffled his son's hair. "Soon, I'll have nothing left to teach you! For now, though, let me tell you a bit about this orb. With this orb, you can communicate with your grandfather, since he has its counterpart. It's about time you got to meet him. To use it, you must first offer up some blood. Just a drop will do. You only have to do this once and then—"

"Father!" Jonathon began but stopped short when he noticed his uncle Rufus among the councilors. King Consort Nils looked up at Prince Jonathon's outburst, concern on his face at seeing his second youngest son doubled over and panting hard from running. Prince Jonathon's mouth opened and closed several times, but no sound came out. He stared at his uncle in confusion. Jonathon then remembered the passage behind the painting of his grandfather in the library. He searched the council room for a similar painting hiding a connecting passage.

"Father," he began again, hurrying to the council table. However, a booming voice from the doorway interrupted him.

"King Nils!" Gregor, the Head Chemist, stormed into the council room. Prince Jacob looked curiously between his brother and Gregor.

"Gregor?" King Nils asked, befuddled. Nils' pale-yellow brows knit together as he glanced at Jonathon, who was trying desperately to catch the king's eye while seemingly pointing at something with his chin. King Nils thought it strange his son was still in his bedclothes.

"My king!" Gregor began again, marching up to the council table. He leaned in too close to King Nils, causing the two Wardens to step inside, reaching for the hilts at their waists. King Nils held up his hand to keep them at bay.

"Yes, Gregor, what is it?"

Gregor chewed his lip, then straightened and announced: "Queen Valencia has been found dead in the library."

King Nils' jaw went slack as his knees buckled, but he managed to stay upright. Prince Jonathon inched closer around the council table toward his father, still trying to catch his eye, but also glancing over at his uncle Rufus, who pinned him with a stare so cold that Jonathon could feel the chill through his bedclothes.

"What?" King Nils stammered.

Gregor bowed his head. "Queen Valencia's head maid noticed that the queen was not in her chambers when she came for the queen's bath. The head maid sent some junior maids to the library to search for the queen, as the head maid knew she oft spent mornings with Prince Jonathon there. However, upon entering the library, the junior maids found the queen on the floor. An overturned teacup was next to her." Gregor eyes quickly darted to Rufus, who gave an imperceptible shake of his head. Gregor cleared his throat and sallied on. "As this seemed unusual, I was called in to test for poison."

King Nils fell hard into his chair. Prince Jacob stared at his brother, but Jonathon continued to look at his uncle Rufus.

"And? Was it poison?"

"Yes, my king. It was. A poison made from the hinterland fern." Gregor inhaled deeply before continuing. "Which, as you know, is a plant only found in the Mersae Mountains."

King Nils looked up sharply at the Head Chemist.

Gregor bowed his head. "There was also a teapot found in the library, one not from our kitchens." Gregor again glanced at Magistrate Rufus. It was a brief look, but Prince Jonathon caught it.

"The teapot bore the colors and maker's mark of Andulsae as well."

King Nils stood up immediately. A small wind rose in the council room, ruffling the scrolls and map on the council table and lifting the hems of the councilors' robes. The orb began to roll toward the edge of the table, where Jacob reached out to stop it from falling off.

"And just what are you insinuating, Gregor? That my homeland poisoned my wife?" King Nils icily asked.

"My king," Magistrate Rufus stepped forward and placed a hand on King Nils' shoulder. "Settle yourself, especially in front of your boys. Gregor is simply relaying the facts. We will launch a full investigation." Rufus directed this last sentence to the councilors at large, who vigorously nodded in agreement. More than one threw suspicious looks at King Nils, however.

The wind died down as King Nils closed his eyes. Prince Jonathon reached up to tug on his father's sleeve, but Nils, preoccupied, didn't notice as he strode to the door.

"Take me to my wife!" he barked at Gregor, who hurried to lead King Nils to the library, the two Wardens close behind.

Magistrate Rufus came up behind Prince Jonathon and placed a hand on his arm, but Jonathon squirmed out of his grasp and rushed from the council room, leaving his confused older brother and an irate uncle behind.

2

uring the three days following Queen Valencia's death, Jonathon worked tirelessly to avoid his uncle while trying to find time to speak with his father. He came close several times, but every time King Nils stopped to listen, Jonathon's throat closed up as he remembered how he did nothing to stop his mother's death. When he could finally find his words once more, Nils had grown impatient and told Jonathon he was needed elsewhere.

Later that morning, after finding his uncle lurking in the entrance hall, Jonathon ran down a corridor, glancing over his shoulder before pushing through an old wooden door in the lower level near the kitchens, down the unlit stone stairs, and into the dungeon. The impenetrable black descended upon him like a comforting blanket. There was no light down here, just the hollow silence of dark, unused spaces.

Prince Jonathon reached out with his powers, for the earth always called to him, a small tingle in his gut. His terramental powers brushed against the iron-barred cells and grabbed the stone corridor beneath his bare feet. The direct connection to the earth comforted him. At the end of the first row of cells, Jonathon sat down on the cold floor, feeling safer in this dungeon than he had the past three days since his mother's death. These cells had sat unused since his grandfather was king, as Queen Valencia commissioned the building of a public prison instead of housing criminals in the castle with her family. At the thought of his mother, tears sprang to his eyes.

Everything went wrong so quickly.

The only thing known was that Queen Valencia had been poisoned, but not by whom. Based on the evidence left in the library, rumors abounded that it was elemental spies from Andulsae in the Mersae Mountains. And even worse, more than one councilor suspected that King Nils, being an elemental and from Andulsae himself, had concocted this plan to take the throne from the humans of Eastport. Yet every time Jonathon managed to get close to his father, his uncle would be there, by his side, a sly smile across his face. And if not his uncle, it would be Gregor.

How could Jonathon tell his father what he saw with his uncle and Gregor right there? Would King Nils believe him?

And it wasn't just when Prince Jonathon sought his father that he found his uncle lurking. When he headed to his room, his uncle was there in the corridor, appearing to examine the portraits lining the hallway, crimson robe grazing the rug. When he and young Prince Joseph, were ushered out to the gardens, under the watchful eye of a maid to keep them from getting underfoot, his uncle was there, sitting on the stone bench under the apple trees or standing near the fountain. Jonathon saw his uncle everywhere, and it was making him more than a little scared. Almost nearly as much as holding in the secret of his mother's death.

King Nils had been struggling these past three days as well. Magistrate Rufus would be seen in private conversations with the various councilors, casting furtive glances and speaking in hushed tones. Eventually, the rumor that started on the day of Queen Valencia's murder grew, the one that said King Nils used his connections with his kin in Andulsae to assassinate his own wife in order to pave the way for an elemental takeover of the kingdom.

Desperately trying to reason with the councilors, his father knew he was fighting a losing battle. The only reason he was tolerated among the elder councilors and staff was because of Queen Valencia's presence. Now that she was gone, old hatreds seeped back into the castle like cockroaches. Queen Valencia was no longer there to stay the whispers and rumblings that King Nils was an elemental spy, grooming his own sons to lead the elemental attack on Eastport and thereby reclaiming the land that was once theirs.

It pained Prince Jonathon to see his father struggling this way. He thought he had finally found the chance to tell his father the truth this morning, when learning that King Nils had come down with a grief-induced malaise and had requested privacy in his chambers. Relieved, Jonathon raced to his father.

But his uncle found him first. Jonathon turned down the hall to King Nils' chambers only to be stopped short by a hard tug on his arm.

"And where do you think you're going?" Magistrate Rufus sneered at his nephew. Jonathon struggled to free his arm to no avail. In a desperate move, he stomped on Rufus' toes, dashing away to the dungeon as Rufus hopped up and down, clutching his foot in pain.

With the hard dungeon floor pressing into his bones, Prince Jonathon guessed that maybe an hour or two had passed since he ran into his uncle. He didn't think that Rufus ascertained to where he fled, and the closeness to the earth had calmed his anxiety quite a bit. Slowly, Jonathon stood up and turned back toward the dungeon entrance, hoping it was safe enough to slip unseen to his room. Or perhaps he could instead go to his older brothers' room. Surely, Magistrate Rufus wasn't guarding his brothers' room as well. Maybe it would be easier to tell Jacob and Jordan what their uncle had done. Jacob could then tell their father. King Nils always did listen to Jacob.

The scuffle of boots on stone sounded behind him, and Jonathon raced through the dark, afraid once more. The tingle in his gut let him know an open cell was nearby. Ducking in, Jonathon clasped a hand over his mouth to quiet a scream while he willed his frantic heart to beat steadily. The soft swish of robes gradually approached as Prince Jonathon's eyes darted around, looking for any escape. He thought he saw a flicker of light, a blush illuminating the darkness from which he had just came. Blinking his eyes a few times, he looked again. Only impenetrable blackness greeted him, leaving him truly trapped.

The rustling noise stopped. Jonathon held his breath and counted to ten, and slowly, one bare foot in front of the other, inched out of the cell. His feet connected with the cool stone of the main corridor, and he guided himself closer to the entrance. The scent of the earthen cell floors provided a small comfort, filling him with a strange warmth. The stone fluttered under his feet like anxious butterflies, eager to do his bidding. His power coiled anxiously in his gut, waiting for the word to strike, when the light of a shuttered lantern flared to his right and a hand grabbed him from behind, shoving him face first into the nearest cell bars. The cool kiss of steel pressed against his throat, and the power in his gut was quickly consumed by fear like a spent candle. Prince Jonathon couldn't keep his entire being from shaking as he heard his uncle's voice drip venomously into his ear.

"Hello, Jonathon."

The blade pressed harder against Jonathon's throat as his uncle's free hand gripped his arm like a vise. Prince Jonathon desperately called upon his power, to make an earthquake or the floor cave in, anything. But nothing was there, just a hollow emptiness. He tried to be still, lest the knife slip. Tears ran freely down his cheeks, and he dared not breathe.

"You think you know what you saw in the library," his uncle's grip tightened on his arm. "The fact is, you're just a boy and I'm the Magistrate. No one will believe you over me. But I also know that you won't tell a soul. Because," Jonathon felt his uncle's warm crooning breath against his ear as his heart pounded forcefully in his chest, "there are worse things than having your throat slit."

*　　*　　*　　*

After what felt like hours of crushing blows, swift kicks, and veiled promises of more should he tell, Jonathon was set free. He remained in the dungeon, slumped against the cell bars in a trance, pain's sharp teeth gnawing his insides. He wanted to cry, to run straight to his father's arms and confess everything. He wanted his mother to cradle him, to tell him he was brave to witness his uncle's treachery. But instead, he just lay there curled against the bars, taking shallow breaths, and shifting out of his body until the nightmare had passed, just as he stood silently by while his mother was killed.

His mother wouldn't call him brave. No one would call him brave. They'd call him a coward. He should have tried to stop his uncle. Then he wouldn't have found himself dumped in a dungeon cell, helpless as a newborn foal.

Prince Jonathon screamed in frustration, curled up on his side, hands raking his face as if he could scratch out the memory before it had time to set. The fight quickly left him though, and he remained on the floor, wrung out like an old dish cloth, wondering that if he never got up again, maybe he could join his mother, wherever she may be, and know happiness once more.

Jonathon closed his eyes and wished death would come quickly. But his mother stayed just out of reach.

Sometime later, he found himself standing before the door to his shared bedroom, unsure of how he got there. He briefly registered that Prince Joseph would be inside, possibly lost to the oblivion of sleep, but just as likely to wake up and ask questions.

No one must ever know. The furious thought raced through his mind as he threw open the door. Jonathon's little brother was curled up on his bed, his blanket fallen to the floor. Jonathon stepped around it and rushed to the washbasin. He silently thanked the maid who kept the basin full and threw off his clothes as if they were diseased. How he wished he had a useful power like his older brother, Prince Jordan, a pyromental. Then he could burn these clothes, and even the flesh, until there was only new skin, shiny and unbroken. Or maybe even powers like his eldest brother, Prince Jacob, an aeromental. Then he could summon the wind to carry him away to where he would never have to face his uncle again.

Jonathon stared at himself in the mirror, the bright light of the full moon through the window highlighting his gaunt eyes in a hollow frame. His uncle was smart, he realized. The bruises wouldn't show around Jonathon's normal clothes. His uncle stayed away from his head or arms, refusing to leave any discernible marks. His ribs and back ached something fierce, though, and Jonathon could see the purple and yellow bruises growing like a virus across his chest.

He turned slowly, scrutinizing his naked self in the mirror. His uncle told him that if he told anyone, anyone at all, this would not be the last Jonathon would see of him, and the next time it would be worse. Jonathon didn't want worse. He didn't even want to look at his battered body now, ashamed that he didn't fight back. His uncle was right. He couldn't tell his father that he didn't defend himself. That was almost as bad as letting his mother die. No. No marks of his uncle's onslaught could remain. Jonathon grabbed the boar bristle brush from the nightstand and slammed it into the water before desperately scrubbing his skin, determined to erase the purple and black welts on his body.

Over and over and over again he thrust the brush into the water and raked it across his chest until blood began to well up in angry red lines.

"No, no," Jonathon muttered, still scrubbing. "I have to get rid of it. I have to. It's not real, it's not real, it's not real…"

"Jonny?" a drowsy voice echoed across the room.

Prince Joseph stirred in his bed, wiping the sleep from his eyes as he tried to focus on the muttering figure near the washbasin. Quietly climbing down, Joseph softly padded over to his older brother.

Prince Jonathon startled as small hands gripped him from behind, causing him to stop abruptly and go rigid in fear.

"Please, not again." Jonathon whispered to the dark.

"Jonny, shh, it's okay." His little brother squeezed him tighter until he dropped the brush into the basin with a splash. His legs quivered, then gave out, and he fell in a broken heap at his little brother's feet.

Prince Joseph quickly ran to his bedside and returned with the blanket, which he draped around Jonathon as gently as placing a shroud. He knelt before his older brother, looked into Jonathon's wide eyes, and knew in his gut that something happened tonight, something that would make the sun dawn tomorrow on an alien world.

"Go back to bed, Joseph. It'll be okay." Jonathon sniffed while scrubbing a hand across his face. His lower lip quivered as he tried to put on a brave face for his little brother.

Joseph scooted closer and with all the understanding a six-year-old could muster, wrapped his arms around Jonathon's shaking body, holding him tight lest he fall to pieces.

"It's okay, Jonny. I am here, so you are safe now."

The tears Jonathon had been holding back finally burst forth, and he sobbed into his brother's arms.

3

agistrate Rufus sat at his desk in his dimly lit room, hunched over a parchment covered in diagrams and hastily scrawled script. He looked over his shoulder to the high window, hunching further over the parchment as if he worried that someone would look into his room on the top floor and see his work. He turned the lantern wick down even lower, throwing the small room into deeper purple shadows. Spinning in his chair, he studied the tapestry behind him for the dozenth time that evening.

The elegantly woven tapestry depicted the battle for Eastport those many years ago, when the land was still called Esdaria and was ruled by elementals. Back then, the human king of Lexington desired more resources and thus looked to the rich forests of Esdaria, having clear-cut those around Lexington in the south. The chief of Andulsae, the elemental capital in the north, seeing the destruction the humans caused to the forests of Lexington, refused to cede any land. Therefore, negotiations led straight to battle, for the human king did not like to be told no. The elementals were not afraid of battle; they had powers far superior to anything the humans had. And yet, they lost and were pushed back far into the Mersae Mountains, all due to a secret advantage the humans had—eusgare ore.

The elementals used eusgare in battle often enough. The ore, crushed into a powder and drunk, would increase an elemental's power. Magistrate Rufus spent years studying the historical texts on the battle, even examined this very tapestry with a fine-toothed comb, but could not find any clue as to how the humans of old used eusgare to defeat the elementals.

It infuriated him. Humans had claimed this land, had proven more powerful than the elementals, yet the elementals returned to Eastport because of the treaty his father, King Rupert, signed. All that was hard fought and won was so easily given right back to the elementals. Rufus could not stand it. If he could only find what that advantage was all those years ago, he could be rid of the elementals for good. If he couldn't be born with powers, then no one should.

A small knock came from behind the tapestry. Furtively glancing at his room door, Magistrate Rufus swiftly got up, ensured the door was locked, and went across the room to push aside the tapestry. Hooking a tiny ring set into the wall with his finger, Rufus pulled, revealing a hidden door. Head Chemist Gregor was waiting.

"What news?" Magistrate Rufus asked as he ushered Gregor in and shut the door, replacing the tapestry.

"From the gilded mouths of the High Tide nobles to the briny tongues of the sailors by the docks, the word is that King Nils had Queen Valencia poisoned. Every elemental is looked on as a spy or conspirator. Neighbor is turning on neighbor, and folks are starting to call on the Wardens more to have those suspected of being an elemental tested."

"Good, good," Rufus said as he sat back down at his desk. "This is exactly what we need to be rid of the elemental scourge of Eastport." He looked at the parchment on his desk, at the experiments with eusgare ore carefully drawn out. The tests had been his idea, one that the elder councilors readily agreed to. It helped that the majority of the councilors were old enough to remember when Eastport was free of elementals instead of being overrun with them as a result of the treaty.

Since Queen Valencia's death was determined to be an elemental plot, Magistrate Rufus suggested that the Wardens begin testing citizens suspected of being an elemental and arrest them if they failed the test, in order to weed out any further attempts of a coup. The test was simple enough. The history books spoke of elementals reacting to a mysterious black substance. Upon further research, Rufus discovered that substance was eusgare, so he had the chemists bring up the eusgare ore left in the old stone tunnels. They chipped away pieces no bigger than coins for each Warden to carry. When a suspected elemental touched the eusgare, the ore would cause their powers to flare up and show themselves. Several arrests had already been made.

The only problem was that Rufus could not figure out how eusgare could be used to defeat elementals, only to oust them. Eusgare was a natural accelerant of power; nevertheless, he had Gregor and his chemists working to find a way to use eusgare against elementals, and to conversely find a way to protect himself against an elemental attack. So far, they had had little luck.

"I think we will need to remove more eusgare from the tunnels," Gregor explained to Magistrate Rufus. "We have nearly used up the stores we have."

"See that it's done quickly, then." Rufus didn't look up from his studying. "I want to add more obelisks throughout the city as well. They must have used eusgare to stop the elementals before; the texts allude to nothing else. And the elementals are sure to rise up sooner rather than later."

"Of course," Gregor nodded. "I will set my apprentices to it immediately."

Rufus fixed his Head Chemist with a hard stare. "Be discreet. I don't want the tunnels to become common knowledge. Some history is best left forgotten."

"As you wish." Gregor bowed and headed back through the hidden door in the alcove.

Magistrate Rufus leaned back in his chair as Gregor left, stroking his short beard in thought. The tunnels were old, remnants from the days of Esdaria. They spread out from the dungeon beneath the castle through the rest of the city, their various access points denoted with ancient elemental symbols. Rufus, in his youth, had explored these tunnels after finding the old stone monument in the woods behind the castle. Even more, Rufus had discovered there was eusgare stored within those tunnels that branched off from the dungeon.

It was from there that he, several months before Queen Valencia's death, had the ore gathered to be made into obelisks by Gregor and his chemists. Just a few to begin with—he had convinced the councilors, and eventually Queen Valencia, that there was no harm, that the eusgare obelisks were a symbol of elemental acceptance in Eastport, being something from their homeland.

Only Gregor knew his true purpose of eliminating the elementals.

Magistrate Rufus looked up at the high window again. There wasn't much wick left to lower in his lantern, and the room was dim as it was. He narrowed his eyes, staring at the darkness beyond the glass pane. The elementals were getting too numerous. They were breeding with humans, creating hybrids like his nephews. He grimaced at the thought. Prince Jacob, the oldest, would soon gain the throne. He would be a tainted ruler, being half elemental. King Nils had been filling his head with elemental nonsense, speaking of the old gods and honing his aeromental abilities. Rufus needed to be sure that Prince Jacob never got the chance to rule.

And he was close. It started with the obelisks, then the tests. Soon, he will be able to convince the councilors to remove elementals from Eastport permanently. He just needed to bide his time.

*   *   *   *

Prince Jonathon sat huddled with his little brother, Prince Joseph, in the corner of their room. He felt his little brother's chest rapidly rising and falling as Joseph struggled to stay silent. It was the middle of the night, and the brothers had been woken up by shouts coming from outside the castle walls. The shouts were just muffled gnats to start with, a tiny buzzing that tried to pull Jonathon from his sleep. But they had steadily become louder, accompanied by bangs that sounded a lot like gunshots. It was this that caused him to leap from his bed, bolt his door, and grab his brother to hide in the corner of their room furthest from the window. He didn't dare look out.

Queen Valencia's death was two months ago. Prince Jacob had taken over as ruler of the kingdom but refused to have Magistrate Rufus as his prime advisor. He instead chose his father, King Nils, much to the dismay of the councilors. The rumors of King Nils poisoning his wife had solidified as fact in the minds of many. The public was becoming more divided, with the increased presence of the Wardens testing and arresting elementals. Fights were breaking out in the streets at the slightest perceived insult. Elementals used their powers to defend themselves, but often they found themselves outnumbered. Nils forbade his sons from leaving the castle.

Prince Jonathon still hadn't had the chance to speak with his father, to tell him of the events surrounding his mother's death. His uncle continued to stalk him, and more so, Jonathon noticed Head Chemist Gregor everywhere he went as well. He couldn't evade both his uncle and Gregor. To top it off, King Nils was never alone. There was always a councilor or Nils' valet hovering nearby. If Gregor was helping his uncle, who else might be? Magistrate Rufus might have an entire network of spies that Jonathon didn't know about. He couldn't risk it.

A gunshot from just outside the window caused both him and Joseph to jump. Prince Joseph slowly unclenched himself and began to crawl across the rug to the window. Grasping at his bedclothes, Jonathon frantically tried to pull his brother back. A sudden pounding on their door caused both of them to freeze. Joseph quietly backtracked to the corner and curled up with Jonathon as they stared unblinkingly at the door.

The bolt on the door creaked, then began to glow red. A sudden gust of wind blasted the door open to reveal the boys' father and older brothers, Prince Jordan's hand still smoking from where he had burned the bolt.

King Nils rushed in and grabbed both boys to his chest, sighing in relief. He stood up, dragging his sons with him.

"We need to leave. The Wardens have turned against us. Quickly now."

He ushered his boys out of the room and into the hallway. The air had an acrid taste and Jonathon heard more shouts echoing off the stone walls. The sound of gunshots grew louder. With Jacob leading the way, the group ran down the hall to the servant stairs and exited near the kitchens. Nils directed Jacob through the kitchens, where the baker was crouched in the corner with one of Nils' stewards. They flinched as Nils and his sons approached at speed. Nils ignored them and urged Jacob onward to the door at the back of the kitchens, which opened into a side courtyard.

Two Wardens were outside. Jacob thrust his hand, palm out, toward the Warden on the right, sending a gust of air that pushed the Warden back a few feet. The other Warden raised his rifle, but before he could aim, Nils swept his arm in front of him, propelling a wall of wind forward. The Wardens were lifted into the air like sheets on a clothesline and slammed down hard against the flagstones of the courtyard. Nils grabbed ahold of Joseph and Jonathon again and ran to the gate, Jordan and Jacob at his side.

From the courtyard, the group reached the gardens and headed for the woods beyond, the night covering their escape. Jonathon twisted in his father's grip to look back at the castle. He saw smoke rising from somewhere and the indistinct figures of men rushing about. The trees quickly blocked his view, but he still heard the muffled shouts and gunshots from behind. He squeezed his father's hand tighter and only felt slightly reassured when his father quick-ly squeezed back.

Soon, they reached the stone monument in the woods, its four sides dappled with shadows cast from the moon and stars above.

"Jordan, some light please," Nils requested in a shaky voice. Jonathon saw the sweat on his father's forehead. A flame sprung to life in Jordan's outstretched hand as he walked around the monu-ment at Nils' instruction.

"Here," Nils had Jordan stop in front of the third side, facing away from the castle, where there was a hydromental symbol carved into the rock. He pushed the symbol and a door silently swung outward to accept them. Nils gathered his sons around him and crouched down to their level.

"Listen to me, and listen well. Follow this tunnel to the docks. There will be hydromental symbols along the way. Those will al-ways point you to water if you ever get lost. Once at the docks, there will be a ship called the *Peridian*. Get aboard it, and stay aboard until it lands in Andulsae. I will meet you there when I can." Nils closed his eyes and inhaled deeply, the scent of smoke beginning to filter its way through the woods.

"Jacob," Nils continued, "you are in charge. Get your brothers to safety as fast as you can, by whatever means necessary. Jona-thon, hold onto Joseph's hand. Do not let him go. Jordan, keep your flames at the ready, just in case."

Jordan nodded solemnly and summoned a second flame to his other palm. Jacob grimaced, his eyes hidden behind the reflected light of Jordan's flames in his glasses. Jonathon grabbed Joseph's hand and squeezed tight. Joseph winced in protest but did not pull away.

"I love you boys," Nils hugged them one by one, then put his hands on Jacob's shoulders, a silent understanding passing between them. He gave them one last look and ran back to the castle, a wind rising at his back.

*   *   *   *

"We need to go straight," Jordan gestured down the earthen tunnel with his flame-lit hand.

"No, we need to go left," Jacob retorted. The brothers had been walking for about ten minutes in the dark tunnel, the dirt floor unforgiving beneath their feet.

"The docks are straight ahead."

"No, they're to the left!" Jacob insisted.

Jonathon kept Joseph's hand clasped in his own as he watched his older brothers bicker. As soon as they entered the tunnels and closed the door, the sounds of fighting ceased. He wondered what his father went back for, to help others or to fight and defend the castle. Jonathon really wished his father had come with them instead.

"Joseph!" Jacob shouted, causing both Joseph and Jonathon to jump. "You're the hyrdromental. Which direction is the sea? Can you feel it?"

Joseph looked up at Jonathon, eyes wide, then back at the ground, his blond hair falling into his eyes.

"I don't know," he replied sullenly, digging his big toe into the dirt. Jonathon realized that they didn't grab their shoes after their father burst into their room.

"What good are you?" Jacob threw up his hands in exasperation. "I could already make a vortex by the time I was your age."

Jonathon frowned at his eldest brother and hugged Joseph to his side.

"Don't yell at him!" Jonathon returned. "Just look for the hydromental symbol. Father said it points to water."

"There's no symbol here," Jacob glared. "Besides, father left me in charge. And I say the docks are to the left." Jacob stomped down the tunnel to the left. Jordan rolled his eyes and shrugged, motioning the other two to follow Jacob while he hurried ahead to light the way.

Shortly thereafter, the brothers came to a stop, unable to move forward. Jordan brought his flame around to inspect the obstacle, only to find it was a short stone door. Jacob grinned triumphantly and shoved the door open. He stumbled out onto rough stones and found himself on the main road leading to the castle. Turning around, he saw that the door he came out of was built into the side of the Agate Bridge where it met the road, hidden in the architecture of the bridge, unnoticeable save for a small hydromental symbol carved near the top. Behind them loomed the castle, yards away from the bridge they were standing on. They were nowhere near the docks. His brothers cautiously exited the doorway and Jordan extinguished his flames.

"This isn't the docks, Jacob. We're too exposed here."

"I'm aware. Come on, let's go." Jacob hurried his brothers toward the middle of the Agate Bridge, hoping the clouds would come to cover the too-bright moon and hide their flight. The Agate Bridge was built ages ago, a link from High Tide to Mid Tide. It was wide, able to fit four horses pulling carriages side by side, and was made of perfectly hewn stone. It was obviously a creation of the elementals of old, for the stones were placed so precisely without any daubing or caulking. It was a wonder the bridge had lasted this long without degradation. The bridge, rising taller in the middle than the two-story houses on its High Tide side and tapering at each end, crossed the fast-flowing Plebeum River, one of the several rivers making up the Jamin Delta. The banks below consisted of large, sharp rocks, boulders that had been deposited and smashed by the raging river centuries before people populated this land. Tonight, with the light of the full moon, the Plebeum looked like a hungry monster eagerly awaiting victims to fall into its maw.

"Jonny!" Joseph tugged on Jonathon's sleeve, causing the brothers to stop and stare behind them to where Joseph pointed.

"Stop!" Several Wardens had spotted them and raised their rifles. Jacob immediately gathered the wind in front of him, circling his hands to create a vortex. Jordan summoned his flames and lit Jacob's vortex, so that the brothers had a column of windy fire between them. Jacob hurled the fire column at the Wardens, who raised their rifles as if to shoot the flames. Yet, the fire column sputtered and died yards short of the Wardens.

Jacob's face paled. "Run!" he shouted, grabbing Jordan's arm and sprinting across the Agate Bridge.

Jonathon pulled Joseph behind him and followed his brothers. Joseph stumbled at the sudden yank on his arm, causing him to fall to his knees. Jacob and Jordan were still racing ahead.

"Stop or we'll shoot!" One of the Wardens yelled from behind.

"Come on!" Jonathon dragged Joseph to his feet and pushed him toward the middle of the bridge. Metallic pings sounded as the Wardens' shots rang off the stone. Jonathon silently urged Joseph to run faster when a hot brand struck him in his right knee. Jonathon bellowed out in pain as he fell to the ground, clutching a hand to his knee, warm blood seeping through his fingers. Joseph stopped and turned back. He saw his brother writhing on the ground with the Wardens closing in, reloading their rifles. The roar of the river below echoed in Joseph's gut, a strong cramping sensation that spread throughout his midriff. Without thinking, he tried to summon the river to him. He held out his hand, but the river was too far away. He was not strong enough. Another shot cracked the air like lightning, striking the stones near his feet.

Jonathon rolled over onto his stomach to face the oncoming Wardens. The pain in his knee blurred his vision, but the Wardens were shooting at his brother and he had to do something. Father told him to never let go of Joseph, and Jonathon would not let him down. The stones around him hummed in anticipation, the pressure in his gut intense enough to rival the pain in his knee. Jonathon used that pain to focus his mind, clearing it of all thoughts other than the Wardens aiming their rifles at his little brother. He concentrated on the stones at the Wardens' feet, imagining the bridge convulsing like a dug-up worm to topple them. With a yell, Jonathon thrust out his hand at the Wardens and felt the stones around him immediately respond. The bridge under the Wardens' feet bucked and heaved like a wild horse, throwing the Wardens violently to the ground.

But Jonathon had released too much power. The stones continued to heave in a wave, bearing down on him and Joseph. He then watched in horror as the bridge lifted both him and his little brother high into the air. Jonathon's stomach flew to his throat as he left the ground, his light body rising much higher than the Wardens' had. He was suspended for a second, watching the blood from his shot knee drip down like rain onto the thrashing bridge below. Then he started his descent, the stones rushing up to meet him. He was abruptly snapped back, like a marionette string jerked too hard, and was gently placed onto the now calm bridge.

Hearing panting, he turned to see Jacob behind him, hands on his knees, Jordan holding onto his shoulder. Jonathon frantically searched for Joseph, but didn't see his little brother on the bridge. Desperately, he looked at Jordan, who simply shook his head and pointed over the side of the bridge. Jonathon crawled to the railing and pulled himself up, his bloody hands slipping on the stone, his right knee refusing to hold him. Finally, he managed to haul himself upright enough to peer over at the river below.

There on the bank, was Joseph, a small, unmoving figure among the rocks. The moonlight showed Jonathon the horrible sight. Joseph's arms were splayed at an awkward angle, his face and head bloodied. His eyes were closed. He wasn't moving.

Jonathon screamed but no sound came out. He tried to gather his injured leg beneath him, but it wouldn't hold. He dimly registered Jacob at his side, pulling him away, Jordan coming to help. Jonathon struggled in their grasp as his brothers dragged him off the bridge and into the night.

4

Fourteen years later

Joe takes a long drag on his cigarette, holds for a beat, and exhales a cloud of blue smoke. Another one down. He throws the butt on the dock and watches as the orange embers die. Too slow. He squishes the butt with the heel of his boot, making sparks, the last breath of his cigarette shooting everywhere before being completely extinguished. Much better.

He pulls out one more and lights up. That makes three this evening. Joe's on edge tonight. The Magistrate had called for another hanging, and he expected all citizens to watch. Each hanging is an example. One more elemental arrested and executed for being born a certain way. This time it was Felix, another sailor who Joe would occasionally have drinks with at the Black Goose, but not a close friend. Joe hadn't even known Felix was an elemental. But he did know that Felix was recently married and that his wife is now a young widow. Not only that, but she will also face persecution and will be publicly shamed if she is allowed to live. But even Felix's widowed wife isn't the source of his unease.

What Joe can't figure out was why Felix looked the way he did when he died. Everyone in Eastport knows that the ore from eusgare is used to root out elementals in hiding. It's for protection, the Magistrate claims, protection for the humans. For some reason, Joe doesn't know why, the eusgare affects elementals. It makes them reveal their powers somehow. He's seen the arrests. Heck, he was there when Felix was arrested a week ago.

They were all at the Black Goose having a pint. Joe and his crewmates, Matt and Nell, joined up with Felix and several other sailors from the *Wodon,* another Eastport merchant ship. It was a quiet evening, and the tavern was filled with muted conversations broken up by the occasional laugh. All of a sudden, the establishment's door was thrown open, and three Wardens walked in.

Joe put down his drink, assessing the situation. The only exit was the door in front of him or through the kitchen behind. He was sitting at the end of the bench at their table; he could spring up quickly enough. Taking a few deep breaths, he calmed his racing heart. No one here knew he was an elemental. The Wardens were not here for him. His crewmate Matt looked curiously at him, noticing the change in Joe's demeanor.

Joe nodded his head in the direction of the Wardens still standing by the door, examining the patrons of the Black Goose. Matt sighed and set his pint down with a thud.

"Wonder what they're here for," Matt blew some curly black hair out of his verdant green eyes. The rest of the table turned to look at the Wardens. Joe felt a twinge in his gut, the tell-tale sign of a new water source begging for his attention. Not only was this source new, it was close. He scanned the table and saw a line of sweat break out on Felix's forehead as Felix quickly turned his back to the Wardens. Joe gave him a puzzled look, but Felix quickly shook his head, not willing to meet Joe's eyes.

Shortly, the Wardens approached their table. With dismay, Joe saw that the one bearing the captain's badge was none other than Bernard Lowain, the thorn in Joe's side during ship inspections at the docks. At that moment, Bernard looked up and noticed Joe staring. Joe quickly looked back to the pint in his hand, but not before he caught Bernard's smirk.

"Felix Dunworth?" Bernard intoned, coming to a stop before their table. "You have been randomly selected to take the test." Bernard pulled on a pair of leather gloves from his uniform's pocket and reached for a coin-sized disc of black eusgare ore that hung on a chain around his neck.

"Randomly selected?" Felix stammered. "Surely, there's been a mistake?"

Bernard raised one eyebrow at Felix's quivering form. "Surely, you're not an elemental and therefore have nothing to hide?" Bernard held out the disc in his open palm.

"Touch the eusgare. Show me you're not an elemental, and we'll be on our way," Bernard commanded Felix.

Joe clenched his fists and stared down at the table, furtively glancing up at Felix. With how badly Felix was shaking, there was no way he wasn't an elemental. Would Bernard and the Wardens insist that everyone at their table take the test?

Felix regarded the disc in Bernard's outstretched hand before looking at Joe, resolve steeling his eyes. Joe gulped. He knew. Somehow Felix knew that Joe was an elemental. Felix's gaze was pleading. Joe brought his pint up to his mouth and gave an imperceptible shake of his head. Felix's shoulders slumped in defeat. He put his hands on the table and sprang backward off the bench, knocking both it and his companions over. Joe, Matt, and Nell all jumped back.

Circling his arms wide in front of him, Felix summoned a disc of fire and hurled it at the Wardens. Bernard and his cohorts immediately drew their bronze-colored cloaks up for protection. The fire disc bounced harmlessly off the cloaks and Felix turned and ran out the door.

Bernard calmly pulled a mini crossbow from its holster on his back and loaded it with a bronze dart. The tavern door swung open with a thud as Bernard strode out, took aim, and hit Felix squarely between his shoulder blades. Felix dropped like a stone.

Walking over to Felix's prone form, Bernard yanked the dart free. He entered the Black Goose once more and approached the barmaid at the counter, dropping two coins before her.

"Send for me if you notice any more elementals in your establishment." Motioning for the other two Wardens to follow, all three went out to collect Felix and dragged him off into the night.

"Serves him right," Nell muttered as she helped Matt and Joe right the overturned table. "Did either of you know he was an elemental?"

"Not a clue," Matt responded.

Joe shrugged and stuffed his hands in his jacket pockets to hide how badly they were trembling.

Shaking his head now to clear the memory, Joe tries to quell the shudder running through his body. He could have helped Felix that night, but he was too afraid of being found out himself. And now, Felix was dead, publicly executed, the same as all other elementals arrested in Eastport. But worse than that, Felix, while up on the gallows waiting for his end, looked consumed. Black webbing crisscrossed his face, and he had a deranged visage. The torch in the executioner's fist had flared two feet high without Felix even moving a hand. It almost appeared that he could take down the entire gallows with just a thought. What was the Magistrate doing with the elementals he arrested? Joe knows that elementals seem powerless to suppress their abilities when in contact with eusgare, but Joe has never heard of it doing that to an elemental before.

Joe leans his head back and stares at the blanket of stars in the night sky as he takes another drag. Footsteps patter up to him. Captain Merrill.

"Joe."

"Hey, Captain." Joe wearily greets him. Captain Calvin Merrill is a stocky, middle-aged fellow, who believes that being a sailor isn't an excuse for sloppy dress. He's a pious man, which Joe doesn't hold against him, even if the gods leave something to be desired. The captain sighs and looks out at the moonlight playing over the still ocean and his merchant ship, the *Moro,* bobbing complacently on the harbor waves. The *Moro* is where Joe spends most of his days, sailing the route from Eastport to Lexington, the southern free city, to gather goods to trade. Occasionally, Joe uses this route to smuggle contraband out of Lexington and into Eastport, such as fruits and medicines from Andulsae. Magistrate Rufus has forbidden trade with Andulsae as he wants to keep Eastport free of the taint of elementals. However, there is a decent black market in Eastport for Andulsaean goods, and Joe finds that his hydromental abilities are conducive to helping him make some extra cash smuggling, something he'd rather keep secret from Captain Merrill.

"Seems like this one really got to you." Captain Merrill doesn't face Joe, but directs his words toward the sea, as if the water will absorb any accusation that might be perceived. Joe stiffens, but no one knows his secret. Only his parents. And Meg and Sara, his cousins. But he trusts them with his life. He knows they would never tell, and he knows that the captain couldn't have possibly figured it out.

Stamping out his cigarette, Joe faces Captain Merrill, head down and shoulders hunched as if this posture will make him seem less threatening, or at least protect him from the captain's disapproval.

"It just seems unfair, sir. Elementals can't help how they were born. Everyone sees them as monsters, but when humans are the ones doing the killing, how do you decide who's the monster?"

Captain Merrill is quiet for a minute. When he speaks, he chooses his words carefully. "You're not the only one who questions. But I'm certain the gods have made it so for a reason. Keep faith." He clasps Joe's shoulder briefly before glancing up at the castle in the distance, then walks back down the dock and up the gangplank of the *Moro*.

Joe watches him leave, filled with regret. The captain and his gods irk Joe. Joe loves the man like a second father, but Captain Merrill's gods are human gods who preach the purity of humans. There is no room for elementals in Captain Merrill's gods. Joe sighs at the now empty dock and heads into the city. He starts off close to the shore, keeping the harbor to his right, on roads that quickly leave the sea behind as they follow one of the many tributaries of the Jamin Delta further inland. The houses become smaller and shabbier the further up the river he goes, heading toward the Low Tide neighborhood. He continues following the road until it becomes little more than a dirt path that winds inland through the northern edge of Eastport, where the poorest live.

Though it's late at night and the nearby roads are empty, he glances around, feeling the hairs stand up on the back of his neck. He shakes his head, trying to dislodge the nervousness. He's only going to visit his cousins; there's no reason for anyone to be suspicious of him. Convincing himself once more that there's nothing amiss, he walks up to a small cottage and knocks softly three times on the door. After a heartbeat, the door flings open and he's tackled by a hug from a short mass of brown hair.

"Joe!" the little girl squeals.

"All right, easy there, Meg!" Joe laughs. "I'm glad to see you too!" Joe picks her up and carries her inside. Her mother, Sara, suppresses a laugh as he enters.

"Make a pony, Joe! Make a pony!"

"A pony? Again? You sure you don't want to see something else, like maybe a dog? Or how about a dragon?"

"No, I want a pony!"

"I think you'd better make her a pony, Joe." Sara smiles as she brings over a bucket of well water.

"Well, Meg, if you insist. How can I deny my best girl?" Joe winks as he holds out his hand above the water. He's done this trick so many times that it barely takes any effort. With a simple thought, he coaxes the water out of the bucket, where it hovers in the air. Meg watches, clinging to his jacket, bright-eyed. Gradually, he convinces the water to rearrange itself. It spirals into a miniature tornado, revolving slowly at first before picking up speed until it's a whirlwind of blue and white. With a big flourish, the water comes to a stop in the form of a pony in mid-gallop, its watery mane flying back in an unseen wind.

"It's so pretty," Meg says, her mouth agape in awe.

With a smile, Joe makes the water pony trot around the room. Meg follows it, clapping in glee. After several rounds, he brings the water pony back to the bucket where it collapses with a splash.

Still giggling, Meg hugs him again. "Thank you, Joe! I always love when you visit! But next time, maybe do a dragon."

"What? I specifically remember asking you if you wanted a dragon, but you insisted on a pony. I think I'm offended."

"No, you're not!"

Joe laughs. "Okay, I'm not. But I think it's time for you to go to bed."

"Yes, it is very much past your bedtime, young lady." Sara reaches down to pick up Meg.

"Okay, fine." Meg squirms in Sara's arms to face Joe again. "When are you coming back?"

Joe reaches up to ruffle her hair. "Oh, it will probably be a couple weeks. Don't worry, though. I would never miss a chance to come see you."

Meg smiles and lays her head on her mother's shoulder as Sara carries her up the ladder to the sleeping loft. After setting Meg down to sleep, Sara climbs back down and motions Joe to take a seat at the table in the back of the cottage. Joe pulls out a chair and gives a start when he notices his father, Ian, already sitting there. The lanky fisherman's dark, slimy hair is plastered to his forehead in the early fall humidity. His dour expression immediately extinguishes any happiness Joe managed to gain from playing with Meg. Sara notices the tension as she pours them both a cup of tea before joining them.

"Is everything okay, Uncle Ian?" she ventures.

"You shouldn't be using your powers, Joe," Ian grunts.

Joe rolls his eyes, knowing where this conversation is going. "No one but you, Meg, and Sara were here to see. It was just a little harmless fun, Dad."

"It's too risky. Eventually you'll slip up, someone will find out, and then where would we be? You're always too willing to put our lives," Ian gestures to Sara and himself, "at risk for a little 'fun.'"

"Dad…" Joe puts his head in his hands.

"No," Ian holds up his hand, "I don't want to hear it. If the rest of us can get along just fine without powers, I don't see why you can't as well."

"It's a part of me. What do you expect me to do?"

Ian glares daggers at him as Sara quickly interjects.

"It makes Meg happy, Uncle Ian. There's no harm in it."

"Using it to smuggle contraband from Andulsae—"

"Meg needs that medicine!" Sara throws her hands up in the air.

"I don't need my powers for that," Joe smirks, sitting back and crossing his arms over his chest.

Ian stares darkly at him. "This isn't funny, Joe."

"I'm not laughing, Dad." He shakes his head and reaches into his pocket. "Here, Sara. I was able to get two vials this trip." He sets the two glass vials of clear liquid medicine on the table in front of Sara. Sara's eyes begin to water as she reaches across the table to hug him.

"Thank you for everything you do for her. Luckily, you saw her on a good day today. Other days, well, I do what I can to make her comfortable. Ever since the fever took William and almost took her…" Sara trails off.

"Of course, Sara." Joe lays a comforting hand on Sara's arm.

"See, Uncle?" Sara rounds on Ian. "This is why I need, why *we* need, Joe to do what he does. Your grandniece would be bedridden without this medicine. Would you rather see her like that? Or dead, like her father?"

Ian sighs, wearily raking a hand down his face. "Sara, you know I don't wish that. But there are other ways…"

"There's not! The Magistrate doesn't allow trade with Andulsae because they're elementals. But the elementals of Andulsae are the only ones who can make the medicine Meg needs! The ingredients are only in the Mersae Mountains. If it wasn't for Joe, putting his life on the line to sneak this 'contraband' in from the markets in Lexington, Meg wouldn't stand a chance."

"Maybe if we got an audience with the Magistrate, told him of Meg's condition, he could have his chemists concoct a different medicine," Ian suggests.

"You know that will never happen." Sara places her hand over Joe's. "But that's why we have you." Sara gives him a sad smile, but then turns serious. "Joe, I appreciate your getting the medicine for us, but please be careful. Things are getting worse." She throws a glare in Ian's direction.

"I know," Joe replies grimly. "But don't you worry about me. I'll be alright."

"I just wish everyone could see that not all elementals are bad."

Joe gives a bitter laugh. "In a perfect world, maybe. Well," Joe, glancing between the two of them, stands up. "I best be going. Short leave this time. Dad, are you coming?"

Ian opens his mouth to speak, but Sara once again interjects. "I think we've had a long enough visit. He'll want to be getting back home to Aunt Matilde, won't you, Uncle?" Sara asks him pointedly.

Ian sighs in surrender and follows Joe out into the dark night.

5

Ian and Joe make their way back home, wending across bridges and through the business district until the castle is a looming presence above them. They come to the foot of the Agate Bridge and head down the path to its left until Ian and Matilde's quaint house comes into view. It's a squat cottage at the edge of the Plebeum River, the Agate Bridge casting an eternal shadow over the place. Joe always had an eerie feeling looking at that bridge. It seemed so tall and foreboding and more than once made him shiver as he passed beneath. The cottage, as with the other houses nearby, looks out of place on the boulders of the Plebeum's banks. Matilde does her best to bring a spot of sunshine to combat the dreariness. The soil is too tough and rocky for flowers to grow, but Matilde manages to coax some orange veralillies and snowy white daydrones to grow in boxes on the windowsills.

Ian and Joe enter the cottage and are greeted by the enticing scent of brumbuck stew and fresh baked onion bread.

"Joe!" A plump woman, more than a head shorter than Joe, bounces over to wrap him in a hug.

"Dinner smells delicious, Mom," Joe smiles into Matilde's hair. Pulling back, he wipes a bit of flour off her cheek.

"And it's just about ready. If you could grab the bowls off the shelf?"

Joe swiftly takes three bowls and spoons from the shelf over the washbasin and sets the table, flopping down in a chair as he finishes, trying to keep from drooling. Ian sinks down directly across the round table, sharing none of Joe's enthusiasm.

"How long are you here this time? Will you be staying the night?" Matilde questions Joe as she ladles out stew to both her son and husband before ladling some for herself. She puts the pot back over the fire and sits down.

"Not long," Joe replies around a mouthful of stew. "Short leave this time." He tears off a chunk of bread and stuffs its oniony goodness into his mouth. "I'll probably just stay on the *Moro* tonight. Don't feel like hanging around the city too long."

Ian grunts at this confession. Matilde frowns, her usual smile lines unsure how to bend in the opposite direction.

She reaches a hand out toward Joe. "Because of the execution? Did you know him?"

Ian looks up expectantly from his stew waiting for Joe to answer.

The bread in his mouth becomes dry. Joe gulps it down with difficulty.

"No, I didn't know him."

"This is what I mean," Ian slams his spoon down on the table. "You keep on as you are, using your powers out in the open, and it will be you next up on those gallows."

"I don't use my powers out in the open for everyone to see, Dad. You know I'm more careful than that." Joe says through a clenched jaw.

"I don't think you are," Ian shakes his head. "That show at Sara's and all the smuggling. Someone's going to catch on sooner or later." Ian wags a finger in Joe's direction. "Did you ever stop and think what would happen to Matilde and me if you are caught? What the Magistrate might do to us? I've said it before," Ian picks up his spoon and turns back to his stew, "we should never have taken the boy in, Matilde."

"Ian!" Blushing, Matilde absently pushes her graying brown hair back into her bandana, a gift Joe had brought back from the markets in Lexington. It is a beautifully patterned fabric with red and orange suns, handmade by a tribe from the Wastes.

"What?" Joe's spoon stops halfway to his mouth. "What do you mean, 'never have taken me in'?"

Ian shares a glance with Matilde, who coughs into her napkin.

"Mom? What does he mean?"

"Oh, it's nothing, just nothing, dear. Your father didn't mean anything." Matilde pats his arm comfortingly.

Joe sets his spoon down and looks back and forth between Matilde and Ian. "Neither of you have powers," he states slowly. "Neither of you are elementals. Does that mean," Joe's eyes go wide as he finally pieces it together. How did he not know this before? "Does that mean you are not my parents?"

Matilde breaks apart the chunk of onion bread in her hands, crushing the crust into smaller and smaller pieces. She sighs and looks Joe in the eyes.

"You are my son, Joe. I love you and always will. But no, I did not give birth to you." She glances at Ian for support, but he resolutely studies the brumbuck tubers in his stew. "During The Expunging, we found you, injured under the bridge. You were very young, Joe, and very hurt. I couldn't leave you. I was never able to have children of my own. Finding you that night answered my prayers." She smiles a watery smile at him.

"Then who are my parents?" Joe gapes.

"We don't know, dear." Matilde reaches out to Joe. He hesitates a moment, but then takes her hand in his. For as long as he can remember, Matilde and Ian have been his parents. While Ian didn't always agree with Joe experimenting and expanding his powers, he also never hit him or treated him as less-than for being an elemental. And Matilde has been nothing but the kind, gentle mother he's always known her as.

"If you found me under the bridge, then that means my real parents are probably dead."

Matilde quickly looks away. Joe squeezes her hand to catch her eye.

"While this is a lot to process, you are the only mother I have ever known. And you the only father," Joe directs to Ian. "I am glad to have you as my parents."

Matilde dabs her eyes with the hem of her apron, and they finish their dinner in silence.

6

att Fletcher sits at the middle table of the Siren Club, hoping that tonight is the night he catches the eye of his crush. Every shore leave he comes to the club, certain that he will get up enough courage to talk to his crush, and every time he chickens out. But not tonight. Tonight, he promised himself that he would finally find his voice. It's been months, *months*, that he's been silently waiting, and sometimes one just has to jump up and do something.

So tonight, Matt sits in the one place where he can't be missed, dead center of the room, out in the open with no shadows to hide in. The stage where dancers perform is illuminated in red just a stone's throw before him, but his crush is not a dancer. Rather, his crush waits on tables and seems to occasionally take patrons to the curtained-off alcoves at the back of the room. In fact, that's probably where his crush is now.

Matt roves the circular room, squinting into the dark red booths at the edges, trying to glimpse behind the curtains at the back. He doesn't want to appear too obvious though, so upon find-

ing several women in short dresses and two men in suit vests ply-
ing the patrons, he turns back to his drink, disappointed. His crush
does not seem to be here tonight. Matt sighs forlornly and plays
with the edge of the black tablecloth. He supposes he should just
wander back to the *Moro* and try again next shore leave.

Downing his drink, he moves to get up when a lithe shadow
falls across his table.

"Need a refill?" A sultry voice in tight trousers and a loose
shirt holds up a pitcher of ale.

Matt gulps. *Finally!*

"Um, yeah, sure." Matt holds out his mug, trying to keep his
hand steady. His crush refills his mug and sets it back down with a
grin.

"Would you like to have a seat?" Matt gestures to the chair
opposite.

"Oh, sorry. I'm about done for the night. No time to head to
the back." His crush points to an alcove with his eyebrows.

"Oh, no, no, I didn't mean that," Matt blushes. "I just wanted
to sit a bit and, um, talk, maybe?"

His crush laughs softly. "Sure, I have a few minutes for that.
What's on your mind?"

Matt wipes his sweaty palms on his pants. "Oh, well, I see you
here often, and I just wondered…what your name is," he finishes
lamely.

His crush's grin fades a bit.

"You can call me Jonny."

"Nice to meet you, um, Jonny. I'm Matt." Matt awkwardly
holds out his hand to shake. Jonny gives him a curious look as he
takes it. "I don't know why I did that, sorry." Matt takes his hand

back and stares into his mug, wishing he could disappear. This wasn't going at all like he planned.

"No, it's fine," Jonny reassures him. "So, let me guess, a sailor? On leave?"

"Oh, yeah!" Matt perks up a little. "I'm on the *Moro*. We actually ship out tomorrow for Lexington."

"Going to the markets?" Jonny looks thoughtful. He leans in close and brushes a finger across the back of Matt's hand. "If I needed to send something to Lexington, discretely, would you be the person to talk to?"

Matt's mouth goes suddenly dry. He wants to reach for his mug, but Jonny's still touching his hand, and he would die if he didn't relish that touch for just a second longer. Swallowing hard, Matt looks up into Jonny's bright blue eyes.

"Not me, no. But," Matt quickly resumes, assuaging Jonny's crestfallen expression. "I do know a man who could help you out."

*   *   *   *

Joe leaves Ian and Matilde's and heads back toward the business district, thinking he might stop at the Black Goose for a pint, or at least for comfort in the distraction of strangers.

The Black Goose is one of the many taverns that rings the city square. A wooden three-story structure with black trim and a black goose for a sign, the tavern is planted between a cobbler and a bakery. It isn't the classiest tavern in the city, but being the local haunt for sailors, it happens to be the best place Joe has found to escape into obscurity, most of the time. He shudders off the memory of Felix's arrest and pushes into the tavern.

Ordering a pint, he finds a booth near the back and sinks down, sitting with his back to the wall, so he can keep an eye on the door, just in case. The tavern is warm and dim and full of raucous conversation tonight. Its population steadily increases as the night progresses until the Black Goose is packed to the brim with smelly, unwashed sailors home on leave. They stand shoulder to shoulder at the wooden bar, shouting out their orders. A fiddler pops up near the fireplace and plays a jig, causing a few sailors to take turns dancing with the barmaid. All in all, it's a cozy night at the Black Goose and Joe relaxes just a bit.

Joe returns to his booth with his second pint when a burst of cool night air rushes in. The open door admits an overly-dressed man. In a pressed shirt and trousers, topped off with a suit jacket and an elaborately carved cane, he looks like he should be headed to a party in the High Tide neighborhood. The man looks around with a haughty air and flicks a speck of dust off his jacket sleeve. Joe takes a drink, smirking at the out of place character, but quickly frowns as the man approaches his table.

"Joe, is it?" The man offers his hand. Joe gives him the once over. Upon closer inspection, the man isn't as fancy as he appears. The scuff marks on his shoes and frayed edges of his sleeves give him away. It even looks as if the man's dyed his hair brown, perhaps using the pigments from Lexington that were often sold to the noblewomen of High Tide. Joe's seen his type before, a man parading around as something more than he is. But what catches Joe's eye is his cane. What he thought was carved wood turns out to be elegantly designed stone. *Interesting*, Joe thinks. He assumes the man doesn't come from money, so how would he be able to afford an artisan to create such a cane out of stone?

"Who wants to know?" Joe responds, not taking the proffered appendage.

"Yes, well," the man begins, pulling his hand back to rest atop his cane. "I hear you are the one to speak to about moving items?" Joe doesn't answer and instead takes a swig of his pint. The man smiles. "Mind if I sit? Unfortunately, my leg isn't what it used to be."

Joe stares at the man's legs before gesturing to the seat opposite. The man sits, carefully stretching his bad leg on the bench seat.

"Ah," he sighs, rubbing his right knee. "Much better." Resting his arm on the table, he studies Joe for a moment. Joe sheepishly stares into his drink. He's not usually intimidated by people. Generally, he challenges every look thrown his way. There is something about this man that is familiar though, a strange sense of kinship nags at the back of Joe's memory.

"Let me start over. My name's Jonathon. And I have a job for you, if you'd like it." The man's name bounces around Joe's brain, vaguely recognizable but unplaceable. Joe squints, trying to remember if this Jonathon is another sailor or the owner of a merchant ship, but he doesn't think so. Jonathon simply grins and reaches into his jacket pocket, removing a small cloth pouch. He loosens the pouch's leather tie and upends its contents into his palm.

"You want me to move a marble?" Joe asks, unimpressed. Most items he smuggles are more obviously worth the risk. This small greenish-blue orb, no bigger than a pocket watch in Jonathon's palm, looks like nothing more than a sea stone washed ashore. Insignificant, and clearly not worth paying to smuggle anywhere, really.

Jonathon smiles, closing his fist around the orb and placing it back in its pouch. "Doesn't look like much, does it? I'd take care of it myself, but I'm not that fond of sailing. Was in quite a wreck several years ago and haven't had much of a taste for the ocean since. Which is why I need you." Jonathon lingers on Joe's face a bit too long, causing Joe to squirm slightly in his seat. Setting the cloth pouch with the orb next to Joe, Jonathon draws out another pouch from his other pocket. This he drops directly in front of Joe's pint, with enough force that Joe can't help but hear the heavy clink of coin.

Joe's eyes widen slightly as he brings the pint up for another gulp, but he recovers quickly. Working aboard the *Moro* isn't a bad gig. He makes enough to send some money to his parents and to save some for himself, but extra coins could never hurt anyone.

"Where to, sir?" Joe asks, palming the pouch. Satisfied with the weight, he shuffles it into his own pocket.

Jonathon steeples his fingers and smiles. "I thought that might appeal to you. You ship out tomorrow, yes? I need this delivered to Lexington. I'm sure that for someone of your abilities this won't be an issue. I'll have a man waiting. You should know him when you see him, but for reference, his name is Jordan. Tallish. Long blond hair. Probably has some ash on his jacket or smudged on his forehead. Once you deliver the package and return, in about a fortnight, correct? I'll meet you right back here to double your payment."

Double payment. Seems easy enough. Joe could take an hour out of his night after the *Moro* is docked and unloaded, join a group going to a tavern, as there is always someone going to a tavern, and the captain would never know. He sits back, crossing his arms.

"How did you hear about me?"

Jonathon grins again, showing none of his teeth. Joe winces, studying Jonathon's face, thinking that it would be more familiar if Jonathon had a different hair color.

"Oh, there are many loose lips where I work. Word gets around."

It's not an answer Joe likes. He thinks he is careful, discreet with his side hustle. To hear that perhaps he is not, or that his clients feel the need to share the details of how they get their goods, leaves him uneasy. The coin pouch in his pocket weighs heavily on his mind, though. Joe can tell it is a lot of money, with the promise of more. And the job seems simple enough. The item is small, easily concealed. The risk seems low.

Joe scratches his chin then holds out his hand. "Sir, you've got yourself a deal."

7

Absent-mindedly fingering the folded paper bird crumpled in his pocket, Jonathon briskly walks toward his apartment. The paper bird, a message from his older brother Jacob, is nearly worn out from Jonathon obsessively opening and closing it to read and reread the words written within. The message asked, no, ordered, him to steal the orb from his uncle, Magistrate Rufus, and deliver it to Jordan, his other older brother, waiting in Lexington. Magistrate Rufus has always been one step ahead of Jacob; by sending the orb to Port Green via Lexington, Jacob hopes that this time, he'll be the one who is a step ahead.

The stupid, elusive orb. Jacob first learned of it from their father, back all those years ago before The Expunging. His father brought the orb with him when he moved down from Andulsae, saying it was a gift from the chief to help solidify the new peace treaty. Jonathon had never seen his father use the orb, so he's not really sure it does anything of significance, but Jacob believes it does. More so, Jacob believes it's rightfully his and should never have fallen into their uncle's hands. After fourteen years and numerous plans to reclaim the throne, Jacob determined the orb was the answer. So, he sent the message bird on the wind, and lucky Jonathon was stuck with the task.

But now the orb is out of his hands and on its way to Lexington. It had been a stroke of luck that the awkward young man in the Siren Club tonight happened to know of a smuggler. Once this green-eyed patron told Jonathon the smuggler's name was Joe, Jonathon almost fainted on the spot. Could it be, seven years after his return to Eastport, that Jonathon had finally found his long-lost little brother? Joe is a common enough name, but Jonathon couldn't stop the flutter of excitement in his chest. Jonathon had searched the best he could while working at the Siren Club, but no sign of Joseph turned up. Tonight at the Black Goose, however, Jonathon finally got to see Joseph after all these years.

At first, Jonathon had stalled, almost not wanting to approach the booth Joseph was sitting in, unwilling to get his hopes up. But as he stepped closer, Jonathon was certain that this man was in-fact his little brother. He had the same ice-blue eyes and cowlick of blond hair against his forehead that Jonathon remembered from their youth. But there was wariness to Joseph's manners, a guardedness that Jonathon didn't recognize. His little brother had always been carefree, rushing headlong from one place to the next. Jonathon wishes he could have asked Joseph what happened these past fourteen years to make him seem jaded.

Yet, Joseph looked healthy, and relatively happy, Jonathon supposes. He is curious as to how Joseph managed to become a smuggler but is glad to know that he would be the one to deliver the orb. *Won't Jordan be surprised,* Jonathon chuckles to himself, *seeing Joseph arrive instead of me.* However, when Jonathon introduced himself, Joseph showed no sign of recognition. Jonathon frowns. Maybe it had been too long, and Joseph had forgotten what he looked like? Clapping his hand to his forehead, Jonathon realizes that he has brown hair now, dyed as a precaution to hide from his uncle. Last time Joseph saw him, it was blond. Maybe that was why Joseph seemed not to recognize him. Either way, Jonathon is glad that his role with the orb is over, and Jacob could finally admit that Jonathon has a part to play.

Jonathon knows he isn't the best one for this job. Rather, he is the only one with the means of carrying it out, something that Jacob would only begrudgingly admit. Jonathon's work at the Siren Club gives him access to many varied patrons, one of whom just happened to be Bernard Lowain, a regular who became a long-term commitment. Bernard had formerly been a simple Warden but was promoted to captain just last week. The Magistrate fast-tracked Bernard's progression through the ranks, which struck Jonathon as odd, since Bernard is no older than Jonathon himself, and therefore is rather young to be a captain. All Bernard told him was that the Magistrate saw promise in him and needed Bernard's expertise on a certain matter. Jonathon pried, but Bernard would not explain further.

Stealing the orb had been easy work. For a year, Bernard had been trying to get Jonathon to come with him on a tour of the castle, trying to impress Jonathon by showing he could sneak him in. Bernard fancied himself somewhat of a rebel, which was rather ironic to Jonathon, but also very endearing. As clumsy and naïve as that boy was, Jonathon couldn't help but fall in love.

After endless needling, Jonathon, against his better wishes, finally took Bernard up on his offer last week, the message from Jacob compelling him to act. They snuck in and around the castle, feeling young and dangerous once more. Jonathon played the role of amazed boyfriend well, asking to see the council room and throne room. When finding that the orb was not in either, he convinced a reluctant Bernard to show him the Magistrate's chambers. He smiles at the memory. *"It was your idea, Bernard!"*

Jonathon immediately spotted the orb upon entering the chambers. It was resting softly in a cushioned box on the nightstand next to the bed. He remembers how appalled Bernard had been when he suggested they test out the lavish red silken sheets. Bernard had dragged his feet and turned pink as Jonathon pulled him toward the bed. Jonathon found this amusing, considering that Bernard had come to the Siren Club almost nightly. After they were done, Bernard fussily rearranged the red sheets. Jonathon took the opportunity to snag the orb from the nightstand and stuff it into his pocket as they left.

He sighs now, thinking back on that day, on how he used Bernard for his brother's end. Sometimes, Jonathon envied Bernard and the rest of the humans of the world. Sometimes, he would rather give up his powers. Oh, life would be so much easier without them. He wouldn't have to lie to Bernard about who he was. He wouldn't have to concern himself with the stupid war for the throne that Jacob wants to wage. But, of course, he'd never mention this to anyone. Jacob would disapprove, saying that to even think such a thing would be to turn his back on his people, to forget what happened to their mother and father. Sometimes he hated Jacob for being so short-sighted. Of course Jonathon would never forget what happened to his parents. How could he? That fateful first night of The Expunging, and the weeks following, would always haunt him. And even though he hated Jacob every time he was reminded that what happened to their mother and father was his fault, Jonathon couldn't help but agree.

Exhaling, his breath misting in the cool night air, Jonathon leans more heavily on his cane as he passes by a bronze obelisk carved in the likeness of the Magistrate, one of many that are scattered throughout the city in concentric circles, cinching tighter the closer they are to the castle. The supposed protectors of Eastport used to be black rock-like pillars made of eusgare, forbidding, yes, but not as intimidating. Just this past spring, however, the Magistrate replaced, to the confusion of many, the black obelisks in favor of these bronze ones, carved to resemble the Magistrate. Magistrate Rufus tells the city that the obelisks will deter elementals from attacking, the material supposedly being a weakness. Jonathon finds it stupid and wonders briefly where his uncle found bronze eusgare when Jonathon's only ever seen black before.

Jonathon hates to admit it, but the obelisks' resemblance to the actual man is exact. He stops at the next corner to stare at the severe visage of his uncle. The obelisk's features are just as Jonathon remembers, even though he hasn't seen his uncle in person for quite some time. The cold eyes looking down the nose in disdain. The overbearing short stature. The hands clenched into fists as Jonathon's skin purpled beneath blows. Jonathon shivers despite his coat and hurries on.

The obelisks aren't enough to cause Jonathon more than a pinch behind his eyes, but it is sufficient to keep him from venturing closer. He has heard stories, though, whispered by patrons in the Siren Club, of elementals that have been exposed to eusgare for long periods of time. In each story, the elemental was eventually driven mad, eusgare acting like a drug. Being in contact with raw eusgare, such as the obelisks or the discs the Wardens carry, increases an elemental's power, eventually consuming them entirely. Only the strongest elementals can resist the raw eusgare for more than a few days, but even they succumb and die. Burning up from the inside out, their power races through their veins in a last attempt to live until their hearts literally burst in their chests.

Rumors in Lexington tell of elementals from Andulsae purposefully using eusgare to enhance their abilities on hunts to take down the great mammoths that roam the Mersae Mountains. Jonathon isn't sure how eusgare helps them, it being so deadly, but assumes there is more to the ore that he doesn't know. It's at moments like these that he wishes his father spent more time teaching him about their elemental side instead of focusing on Jacob, so he could understand where he came from. Too late for that now.

Looking up from his thoughts, Jonathon notices that he has overshot his building by many blocks and is at the foot of the Agate Bridge. He stands for a moment, not willing to step foot on that bridge again. Gazing up at the moon-washed towers of the castle looming like a giant over the Mid Tide neighborhood, he remembers a time fourteen years ago when he called the castle home. When his family was whole and happy. To his right, he spies a light flickering in the throne room of the closest tower, and his mind clouds over with the dark memory of the last time he saw his mother alive that he can never seem to escape. Shaking his head, he turns back in the direction of his building.

A slamming door accompanied by loud voices causes him to pause. People gather outside one of the row houses to his left. Startled, he shuffles into the shadow of the bridge, hoping he isn't seen. Two Wardens lead a woman away from the row house. She struggles against them, appearing to plead for release, but Jonathon is too far away to make out any words. Rearing back, the woman breaks free of the Wardens' grip as a jet of air knocks them to the cobblestone street. She sprints forward, but is stopped short as the cobblestones shoot up from the ground in columns, surrounding her in a stone cage. Turning, the woman shoots another jet of air at the Wardens and then aims her hands down at the ground, gathering wind beneath her to lift her up and away. The cobblestones swiftly rise higher to intertwine above her head, blocking her escape.

Jonathon fretfully examines the ground at his feet, wondering if somehow his powers reacted without his knowledge. Yet he knows this is not his doing. Stampeding boots snap his attention back to the woman, where the two Wardens approach once more. Behind them, a third Warden steps into the light of the streetlamp, pulling a man along by a collar clasped at his throat. The collared man has both hands up, focusing on the stone cage trapping the woman. Black veins run from his forehead down his neck, disappearing beneath his shirt and his eyes are solid white.

Trying to still his pounding heart, Jonathon slowly backs away, but his shaking hands lose their grip on his cane and it clatters to the ground. Jonathon holds his breath as he glances at the Wardens, hoping they didn't hear him. Instead, he finds the terramental's white eyes zeroing in on his position in the shadows. Stomach clenching, Jonathon sprints down the hill beneath the Agate Bridge, not daring to look back. Reaching the bottom of the hill, he slides into a dark alley between two apartment buildings that huddle below the bridge. There are no streetlamps down here under this part of the Agate Bridge, and the apartment buildings tower like menacing giants over him.

Pausing a moment, Jonathon tries to catch his breath. The Wardens used an elemental to arrest an elemental. What's more, the terramental's eyes were white. And what were the black veins on his face? Jonathon opens his jacket and fans himself, wiping a sleeve across his forehead. That terramental saw him. Jonathon needs to get home, fast, before the terramental leads the Wardens right to him. Will they take him to his uncle if they catch him? What would his uncle do to him then? Turn him into a white-eyed attack dog like the terramental tonight? His right knee is screaming, and he wishes he hadn't dropped his cane. Jonathon longs to create another, but he knows he can't risk it. Not with that terramental helping the Wardens.

A rat scurries over his foot, and Jonathon nearly yelps. That's all the prodding he needs. Gulping in a big breath of air, Jonathon limps his way out of the alley to the other side of the bridge, hiding in the apartment buildings' shadows as much as he can. He slowly climbs the hill to the right of the bridge and peeks to see if the Wardens are still there. The woman and Wardens are gone. So too is the white-eyed terramental. Jonathon hurries past the spot of the arrest, not willing to look down at the disarrayed cobblestones, and heads away from the castle back into the city.

Turning down an unlit alley three blocks from the Agate Bridge, Jonathon stops before a green door set back into a stone wall. The window next to the door has its curtains drawn, but he sees a soft glow emanating from the fabric's edges. Exhaling in relief, he unlocks and opens the door to his and Bernard's apartment, sighing shakily as he inhales the warmth emanating from the stove. The apartment is small, with the iron stove nestled in the far-left corner. Near the stove is a double bed, covered in a blue and green quilt made for him by Madame Barnaby, the owner of the Siren Club. A nightstand with a washbasin stands along the right-hand wall next to a wooden screen to block off the chamber pot.

Bernard thinks the screen ridiculous, but Jonathon insisted. Some things should remain private. Further down the wall, two chairs and a table crowd underneath the window. Jonathon slumps against the closed door, happy to be far removed from whatever he just witnessed near the Agate Bridge. He removes his coat and hangs it on a hook to the left of the door then heads over to the stove to shake off the cold.

"Bernard?" he calls out as Bernard returns from the chamber pot. "How was your day?" Jonathon takes a deep breath to calm his shaking hands, an attempt to appear normal so as to not give any hints about what he just saw. But surely Bernard knows about the Wardens using elementals. *Would he ever turn on me like that?* Jonathon shudders at the thought.

Bernard shrugs as he joins Jonathon at the stove and puts a pot of water on to boil, starting supper. "Interesting news from Gregor and the chemists," he replies, angling away from Jonathon. "You know how I've told you Magistrate Rufus has been experimenting with eusgare?"

Jonathon pauses approaching Bernard for just a second. "I think I remember you mentioning he was testing eusgare's full abilities on elementals, yes."

"Right. I think Gregor has just about solved it, especially with the success they had with this last one. I was told the subject responded better than expected. Shame he expired so soon."

Jonathon thinks back to the hanging in the square just a day ago, and how the elemental had black veins all over his face. The terramental tonight had the same black veins. Would he "expire" soon as well?

"Gregor's chemists have invented a new drug they call Ink," Bernard continues, glancing up from the pot on the stove. "It's made from liquefied eusgare. Magistrate Rufus is very pleased with the results."

"Oh?" Jonathon comes up and rests his head on Bernard's shoulder, weary from the day and wanting some peace, the murmur from the boiling water soothing him.

"Apparently, elementals who use the drug become more powerful for a while. The Magistrate plans to use this drug to make a small militia of elementals that he can control. Extra protection for us should those from Andulsae ever attack. The only good elemental is a dead one—or one that is in our control." Jonathon is only half paying attention, but this last phrase flips his stomach. Controlled elementals? Is that what he witnessed? He feels Bernard tense beneath his ear. Jonathon stands up straight and examines Bernard's face.

"You look troubled," Jonathon says.

Bernard turns toward him with his deep brown eyes, like two pools of melted chocolate. Jonathon loves how those eyes match his hair perfectly. He reaches up to brush a strand of that chocolate hair from Bernard's forehead.

"Magistrate Rufus also had interesting news." Bernard looks down at his feet. "And I am conflicted."

Jonathon drops his hand and takes a step back, the air suddenly heavy. "Oh?" is all he can manage in reply as pressure builds in his chest.

"That night, when I snuck you into the castle to give you a tour?" Bernard stutters, unsure, but forces himself to continue. "Apparently, we weren't as sneaky as we thought. Gregor saw us. And he recognized you."

Jonathon gulps the lump of fear building in his throat. Glancing down, he notices that Bernard's boots are still on, as is his belt with his nightstick. Jonathon almost falls to his knees, the weight of what he must now do unbearable.

"Gregor said you look different now, that your hair is a different color, but that you are one of the lost princes," Bernard whispers with a barely concealed rage. "An elemental."

Quickly, Jonathon lunges for the pot on the stove and flings the boiling water in Bernard's face.

Bernard howls with pain as he crashes to the floor, desperately trying to scrub the burning water away with his shirt sleeves. For a moment, Jonathon thinks of running to the well outside to grab a bucket of cool water for Bernard. He had only known Bernard for just over two years, but for the first time in his life, Jonathon had felt safe. He loves Bernard and causing him this much pain crushes Jonathon's heart. But if he lets Bernard catch him, Jonathon fears he will end up like that terramental he saw tonight.

Steam fills the air, and Bernard struggles to rise, blindly tearing at the nearby bed. Squinting through red eyes Bernard searches the room, seething. Jonathon stumbles as he hobbles for the door, catching Bernard's attention. Bernard draws his nightstick and quickly strikes Jonathon in his bad knee, which immediately goes limp, and Jonathon falls back to the ground with a heavy thud, stunned.

Using the bed for leverage, Bernard slowly pushes himself up and towers above Jonathon, chest heaving, fury further reddening his now marred face. "I can't believe I ever fell in love with a dirty elemental," he spits.

His heart breaking, Jonathon desperately wants to call upon his power, but he can't bring himself to truly hurt Bernard. Loving Bernard had given him hope that things would get better, and he hoped that one day, Bernard would see past his being an elemental.

Unfortunately, Jonathon thinks remorsefully as the nightstick comes at him once more, *some people will never change, no matter how much I hope.*

8

hrilled at his new wealth, Joe, slightly drunk, stumbles back to the shipboard cabin he shares with Matt, his fellow crewmate. On the way, he stops by the bakery to grab two cinnamon buns, one for both him and Matt, before the bakery closes for the night. They're stale, being the leftover pastries that didn't sell during the day, but Joe didn't think Matt would mind. Continuing to the harbor, Joe approaches the *Moro*, stopping to take in the sight of the ship floating gently in the water before him, its polished wooden sides dimly illuminated by the lamps of the docks.

The *Moro* is a simple merchant ship with a small crew of about thirty; three-masted and squat, it sits low in the water. Its keel is as wide as a fat-bottomed barmaid, providing greater stability in rough water. The *Moro* doesn't carry any guns, freeing up its innards for more cargo. The berth deck holds the crew's cabins. Captain Merrill prefers small rooms for his crew instead of crowding them together in hammocks. The berth deck also houses the ship's galley and sick bay. The stern of the ship holds the captain's cabin and navigation room. The bow of the ship has a wooden fig-urehead carved in the likeness of Captain Merrill's wife.

Joe walks up the gangplank of the *Moro*, crosses the main deck, and heads down the stairs to his cabin, but something makes his hand pause above the doorknob. A noise. A sort of shuffling sound coming from behind the wooden door. Slowly, he lowers his hand and turns the knob. The door swings open wide as Joe bursts into his room, but he quickly stops when he sees that it's not a bur-glar. *I should've known better,* he thinks as he slumps against the doorframe.

"Nell, what're you doing?" Joe crosses his arms, watching Nell throw his socks and underwear out of the top drawer of his dresser. Nell tosses her long brown braid over her shoulder as she straightens.

"Rearranging. You should really clean up in here. Your room's a mess." She comes and stands in front of Joe, a sly smile on her narrow face.

"They're not in there, Nell." Joe takes out his pack of ciga-rettes and offers her some. "You know, you could've just asked."

Nell grabs five cigarettes and stuffs them in her pocket. "I know. But maybe I just wanted an excuse to come into your cabin. Maybe I wanted an excuse to see your underwear."

She moves closer to him as she talks until their noses are an inch apart. Nell puts her hand on Joe's chest and leans in close. Oh man, can she feel how fast his heart is beating? Joe reaches out to cup her face; he can already taste her lips.

Nell pushes him hard into the doorframe. "Sucker. Not on your life, Joe. Thanks for the cigs."

"Dammit, Nell! Don't tease me!" Joe follows her raucous laugh down the hallway and up the stairs. And she's gone. *One of these days. One of these days, I'll get that kiss.* Joe shakes his head and closes the door. Nell. He's had a crush on her ever since he started on the crew. She's most definitely noticed and loves to toy with him. Joe sighs as he takes off his jacket. He goes to hang it up, but then remembers the money pouch in his pocket. Taking it out, he heads over to his bunk and puts it under his pillow. *Ah, I'm going to sleep well tonight,* Joe thinks as he smiles to himself. Changing out of his street clothes, he climbs into bed and falls asleep instantly. Then the nightmare starts.

This nightmare has haunted him for several weeks now, seemingly more real each time it comes. Joe is young in the nightmare, maybe five or six years old, sleeping in a large room. In the dream, loud bangs wake him abruptly from sleep. Another boy, maybe a year or two older, pulls him out of bed, and they huddle together in a corner. Everything is dark and loud, and the smell of gunpowder fills the air. The next thing he knows, he and the other boy are racing through the night, hallways and rooms and tapestries blurring together in one mirage of color until they emerge outside with a castle at their backs. Joe is then transported to a bridge. The other boy grips his hand as they race across. Shouts resound from behind and his hand is yanked from the other boy's. Joe looks down and sees that this time, the boy elongates, his face and torso stretching like a fishing line, until the boy transforms into the man from the Black Goose who gave him a job. The man clutches his knee in pain, blood shining bright against the pavement. He looks up at Joe, opening his mouth to say something. Joe strains to hear but can't make out any words.

A sharp noise brings Joe fully out of his dream. He gasps, then lies still, trying to process the sound he just heard, unsure if it was part of his dream or here in the cabin. Barely moving, he glances out of the corner of his eye at the slowly opening door. Silently, he reaches for the knife on his nightstand, but sends the lantern crashing to the floor instead. *Dammit.* Grabbing his knife, Joe springs from his bed and rushes the door, hoping to catch the intruder before his blunder sends him too far. But swinging open the door, Joe only finds Matt, a startled expression on his face.

"Um…Is this a bad time? Do you have, like, company, or something?"

"Ah, sorry, Matt." Joe quickly stows his knife and heads back into the room. "Bad dream is all."

"Again? Maybe you should pick up some nightfern this next trip. Supposed to help you sleep. Either that or you should drink more. Maybe you could join me at the Siren Club." A mischievous grin spreads across Matt's impish face as he quickly changes and climbs into his bunk above Joe.

"Score!" Matt crows as he spies the cinnamon bun on his bunk that Joe brought him. "These are the best!" he mumbles through a mouthful of pastry.

Joe gives a wry smile as he sits back down on his bed. "No luck with that fellow you've had your eye on?"

Joe hears Matt flop down above him, emitting a dramatic sigh.

"No. I spoke to him, finally, but unfortunately, I just made a fool of myself in front of the love of my life."

"Love of your life?" Joe laughs.

"Some things are just fate, dear Joseph."

Joe punches Matt's mattress and settles back down on the covers, a strange sense of dread creeping in. He closes his eyes as he pinches the bridge of his nose. These nightmares are really starting to get to him. He feels like a spool of thread, slowly unraveling, and he's not sure why. Laying his head on his pillow, he wishes that it had been an intruder at the door instead of Matt. At least an intruder is something he could handle, something tangible that he could grab and punch. But these nightmares, well, they're not something he can escape. They scare him more than any intruder would because he's certain that these nightmares are memories trying to claw their way to the surface. Memories that he can't even begin to understand. What was he doing at the castle? Who was the other boy with him? Could these nightmares have anything to do with his real parents? Joe hasn't yet taken the time to truly think through the surprise Ian and Matilde dropped at dinner. Perhaps he should. But the *Moro* is shipping out tomorrow and there's little time to sort these thoughts out. Sighing, Joe puts the knife under his pillow, next to the money pouch, and tries to get some sleep.

*   *   *   *

Joe wakes the next morning to pounding on his door.

"Go away!" He shoves his face into the pillow, trying to block out the noise.

"Get up, Joe! Everyone else is already up and at it! I don't know why I even bother with you."

Nell. Pounding on the door. Pounding on the door...*Dammit! I'm late!* Jumping out of bed, Joe rushes to get dressed.

"Joe, come on!"

"I'm coming!" he shouts as he fumbles with the ties on his shirt. Falling against the wall as he pulls on his boots, he stumbles down the hall, up the stairs, and onto the main deck. Captain Merrill gives Joe a stern look, causing him to hurry down the gangplank to the dock where cargo is being loaded onto pallets. Patting his jacket, Joe desperately searches for the ship's manifest.

Nell saunters past, pushing the leather-bound book into Joe's chest. "Nell, what would I do without you?"

She turns, walking backward down the dock, "Crash and burn, Joe. Definitely crash and burn." Joe shakes his head and smiles, opening the manifest as he walks over to where Matt is loading pallets. They are shoving off in an hour, and there is still a lot to do.

"Matt, why didn't you wake me up?" Joe shouts to his foreman. Matt cups a hand over his ear and shrugs at Joe, not hearing above the din of the crew loading cargo. "Oh, never mind," Joe mutters to himself. "We need to pick up the pace if we're going to catch high tide. How many more loads?" Joe bellows up to Matt.

"Calm down, Dreamland. We'll make it. Only two or three more." Matt nets another pallet to the winch.

Joe smiles to himself and breathes in the fresh salt air, the strangeness of last night almost forgotten. Everything is going to plan. Soon they'll be on their way, landing in Lexington right on schedule. Joe will unload his latest package, collect the rest of his pay, and have extra to bring home to his parents.

Pounding footsteps like a herd of elephants resound on the dock. Looking up, he sees a patrol of Wardens drawing nearer, with none other than Bernard Lowain in the lead. Joe rolls his eyes. Bernard, all proud in his new role as Captain of the Wardens, has been trying nonstop to arrest Joe for smuggling. Of course he has no proof. And without proof, Bernard could never hope to detain him for longer than half a day. Joe sighs as Bernard halts in front of him.

"What do you want, Bernard? We're on a schedule."

"You're under arrest, Joe." Bernard steps forward primly.

Joe gives a short laugh. "On what charges?" The rest of the crew stops loading cargo to watch the scene unfold, smirks on most of their faces.

A cruel smile spreads across Bernard's face. "Joe, Joe, Joe. Seems like someone let your secret slip."

Joe's heart skips a beat. Surely he's just talking about his smuggling, not his being an elemental, right? Quickly disguising his worry, Joe slams the leather cover of the ship's manifest shut and leans against a crate, arms crossed. "Out with it, Bernard. We have a schedule to keep. I don't have time for your games."

"Pity." Bernard eyes Joe, assessing him. A puzzled look crosses Bernard's face as his mind appears to drift. Shaking his head, he rights himself. "Fine. You know you're taking all the fun out of this, Joe. But I'll be brief. You're under arrest for being an elemental."

Joe stands up, shocked and silent, but keeps his face blank. Obviously, this is just one of Bernard's tricks to try and get him to admit to smuggling.

"I'm sorry, a what?" Joe scratches the back of his neck in exhaustion.

"An elemental? Who, Joe? Good one, Bernard!" Matt jokes from beside the crate he's winching. The rest of the crew chuckles.

"Laugh all you want, but I have my sources. A certain someone who met you at the Black Goose last night."

Joe rubs his brow. *The man from last night? Jonathon?*

"Bernard, this is ridiculous. Look, we've got a schedule to keep, so unless you have something substantial, can you leave?" He turns his back and opens the manifest to continue inventory.

"Yes, yes. I know about your precious schedule," Bernard sighs with mock dramatics. "But either I arrest you now for being an elemental, or I have my men arrest the entire crew for harboring one."

Joe sets down the manifest and slowly turns to face Bernard, steel in his eyes.

"Your move, Joe."

Joe clenches his fist, dying to show Bernard just what kind of moves he can make. Who does Bernard think he is, threatening his crew? He slowly counts to ten, the heavy realization settling on him that there is nothing he can actually do except get arrested. Him or his crew. It's not even a choice. Heavy footsteps behind him announce Captain Merrill's arrival.

"Bernard, why are you harassing my crew?"

"You would address me as Captain, Merrill. I'm here to make an arrest."

Captain Merrill slowly crosses his arms. "Of whom and on what charges?"

"Joe. For being an elemental."

"Do you have proof?"

"I have what I need. But, per procedure, I did bring eusgare." Bernard pauses to put on gloves from his waistband before grabbing the eusgare disc from a chain around his neck, handling it as if it were poison.

Captain Merrill looks at the disc and motions to Joe. "Take the test. Prove him wrong, so we can ship out."

Joe stares at the disc. He doesn't know much about eusgare except that extended contact with the ore causes an elemental to show his powers. Felix was afraid to touch it when he was arrested. What would actually happen if Joe did touch it? Would it burn him, or cause him to go mad, or something equally as horrible? Joe uses his powers, but not often. Matilde taught him that while his powers were nothing to be ashamed of, he shouldn't make it known that he had them, lest one day someone finds out. It appears today would be that day. Could he somehow beat the eusgare? Keep pretending that he's human? He's walked past the obelisks in the city often enough without any major incidents, so it was possible he could beat the test, right? Heck, Joe's never truly tested the limits of his powers, so maybe his powers were weak enough that the eusgare wouldn't detect them?

"Joe?" The captain looks at him. "Hurry up, we don't have all day."

There is no way out of it. If he doesn't agree to the test, it will only prove his guilt. Joe takes a deep breath and steps forward, holding out his hand.

That cruel smile comes to Bernard's face once more as he removes the disc of eusgare from its chain and places it in Joe's open palm. The eusgare looks rather beautiful, even a bit mesmerizing, appearing to shimmer in the morning light, but Joe knows not to be enticed. Great beauty can often hide deadly foes.

Bernard forces Joe's palm closed over the disc. Joe feels a pinch in his gut, but nothing more. He smiles to himself. He can beat this test.

"I wouldn't smile just yet, Joe," Bernard hisses as he pulls his bronze-colored cloak in front of his body. Joe notices the other Wardens do the same, and he quizzically glances at Matt over his shoulder. Matt just shrugs and makes a "get on with it" motion with his hand. Joe turns back to the disc in his closed palm. He expects there to be a force to strain against, but he feels nothing.

Just the smoothness of the eusgare in his hand. He chances a glance at Bernard, who remains frozen in anticipation.

Joe sighs. "Look, Bernard, nothing's happening. Can you stop this nonsense and let us…" Joe pauses as he feels a curious sensation in his gut. There is a slight pressure there, as if he has to pee, but he's sure he doesn't. This isn't like the other times he's used his powers. Those times he just used them, and that was it. But now, Joe finds himself wanting to explore this feeling he's never felt before, this feeling of not quite pain and not quite pleasure.

He clenches his fist tighter around the eusgare disc, sinking deeper into the sensation in his gut, willing it to expand. Almost at once, Joe feels the full brunt of the eusgare's power. The strain in his gut makes a wave of energy that pulls at him, filling him with a lightness, as if he could float away. He feels strong, so strong, like he could command the ocean to do anything, everything. And not just the ocean here, but all water, everywhere. He senses the sharp tug of the underground rivers, the pull of the rain in the sky far above. The sensation builds up in him, threatening to overtake him, and he so desperately wants to give in to the release, to revel in this power, to let it break forth.

Losing himself, Joe feels the ocean at his back rising, churning, wanting to burst over the docks and wash away all of Eastport. He feels geysers of water racing through the ground, ready to break through the surface and add to the destruction that is building. But, as if from a great distance, he hears astonished gasps of fear, and he struggles to come back to himself. Gaining awareness, he notices that the power he feels isn't just inside him, but that he is actually causing a massive tidal wave to bear down on Eastport, and that geysers of water are, in fact, bursting up from the ground. In his periphery, he sees his crew's scared faces as they cower from the towering columns of water. He sees Nell, a look of utter betrayal etched on her face, Captain Merrill, trembling in fear, and Bernard, still hiding behind his bronze-colored cloak, laughing because he is right.

Joe needs to stop, to make everything normal. But the eusgare is so insistent, and he knows that if he stopped, he'd lose the best thing that could ever happen. But from somewhere deep in his mind, he hears Matilde saying to him, as she usually does when he questions why he is burdened with this curse: "You are not a monster."

I am not a monster, he thinks to himself. From out of his throat comes a guttural scream as he forces the ocean back. The eusgare fights him every step of the way, but these are his friends, his family, and he can't do this to them. With one last push, he makes the ocean retreat and the geysers return to the earth. Joe falls to his knees panting with exhaustion at using so much power. Yet, the tingling sensation still remains, filling him with a warmth reminiscent of hot cider on a cold day.

Before him, he notices Bernard draw a small crossbow from a holster on his back and notch a bronze dart. Joe puzzles at this image. This is supposed to be an arrest, not an execution. Bernard releases the dart, and Joe feels a punch to his shoulder. The wooden planks of the dock tilt toward Joe as his back hits the ground, the eusgare disc rolling from his hand.

9

onathon shifts his hips so that he is resting on his left side, letting his injured knee have a bit of a break. His arms are shackled to the stone wall over his head, not giving him much room to maneuver. He's back in the castle dungeon, once his safe place where he was comforted by the direct contact with the earth, but now the place of nightmares and bad memories of his mother's death fourteen years ago.

Magistrate Rufus reopened the castle dungeon after Queen Valencia's death, using it only for arrested elementals. When he was dragged in, Jonathon could dimly make out bronze pillars marching down the corridor between cells in the lantern light. He thought it was a strange addition, as he is positive these pillars weren't present fourteen years ago. As he passed them, he felt a suctioning in his gut, as if his powers were retreating down a drain. Jonathon doesn't give much thought to it now, sitting in the pitch-black dungeon and hearing the whimpers of what he assumes are other elemental prisoners.

Like Bernard said, Jonathon's uncle has been experimenting.

Jonathon had only been arrested last night, but since then, Bernard and Gregor have come to visit him every couple of hours. And each time, they bring Ink.

Jonathon fought back the first time they came, several hours after his arrest. A lantern flared to life as the heavy dungeon door opened. Bernard held the lantern aloft as Gregor stepped in, a large wooden case slung over his shoulder. Jonathon shook upon seeing Gregor, forbidden memories invading his mind of Gregor and his uncle whispering in the library before his mother was murdered. A flutter of hope twinged in Jonathon's chest as Bernard approached, the absurd notion that Jonathon might be released drowning out his rational thoughts. But Gregor and Bernard strode past his cell, Bernard resolutely refusing to glance at Jonathon. Pausing in front of a cell three down from Jonathon's, Gregor unslung the wooden case while Bernard unlocked the cell. The lantern flickered as they both entered, Bernard blocking Jonathon's view of their actions. Jonathon strained to see around Bernard's broad shoulders. There was a thud as the wooden crate was set on the floor, and then Jonathon heard a clinking, followed by silence.

The silence lasted an unbearably long time. Jonathon hardly dared to breathe. It seemed that any noise would disrupt the delicate process that Bernard and Gregor were undertaking. Jonathon figured this must be the experiments Bernard had mentioned yesterday. Part of him wished he could see around Bernard, to understand what it was him and Gregor were doing to cause the white eyes and black veins he saw in that terramental. But the logical part of Jonathon knew that whatever it was they were doing, he never wanted to experience it. Their surgical silence instilled more fear than his uncle's beatings ever had.

An agonized howl caused Jonathon to jump back. Bernard set the lantern on the ground and rushed to help at Gregor's command. Without Bernard blocking the way, Jonathon could see the grisly scene unfolding in the other cell. An elemental was writhing on the ground screaming, Gregor holding his shoulders while Bernard held his feet. The elemental wore no shirt, and Jonathon could see black lines crossing his chest, traveling all the way up his neck to his forehead. The elemental's eyes were pure white.

Jonathon gasped in recognition. This was the terramental who helped the Wardens arrest that woman last night.

"Gregor! Do we administer another dose?" Bernard shouted over the ravings of the terramental.

"No. It's too late for this one," Gregor's deep voice responded without emotion.

"We'll bound him tighter and prepare the gallows for his hanging."

"Not this one, Bernard. As I said, it's too late for him." Gregor reached into the wooden case and withdrew a dagger. The terramental's screams intensified.

"The Magistrate wants them publicly executed when you're done with your experiments. As a reminder to the people. You cannot kill him here." Bernard struggled to keep ahold of the flailing terramental's feet.

"This one won't shut up long enough for a hanging. If the people see him screaming on the gallows, they'll mistake it as fear and might have pity on him. Then they would question the necessity of these hangings, which then leads them to question the Magistrate. The dosage and the frequency are wrong. This is a failed experiment, and failed experiments are disposed of."

Gregor slashed the dagger across the terramental's neck in one quick movement, a spray of blood striking him in the face. Gregor calmly wiped the blood off his check with his shirt sleeve.

Jonathon tried to cover his ears to block out the gurgling coming from the terramental's neck but was unable due to his shackled hands.

"Let's get the other one started before we clean up this mess." Gregor cleaned his dagger on a cloth from the wooden crate and picked it up as he motioned for Bernard to follow. They came to a stop outside of Jonathon's cell.

"Hello, Jonathon. It's been a while since I've seen you around here." Gregor tipped his head in greeting, as if he was meeting Jonathon on the street instead of preparing to experiment on him in the castle dungeon. Bernard unlocked the cell as Gregor continued his conversation with Bernard. "I think smaller doses in a higher frequency will achieve the results we want. Enhance the power but leave them subservient, craving that next dose. Hold this one down."

Bernard set the lantern on the ground and stepped toward Jonathon. Jonathon squirmed in his shackles, trying to break free. He tried to call forth his power, but it felt buried deep down, out of reach. Soon, Bernard was before him, and Jonathon stopped trying to access his power when he saw the burned skin on Bernard's face. Jonathon couldn't bring himself to hurt Bernard again.

"Bernard, please, let me go," Jonathon pleaded. "This is just a big misunderstanding." But Bernard forcibly grabbed his arms, pinning him to the wall.

"Now don't try anything," Gregor said as he withdrew a glass vial from the wooden crate. "We're wearing gwarem armor. Your powers have no effect on it."

Jonathon's eyes grew wide as Gregor filled a syringe partway with the black liquid and brought it to his forearm, injecting it into the fleshy part just below Jonathon's elbow. The eusgare hit Jonathon's veins like a gunshot, filling him instantly with the sense of unbridled power. Every minute detail of the earth around him became shockingly clear. The dungeon he could always sense, being in it, but now he felt the enormity of the castle rising above him, the great stone towers stretching like fingers toward the sky. He felt the stone monument out in the woods, just beyond the castle grounds, the escape tunnels he and his brothers used so many years ago. But the biggest pressure in his gut, the almost painful sensation of his stomach exploding, was the sheer cliff face just behind the castle, standing tall like a giant bearing down. Jonathon reached toward the cliff, the sweet ache in his gut wanting to be satiated. He felt the floor of the dungeon beneath him rumble before another pinch to his arm brought him crashing down.

That was all within the first few hours of his arrest. Now Jonathon has had so many doses of Ink that his sense of being is absurdly distorted. Immense guilt washes over him as a memory of early this morning returns. Bernard and Gregor had come, demanding Jonathon to tell them what he did with the orb he had stolen. Gregor continued to inject him with Ink, then enveloped him with a bronze cloak, over and over until Jonathon could barely keep his eyes open, the high and resulting crash tossing him about like a ship on a tempest sea. During one of these crashes, eager for the next high, Jonathon let it slip that he had given the orb to a smuggler, one who could get the job done because he was an elemental.

A headache builds, and Jonathon squints his eyes shut trying to make it go away. Jonathon hasn't had a dose of Ink for a few hours now, and he craves it with the hunger of a man who hasn't eaten for days. He hadn't meant to mention Joe's name, nor that he was an elemental, but all he can remember is wanting the pleasurable power of Ink to return. He said anything to make that happen.

Pushing past the hunger, he reassures himself that Joe's ship had probably already shoved off before Bernard and his Wardens could have shown up. Joe had to be safe. Jonathon holds onto this thought as the dungeon door bursts open. Light from the lanterns outside instantly floods the dark space, bouncing off the bronze pillars and making Jonathon and the other elemental cry out at the sudden assault to their eyes.

"Put him in this one." Bernard strides over and unlocks the cell across from Jonathon. His Wardens place an unconscious man into the empty cell. Bernard glances at Jonathon as he relocks the cell, and Jonathon's heart flutters. But just as quickly, Bernard stomps away, taking the light and the Wardens with him. Jonathon slumps and squints against the dying light into the cell across from him. Recognizing the blond hair and dusty blue jacket, Jonathon gulps, a cold fear gripping his throat as he sees that the unconscious man is Joe.

*   *   *   *

The cold slowly wakes Joe. Lying on his side, the hard dirt floor numbs his bones. Something sticky runs down his face, and it takes him a minute to realize that his nose is bleeding. Blinking his eyes, all he sees is darkness. He tries to move his hand in front of his face, just to check that his eyes are in fact open, but realizes that his hands are shackled behind his back. Craning his neck, he takes in his surroundings. The dark is impenetrable, but he is surely in the castle dungeon. Where else would the Wardens take him? Joe feels the floor beneath his fingertips and crawls his fingers back as far as they can reach. Shortly, they hit a stone wall. He sighs in defeat and closes his eyes. He can't see anyway. He can't even hear the scurrying of rats that he's grown accustomed to on the *Moro* and assumed would be in the dungeon.

A wave of nausea overtakes him as he sits up, moving to rest his back against the wall. He feels a miniscule tug in his gut drawing him to a well somewhere nearby, but the pull makes him nauseous, and his shoulder is starting to hurt from where the dart hit. Not wanting to pass out again, Joe resists the urge to send a flood through the prison. Wincing, he rests his head against the wall, trying to remember what the hell happened.

Bernard. The guards. Losing control. The entire crew watching. Which means that Nell saw everything. Nell would never forgive him for lying to her. She hates elementals almost as much as the Magistrate since her father was killed by a hydromental during The Expunging. Any chance he had with her is effectively dead now.

Nell only told him the story once, a night two years ago while on shore leave in Lexington. They had grabbed a few bottles of ale from the tavern and worked their way down to the seawall that overlooked the south tides, which stretched out to the Whalen Archipelago in the distance. Hopping up on the wall, they watched a pod of whales swimming their way past the harbor. It was late in the evening, and the sun had long ago set. The sun set early in the south during the spring and summer, leaving the southerners to enjoy longer bouts of nighttime, a fact Joe was more than happy to take advantage of. The full, bright moon was accompanied by a slight breeze, just enough to blow away the humidity, and Joe was already a couple of pints in when he and Nell had decided to head to the seawall.

Joe had one thought on his mind when they sat down and cracked open a bottle of Murky Bottom, the local ale of Lexington made from fermented bangerine fruits. He took a long drink to build up his courage and leaned in toward Nell, but she was staring out at the pod of whales breaching in the harbor, chin resting on her drawn-up knee. In the vivid moonlight, Joe could see the streak of tears leaving tracks in the dirt on her face, and all thoughts he had of getting lucky flew away.

"Nell! What's wrong?" He slurred drunkenly at her, a smokey citrus flavor coating his mouth.

Nell wiped a hand across her cheeks and opened the other bottle of Murky Bottom, draining half the bottle before she stopped for a breath. She set the bottle on the wall next to her while she pulled a daydrone out of the ground and started ripping off the petals. Joe just stared, unsure if she heard him or if he should be quiet and wait. He set his own bottle of Murky Bottom down and chose the latter.

"My dad and I used to come here to watch the whales," Nell began. "We used to live here in Lexington, did you know? We moved up to Eastport when I was ten. It was a city. He thought he would have more opportunities there. He wanted to quit fishing and open a bakery." Nell smiled at the memory. "Like, five months after we moved, the Queen was killed, and The Expunging started. We lived in the Mid Tide neighborhood, back then, near the mouth of the Jamin Delta."

Joe shuddered. He had heard the stories. The Mid Tide neighborhood was flooded by escaping hydromentals during The Expunging.

"I wasn't home when it happened," Nell continues, picking another daydrone out of the ground now that her first one was stripped bare. "I had been at the library, looking at books of the different whale species near Eastport when someone came in to say that the hydromentals had flooded the Mid Tide. I ran back as fast as I could, but I couldn't even get down the road to our house. The Wardens were fighting with some hydromentals. They shot and killed them all in the end but wouldn't let anyone pass. They kept saying there was nothing left."

Joe gulped down some more Murky Bottom, thinking that as long as he kept his mouth busy, he wouldn't let anything slip about being a hydromental himself.

Nell sniffed, drained the rest of her bottle, and stood up.

"Come on." She pulled Joe to his feet. "We need to get back to the *Moro*." And that was the last Joe ever heard Nell speak of her father.

Looking back on it, Joe should have said something comforting to Nell. But she is so stoic; nothing Joe could have said would have been sufficient. Especially now that he has been outed as an elemental. He would be lucky if he could ever talk to Nell again.

"How did everything go wrong?" Joe mutters to himself.

"Well," comes a quiet raspy voice from the opposite cell, "I sincerely hope it wasn't my fault."

Joe startles, searching for the voice's owner, but the blackness of the dungeon gives up no secrets.

"Who are you?" Joe asks of the darkness.

"Ah, yes. Last time we met, I was looking quite," Joe hears a grunt of pain, "better. I believe I was giving you a job."

"You! From the Black Goose. You turned me in!" Joe accuses.

"That was not my intent, dear Joseph," Jonathon softly rebuts. Joe cringes at hearing his full name. He waits for Jonathon to say something more, but instead, an uneasy silence fills the dark.

"It just doesn't make any sense," Joe sighs.

Jonathon gives a bitter laugh. "Life doesn't make sense, Joseph. We just have to accept that, for the time being, we are royally screwed." Jonathon snorts and starts to laugh loudly until he is heaving. As quickly as the laughing begins, it briskly ends. "That was a bad joke, wasn't it?"

Joe stares at him, unsure what to make of this man. At the tavern, he was so clean and well-kept, but now he sounds unhinged.

"You really don't remember anything, do you? Even after meeting me?" Jonathon continues.

Remember him? What is that supposed to mean? Joe fiddles with the hem of his jacket behind him, needing to release some of his building anxiety.

"I remember meeting you at the Black Goose and you giving me a job. Then, I remember Bernard arresting me, saying that the man I met at the Black Goose turned me in. That's you." Joe stares pointedly in the direction of Jonathon's voice even though he knows Jonathon can't see him. Jonathon snorts again before falling quiet. Joe looks around the cell, trying to see if there is any way out, should he decide to call upon his power, but, of course, all he sees is darkness. Could he bust a hole in the wall behind him? It shouldn't be a problem to call upon the well he felt earlier, yet his power seems to have shriveled. He can barely feel the pull of the well. Should he help Jonathon escape too? The guy creeps him out and turned him in. He doesn't deserve to be saved in Joe's mind.

As Joe's eyes further adjust to the gloom, he finally notices a faint flickering light near the ground. To his left, slivers of orange outline the bottom of a substantial door, the faintest light seeping in through the frame. To his right is nothing but the immense blackness.

"That's an outer wall. At the end of the corridor where it comes to a tee," Jonathon's raspy voice cuts through Joe's thoughts. "I'm guessing you're trying to figure a way out of here. You could probably do it. Get away, I mean. I could make a hole for you under the bars. I can open that wall for you, give you a chance. I have enough left in me for that, at least." His voice holds an edge of pain, but mostly, he sounds exhausted.

It then dawns on Joe. "You're an elemental."

Jonathon gives a strained laugh. "So are you."

Joe ponders a moment. Escape. He couldn't go home, nor to the ship. He couldn't put his family and friends in any more danger. But surely there are elementals hiding in Eastport, somewhere. Maybe they would help him. Help him to do what, he isn't sure. Eastport is the only home he knows. His crew, his parents. He's only lived with humans. To try to live with other elementals, what would that be like?

"Wait," Joe starts. "How did you know I was an elemental?"

He hears Jonathon shuffling along the floor, as if he's trying to move further away from Joe. "How did you know?" Joe asks again.

Jonathon's response comes in the tiniest whisper. "There are many things you don't know, Brother."

Brother?

Joe's shocked into silence. It's not possible. Perhaps it's simply the delirium of being trapped in this dank dungeon, hidden from the light of day. It's scrambled Jonathon's mind so badly that he sees Joe as his brother, maybe as a last resort to keep sane. Joe shifts the shackles, trying to stretch his sore wrists. He turns his back to Jonathon, not wanting to add to his delusions any further.

"I know you don't believe me," Jonathon whispers, his voice dying in the surrounding darkness. "I know that it seems crazy. And maybe I was crazy for giving you the orb once I recognized you at the tavern. But I've missed you, Joseph. And I know that if I could just talk to you, you would remember. Remember who you were to me."

Joe tries to swallow the growing lump in his throat. He recalls the nightmare, how the boy who was shot became Jonathon. In the nightmare, they were running away from somewhere. And the boy fell, clutching his knee.

"You were shot, weren't you? In the knee, as we were trying to escape?"

"You remember?" Jonathon asks, hope rising in his voice.

"It's not really a memory. More like a nightmare. I don't know what it means, but I think you're in it."

"Yes. Yes, it's a memory." With his powers, Joe feels the tears running down Jonathon's face. "It was the first night of The Expunging," Jonathon begins. "We were trying to escape. Uncle had set the Wardens on us. Jacob and Jordan, our older brothers, they left us behind. We got to the Agate Bridge when the Wardens began firing, and a bullet struck my knee. Blew it out, actually. I told you to keep going, but you were always the brave one. You stayed, ready to take on all of them."

Jonathon pauses, giving a shaky sigh.

"You were my little brother. I couldn't let them kill you. I hadn't practiced using my powers much, but I thought I could do it. I thought I could cause a quake strong enough to knock the Wardens down, give you the chance to run away. But I did too much. The quake I made took care of the Wardens, but it also made you fall over the side of the bridge."

Joe's eyes widen. The Agate Bridge is the tallest bridge in Eastport. Just south of the castle, it crosses the Plebeum River, whose banks consist of big boulders and sharp rocks. The height from bridge to ground had to be at least fifty feet. Joe couldn't begin to imagine what falling off that bridge would be like, but it seems as if he's already experienced it.

"When it was over," Jonathon begins again, "all I could do was scream your name. You were so still, lying at the bottom. I knew you were badly hurt, but I couldn't get to you. Next thing I knew, Jacob was there, pulling me away through the city toward the docks. I tried to tell him what happened, that we had to go and get you, that we couldn't leave you behind, but when I turned back, you were gone."

No. No, no, no. A memory comes flooding back to Joe. A sense of being thrown from a cliff, his stomach swimming up to his throat. Sandpaper stone cutting into his palms as he crawled toward a cottage. A woman looking down at him with concern and fear, asking his name. Darkness, then waking up to that woman's smiling face, telling him it would all be okay, that he just had a little fall.

Joe rubs his left thumb over his palm, tracing a tiny scar that Matilde told him was caused by a fishing hook that got caught one day as Ian was teaching him. Now, Joe starts to wonder if that's true.

"What were we escaping from?" Joe begins cautiously. "Who are my parents?"

A grating sound assaults Joe's ears as the dungeon door shoves open. "They were that no-good aeromental and my weak-hearted sister," says a new voice. Magistrate Rufus, lantern held high and red robes swirling around his feet, strides in.

The sudden light blinds Joe as he tries to raise his arms to block it, but he can only manage a shrug with his hands still shackled behind him. With the intrusion of light, Joe can see bronze pillars in front of his cell, about waist-high, marching down the corridor with an even stride. In the cell across from him, he sees Jonathon flinching away and almost gasps. Jonathon's face is bloody and bruised, his shirt torn and slashed, blood seeping through the fabric like mites from a mattress. There's a hunger to his gaze, as though cautious of the Magistrate's intrusion. He also seems to be searching for something Magistrate Rufus might have brought. Jonathon's right leg glides along limp as he tries to pull himself away from the invading lantern light. Barely glancing in Jonathon's direction, Magistrate Rufus stops in front of Joe.

"Yes, you were left for dead. And what's worse, your brothers, your true family, never once came to look for you. They left you behind like a stray dog. And this one," he gestures back to Jonathon, "turned you in as an elemental. Really, dear Nephew, you deserve so much better."

10

"Wait, what? Nephew? You're my uncle? And you say you're my brother," Joe points to Jonathon. "So that would mean I'm one of the lost princes?" Joe shakes his head, looking from the Magistrate to Jonathon, who shrinks back even further, as if trying to be absorbed by the wall. "And then you turned me in." Joe stares at Jonathon, voice dripping with betrayal, but Jonathon at least has the decency to look away.

"It's all true. Whether you choose to believe it or not, I could not care less. Pity that family can never be trusted, though." Magistrate Rufus shakes his head and continues. "I'll make you a deal," he starts. Joe finally turns away from Jonathon and squints at the man, trying to find any resemblance to his supposed "uncle." Is he really supposed to believe that the short man in front of him, his face deformed by a permanent sneer, is truly a relation? More to the point, is he really supposed to believe that Jonathon, the man who got him arrested, is his brother, and that they are two of the lost princes?

"You work for me, and I'll let you out of this cell," the Magistrate proposes as he carefully watches Joe's face.

Joe straightens up against the stone wall. "Work for you how?"

The Magistrate grins. "As you know, the elementals have a stronghold on Port Green. How they managed to turn that uninhabitable jungle into a stronghold, I'll never know. I have ways of tracking their movements from a distance, which is how I learned of the plan to have that idiot over there steal the orb, but I need a way to attack them from a distance. To rid Eastport once and for all of the elemental scourge." Magistrate Rufus closes his hand into a fist, staring off into the distance as if speaking before a crowd of acolytes.

"Let's say such a thing was possible," Joe starts. "Do you really think I'd help you attack my own people?"

"Your own people?" the Magistrate snorts, turning back to him. "And what have they done for you? They left you behind, to fend for yourself. Their actions," he turns to stare pointedly at Jonathon, "caused you to forget who you were. You owe them nothing."

Joe stares at the floor between his knees. What Magistrate Rufus says is true, but even if things had gone differently, if both he and Jonathon had escaped to Port Green that night long ago, would his life actually be better? Instead of having a home, parents who loved him, friends, a good job—what would he have had? His true family, maybe, but a life of exile? A life of hatred toward humans? A life of hardships? A life without Nell. Joe winces at the thought. His life may have been a lie, but he wouldn't trade the past fourteen years for anything. And he can't justify attacking a whole island of people just to satiate the Magistrate.

"Maybe what you say is true. But the way I see it, both humans and elementals are to blame for the current state of things. I won't help you condemn the lives of one while ignoring the fault of the other."

Clasping his hands in front of him, Magistrate Rufus smiles down his nose at Joe.

"Such a shame your mother isn't alive to see this. You have the makings of a true diplomat in you."

"You're one to talk," Jonathon spits. "I wonder if your people would still love you quite as much if they were to learn that you were the one who killed Queen Valencia, your own sister."

The Magistrate fixes a cold gaze on Jonathon, one which Jonathon meets with his own.

"I think I'll send Bernard back down in a while, this time without the Ink, and see what further information he can gather from you. And perhaps I'll come and watch." Jonathon gulps and shrivels into himself.

Turning back to Joe, Magistrate Rufus resumes. "I figured you would be hard to convince. So, as incentive, I've brought two people near and dear to you." He gestures to the door, through which a Warden shoves Ian and Matilde into the dungeon.

Joe immediately stands and runs to the cell door.

"Why did you drag them into this?" he demands. Ian's face is bruised, the skin beneath his left eye turning purple, and Matilde cowers near the door, her bandana askew. She doesn't try to hide her fear, but she finds the strength to give Joe an encouraging smile.

"We're all right, Joe," she wavers. "Don't worry about us."

"Hardly," the Magistrate says, turning toward Matilde and Ian. "But they won't be harmed any further if you agree to help me."

Joe strains against the cell bars, wishing he could do something, anything, to ease Matilde's fear, to relieve Ian's pain. Without stopping to think, Joe plants his feet and begins to reach for the well he felt earlier. Instead of feeling the familiar tug of water reaching out to him, Joe feels like his stomach is caving in. He lifts his head, confused as to why he can't access the well and steadies his posture, ready to try again when he catches Matilde's eye. Somehow, she always knew when he was about to use his powers. She gives an imperceptible shake of her head. Joe stares for a beat, still trying to reach for the well, but Matilde is right. If he does this, drowns the entire dungeon, he will only prove that the Magistrate is right about elementals.

"Let them go," he says again with gritted teeth. "Whatever this is, it doesn't concern them," he snarls at the Magistrate.

"That's to be seen," Magistrate Rufus replies. "Enough talk." He motions to the Wardens, who stride over and unlock Joe's cell. A Warden on each side, Joe is led past Jonathon in the opposite cell and out of the dungeon. More Wardens follow with Ian and Matilde in tow. The Magistrate closes and locks the heavy door, taking the torch with him and plunging Jonathon back into the inky darkness.

"Stay strong, brother," Jonathon whispers to the door and hallway beyond. "I won't fail you again."

J oe squints against the blinding sun as he is shoved into a large square room. The stone walls are empty save for one tapestry hanging behind the throne, which depicts a battle scene. It's not a scene Joe recognizes, but he is not one for history. The only other object in the sparse room is a raised red throne. To the throne's left is an odd circular stand, strangely vacant, waiting for the last piece of the puzzle to make it whole. To either side of the throne are floor-to-ceiling windows, displaying an expansive view of Eastport: the castle grounds rolling downhill to the Agate Bridge, the High Tide, Mid Tide, and Low Tide neighborhoods, the business district straddling the Jamin Delta, and finally the docks and sea beyond.

The sea calls to Joe so badly that his heart aches. Somewhere out there, his crew has already set sail on their next voyage, heading south to trade with the Lexington merchants. Forgetting his situation for a minute, he lets his mind drift shipboard. He imagines the sea spray beading on his skin as he goes about his tasks. The symphony of wind and ocean as the ship cuts through the waves, sails snapping. The steady murmur of his crewmates' voices. Nell, sneaking into his cabin to steal a cigarette. To think, all it took was a few hours, and his whole life had changed.

Matilde stumbles and falls to her knees as a guard pushes her in front of the throne. Joe rushes to her side and wants to put a comforting arm around her, but he can only manage a shoulder bump due to his still-shackled wrists.

Magistrate Rufus steps around the pair, his red robe brushing Joe's cheek as he walks past to sit haughtily on the throne. Joe can't keep the disgust from his face. The Magistrate simply laughs and steeples his fingers.

"How do you like my changes? I was always fonder of red," Magistrate Rufus gestures to the room. "But I suppose you wouldn't remember much, since you were so young. You know," the Magistrate taps his chin thoughtfully, "I had lost track of you after The Expunging. I knew you weren't on Port Green with Jacob and Jordan, since I never saw you through the orb. I thought I would find you once I learned that Jonathon had returned to Eastport, but alas, I lost track of him as well. It wasn't until Gregor here," Magistrate Rufus gestured to a burly man on his right, "recognized Jonathon that I realized he was under my nose the entire time, that he had simply dyed his hair. So were you, too. There were so many little blond delinquents running around; how was I to know which one you were? But imagine finding out that you were only a stone's throw away from me the entire time. If I had known earlier, I might have had you killed, just to eliminate the threat. Trust me, Jacob is enough to handle on his own, I don't need the rest of you boys vying for this throne." Magistrate Rufus pats the arm of the throne lovingly.

Joe glances from Matilde, to Rufus, and to Gregor, the man on the Magistrate's right. *What is he blathering on about? None of this makes any sense.* Joe tries to focus on getting himself, Ian, and Matilde away from here. He fixates on the tapestry behind Magistrate Rufus' head, hoping for some inspiration on how to get out of this mess.

Magistrate Rufus notices him looking and turns to admire the tapestry.

"Are you familiar with our history, Joe?" he asks, turning back around.

Unsure why this is relevant, Joe shakes his head.

The Magistrate tsks. "History is such an important thing. Take this tapestry, for example. It depicts the battle for Eastport, when humans defeated the elementals and took this kingdom for their own. I have studied this tapestry for years, trying to figure out the secret of how this was accomplished. All signs pointed to eusgare, but I could find no mention of it. Finally, I found my answer, just this year. It was never eusgare. That is for the elementals. But if you look closely," Magistrate Rufus gets up and circles the throne to point to a group of soldiers on the tapestry, "you'll see that these soldiers have bronze-colored armor and swords. At first, I thought it was a stylistic choice of the weaver, but I realized that this was the key." Magistrate Rufus prods the tapestry several times in emphasis.

Joe takes a closer look at the tapestry. The woven castle overshadows the city, which is depicted as nothing more than a few houses and the docks at the delta. Rising above the castle is the mountainous cliff, on which the weaver has added several figures who must be elementals. Bright threads of orange, blue, silver, and brown flow in an attack from these figures down to the soldiers astride horseback below. Focusing on the soldiers that Magistrate Rufus indicated, Joe doesn't quite see the gleam of bronze-colored armor. He only sees tightly woven tan threads used to represent the soldiers, and the threads themselves look insignificant, like the many spools of thread the *Moro* has brought from Lexington to sell at market.

"The bronze color depicted here comes from gwarem, an ore that is found in abundance in the very cliffs behind this castle." Magistrate Rufus continues. "While eusgare expands an elemental's power, gwarem inhibits it. That's how they did it!" The Magistrate laughs and returns to his seat on the throne. "And that's how I'll do it now, to ensure all elementals in Eastport are eradicated and can never question my right to this throne." Magistrate Rufus stares daggers at Joe. "And if you think about trying to attack me, I'll have you know that I am always protected." He reaches for the hem of his robe and lifts it enough that Joe can see the shimmer of bronze on the other side. "All my clothes have gwarem woven within. All my Wardens and soldiers have gwarem armor and weapons. You elementals have no chance of besting me."

An uneasy silence fills the space between Joe and the Magistrate. Joe shifts his knees on the stone floor, unsure why his uncle felt the need to explain all that to him. There is not an elemental plot to overthrow the Magistrate, as far as Joe knows. Sure, there are some angry whispers at his policies and the killings of elementals, but that's as much as Joe's heard.

"I digress." Magistrate Rufus sits back on the throne. "Let us get to the matter at hand. Joe, as you may know, we confiscated an item that you stole from us. Or rather, that Jonathon stole and gave to you for who knows what reason."

"Because I'm the best," Joe can't help but retort.

"Perhaps," the Magistrate snorts. "But clearly that's not quite true." With a hand, he beckons to one of the Wardens, who brings forward a small cloth pouch. Joe recognizes it immediately. It's the pouch the orb is in, the orb he was meant to deliver to Lexington.

"I don't expect you to know just how important this orb is, or just how stupid your brother was for stealing it," Magistrate Rufus says as he holds the small marble aloft.

Light streaming through the windows catches the orb, turning it as iridescent as a pearl. Walking over to the circular stand, the Magistrate drops the orb. To Joe's amazement, the orb expands as it falls, until it settles comfortably in the stand, as large as an ocean buoy.

The Magistrate pats the orb like a dog, caressing it as he slowly walks behind it to face Joe. "Do you know why this little bauble is so special, dear Nephew?" The Magistrate looks at him expectantly. Dumbfounded, Joe simply shakes his head.

"Of course not," Magistrate Rufus sighs. "Neither do your brothers, I assume. Otherwise, they wouldn't have left the task to a dimwit like Jonathon. This orb was a present to my father, the previous king. A sign of goodwill from Chief Andulssan of Andulsae upon signing that stupid peace treaty." The Magistrate's jaw clenches. "My father was an idiot for thinking that peace between elementals and humans should ever be achieved. My sister was just as dumb for marrying one. Look where it got her."

This is one story that Joe did know. Queen Valencia assumed the throne after the death of her father, King Rupert. She believed in her father's mission to unite the two races, seeing the elementals as allies and friends as opposed to a danger and threat. To her brother's chagrin, Queen Valencia insisted it was not for mere mortals to judge how one is born, be it with or without powers.

After accompanying her father on several peace keeping trips to Andulsae, she fell in love with the chief's son and he with her. The king and chief thought that a marriage between their two peoples could help bridge the divide and end years of fighting. Surprisingly, the example set by Queen Valencia and her new husband seemed to quell the mutual hatred between the elementals and humans, even after King Rupert's death. There was never one before her who could rally everyone and anyone into forgiveness and acceptance. After her father's death and assuming the throne, she bore four sons. For several years afterwards, Eastport and Andulsae celebrated this union and seemed to embrace a new life of peace. That was until Queen Valencia was seemingly murdered by her husband fourteen years ago. It was then that the Expunging began, along with the systematic elimination of elementals in Eastport.

"Alas, I digress yet again," the Magistrate says with a wave of his hand. "This orb is the most powerful object the elementals have ever possessed. They were fools to part with it, yet another example of why we should never let an elemental gain any power of state. I have found that the magic of this orb allows the user to see any place or any person and to act upon that vision. One only needs to know what they seek and must have first imprinted with the orb by offering up some blood. In other words, all I have to do is ask it for what I wish to see. I didn't use it to find you because you were so young and not a threat when compared to your brothers. Nor could I use it to find Jonathon because he had dyed his hair, and here I was picturing a blond man. Jacob was easy to track because I had a better image of him in my head when you fled. I tracked him for years. I saw him send the message bird a few weeks ago and figured out his plan from there. I can find whomever or whatever I want, but I cannot act through the orb, since I am not an elemental and have no powers. That's where you come in."

Magistrate Rufus beckons to a Warden who hauls Joe to his feet and brings him to stand in front of the orb.

"Allow me to demonstrate," the Magistrate gestures for Joe to watch. "Show me the elemental stronghold on Port Green," he whispers gently to the orb.

Before Joe's eyes, the orb pulses a cloudy blue. The blue fades away to show a small cluster of wooden buildings nestled among tall trees. Beyond the trees and maybe a hundred yards from the shoreline is a crop field in a small clearing, not much to be afraid of. Joe can make out figures going about their daily routines, unaware of the intruder in their midst. But the Magistrate is human; he has no powers. Joe wonders briefly if the Magistrate is half-elemental. Otherwise, how is he able to use the orb? Joe's thoughts are abruptly cut short as Magistrate Rufus whispers again to the orb: "Show me Jacob."

The images in the orb rush by so fast that Joe can barely keep up. Traveling upward from the village, the images cross through dense forest and climb a steep hill. The whirlwind of color comes to a sudden stop at the top of the sandy hill overlooking the ocean. Sitting cross-legged, facing west toward Eastport, is a tall, lanky, bespectacled blond man, eyes closed in concentration.

Magistrate Rufus snorts. "Jacob, Jacob. Always trying to eavesdrop. No matter," he says, looking up at Joe. "I think you'll be more than a match for him."

But Joe doesn't listen. He is preoccupied with the man in the image. The man bears a striking resemblance to Jonathon, and, Joe supposes, to himself. The Magistrate called him nephew. Jonathon called him brother. Queen Valencia had four sons, supposedly none of which had ever been found after The Expunging. Most believed that the four princes had escaped, but there's never been any proof. Now, most believed them to be dead. Yet, Joe feels a tickling in the back of his mind, a small ripple on the surface of the ocean, one that began in the dungeon with Jonathon. Maybe he really is one of the lost princes.

"What do you want me to do?" Joe asks warily.

A wicked grin spreads across the Magistrate's face. "That's more like it."

"I didn't agree to help you yet."

"Perhaps not. But you will. You will attack Port Green. Wipe them all out. Prove to Jacob that he is in over his head, and that he cannot beat me. That the throne is and will forever be mine," Magistrate Rufus spits at the image in the orb.

"You want me to attack Port Green? From here, by myself?" Joe gives a humorless laugh. "The island has at least a hundred elementals. You're outnumbered."

Magistrate Rufus drums his fingers on the orb, still staring daggers at Jacob's image. "I have the element of surprise. Namely, you."

Does the Magistrate really think that Joe will attack an entire island of innocent people? Yes, maybe this Jacob and Jonathon are his brothers. Maybe he is a lost prince, and maybe his brothers did leave him behind, not once trying to contact him. Any fairytale is possible if repeated enough. If he wants to believe that fantasy, he supposes he would be a little bitter about being forgotten and would maybe want some justice. But not enough to eliminate an entire island. Both humans and elementals are at fault for the current state of Eastport, but that doesn't give one the right to eliminate the other. It seems like a lose-lose situation to Joe. Besides, he couldn't, in good conscience, use his powers to hurt others. Not in this way, unprovoked and unable to defend themselves. Then a thought occurs.

"Even if I wanted to, I'm not powerful enough to take on an entire island, miles away, by myself. You're out of luck. Looks like you'll have to wage your war the old-fashioned way, you know, by growing a pair and facing your enemies in person."

Magistrate Rufus raises his head and slowly fixes his steely eyes on Joe. Immediately, Joe tries to retract his misstep. But before he can say anything, the Magistrate snaps his fingers, and a Warden approaches Matilde. She cowers back into Ian, but the Warden grabs her by the arm. A cry of pain emanates from Matilde, causing Joe to strain against his shackles. The Warden twists Matilde's arm behind her back, pulling so hard that Joe knows the bones will break. One more yank, and Joe hears a snap. Immediately, his vision goes red.

He gives into the power that has been building in his core, and searches for something, anything, to avenge Matilde. A strange shiver tickles his gut, just a trickle of water unlike anything Joe has felt before. Closing his eyes, Joe narrows in on this tickle and traces it to the Warden hurting Matilde. Blood. The water in the Warden's blood that flows through his veins. Without thinking, Joe reaches out and forces that water into the Warden's lungs. The Warden drops Matilde, who cowers on the floor, clutching her broken arm. Grasping at his chest, the Warden struggles to find air. Joe continues his onslaught as the Warden falls to his knees, coughing up water in a seemingly never-ending stream. *More water. This is what he deserves.* It's so easy. One flick of his wrist behind his back and the blood moves at his command. Joe smirks at the Warden flopping on the floor like a fish.

Joe. Stop. Please.

A tiny voice, like an annoying gnat, rings in his ears. It's urgent, pleading, but insignificant.

"Joe, please! You are not a monster!"

That voice, his mother. Matilde. Reminding him again that he is a better person than most humans make elementals out to be. Better enough to not be a killer.

"I know you are stronger than this." Matilde's voice cracks as she watches her only son drown a man.

With tremendous effort, Joe pulls back from the power and releases the Warden, who continues gasping on the floor.

I could have killed him.

Joe looks at Matilde and sees tears running down her face. She looks back at him with sorrow in her eyes, but to his great relief, not fear. Ian, terror etched on his face, strains to back away, forcing his Warden toward the door of the throne room.

"It's okay, Joe," Matilde says with a quiver, cradling her arm to her chest. "This isn't your fault. You don't have to be like them."

Joe stares puzzledly at her. Like whom, elementals? Or humans?

"Mom," Joe begins, falling to his knees on the cold, damp floor. "I'm so sorry."

Three short claps sound from behind him.

"Well, well, well. That was impressive. Think of how powerful you could be on Ink." Magistrate Rufus places a hand on Joe's shoulder. "This could be fun."

Joe trembles beneath his touch, head swimming, breath coming in shallow gasps. How could he have so easily given in? The answer is clear, though: the rush of using so much power to kill.

He never felt that powerful before, holding a person's life in his hands. It is intoxicating to know that he could do that, drown a person from the inside out without much effort. Maybe this is what it means to be an elemental. *Maybe Magistrate Rufus is right to fear us*, Joe thinks proudly. Steadying his breath, he looks up to the Magistrate.

"If I help you, promise me you won't hurt her."

"Joseph, no!" Matilde begs. "Don't sacrifice yourself for me."

Joe gives her a pained look. He wants to keep Matilde safe, and he wants her to be proud of him, of how he has proven throughout his years that elementals can be something more, something good, something not feared. The shackles bite into his wrists, sending an ache through his core. He wants to give Matilde no reason to doubt that she has raised a good son, elemental or not. He can't attack innocent people. He won't. But the power beckons so sweetly.

Magistrate Rufus regards him for a moment and gives a small nod. "But of course. Where are my manners? No further harm shall befall either Matilde or Ian here."

Joe can't meet Matilde's eyes. He's doing this for her. He's only doing this for her. He won't hurt them. The bloodlust is still running through his veins, but these people are innocent, unlike that Warden. He'll just give them a little scare. No one will get hurt. And the Magistrate will be none the wiser. After all, he is the best, a master of subterfuge. Still a bit shaky, he rises awkwardly to his feet.

"All right. I'll help you."

"Excellent." Magistrate Rufus grins wickedly, and Joe swears that he sees teeth as sharp as a shark's peeking out of his uncle's mouth. The Magistrate beckons a Warden, who brings Joe forward to the orb and unlocks his shackles. Joe glances at Magistrate Rufus.

"You know what to do," Rufus nods.

Joe steals a look back at Matilde, still kneeling on the floor, holding her broken arm. Silent tears flow down her cheeks, leaving shiny trails, but Joe knows the tears aren't from the pain of her broken limb: he knows he's breaking her heart. But it is destroying him even more to see the Magistrate hurt her. And he will do anything in his power to make sure that the Magistrate never lays a finger on her again, the woman who loves him, who has always loved him, despite his flaws, despite him being an elemental.

Just put on a good show, he reminds himself. *No one else has to get hurt.*

"Well?" Magistrate Rufus prods. "I can break her other arm."

Joe glares at him but nods his head.

"Excellent." A hungry smile spreads the Magistrate's lips as he motions the Wardens to hold Joe still. Immediately, Joe tries to break free of the Wardens' grip, but they hold on like vises.

"What are you doing?" Joe struggles as Magistrate Rufus beckons Gregor to approach him. Joe had forgotten the man was there. Gregor had been standing silently, blending into the stone walls, waiting to be summoned. He pulls a vial of jet-black liquid from his robes, followed by a syringe.

"Don't fear, Joseph. This is just a special little treat Head Chemist Gregor whipped up for me. Liquefied eusgare. Ink, we call it. While gwarem inhibits your powers, eusgare amplifies them. You might be wondering why I would risk making you even more powerful. Let's just say I'm experimenting to find eusgare's limit. And if making you more powerful for a little while helps me defeat Jacob, it's a risk I'm willing to take." He lackadaisically waves Gregor on.

Gregor first pricks Joe's finger with a pin from his robes. The bright red bead of blood drips onto the orb, immediately disappearing into its murky depths. Gregor then carefully, almost fondly, rolls up the sleeve of Joe's jacket, and there's a flicker of pain as a needle shoves into his arm, followed by an icy surge that shocks all his senses awake. Gasping for air, Joe slumps against the Wardens behind him, his head swimming with the sensation of eusgare flooding his veins. Then, like a bolt of lightning, the world becomes preternaturally clear. Joe can feel every little bit of water, from the ocean, to the delta, to the well somewhere on the castle grounds, to the boiling pots of water in the kitchens, to the blood running through the ten beings in the throne room. Out of the corner of his eye, he sees the Magistrate point.

Joe turns his attention to the orb in front of him. Manipulating water has always been easy in small amounts, but he's never tried to do so indirectly or on the entire ocean. He doesn't even know if such a thing is possible. Taking a deep breath, he closes his eyes and reaches out toward the picture in the orb, imagining it as if he were standing at the bow of the *Moro*, looking out at Port Green, as he's done before on various trips to the southern markets. In his mind, he sees the coastline of the island, the bay in which Port Green is settled, the village with all of its huts, the crop field near the shore, and the sandy hilltop in the middle. Joe can feel the waves thumping steadily against the sand. He attempts to mimic that rhythm, timing each beat of the pounding surf to that of his heart. Slowly, he feels himself drifting, as if he's leaving his body and is suddenly transported to a ship docked off Port Green. The salt air stings his nose, and he realizes that he can feel the Eusgarian Sea.

He cautiously opens his eyes and mentally pokes at the image in the orb, coaxing the picture to zoom in on the beach and village just above it. Placing his hands on the orb, he jostles the ocean in the image, urging the waves to grow bigger, to travel further inland with each crest. To his surprise, he feels the ocean obey him, but at a distance. The tug of the connection is a much longer tether than he's ever felt before, but nonetheless, it is there, that familiar pressure in his gut. And he's never felt stronger.

"What are you waiting for? Get on with it!" Magistrate Rufus' voice is muffled, as if Joe is hearing him from underwater. Caught up in this newfound sensation, it takes Joe a moment to remember the gravity of his situation, his parents' lives.

Urgently, he forces the ocean to swell, building up the water higher and higher until it's looming over Port Green, a threatening wall of blue ready to smash down. Joe's head pounds with the pressure of holding back the ocean, but he knows he needs more, more to convince the Magistrate. With any luck, the elementals on Port Green will notice the impending tsunami about to strike and will flee for higher ground.

He draws in more water, directing the surrounding currents to the onslaught that he is barely holding back. Something slimy runs down his face, and he realizes that his nose must be bleeding again. The Eusgarian Sea is not meant to be contained, especially not for this long. The edges of his vision begin to turn black. Dimly, he notices the Magistrate hovering out of the throne in anticipation, Matilde still crying on the floor behind him. He can only hope that those on Port Green have had enough time to hide. With a yell of rage and relief, he lets go, flinging his power out through the orb and toward the island. The tsunami crashes onto shore, annihilating huts, fences, trees, everything in its path. He keeps feeding the waves, adding more and more into the swirling morass of debris that was once the village center. He pulls back just a little, not wanting to completely drown the island. Ever so slightly, he reverses the flow of the ocean, hoping the change is too small for the Magistrate to notice.

It's a fine balance between destruction and salvation, but Joe holds on to the belief that he can do both. The pounding in his head increases and he can feel himself beginning to wane. The drug is wearing off, being spent too quickly. The ocean proves too much for him. Gasping for air, he tries to regain control of the melee, but instead falls to his knees and surrenders to the blackness.

12

"**P**lease, Bernard, don't do this. You loved me once, remember?" Jonathon pleads, trying to catch Bernard's eye, but Bernard refuses to look at him.

"That was a mistake I regret every day."

"Please, Bernard," Jonathon tries to keep the hurt from his voice. "I don't want any more Ink."

Jonathon struggles against the chains holding him to his cell wall, knowing that if he tried, he could break free and cause the entire dungeon to come crashing down around them both. If only he wasn't so tired. If only it wasn't Bernard in here with him. If only he didn't have Joe to worry about. He's already failed him too many times.

He flinches as Bernard jams a needle into his arm and presses the plunger, sending yet another dose of Ink into his veins. Sighing, Jonathon drinks in the drug's strength, relishing the freedom from the constant pain in his bad knee. He feels his power rise, threatening to spill out, but he holds back. There are too many people he cares about in this castle to let it go. He swallows, forcing the power back down into his core. He is so tired. Maybe he should just let it all go, bring the castle down. That's his uncle's end game, is it not? To have Bernard, the man he loved, torture him in hopes that he'll lose all control? To prove that elementals are nothing more than dangerous dogs that must be put down? It would bring such sweet relief. He knows he can do it. He knows that he is strong enough. And maybe his uncle would die in the process.

Think of Joseph, Jonathon reminds himself. *You didn't come all this way just to lose him again.*

Wearily, he opens his eyes to find Bernard quickly turning away.

"Bernard. Please. Stop this. We can leave, we can start over. You don't have to listen to him. I can't believe that you don't still have feelings for me, I can't believe—"

"Shut up!"

Jonathon reels as Bernard strikes him across the face, his teeth clicking upon impact. Bernard stands up, backing away toward the cell door.

"Just shut up!" He gathers up the wooden crate full of Ink vials and walks out of the cell, locking it before racing from the dungeon, leaving Jonathon alone in the darkness.

Jonathon watches the door for a minute, trying not to hope that Bernard will come back and free him. It's too much to hope for. He feels stupid for even thinking it. He scans the dungeon, feeling his power rise like bile. *A stone castle. You really need to do better, Uncle.* His eyes come to rest on Joe's empty cell across from him, and Jonathon hangs his head in shame. Joseph needs him. He just needs to bide his time, and then they can both be free.

He shifts on the dirt floor, trying to get comfortable, when his thigh bumps something. The vial and syringe filled with Ink. The obsidian liquid beckons to him, like a sweet taste on his tongue. With difficulty, he opens the lid to the power that's been building inside, fighting against the gwarem pillars that stifle his efforts. The Ink flowing through his body provides him just enough strength to roll the vial and syringe along the dirt floor, like pulling a rug, inch by inch, until the objects hit his thigh. Raising the dirt like a hand, he pushes the drug into his pocket before tamping the power back down.

A whole vial. He thinks. *Bernard should be more careful. You never know when something like that could come in handy.*

The door to the dungeon thuds open, causing Jonathon to jump as if he were just caught stealing pastries from the kitchen. A light blinds Jonathon as a lantern is hung on a hook near the door. Two Wardens drag an unconscious Joe around the bronze pillars to his cell and unceremoniously dump him on the ground. A trickle of blood runs down his face. Seeing him lying so still on the dirt brings back unwanted memories. Jonathon tries to calm his frantically beating heart in an attempt to convince himself that this will not end up like last time. Joseph merely exerted himself too much, that's all.

He glares as the Wardens stride out of the dungeon, and in his mind, he forces the earth to swallow them whole for what they have done to his brother. Yet, these are only vengeful fantasies. Even though he is stronger than that night fourteen years ago, so much stronger, he doesn't want to risk it. Not when he is so close to regaining the brother he lost. If Joe forgives him.

Jonathon sighs as the Wardens close the door and walk back upstairs. From the corner of his eye, he sees Joe stir slightly, a tiny twitch that lets Jonathon know he will be okay.

The door opens again, and this time the Wardens bring in Joe's adoptive parents and place them in the cell next to Jonathon's. The Wardens exit, leaving the lantern hanging by the door. Eyes having adjusted to the light, Jonathon notices that the woman is holding her right arm close to her chest, as if broken, and his anger toward his uncle only intensifies. A tremor rumbles under him as Matilde lowers herself to the floor, defeated. Maybe he should bring this castle down. Being buried under a pile of rubble is a more generous death than his uncle deserves.

Once again, Jonathon struggles to quell his anger and the tide of power from the drug. "This is bigger than you," he whispers quietly to himself.

"You're his brother, one of the lost princes, aren't you," Matilde directs the statement at Jonathon, but gazes in sorrow at Joe's still form.

Surprised, Jonathon swivels left as far as his chains allow him to face her.

Matilde gives a small laugh, almost a sigh. "You look so much like him." She turns to face him, meeting his eyes directly. "He's a good person. He deserves so much better than this."

Jonathon hangs his head in shame. *He would have been in a better place if only I had been brave enough to tell Father what I saw that morning in the library.*

Seeing the pain on Jonathon's face, Matilde scooches over and reaches her good arm through the bars, patting his leg. "I'm not blaming you, dear. It's this system the Magistrate enacted. If only

Queen Valencia was still alive…" she trails off, and Jonathon catches tears forming in the corners of her eyes.

"It's selfish of me," Matilde sighs. "It must've been a horrible thing for you boys to go through, losing both your parents like that. But if that never happened, I would never have had the chance to have a son. He was the answer to all my prayers."

As hard as it was to lose his brother, Jonathon never stopped to think what it would be like for Joe's adoptive parents. If things had gone differently—if he and Joseph had never been arrested and he had somehow convinced Joseph to join him, Jacob, and Jordan on Port Green—Matilde and Ian would have lost their only son. The child they raised and loved as their own. For the first time, Jonathon realizes that Joseph has built a life without him, without anything to do with Port Green or elementals. And Jonathon would never have fit into that life. That clarity hits him like a blow to the stomach. Jonathon was so focused on getting his little brother back that he didn't think about what he would be taking from Joe.

"I'm sorry," is all he can think to say to Matilde. She smiles at him, the skin around her eyes crinkling.

"It was your father, King Nils, who believed in me," she says. "The day he was hanged."

Jonathon grits his teeth. About a month after Jonathon, Jacob, and Jordan escaped Eastport and wrecked on Port Green with the other elemental refugees, they heard word brought by Lexington traders that King Nils had been publicly executed by their uncle. That was the day twelve-year-old Jacob vowed revenge on Magistrate Rufus. Jonathon is in no mood to hear the gory details of that execution now.

"King Nils' only concern that day was making sure his youngest son was safe. He somehow knew Joe didn't make it out of

Eastport. He pleaded, begged for someone to please watch over his son, to not hand him over to the Magistrate. King Nils cried out that his son was only six. We were there, Joe and me. Everyone was there. We had no choice. Joe was frightened, and I held him close, not wanting him to see your father, to see what was about to happen. Then your father looked at Joe, and looked at me, and he smiled. He smiled and nodded to me, like he knew I would raise Joe as my own and protect him. That's when I knew who Joe was. I never told Joe that."

"Our father would have been proud of you," Jonathon says, turning his head so she wouldn't see the tears streaming down his face.

"He would have been proud of you too," she whispers.

Jonathon shakes his head. "For what? All of this, this mess, is my fault. If only I were braver, if only I had done something."

"You were just a child."

"I should have done something." Tears run freely down his face, and not for the first time, he wishes his mother was there to hold him and tell him everything would be all right, the way she used to when he had a bad dream.

You're not a child anymore, Jonathon. You have to fix this on your own, he thinks to himself. But from the back of his mind comes the fear he's been trying to smother for hours: *What if I can't?*

13

oe stirs to the sound of murmuring.

"You were just a child," says a voice he recognizes as his mother.

"I should have done something," says a second voice of broken glass. *Jonathon?*

As their muted conversation continues, Joe slowly stretches his fingers and works his way up his forearms to his shoulders, contracting and releasing his muscles. He squirms against the hard floor, trying to inch his way up to a seated position. His entire body aches from the power he released, and the spot on his arm where the needle entered is sore. Reaching up to rub the sore spot, Joe notices that his hands are now shackled in front of him instead of behind. He keeps his eyes closed a while longer, listening to Jonathon's voice, trying to match it to any sort of memory he had from when he was young.

It strikes Joe as odd to hear Jonathon sound so defeated, like a child who has been repeatedly told no. The first time Joe met him, he seemed confident. The second time, here in the dungeon, he was broken. But now? Now, it almost sounds like he's given up. To his surprise, Joe feels a sudden pang in his chest at that thought. A protective urge races through him, and all he wants to do is reach through the cell bars, grab Jonathon's hand, and tell him everything will be all right. Surprisingly, that feels familiar. A brief memory of him wrapping a boy in a blanket flits through his mind. Did he used to comfort Jonathon a lot when they were younger?

Joe finally opens his eyes and immediately closes them, surprised to see lantern light in this normally black dungeon. He waits a second for his eyes to adjust then carefully sits up.

"Joseph!" Matilde notices the movement and turns toward him.

"Mom. Are you okay?" He remembers her broken arm and realizes that this is a stupid question. He quickly scans the rest of her. She's slumped against the dungeon wall, still cradling her arm, but otherwise she appears unhurt. Just incredibly tired, judging from the pale pallor of her face. Next to her is Ian, facing the corner of the cell with his back to them all, refusing to acknowledge them.

Joe hunkers down in his jacket, ashamed of making Ian so scared. Joe almost killed that Warden, and he never felt more powerful. The feeling lingers like an aftertaste, but looking at Ian and Matilde, his wishes he could take it all back.

"I'm so sorry, Mom. This should have never happened to you."

"You're safe. That's all that matters." She gives him a small smile.

"If this is what you call being safe, sure." Joe snorts.

"You're alive. And I'm alive. That counts for something."

Does it though? Joe wonders if spending the rest of his days in this dungeon is truly better than the alternative. If only he could be sure that his mom would be okay. Magistrate Rufus won't offer her protection, that much is obvious. And as long as Matilde is here, Magistrate Rufus can use her against him. There's nothing he wouldn't do to make sure she comes out of this mess in one piece. Joe would happily give his life for her. She's his mother, the only one he's ever known, at least. She deserves better than this.

"Hey!" He shouts across to Jonathon's cell. Jonathon doesn't stir. "Hey! So called brother of mine. I'm talking to you!"

Jonathon slowly lifts his head. Again, Joe feels a pang in his chest at the sight of Jonathon's tear-streaked cheeks. He quickly pushes the feeling aside. Bigger issues.

"You're a terramental. You said that you could get me out of here. Well, put your power where your mouth is. Get her out of here."

Jonathon glances at Matilde but drops his head. "I can't," he whispers.

"Yes, you can. Make a tunnel. Get her out."

"I can't," Jonathon repeats.

"Can't or won't?" Joe feels anger bubbling up through his chest. "Hey! This is your fault. She's not part of this. Prove that you're actually good for something, and get her out of here!"

Jonathon lifts his head and fixes a steely gaze on Joe. "I told you, I can't."

"Why not?!" Joe screams.

Jonathon holds Joe's gaze a moment longer before slumping back to the floor in defeat. Joe has every right to be mad at him. This is his fault. Not Joe's adoptive parents, perhaps, but he might as well take the blame for that too. All he wants is his little brother back. He imagined that as soon as he met Joe, as soon as Joe truly saw him, he would remember. Jonathon could apologize for leaving him behind those fourteen years ago, and they could start over. He could have someone who would believe in him, unlike Jacob. But now, Jonathon accepts the truth. That was all merely a fantasy, an impossible dream he will never attain, because deep down he knows that he is not worthy of such happy endings.

"Why not?" Joe asks again.

"Because I'm not strong enough. Something down here is draining me."

Then Joe realizes just what the bronze pillars in the corridor are. Gwarem. Magistrate Rufus made sure that the elementals he locked up couldn't act against him. Joe wonders how many more gwarem pillars have sprung up throughout the castle. *The obelisks in the city! They're bronze now; how did I not notice that?* Joe's dumbfounded that he could be so oblivious. Before he can process, the dungeon door slams open, and the Magistrate strides in. Immediately, Ian leaps to his feet and races to the front of the cell.

"Sir, please have mercy! Let me and my wife go. We are not elementals or elemental sympathizers. We are loyal subjects!" he begs, gripping the bars tightly.

Magistrate Rufus looks at him in disgust, as if Ian is nothing more than horse dung he had the misfortune to step in. "Quit your sniveling. It's most unbecoming." He motions to the Wardens, who, in turn, ensure that the prisoners are shackled with hands before them as they haul Joe, Ian, Matilde, and Jonathon out of their cells and back up to the throne room.

Try as he might, Jonathon can't help but lean heavily on his Warden. Even with Ink running through his veins, his knee is too stiff to move without support. He is just thankful that his uncle didn't make Bernard fetch him. Gone was the gentle, caring man Jonathon had come to love. Instead, there is a callous demon, blindly following Gregor's orders. While Bernard didn't appear to enjoy this torture as much as Gregor did, Jonathon noticed that he didn't refrain from it either. Jonathon thought Bernard would be different. Life had been so comfortable, but now, Jonathon wonders if maybe it was all a ploy from the beginning. Perhaps Bernard had never truly loved him at all.

But even as he thinks this, he remembers the look in Bernard's eyes on the last trip he made to the dungeon. He looked, perhaps, remorseful? Jonathon shakes his head. No, he will not let himself hope like that. It will only make things worse.

Jonathon blinks and shields his eyes as he's shoved into the throne room, the room painted a fiery gold in the dying light of the evening sun. His Warden directs him past Ian and Matilde to the throne and the orb lying in its pedestal, where Joe already awaits. Jonathon's knee is throbbing, having to endure movement when it has been denied for the past day in the dungeon. He would like nothing more than to sit down, to relieve the pressure. His arm bumps a bulge in his pants pocket as the Warden jostles him. The vial and syringe. Or maybe another dose of Ink would do the trick. Just one quick shot of the obsidian liquid, and the pain would go away.

"Joseph," Magistrate Rufus demands, breaking Jonathon out of his thoughts. "Ready to try again?"

Joe drags his eyes to the Magistrate. "You have to let my parents go first. Both of them." Joe tries to keep his voice steady, but even he can hear the desperation seeping in.

"Give me what I want, and I'll set them free." Magistrate Rufus glares from his throne, challenging Joe to counter. Joe turns to face Matilde, sees the fear in her eyes as she tries to reassure him with a smile, the orange and red suns on her bandana out of place in this gloomy situation. For as long as Joe can remember, she has always been there for him, protecting him from harm, surrounding him with love. He can't fail her, not again. There are just a hundred souls, give or take, on Port Green; surely, some of them will escape. Sighing, he faces the Magistrate, resigning himself to his fate.

"I do what you want, and you have to promise to let them go. If you are truly my uncle, and we are truly family, then please respect my request, and set them free. I'm begging you."

Magistrate Rufus places a hand on his chest, shocked. "Of course. Say no more, my nephew. On my honor as your kin, flesh and blood, I will release them as soon as you destroy Port Green. Until then, they will remain as collateral."

Joe hardly believes him, but he doesn't have a choice. Maybe, just maybe, the Magistrate does have a heart. Maybe he'll see the pain in Joe's face and soften just this once. Drawing a deep breath to steel himself, Joe approaches the orb. It's still large, sitting in its pedestal, throwing glimmers of the evening sun around the room in brilliant mosaics. A light within the surface, like a distant fog, pulses and twists as he steps closer. He reaches out his hands, an image of Port Green already forming in his mind, when a rough weight on his shoulder stops him.

"Just a minute, Joe," the Magistrate calls as he motions to Gregor. The Head Chemist holds up a syringe filled with black liquid. "Let's call this a security measure. No holding back this time, yes?" A knowing look crosses Magistrate Rufus' face. "Besides, Gregor tells me the first dose should have worn off by now."

Gregor rolls up Joe's sleeve and administers the drug. Immediately, Joe feels a rush as the drug races through his veins. His senses now electrified, he reaches out to the orb to begin his assault.

"Just one more minute." Magistrate Rufus stops Joe again as Gregor pushes Joe's hands from the orb. "I'm going to add one more element to this mix. The two of you working together should be unstoppable."

Magistrate Rufus snaps his fingers at the Warden holding Jonathon, who pulls him over to the orb next to Joe. Gregor pricks Jonathon's finger, smearing the blood on the orb, before filling another syringe and injecting it into Jonathon's arm. Beside Joe, Jonathon's knees buckle, and the Warden struggles to keep him upright. Gregor places the brothers' hands on the orb, and Joe is relieved to finally release the power that has been building inside his gut.

Everything quickly falls away around Joe. The throne room, the Magistrate, Ian and Matilde, and even Jonathon next to him all fade into a distant background as he focuses in on Port Green. It's so much easier this time. The ocean responds to his command as if an old friend, with barely a thought. He moves his hands in a small undulating motion, restricted due to his shackles, causing the Eusgarian Sea around Port Green to rise and fall, collecting more water with each rise. The wave builds, taller than the last time.

In the orb, Joe sees the elementals of Port Green rushing about, various aeromentals whisking children away to the sandy hill at the center of the island. A contingent of terramentals attempt to build a wall around the village, pulling up pumice and bedrock from deep within the earth. With the Eusgarian Sea climbing ever higher above them like a giant raising a club, the terramentals give up on their wall and flee for the hill. Four hydromentals race to the shore, trying to draw the water back down into the ocean to allow the other villagers time to escape, resulting in a tug of war with Joe. He can feel their combined strength pull against his own, the water receding back into the ocean and rising up to tower over the island, like some intimate dance between partners.

"Attack!" A muffled yell echoes in Joe's head. "Stop just standing there!"

Joe hears a thud and short yelp from Jonathon but doesn't break his focus. If he stops now, Matilde might be the next one hit. He doubles his efforts against the hydromentals, digging deep into the pressure of his core to force the Eusgarian Sea to do his bidding. Straining, his face turning as red as a tomato, Joe bends the wave closer and closer to the hydromentals on shore. If he can wipe them out, he'll be clear to flood the whole island. The monstrous wave looms over the hydromentals, blocking out the sun and casting the beach of Port Green into an early twilight. The raging dark green morass advances relentlessly on the island, and one hydromental falls to his knees. A bit of resistance disappears. Joe pushes harder at the image in the orb, and another hydromental wanes. Joe gives the wave a final shove, and the Eusgarian Sea comes crashing down.

Just before the wave pummels the sand, a group of ten aeromentals, safe on the sandy hill, sends down large hightower fronds. The hydromentals grab hold of the fronds on either end as the aeromentals whisk them away on the wind before the wave can drown them. Joe frowns, wanting to see the wave crush them. He took on four elementals by himself, and he had won. He barely feels tired, even though he just commanded the entire ocean. And yet his quarry escaped. He tracks their progress through the sky and to the top of the central hill. A hundred elementals all gather there, seeking shelter from the flood that has wiped out their village. Terramentals have hastily built stone huts for protection, the masses huddling inside.

Below, the village is in shambles. The wave explodes the pumice and bedrock wall, sending huge chunks of rock through the wooden huts. The crop field is a soupy mess, stalks bent in half like a stork's legs. The hightower trees take the brunt of the wave, shattering like ice falling from a roof to the road. The Eusgarian Sea drowns the entire west side of the island, a soggy wasteland rising up to the untouched sandy hill.

Joe redoubles his efforts, pulling in more ocean to sink that hill, but is surprised to feel resistance, like a brick wall blocking his attacks. He throws everything he's got at the invisible wall until sweat pours from his forehead and his knees threaten to buckle. In the orb, he spies a lone, bespectacled figure in a vortex of wind, at least twenty yards wide, holding back the ocean, trying to protect the stone huts from being flooded. One man is no match for him. Grinding his teeth, Joe pushes harder. The Eusgarian Sea pools at the man's feet but goes no further toward the stone huts. Joe quickly becomes out of breath, as if he's run for miles. The Ink must be beginning to wane.

Yet, in the orb, Joe sees a whirlpool form around the man. Confused, Joe tries to figure out where the whirlpool is coming from when he notices a new sensation, almost like sand scraping against his palms. He spares a quick glance to his left and realizes that Jonathon must finally be lending a hand. Jonathon's brow furrows as he glares at the man holding back the sea. Jonathon moves his hands together in a circular motion over the orb, and Joe senses the sandy hilltop reacting. Then Joe gets it. Jonathon is adding his terramental powers to the flood at the man's feet to create quick-sand. The man yells something, but the brothers can't hear over the storm they've made. The man struggles to hold back the wall of water while trying to unstick himself from the ground. A woman runs out of one of the stone huts to help, and a young girl of five or six follows her, crying out for her mom.

The sight of the little girl stops Joe short. She has wild brown hair and reminds him so much of his little cousin, Meg. Joe pulls back, and the man on the hill takes advantage of the moment to force a gust of wind downward and break free of the quicksand. He runs to the woman and girl and hurries them to the nearest stone hut. Joe steps back from the orb. Jonathon also stops, and he glances at Joe, a puzzled look on his face.

Why are they stopping when Jacob is right there? Jacob, who ordered Jonathon to steal this very orb. Jacob, who thinks less of Jonathon because he works at the Siren Club. Jacob, who blamed Jonathon for their mother's death after he found the courage to confess what he saw that night. A red rage consumes him. For the first time in his life, Jonathon is more powerful than his oldest brother could ever dream of being. For the first time, Jonathon has the upper hand. He and Joe were finally working together again, a united front. And they were winning. Spying Jacob safe in the stone hut instead of slowly sinking into the ground, Jonathon's shoulders slump in defeat. His fun is over too soon.

"Why have you stopped?" The Magistrate thunders from his throne. "I was winning! Jacob was almost defeated! Again, hit them again!"

Joe braces himself once more on the orb. *That little girl was just like Meg. I can't do this. I can't do this to them.*

"What are you waiting for?" Magistrate Rufus leaps from his throne, grabs Joe by the back of his jacket, and yanks him upright, pushing him against the orb. "You can rest once the job is done!"

"I can't," Joe whispers. Now that he's stopped, he can feel the effects of the drug wearing off. Something sticky runs into his mouth, and he knows his nose is bleeding once again. His body aches all over, and he would like nothing more than to lie down, close his eyes, and pretend that none of this is happening.

"You can, and you will. Gregor!" the Magistrate commands. Joe feels a jab in his arm as another dose of Ink crashes into his veins. A burn like fire ignites his skin and bones, and his joints seize at the drug's onslaught. The pull to act, to destroy, is so strong that he quickly gives in and tries a half-hearted attack on Port Green once more. Only, something's wrong. Instead of the ocean flooding the island, it's retreating.

"What are you doing?" Magistrate Rufus yells. "I order you to attack!"

But the waters continue to sink back into the ocean. The only thing on Joe's mind is the image of that little girl, the terror etched on her face, and the shame of knowing he caused it. Behind him, he hears the snap of fingers and turns in time to see Ian and Matilde slump to the ground, their throats slit, and a stabbing pain fills his heart. Matilde's blood pools beneath her hair, blending in with the red suns on her bandana.

14

"Clearly they weren't enough motivation for you," the Magistrate sneers. He gestures for Gregor to bring another dose of Ink and approaches Joe, whose knees begin to buckle. "Now, you will do as I say."

"No!" Jonathon reaches out as Joe crumbles to the floor of the throne room, memories of Joe lying broken on the bank of the Plebeum flashing through his mind.

The Magistrate motions to the Wardens, who surge forward to haul Joe up off the floor. Joe slumps in their grip, barely able to raise his head, the effort of his last attack draining him further. Blood is pouring from his nose, and his eyes are pure white. Jonathon knows the struggle between the pain and pleasure of Joe's increased power.

"Joseph," Magistrate Rufus drawls, drumming his fingers on the arm of his throne. "I know you're holding back. I know you can do better. Those people, they are not your people. They abandoned you. Your own brothers even abandoned you. You owe them nothing. Stop fooling around, and kill them already!" Spittle

137

flies from the Magistrate's mouth as he half-rises from his throne in anger.

The waning sun dances across the stone floor and upon the faces of Ian and Matilde in mockery of the horror that has happened within these walls. Slowly raising his head, Joe fixes his blank white eyes on the Magistrate.

"Why?" he rasps, his voice like sand against the keel of a rowboat. "Why should I do anything for you?" Joe takes a deep breath, succumbing to the power coursing through him, feeling his sanity slip further and further away. Outside the windows, the Plebeum River rises into a tempest, white-capped swells gathering like a flock of seagulls.

"Don't give into it, Joseph! You're stronger than this." Jonathon knows his pleading won't stop what Joe has already set in motion.

"Why should I do anything for you?" Joe asks again, spitting blood from his mouth. "Seems to me that there's only one way out now." A smile splits his face, blood-stained teeth showing the monster inside.

"Agreed." The Magistrate sits back on the throne, as still as one of his obelisks, and examines Joe with disappointment. "There's only one way out for elementals who've outlived their usefulness." Magistrate Rufus snaps his fingers. "Gregor." Gregor approaches Joe like a mountain lion sizing up its prey, slowly withdrawing a dagger from his waistband.

"No!" Jonathon shouts. Summoning all his willpower, Jonathon wrenches free from his Wardens and limps over to his brother, sending spasms through the stone floor in his wake.

Unbalanced, the Wardens and Gregor topple like chess pieces as Magistrate Rufus clings to his throne. The orb rattles in its stand as the tapestry behind the throne sways. Jonathon himself stumbles, falling on his bad knee. With Ink still in his veins, he doesn't feel the pain as the stone floor scrapes against his skin through the tears in his pants. He tries to get his feet back under him, but the floor is shaking too much for him to regain an upright position. He continues toward Joe on elbows and knees, the best he can do with his hands shackled, urgency speeding his crawl.

Reaching Joe, Jonathon grabs his collar and hauls him about. The vibrations beneath Jonathon's knees slow and eventually come to a stop as the earthquake peters out. Turning, Jonathon sees that Gregor is the first to recover. The Head Chemist grabs his dagger by the blade, aiming it at the brothers as he lines up his throw.

Jonathon doesn't think twice as he brings his hands together in a downward motion, cleaving the throne room in two and dragging Joe down with him into the chasm. Large chunks of stone fly into the air as the room is torn asunder. Catching the surprised look on his uncle's face, Jonathon is swiftly engulfed in the debris avalanching through the floor.

They land in a heap in the library below, startling a gaggle of councilors reading in the chairs by the windows. Dirt and dust coat the brothers, giving them the pallor of ghosts and eliciting more than one cough. Jonathon dimly registers where they have landed as he spies shelf upon shelf of books, and a sharp pain fills his heart. Looking up at the hole in the library ceiling, Jonathon sees Gregor and several Wardens gathering with crossbows drawn.

"Shoot them! What are you waiting for?" Magistrate Rufus bellows like a wounded whale.

Gregor launches his dagger at the brothers. The spinning blade refracts the low light streaming in from the floor-to-ceiling windows, sprays of sunshine blinding the library patrons. Jonathon pushes Joe aside as he barely dodges the blade. It catches the hem of Jonathon's pant leg, but he rips the fabric free and hauls Joe to his feet as the Wardens release their volley of arrows. A dozen crossbow bolts splinter the ruined library floor where the brothers were just a moment before.

Clinging as tight as a lamprey to his little brother, Jonathon manages to hobble them out of the room and into the main entrance hall. An assistant gasps and drops her stack of books upon seeing these two dirt-covered phantoms emerge from the usually pristine library. Jonathon bumps her aside as he races down the hall to the servant stairs, his right leg dragging like a cart with a broken wheel as the Ink begins to wear off. Joe cranes his neck back and forth as they run down the stairs to the kitchen, a familiar memory tickling at the back of his brain, just out of reach.

Jonathon bursts into the kitchen, dragging Joe along by the shoulder. Several cooks jump at the intrusion, but none say a word. Muscle memory kicking in, Jonathon marches them through a door at the back of the kitchen and into the side courtyard, the same escape route they had taken fourteen years ago. Two Wardens patrolling yell at them, but Jonathon simply flicks his wrist, and the ground falls away beneath the Wardens, swallowing them up to their knees. He continues to speed himself and Joe through the courtyard and into the garden beyond, not pausing to look back and see if the Wardens are following. The brothers rush into the woods and are quickly enveloped by the dense tree cover.

Joe trips on a root protruding from the ground like an unburied bone and pulls Jonathon down in a tangle of legs. Jonathon's bad knee twists, and he yelps in pain like a kicked dog. Joe pants, exhausted, and flops onto his back, wanting the forest to engulf him. Jonathon, extricating himself, awkwardly reaches both shackled hands into his pocket and pulls out the vial and syringe Bernard forgot in his cell.

Jonathon pauses a moment, contemplating the dark liquid swirling within. He cleaved the throne room in two and ran the length of the castle with almost no pain in his bad knee. When Bernard and Gregor were forcing Ink on him in the dungeon, Jonathon could only think about the terramental that had been a few cells down from him. How the terramental's screams ricocheted off the dungeon walls until he was abruptly silenced by Gregor's dagger. If Jonathon takes more Ink now, will he end up a dead man, like that terramental? On the other hand, to walk without pain, to be more powerful even than Jacob, is surely worth the risk.

A loud shout from the direction of the garden springs him into motion. Jonathon licks his parched lips and carefully reaches for the syringe and fills it. Pushing up his sleeve, he injects a dose into the flesh just above his wrist, which is as far as he can reach while shackled. An instant rush of power fills him, the pain in his knee subsiding once more. The shouts from the garden draw nearer. If they stay here much longer, all of Jonathon's efforts will be for nothing. He stands and grabs Joe's jacket, hauling him up from the ground where Joe's sprawled on his back. Jonathon then forces them to continue on. Joe doggedly puts one foot in front of the other, barely keeping upright.

Jonathon vaguely remembers the stone monument their dad brought them to the night of The Expunging. He knows it is somewhere close by but is unsure of the direction. Closing his eyes, he reaches out with his power, sensing the dirt beneath their feet and the cliffs behind the castle, until he feels a change, something out of the ordinary, nearby. It is still earth, but clearly man-made. Jonathon latches onto this man-made stone and uses the tether he creates between it and himself as a guide.

The brothers stumble onward, closing in on the monument. It soon appears before them, and Jonathon finds the side with the hydromental symbol and presses it, opening the door. They hustle inside and are engulfed in darkness. Jonathon lets out a sigh. He can tell that Joe is quickly fading. Each step Joe takes seems to drop him lower to the ground. Joe's eyes flutter closed every few minutes, and Jonathon sharply pulls against Joe's jacket to keep him awake. Jonathon wants to pause for a moment, for Joe's sake, but he knows they need to get away. Away from the castle, away from Eastport entirely. There's nowhere safe here. He can't risk taking Joe to Madame Barnaby at the Siren Club. He can't risk her getting arrested and killed like Joe's adoptive parents. He tightens his grip on Joe, and they march on.

Presently, they come to a fork where years ago Jacob made the decision to turn left, leading them to the Agate Bridge exit. Jonathon doesn't even pause at the intersection but maintains a steady course straight ahead. He can feel the tunnel going deeper, even though he can't see well in the dark. Pausing for a moment, Jonathon kicks off his shoes, planting his bare feet on the soil of the tunnel. The tunnel's loaminess fills his heart with peace. The soil is rich and waiting to do his bidding, to be formed into whatever Jonathon pleases. It's a comfort to him to know that some things are malleable in a world that is becoming increasingly rigid.

Stumbling on, Jonathon lets the dampness of the soil guide him. They continue for another ten minutes, Jonathon occasionally readjusting his grip on Joe's waist, until they reach a dead end. Jonathon props Joe against the side of the tunnel. Turning to the darkness in front of him, Jonathon slowly reaches his hands out, running his fingers over the stone wall, feeling for a crease or crack to denote a door. Instead, his fingers brush up against another hydromental symbol carved into the stone, and he presses it.

A door swings inward a fraction of an inch, and Jonathon can smell salt water in the air whistling in. The salty breeze seems to revive Joe slightly, as he opens his eyes and sighs. Scuttling himself to the right, Jonathon grabs the door and pulls it open just enough to peer out.

The tunnel ends at the harbor, hidden in the sewage pipe that brings the offal from High Tide to the sea. A river of refuse flows just beyond the door where it waterfalls out the pipe's opening. Jonathon slides out the door to peer around the edge of the pipe. To the right are the docks, bustling with activity. A small spit of sand extends from the pipe to the first pier, where a ladder allows access to the planking above. Jonathon spies Wardens making their daily patrols, bronze-colored cloaks he now knows are gwarem-lined, swirling behind them.

They're too exposed here. Jonathon looks back through the door at Joe, who is slumped further down the tunnel wall and mostly concealed by the tunnel's darkness. Options race through Jonathon's mind. They can't go back into Eastport, not with how many Wardens would be looking for them. They can't hide out in the woods; they would most likely starve before the Wardens could find them. They can't stow away on a ship without getting caught. Besides, Jonathon isn't fond of sailing. He stares out across the ocean, a plan forming. Well, he wouldn't be bringing Jacob an orb. Perhaps Jacob would settle for a once-lost little brother instead.

Jonathon turns around, scuttles back into the tunnel, and closes the door. He's never attempted something like this before, but with the help of Ink, he has no doubt he can handle it. Jonathon feels stronger than Jacob, who is the strongest elemental he knows. Holding out his hands in front of him, Jonathon imagines the earth beneath the door hollowing out into a new tunnel. He jumps back in surprise at how easily the earth before him moves. It rumbles like some disturbed beast, arched earthen walls springing to life. Jonathon once more grabs Joe by his jacket, and begins the arduous trek under the Eusgarian Sea to Port Green, the farthest he can get from his uncle. He pauses briefly to once again inject a shot of Ink from the stolen vial, knowing that he'll need as much help as he can get to make a tunnel all the way to Port Green. Relishing the extra strength, Jonathon continues, half-dragging his brother toward freedom. With each step, the pain in his leg lessens, and he feels the earth's power fill him. With the briefest thought, the tunnel continues to form in front of them, dirt and stone leaping aside as if being thrown by a burrowing mole. He tightens his grip on Joe and trudges on.

Jonathon is unsure how much time has passed, the monotony and darkness of the tunnel removing all thought, but he does notice the ground beneath his feet turn from a loamy soil, to a thicker damp sludge, to finally a firm, cold clay. The air has become moist and harder to breathe. Jonathon guesses they are well under the Eusgarian Sea now. He can feel the weight of the water above pushing down, wanting to crush them like ants. He knows he is stronger than the measly ocean. His tunnel will hold. But this escape is taking too long. Surely, they should have reached Port Green by now. He should have felt the change in earth—a transition from cold, silent, and damp to warm, dry, and teeming with forest life.

It's Joe. Joe is slowing him down, barely able to place one foot in front of the other. Leaving him here would make things much easier, Jonathon begins to think. No one would be able to use him if they couldn't find him down here in the dark. Jonathon's grip loosens, and Joe almost falls to his knees.

With a start, Jonathon hauls Joe back to his feet. *The Ink,* Jonathon thinks as he slows. *It must be the Ink. I wouldn't spend all these years looking for Joseph just to leave him here.* The earth stops moving ahead of him as he comes to a halt. If he continues on, drawing strength from the drug, he's sure that he'll end up doing something he regrets, like leaving his brother to the forbidding subterranean ocean. But without Ink's power, they'll never reach Port Green. They are both too weak.

"Joseph." Jonathon nudges his brother. "Joseph. Wake up. You must wake up." Joe's head lolls from one side to the other as Jonathon continues to shake him. "Joseph!" With a great effort, Joe turns to the insistent, annoying voice on his left.

"Joseph. We can't go forward anymore. We need to go up. You need to get us through the ocean. Can you do that?"

Joe notices a man talking to him, but the words are distant, and the haze in his mind is invitingly drawing him back in. "Joseph!" Something strikes his cheek.

"What?" Joe raises his head, focusing on the blurry shape in front of him until it clears. The gentleman. The one who claims he's his brother. "Jonathon?"

"Did you hear me? We need to go up. We must be miles under the Eusgarian Sea by now, and we can't go back to Eastport. Can you get us to the surface?"

"Up?" Joe cranes his neck upward, seeing nothing but dirt. "Where are we?"

"Under the Eusgarian Sea. About ten miles from Port Green, I think."

"Seven miles."

"What?"

"We're seven miles from land. At least, there's an obstacle that's not ocean seven miles from us."

"Well, if that's true, hopefully there's some ship we can jump. Can you get us through?"

"What?" Joe asks, still not quite comprehending what this man is asking. Joe looks up, straining to see the tons of water he can feel weighing down on them. It's almost comforting, that weight. Knowing that it's there, knowing that it will always be there. *It wouldn't be so bad to stay here*, he thinks. Ian and Matilde are dead. His crew is gone. There is nothing left for him above. It would be nice to stay here, in the dark, with the comforting weight of the ocean, his ocean, to protect him. Joe's knees buckle, and he gladly begins to sink to the ground. But there's a sharp jolt on his arm, and that pesky voice is yelling at him again.

"Joseph! Don't pass out on me! Stay awake! We can make it, but you have to help me!"

"If I help, will you shut up?" Joe doesn't bother waiting for an answer. He begins to draw the ocean toward him, calling forth the sea to break through the earthen walls and carry them away into the abyss. Frantically, Jonathon pulls down the earthen ceiling above them like an avalanche as he realizes what Joe is doing.

The current reaches down like a punch, lifting them up into the watery vastness. Surrounding them are the blue-green fathoms of the Eusgarian Sea. The surface shimmers above, a thousand tiny lights beckoning them to freedom. Joe feels the grip on his arm loosen and turns to see Jonathon sinking back down. And for a minute, Joe just watches. That man slowly sinking into the blue twilight is the cause of all his problems. Every bad thing that's happened is because that man came into his life. Joe can't help but think that if he lets this man drown, all his problems will be over. Jonathon sinks lower, his hair forming a halo in the current, bubbles of air escaping from his lips.

After what feels like ages but must only be a few seconds, Joe reaches down and drags Jonathon up to him, pushing the ocean away to create an air pocket for the man who claims to be his brother. A ragged gasp sounds in his ear as Jonathon sucks in a breath. Jonathon clutches one of Joe's shoulders, shaking. Joe sees the terror in his eyes and feels a quick brush of shame as he realizes he was about to let Jonathon drown. Gripping Jonathon's arm, Joe kicks upward, continuing to repel the ocean away from them. They slowly continue their ascent. Finally, the tiny twinkling lights of the ocean's surface break way to salt air. Satisfied that his work is done, Joe releases his grip on the ocean and slings his shackled arms around Jonathon's neck, unwilling to help any further.

Jonathon gulps in air as they breach the surface. He flounders in the water, frantic, until his legs start kicking and he treads water. Joe clings to him like wet paper, and Jonathon latches onto his little brother, struggling to keep them both afloat. Water has never been his friend, but he'll be damned if he is going to be stymied by it now. They had made it this far; he will not give up. Turning in a circle, all he can see is ocean. The last rays of the setting sun illuminate the water, blinding him, but land is nowhere in sight. Panic begins to creep in, but Jonathon shakes his head and tries to take a deep breath without gulping in the salty water. Centering himself, he feels a slight tug of earth to his right, so he angles in that direction, hoping Port Green will soon appear. Instead, a smudge of a shadow noses its way into his sightline. A ship.

"Help!" He tries to yell, but his voice comes out hoarse and garbled. Jonathon gathers his breath to try once more when a monstrous wave knocks him and Joe under. Clawing his way back to the surface, he sees that the ship is moving away from them, becoming smaller on the horizon. His strength quickly fading, Jonathon thinks longingly of the vial and syringe in his pocket. If only he could have one more dose, he could easily save his brother by summoning the sea floor to rise up to him, forming an island. But, as it is, Ink is not an option. With his hands still shackled, and Joe using him as a buoy, Jonathon has no hope of reaching the Ink in his pocket.

Summoning every last drop of power in his body, Jonathon focuses on the ship, willing it to stop, turn, come back. He latches onto the stone ballast in the cargo hold and urges the ballast to come to him. He feels the resistance of the rudder against the current, like a fish trapped in a net, fighting against him, but he hardens his resolve and, feet kicking desperately to stay above water, slowly draws the ship to him like a magnet.

Jonathon lets go as he feels the last of his strength leave him, and with one last desperate breath bellows "Help!" once more. The ship is closer than before but is still such a long way off. He tries to kick out toward the ship, but it's all he can do to keep them both afloat. Bobbing further down into the waves, Jonathon almost dismisses the distant cries for seagulls. Straining his ears, Jonathon now hears shouts from across the water and sighs in relief as he realizes that the ship has spotted them. The ship's sails rise, and the wind speeds it ever closer to where Jonathon flails under Joe's weight. Soon, the ship is close enough that Jonathon can barely make out the scurrying of men onboard and a longboat being lowered, oars pushing out to meet them.

Before Jonathon knows it, he and Joe are being dragged aboard the longboat and rowing through the waters back to the ship. The crew hauls the unconscious Joe up first before tugging Jonathon over the railing. Landing in a heap on the deck, Jonathon is surprised to hear a voice speak his brother's name.

"Joe?"

15

onathon looks up, searching for the owner of the voice. Blinking several times to clear the seawater from his eyes, Jonathon sees a small group of sailors staring at him and Joe. Most are men, but there are a few women scattered about. One sailor in particular catches his eye, a young man with a mess of curly black hair. Jonathon then notices a one-handed tall man at the head of the group in untorn and clean clothes, differing from the rest of the crew.

"You know who he is?" Jonathon struggles to catch his breath as he questions the tidy sailor, who he assumes to be in charge. Captain Merrill peers down at them both, absently fiddling with the sleeve of his missing right hand, freshly bandaged. His eyes land on Joe, slumped on the deck, water pooling around his clothes.

"Yes." The captain's gaze hardens.

"Then please help him," Jonathon pleads. It's a fight for Jonathon to stay conscious, the edges of his vision blurring as he looks

151

from the captain to his brother. "Please help him. I can't lose him again."

"I don't understand why he didn't just tell me. He was like a son to me."

Jonathon's stare bores holes into Captain Merrill's anger, fraying the edges with the immense sadness he finds there.

"Often we are betrayed by the ones we love most."

Who is this man? Captain Merrill thinks. Clearly, he is another elemental. He looks familiar, like maybe the captain has seen him around the docks before, but it's something a bit more than that. The blue eyes and round face. Then it hits him. Aside from the brown hair, this man looks like Joe.

"Who are you, son? Why is Joe so important to you?" the captain asks as Jonathon slumps back against the deck railing, defeated. The wind whips sea spray on the deck and ruffles the sails overhead. The ship's timbers creak hypnotically, lulling Jonathon into a stupor.

"He's my brother," Jonathon finally admits.

Surprise fills Captain Merrill's face, but understanding follows shortly after, and a suspicion that has been brewing in his mind since Joe's arrest begins to solidify.

"Nell," Captain Merrill gestures behind him. "See to it that Joe is taken to the sick bay, and tend to his injuries."

"No," a slight woman with a stern face answers. She's frowning at Joe, body stiff with her fists at her sides, as if she's preventing herself from storming off.

"Excuse me?" Captain Merrill turns to face her.

Nell fixes her steely gray eyes on the captain and crosses her arms over her chest. "You may be able to forgive his lies so easily, but maybe you've forgotten that a hydromental killed my father."

She turns, her long chestnut braid slashing through the air, and strides away.

Sighing, Captain Merrill rubs his forehead. "Shorty," he gestures to a scruffy mate with a patchy beard, "take Joe below, and see to both him and his brother. Matt," the captain turns to the curly black-haired young man hovering nearby. "Go help."

"Thank you, Captain." Jonathon's eyes flutter closed in relief.

*   *   *   *

Jonathon follows the two men into the ship's belly. Using the wall for support, he hobbles down a set of stairs and through a long corridor lined with doors. They stop in front of the last door on the left.

"Here we are. Sick bay." The black-haired man points awkwardly at the sick bay entrance. Shorty gives Matt a knowing look as he carries an unconscious Joe through the door.

"Thank you…" Jonathon begins.

"Matt."

"Thank you, Matt."

Jonathon trips as he crosses the threshold after Shorty, his bad knee giving out in protest. Matt catches Jonathon's arm before he can hit the floor.

"Steady on there, mate."

Head spinning from the pain, Jonathon grips Matt's arm as they make their way to the room's other cot. He sits down heavily on the thin straw mattress, sneezing as a cloud of dust flies up. The sick bay is small, with two straw mattresses on either side of the room. A worktable, with a wooden railing around the edge to keep utensils from rolling off in rough seas, takes up half of the back wall. Above it is a shelf with various implements stacked upon it: tools for cutting, prodding, and stitching. A cabinet takes up most of the rest of the back wall, filled with tinctures, salves, potions, and bandages, among other medical necessities. A porthole window sits between the worktable and cabinet, showing a view of purple water as the moon begins to rise.

"You're not a pyromental, are you?" Shorty asks from where he's bent over Joe, trying to remove the shackles.

"I'm afraid not," Jonathon says, sitting down.

"Damn. It would be a lot easier if you could melt these off."

After a brief glance around the room, Jonathon points to a stone mortar and pestle on the shelf above the worktable.

"If you hand me that pestle, I can make a key."

Matt raises an eyebrow at Jonathon as he hands him the pestle.

"You're a terramental, yeah?"

"Yes," Jonathon hedges.

Matt frowns, but not judgmentally. Rather, he looks at Jonathon as if trying to figure out a puzzle. Uncomfortable, Jonathon focuses on the pestle in his hand. A skeleton key: one key to fit any lock. With the pestle not being much larger than a pen, it takes hardly any effort to will the pestle into the correct shape. He holds it tightly in his hand and prods at the bulbous end with his finger, encouraging it to narrow. He traces the rough image of a key's teeth onto the pestle, the excess stone crumbling away at his touch.

"Here." He hands the finished key to Shorty.

Shorty unlocks Joe's shackles with ease and moves onto Jonathon's. The moment the shackles are removed, Jonathon falls back onto the cot, absolutely drained of adrenaline. He feels every ache in his body, every throb emanating from his bad knee, and the dark curtain that threatens to close off his mind. Dimly, he hears Shorty muttering.

"This salve is the best bet to heal those blisters left from the shackles and your bruises, but there is not much more to do but rest. I'm not as good a healer as Nell, but it doesn't appear that anything else is wrong with you both."

"Joe definitely ruined any shot he had with Nell now," Matt adds.

"Ya think?" Shorty moves over to Jonathon, who registers a slimy cold on his wrists. "Bah," Shorty continues. "Nell will come around soon enough."

Eyes still closed, Jonathon hears the sick bay's door open and close. Finally alone, he tries to process everything that happened. Joseph's adoptive parents killed. Joseph, using his powers in ways that shouldn't be possible. Their flight through the ocean, and he himself using his powers with an unimaginable strength. Was tunneling under the ocean solely due to the drug, or is he really that strong? Jonathon hasn't used his powers to their fullest abilities ever since that day on the bridge. He didn't want to hurt anyone else. And once he moved back to Eastport, he couldn't risk using his powers much, even in the confines of a safe haven like the Siren Club. His older brother Jacob has always been powerful, more powerful than other elementals according to their father, so maybe he is too. And if that's true, then maybe, once Joseph is safe, he'll go back and finish tearing down his uncle's castle, and his and Bernard's old apartment. Yes, he'd love to tear down that apartment, brick by brick, and watch it all crumble around Bernard.

With that delicious thought, Jonathon feels a cold strength course through his veins. His power reaches out until it hits the closest earthen object. The mortar on the shelf begins to tremble and tumbles into a pile of rubble. Not satisfied, he reaches out once more, searching for something else to destroy.

The first item he comes across is round and gold. A pocket watch. Too small. Reaching further, he senses the ballast in the hold. Interesting, but not quite big enough. Then he latches onto something massive. The ship, with all its metal rivets. Of course. The ship would be excellent practice for his uncle and Bernard, a slight balm to help ease his broken heart.

All around him the *Moro* begins to tremble.

"Hey now, easy there. I don't think you're ready for another swim just yet."

Jonathon's eyes fly open to see startling green eyes in a round face staring down at him. Immediately, the trembling stops. Feeling slightly defeated, Jonathon tries to sit up. Matt helps him lean back against the wall.

"Sorry. I thought I was alone. Must be the stress of everything getting to me."

Matt just silently stares at him, making Jonathon uncomfortable, yet intrigued.

"Why are you still here? Shouldn't you be with the rest of the crew complaining about how you have two elementals on board?"

Matt simply shrugs.

"Joe was my friend. Still is, I hope. I don't really care if he's an elemental. You either, for that matter."

Jonathon grunts. "That must make you rather unpopular," he says, leaning his head back against the wall.

Matt shrugs again. "Not everyone agrees with Magistrate Rufus. Might surprise you to find that a lot of people just want peace."

Jonathon finds himself falling ever so slightly into those bright green eyes.

"An unattainable dream. But nice to think about," Jonathon responds. He searches Matt's face, something familiar about the green eyes peering out through a dimly lit red room. "You're the patron from the Siren Club!" Jonathon exclaims. "The one who gave me the information about Joe being a smuggler."

Matt ducks his head, blushing. "Uh, yeah, that was me," he says while picking at a hangnail, glancing every few seconds at Jonathon.

They sit a moment in silence, listening to the ship's timbers creak. Above them drifts down the faint bustle of the crew on deck. Jonathon closes his eyes and tries to adjust to the swaying rhythm of the ship. He feels uprooted, being so far from solid land. He'd give anything to be back in Eastport or Port Green, or even a deserted island as long as the ground is firm and stationary.

Jonathon looks over at Joseph and notices the color has returned to his cheeks and that his breathing seems easier, more regular. Whereas he feels pulled up at the roots, the ocean appears to be filling Joseph with vitality. Such is the difference between terramentals and hydromentals, Jonathon supposes.

"Is he really your brother?" Matt's question breaks through Jonathon's thoughts. "He's never mentioned any family aside from his parents."

Jonathon's heart gripping in a sudden vise, he turns away, hoping Matt doesn't catch the wet sheen in his eyes. "No," he whispers. "He wouldn't have. It's my fault he doesn't remember." Jonathon wishes Matt would quit staring at him. Concern written on his face, Matt reaches over and gently places his hand on Jonathon's bad knee. Jonathon flinches, recoiling from his touch.

"If you don't mind, I'd like to be alone now."

"Sure," Matt says after a minute. "I'll bring you an extra set of clothes and some shoes, since yours seem to be missing." He rises to leave but pauses at the door.

"It wasn't your fault."

"What?"

"Whatever it is you're blaming yourself for. It wasn't your fault." Matt gives a small smile as he leaves.

"I don't need your pity," Jonathon mutters to himself as he tries to find a comfortable position on the cot. Matt can believe what he likes, but Jonathon knows the truth. He's spent every day of the past fourteen years trying to shove aside his guilt. He closes his eyes and tries to push those thoughts from his mind. At least Joseph is safe. For now.

16

"This is an outrage!" Magistrate Rufus stomps across his room to the alcove. Reaching the wall, he turns and stomps back to the door. Gregor stands next to Rufus' desk, silently waiting for the Magistrate's anger to subside enough to hold a rational conversation.

"How did you let them get away?" Magistrate Rufus hisses at Gregor.

"While we have added gwarem pillars to the dungeon, we have yet to address the throne room," Gregor monotonously replies. "I did not expect you to entertain elementals in the throne room."

Magistrate Rufus stops his pacing and glares at Gregor. "The opportunity to remove Jacob presented itself. I would not let that go to waste." Taking a fortifying breath, Magistrate Rufus stalks over to his desk and drops into his chair. "No matter. We have the orb back. We must attack Jacob and Port Green soon, before they've had a chance to recover. Are your elementals ready?"

Gregor straightens, not showing an ounce of failure as he responds. "Not yet. The Ink's formula is correct, but we have not yet perfected the dosage and frequency. We will soon, but I do not have elementals to spare if we want to get this right."

Rufus slumps forward onto his desk at this news. Gregor and his chemists have been working on Ink for months now, adjusting the formula and dosage. Once the right combination is found, Magistrate Rufus will have an army of elementals beholden to him. Addicted to Ink, they will do whatever he commands as long as they can get their next fix. Presuming the Ink doesn't kill them first, which has been the result so far. Rufus would still rather see all elementals dead, but he feels the tides slowly turning. With an elemental army at his command, he would be more powerful than any elemental in all of Eusgaria. If he couldn't have powers himself, he could at least control the ones who do.

The light outside his high window pales to a twilight violet as the sun begins to rise. His nephews escaped hours ago; they could be anywhere by now. After their escape, Rufus scoured Eastport with the orb, which showed his nephews in what appeared to be the tunnels. Being surrounded by dark, earthen walls, it was difficult for Rufus to determine where exactly in the tunnels his nephews might be and where they would emerge. He couldn't watch the orb all day, so Magistrate Rufus had set increased patrols of Wardens to search all of Eastport for his nephews. For now, his efforts are better directed elsewhere. Jacob still remains the first priority. One of these days, Jacob will manage to recruit the elementals of Andulsae and lead an attack on Eastport. Magistrate Rufus knows this in his core. His stomach churns at the thought. Getting Jacob out of the way eliminates one threat to the throne.

"So, your Ink is still in development. What about the barrels?"

"Those have shown most promising results," Gregor smiles eagerly.

"Perfect. Gregor," Magistrate Rufus demands, "fetch me Bernard Lowain, our good Captain of the Wardens. I have a mission for him."

Gregor strides swiftly out of the Magistrate's room. The door closes with a satisfying thud. Pushing up from his chair, Magistrate Rufus collects a match from the shelf behind him and lights his lantern. He gingerly pulls out the orb from his robe pocket and sets it gently on the desk as he retakes his seat. The ever-present mist swirls within the orb's depths, awaiting the Magistrate's request. Jacob's gone through great lengths to steal this orb. What does he think he can do with it? It took Rufus many years of trial and error to figure out the orb's secrets. He's not sure that he's even discovered the full extent of the orb's powers.

Around him, the castle is silent. Straining his ears for several seconds, Magistrate Rufus fails to hear the clack of Gregor's returning boots. At this time of morning, Captain Lowain should be just finishing his patrol. It would be some time yet before Gregor returned with him in tow. Bringing the lantern closer, the Magistrate pulls open a desk drawer and removes a small circular stand, no bigger than a serving tray. The arms of the dark wooden stand intertwine, creating a woven basket. Magistrate Rufus places the orb into the belly of the basket, watching in awe as the orb expands to fill the space. No matter how many times he's seen it, a small glee fills him every time Rufus watches the orb awaken.

"Show me what Jacob is doing right now." The Magistrate's breath clouds the mirrorlike surface as he leans over the orb. The orb's mist shimmers and condenses, sending a shiver down his spine. Clearing, the vision in the orb lands on Jacob sitting quietly in a dark room. Magistrate Rufus greedily inhales the scene. There he is, his oldest nephew, listening on the wind per usual. More often than not, this is how Rufus finds Jacob. A shaft of pale dawn light breaks through the darkness in the orb as Magistrate Rufus watches Jordan, his next oldest nephew, walk in. The room is plunged back into darkness as Jordan closes the door. He ignites his palm and sits cross-legged in front of Jacob.

The brothers remain seated still five minutes later, Jordan's flames casting solemn shadows about the room. Rufus is ready to give up; nothing of importance is going to be learned by observing his nephews sit silently in a dark room. Besides, Gregor should be returning with Captain Lowain soon. He moves to grab the orb when he hears Jacob speak. Jacob's voice is as soft as falling leaves, and Magistrate Rufus struggles to hear.

"I think we're in the clear. The best I can hear is Uncle stomping about. I don't think he's listening," Jacob reports to Jordan. "It seems that Jonathon found Joseph."

"Joe's alive?" Jordan's flames burn a bit brighter. "But you knew that already, didn't you."

Jacob's stoic face is unreadable through the reflection of the flames on his glasses. "Yes, I had been keeping tabs on him. Jonathon managed to get him arrested as well."

"So that means we still don't have the orb. Which means the Magistrate will continue to attack us without warning." Jordan's shoulders slump in defeat.

"Precisely, since Jonathon decided to deviate from the plan."

Magistrate Rufus sniggers at Jacob's scorn.

"But," Jacob continued speaking in the orb's vision. "Jonathon managed to escape the castle dungeon. With Joseph. They were just picked up by his ship at sea. A small merchant ship called the *Moro*, if I heard correctly?"

So, there is some news after all. Magistrate Rufus leans back in thought. Captain Merrill had his ship pick up Rufus' escaped nephews. He could work with this. Merrill is already under the black flag; the Magistrate could send word to his naval captain to make haste and intercept the *Moro* before it docks in Lexington. Then Rufus could deal with not only his errant nephews, but that dour captain as well. Apparently taking his hand was not enough.

"This could be the chance we were waiting for," Jordan's tinny voice pipes up from the orb. "If this ship isn't too far from here, perhaps we intercept it and bring it back to Port Green. Lexington won't give us a ship, and Andulsae has made it clear they won't help. But if we take this ship, we can take a small group of our best fighters, sail back to Eastport, and get the orb ourselves." A flame leaps to life in his other palm at his excitement. "Think about it, Jacob. You can't transport the group we need across the Eusgarian Sea by yourself. We need a ship. There's been no other opportunity like this."

Jacob ponders for a moment, toying with the dirt floor beneath him. "You're not wrong. But we've just been attacked. I don't think it's prudent to leave Port Green undefended."

"Well, the island won't be undefended. Our fighters will stay here. Just you and me, then. We'll go out to this ship and get it."

The image goes very quiet. Magistrate Rufus struggles to hear Jacob's response, but all he sees is a small smile creep across Jacob's face. A booming knock echoes throughout the Magistrate's room, causing him to jump. The scene in the orb fades, and the orb shrinks to a marble once more. Irritated, Magistrate Rufus jumps up.

"What is it?" he yells at his door.

Gregor sticks his head in. "I've got Captain Lowain here with me, Magistrate."

Magistrate Rufus sighs and smooths the front of his robes. "Yes, please do come in." He ushers Bernard to take a seat before his desk as Gregor leads him into the room.

"What can I do for you, Magistrate?" Bernard bows, waiting for Rufus to sit before sitting himself. Bernard is a strapping young fellow, fit and determined. Magistrate Rufus has not seen a more ruthless Warden, much to his pleasure. Bernard is exactly the man he needs right now.

"I have a task for you," Magistrate Rufus explains. "It has come to my attention that Port Green will be left defenseless for a time, providing us with the most opportune window to eliminate that elemental threat."

Bernard scooches forward in his chair, anticipation dripping off him like a raincloud ready to burst.

"You will take four ships and launch an attack on Port Green." Magistrate Rufus continues with his plan, describing every minute detail to a rapt Bernard.

"Do you follow me so far?" the Magistrate asks as he pauses to assess Bernard.

"Yes, sir."

"Good." Magistrate Rufus turns serious. "I need you to complete this mission without failure. We will not have another opportunity to attack Port Green without Jacob present." Magistrate Rufus picks up the orb and weighs it in his hand. This bauble has been his eyes and ears for years now. To part with it would be akin to cutting off his right hand. Yet, to defeat Jacob, he must make big moves. He holds out the orb to Bernard.

"I will give you this orb, so you can better plan all the moving pieces once on Port Green. You will need eyes everywhere, and this orb can do that for you. But," his voice lowers to a menacing volume, "you must bring this orb back to me. Should you return without it, consider your life forfeit. Do I make myself clear?"

Gulping, Bernard nods once.

"Good." Magistrate Rufus tightens his fist around the orb as he studies Bernard. It's a risky play, but wars are not won by cowards. "Gregor!"

Gregor approaches at the Magistrate's call, dagger in hand. Bernard involuntarily flinches away from the dagger that has cut so many elemental throats. Yet, Gregor snatches Bernard's wrist and slashes the dagger across his palm. He holds Bernard's dripping hand out to the Magistrate as if an offering.

"You're about to become almost as powerful as me," Magistrate Rufus slyly smiles as he closes Bernard's bloody hand around the orb. Bernard winces at the brief flare of pain, the uncomfortable way the orb digs into his torn skin. Swallowing down his disgust at touching an elemental object, Bernard straightens under the weight of responsibility.

"I won't let you down."

17

An incessant growling echoes through the room. It takes Joe a minute to realize it's his stomach. Damn, when was the last time he'd eaten?

He lies on a cot, staring at the rough wooden beams above him. That's odd. He's fairly certain the dungeon is made of dirt and stone. Also, the dungeon is not this bright. Sitting up, he looks down at his wrists.

I'm not in shackles.

Hearing a soft moan, Joe turns to see Jonathon sleeping in the cot across from him. The *Moro*. Somehow, he's back on his ship, in the sick bay by the looks of it. Someone has left two changes of clothes on the workbench behind him. He's happy to see that whoever it was had the sense to bring him his own shirt and pants from his cabin. Joe quickly sheds his current clothes, smelling of dungeon and dirt, and puts on the soft, clean shirt and sturdy canvas pants.

Nell. The thought enters unbidden to his mind. Did she visit him and bring the change of clothes?

Quietly, he leaves the sick bay and heads topside. The bright sun sears into his brain as he emerges from below. Eyes adjusting, he scans the deck, searching for Nell. He needs to explain it all to her, to tell her he's sorry he lied. But then he remembers her father, how he died. He'd be lucky if Nell ever spoke to him again.

He spies the captain at the helm. Taking a deep breath of salt air, he makes his way over. Stares from his former crewmates pierce his back, and he does his best to ignore their silent judgment. Captain Merrill, sensing a lull in activity, spins around to order his crew back to work when he spies Joe just feet away.

Startled, the first thing Joe notices is that the captain's right hand is missing, the stump wrapped in a dingy bandage. The second thing he sees is the hard frown aimed at him.

Joe is about to blurt out something stupid, like "What happened to your hand?" but it dawns on him that the captain is just one more casualty on his list. The more he thinks about it, the more he knows it to be true. Of course the Magistrate wouldn't let his crew go scot-free. Punishment had to be dealt out for harboring an elemental. He wishes, not for the first time, that he had never met Jonathon, had never taken that job.

Tearing his eyes away from Captain Merrill's stump, he steels himself and meets the captain's gaze. The hot sun bears down on his neck, and sweat breaks out on his forehead.

"I'm sorry," he whispers, dropping his head. "For everything."

Captain Merrill sighs and attempts to rub his forehead with his right hand, momentarily forgetting himself. He crosses his arms instead.

"Joe," he begins. He opens his mouth to say more, but nothing comes out. Frowning, he tries again, but Joe interrupts.

"I should've told you. You've been like a second father to me, and I never meant for any of this to happen and…I should have just told you." Joe bows his head in shame.

Suddenly, Joe finds himself wrapped in an awkward hug. Joe sinks into the captain, exhausted and surprised to feel tears welling up in his eyes, sorrow like a balloon expanding in his chest.

"I understand why you didn't."

"He killed my parents," Joe gulps as the balloon bursts.

Captain Merrill stiffens, then pulls Joe up.

"Come on," he says as Joe wipes a sleeve across his face. "Let's talk further in my cabin."

The crew remains transfixed at the spectacle unfolding before them.

"Back to work!" The captain barks as he leads Joe away. They enter Captain Merrill's cabin beneath the quarter deck, Captain Merrill tightly closing the door behind them before heading to his desk at the back of the cabin. Joe follows and sits in an armless wooden chair across from him.

"I'm glad you're all right Joe, but I can't say that I'm too happy to see you right now." The captain frowns at him, brows furrowed. Joe notices a day's worth of stubble on Captain Merrill's chin. He usually shaves every day. He must be under considerable stress to have forgone this daily ritual.

"I'm sorry Captain, I didn't mean to—"

Captain Merrill holds up his left hand. "Let me stop you there, Joe. You may have your apologies, but they won't change the fact that you've caused undue harm to this crew. Had I known you were an elemental, I would have never taken you on."

Joe stares down at his hands in shame. Captain Merrill tends to keep his politics to himself and prefers his crew to do the same.

Joe hasn't heard Captain Merrill directly disparage elementals; he always took the captain's quietness on the subject, whereas some of the crew was very vocal against elementals, as indifference. Looks like he was wrong.

"Captain, if you would just let me explain."

"No, Joe." Captain Merrill holds up his right arm this time, allowing Joe to examine the full extent of his injury. The wound looks fresh, as blood seeps through the bandage, the skin red and raw where the bandage ends. "Actions have consequences. After your arrest, the entire crew was taken to the public prison. Magistrate Rufus was content to let them all rot there for a month. These men and women depend on this ship and its wares in order to feed their families. Their families can't have them in prison. I was willing to make Shorty captain while I remained in prison instead. At least the *Moro* could continue onto Lexington then. But, the Magistrate had a different plan."

Captain Merrill looks longingly at his missing right hand. Joe gulps, getting the gist of where this story is heading.

"The Magistrate offered a trade. The crew could remain in prison for a month, the *Moro* dry-docked, and our wares auctioned off to other merchants to trade, or I could give up my right hand, and the *Moro* could continue with our scheduled trade in Lexington, under the black flag. Which, as you know, means we are marked. If we don't show up in the Lexington port in a week's time, an Eastport navy ship will be dispatched to track us down and sink us on sight. Once we get to Lexington, if we don't then return to Eastport within another week's time, a navy ship will track us down and sink us on sight. I am no longer in control of this ship."

"Why didn't the Magistrate station a navy officer on the *Moro*?" Joe ventures.

"It was brought up. But that man of his, Gregor? He reminded Magistrate Rufus that they didn't have men to spare. Must be planning something big." The captain's eyes are troubled as he looks to the door behind Joe. "The last time Magistrate Rufus planned something big, all the elementals in Eastport were killed or arrested. Humans and elementals alike lived in fear during those months. Stepping out your door didn't feel safe.

"I'll let you and the other one stay with us until Lexington, but then you must leave, discretely, for we'll be watched. I already almost lost about ten men after your arrest. They fear for their and their family's lives, having been caught sailing with an elemental, albeit unknowingly. I can't be held responsible for what they might do to you if they feel threatened. In fact, I think it would be best if both of you stayed out of sight below deck until we dock."

Joe bows his head. There isn't much to say. His and Jonathon's presence on this ship would only make Captain Merrill's situation worse than it is, and he couldn't do that to the *Moro* and its crew. They are his home and family, even if most of them want to throw him overboard. He nods his head solemnly and gets up to leave just as a loud thud echoes from beyond the closed door.

*   *   *   *

Jonathon suppresses a scream as a searing pain like being kicked by a horse travels up his knee. Gasping, he sits up in the empty sick bay and pulls out the vial of Ink from his pocket, staring for a moment at the loose syringe. He should really find a pouch or something to better carry the drug than risk it falling out of his pocket for anyone to see. He looks around the sick bay at the shelf and cupboard lining the available wall space. Hoisting himself off the cot, he limps over to the cupboard and rummages inside until he finds a small leather case containing slim rolls of bandages and salve. Dumping the bandages and salve into the cupboard, he replaces them with the vial of Ink and the syringe, admiring the way the two implements fit snuggly in the case.

He knows he shouldn't do this, especially after the doses he had in the dungeon. He has seen what happens to elementals who use too much, or were forced to use too much. He felt the beginning of that end himself. He saw how powerful Joseph had become on Ink, but he also saw how it had almost killed him.

He removes the vial again, tilting it one way and then the other, entranced by the way the black liquid absorbs all light, as if it is the mouth of hell itself. Gingerly, he takes out the syringe, uncaps it, and draws up a small dose. He knows the risks, and that is what will keep him safe. *Medicinal interests*, he reassures himself. The fact that Jacob is bound to show up at any moment, a gale at his back and blame on his tongue, has nothing to do with this decision. Just a taste. Not enough to affect his powers, just enough to eliminate his pain, to forget his betrayal. For a little while, anyway.

Rolling up his sleeve, he slides the syringe into his arm. A sigh of pleasure escapes his lips as the drug races through his veins. Jonathon sits back down on the cot for a moment, half-hoping Jacob does show up soon. He'd love to see the look on Jacob's face when he realizes that it was Jonathon who made the quicksand that almost sucked him down during the attack on Port Green. Of course, with Jacob's ability to hear over great distances, he probably already knows. Jonathon frowns at that thought. Jacob always has to one-up him.

A heavy bang echoes down from the deck above, bringing Jonathon abruptly out of his reveries. With a deep breath, he rolls down his sleeve, placing the vial and syringe back in their new-found case and into his pocket before limping his way topside to what promises to be the most disastrous family reunion ever.

18

fter emerging from below deck, Jonathon immediately notices that the entire crew has come to a standstill. Glancing around, he sees his oldest brother, Jacob, looking haughtily about him, threatening anyone to make a move. Jordan stands next to him, having the decency to look a little sheepish at the intrusion. Jonathon's blood begins to boil ever so slightly as he returns his attention to Jacob.

"This is a bit unnecessary, don't you think? Flying over here like that?" Jonathon spits at his eldest brother.

Jacob faces him, the sun flashing briefly off his glasses, making his expression momentarily unreadable before morphing into a disapproving frown. Ignoring Jonathon, Jacob makes a slow circle of the deck.

"Where is your captain?" he bellows out.

A steady voice answers from the direction of the quarter deck. "Here. Care to explain the intrusion?"

Jacob smirks as he spins around to face Captain Merrill. "I'm here to collect Joseph and Jonathon, and we'll be on our way."

Joe steps out from behind the captain.

"I'm not going anywhere with you," he says, drawing himself up to his full height, which is still shorter than the imposing figure Jacob makes.

"You really don't have a choice in the matter."

Jonathon's hands curl into fists at his side. "Lay off it, Jacob."

Jacob finally acknowledges Jonathon. He studies him for a minute before turning away with a sneer. Jonathon feels a humiliated blush begin to creep up his neck, and his fingers itch to call forth his power, to blast his older brother off the ship, if to do nothing more than to prove that he can. He feels a small warmth begin to grow around him and looks up to see Jordan watching him, offering a calming smile. Jordan always was the levelheaded one. Jonathon gives his second oldest brother a brief nod, closes his eyes, and counts to ten. Slowly the anger reduces to a simmer.

"You were the one who attacked Port Green," Jacob returns his focus to Joe, who straightens under his scrutinizing glare. "You shouldn't have been able to hit as hard as you did." Jacob's cheeks redden as he remembers the tsunami that obliterated his village and how he was powerless to stop it.

"Afraid we might be more powerful than you?" Jonathon can't help but remark. Jordan gives a quick shake of his head, and Jonathon immediately looks down at the timbers below his feet. He doesn't need to do this here. Not in front of everyone. Not in front of Joseph.

"That's beside the point," Jacob walks over to Captain Merrill and Joe. "Your actions will be discussed later at the town hall. While there, we can also discuss how to regain the orb." The last comment is icily directed at Jonathon. "If you had just done what I told you, Jonathon, none of this would have happened."

Jonathon grits his teeth and wishes that he was still stuck in his uncle's dungeon. At least there he wouldn't have to face Jacob's scorn.

"It'd be wise to finish this discussion elsewhere," Captain Merrill interjects.

"Agreed," Jacob nods. "We will continue on Port Green. At the town hall, as I've already said."

"We'll continue in my cabin. Here. Now. You don't get to blast your way onto my ship and declare you're leaving with a member of my crew without my say-so first," the captain asserts as Jacob raises an eyebrow, not used to being challenged.

Joe sighs in relief, glad that, even though Merrill is angry at the trouble Joe's caused the *Moro*, he's still willing to stick up for him.

"This is still my ship. That means we play by my rules. No powers are to be used. Whatever it is you have to say will be done civilly, away from the prying ears of my crew." He glances around at the lack of activity on deck, noticing several angry looks after being boarded by even more elementals.

"This way," he gestures for the group to follow him to his cabin.

Captain Merrill's cabin is warm. At least, that's how it appears to Jonathon, who silently applauds the captain's tastes. It's a comforting, yet simple, room. The walls are unadorned except for a large map of Eusgaria, marking everything from the Eusgarian Sea that surrounds Port Green in the east to the Wastes in the west, beyond Eastport. It appears to be hand drawn, and Jonathon wonders if Captain Merrill is the cartographer behind it. A squat bed is pushed against the right-hand side, a sturdy wool blanket stretched across its frame. In front of the porthole sits the captain's desk, a thick wooden structure in deep mahogany that matches the stout chair behind it. Against the left-hand wall is a large weather-worn seaman's trunk, frayed leather straps holding it shut. All in all, the whole ensemble is a picture of reassuring steadiness in what may soon become a storm. It makes Jonathon feel safe. Almost.

Jacob stands in front of the captain, arms crossed, his annoyance evident at the lack of seating. Captain Merrill makes no invitation toward Jacob, a reminder of who is in charge on the *Moro*. Jordan balances precariously on the trunk, not wanting to damage it, while Joe leans against the back wall facing his brothers. Jonathon hovers near the door, out of Jacob's sight and venomous temper.

The captain rests his arm on the desk and slowly glances at each of the boys in turn. "Well," he begins. "Let's start at the beginning."

"Let's start with what the hell Jonathon was thinking when he gave the orb to Joseph. I gave you specific instructions," Jacob retorts.

"It's Joe, not Joseph."

"I had it handled," Jonathon replies glumly.

"Clearly not," Jacob snaps.

A shameful flush creeps up Jonathon's neck. Jacob's right. He didn't have it handled, and everything fell to pieces. He had the orb. He should have just left it at that. Booked passage to Lexington and met up with Jordan by himself. Joseph never had to be involved. But instead, he dragged Joseph into this mess.

"What's so special about that orb?" Captain Merrill breaks the silence.

"Ask Joseph," Jacob says pointedly.

Joe meets his gaze, not backing down from the challenge. He doesn't feel good about what he did to Port Green, but he wasn't in his right mind at the time, and he'll be damned if Jacob shames him for it, though he can't deny that he enjoyed the surge of power.

Joe feels heat rising in his cheeks as Jacob continues to smirk at him. Jacob notices and sends the stale air in the cabin circulating. Joe's fingers twitch, itching to respond in kind by throwing a wave against the aft of the *Moro* and knocking Jacob off balance. Jordan steps up quickly to diffuse the situation.

"Easy," Jordan says with a placating smile. "We're not here to lay blame. Why doesn't everyone take a few deep breaths," he looks pointedly at each of his brothers, "and we can simply have a conversation."

Jacob rolls his eyes. Playing the diplomat never achieves anything.

"Fine," Joe mutters as he goes to stand behind the captain.

Jordan nods at him and then looks expectantly at Jonathon. Begrudgingly, Jonathon sulks his way closer to the desk.

"That's better." Jordan faces Captain Merrill, full of apology. "We don't mean to intrude upon your fine ship, sir, but we got wind that our brothers were in trouble. We thought it best to find them and help them back home."

"How did you know where we were?" Joe asks curiously. Although he doesn't quite trust his new "brothers," he hadn't actually talked to other elementals about their powers before. Everything he learned about his powers came from trial and error, and he can't quite hide his interest in knowing how other elemental powers worked.

"Certainly. It must have been difficult growing up so isolated from other elementals," Jordan gives him a sympathetic smile while Jacob just snorts. Jonathon's blush deepens, but whether from embarrassment or something else, Joe isn't sure.

"I've been just fine living with humans, considering my first encounters with elementals haven't been all that great," Joe retorts, huffy that his question about how Jacob and Jordan knew he was aboard the *Moro* was ignored.

Jordan looks at the rough planks below his feet.

"We are truly sorry for your loss, Joseph. I mean, Joe," Jordan replies softly. "We all know what it's like to lose your parents in such a terrible way." Jordan's eyes travel to the sky outside the porthole. The knuckles of his clenched hands turn white as he takes a deep breath before beginning again.

"As to your initial question, Joe, Jacob is an aeromental. One of his abilities allows him to hear across great distances through the wind. It's how he's been able to keep track of Jonathon's mission, and by default, you."

Joe notices Jonathon's jaw clench.

"And for your benefit, Captain, I am Jordan, and this is Jacob. You've already met Jonathon, and obviously you know Joe. We are Queen Valencia's sons."

Captain Merrill worries the corner of his desk, looking from one brother to the next before finally stopping at Joe.

"I had my suspicions that you were smuggling, but I never thought you were a prince."

"Wait, what? You knew I was a smuggler?" Joe's jaw drops in surprise.

A knowing smile stretches across the captain's face. "You're good, but not quite that good at your little side gig. You would go off with Matt, Nell, and the others, but head in a different direction before reaching the main road to the tavern and the clubs. Or you would come back early and alone. Pretty unusual behavior for any sailor I've met."

Joe's mouth opens and closes like a fish out of water.

"And what about him being an elemental? Would you have turned him in if you had known?" Jordan interjects.

Captain Merrill's brow furrows, deep in thought. He scratches at some stubble on his chin, choosing his next words carefully.

"That's hard to say. Might have saved me some trouble if I had known." Captain Merrill glances quickly at his missing hand. "I think my current surprise and confusion has to do with having all of the lost princes here, in my cabin. Many have been wondering where you four have been all these years. Most assume you were killed during The Expunging. But, if you are the lost princes, I guess it begs the question, where have you been? Why haven't you come back? Are there none left that are loyal to you?"

Jacob's eyes narrow as a small wind begins to rise once again in the cabin. "I'm working on it," he growls.

"With all due respect, sir," Jordan intervenes, placing a hand on Jacob's shoulder. The wind settles down. "We were so young when The Expunging happened. With our father hanged, there wasn't much we could do except lie low."

The captain nods. "Understandable, but you're not kids anymore. Many people are suffering in Eastport, and not just the elementals. The Magistrate has a trade embargo on Andulsae, and they are the only ones who have certain supplies we need, like medicine. Merchant ships are evaluated upon returning from Lexington, and any goods thought to be from Andulsae are confiscated, with more than just heavy fines imposed on the ship's captain."

Captain Merrill looks again at his missing hand, lost in thought for a minute. Joe also finds himself staring at the missing appendage, anger boiling in his gut at the Magistrate.

"Magistrate Rufus wants nothing to do with Andulsae," Captain Merrill continues, "and refuses to accept their goods. Without free trade, we are isolated. Isolated and suffering. If you are able to break into the castle and steal that orb thing from the Magistrate, surely you can do more to help your people."

Jordan leans forward to interject, but Captain Merrill holds up his hand.

"Let me finish. Your mother was greatly respected. Believe it or not, so was your father. Many in Eastport felt abandoned when you left the throne to the Magistrate." The captain rubs his forehead, exhausted. "It just seems that, being elementals, surely you would have some connections to your kin up north who could have helped."

Fixing his icy glare on Captain Merrill, Jacob huffs with derision. "How little you know about the politics of our kingdom is sad," Jacob spits. "We didn't give the throne to our uncle. He stole it. It's rightfully mine, and I aim to get it back. However, with our exile, this has proven to be difficult. Maybe you've missed the abundance of Wardens and hangings in Eastport? Some of which aren't even elementals, but just sympathizers? I hear the interrogations and allegations our uncle pins on them. I know of his plan to eradicate all elementals in Eastport, then Port Green, then even Andulsae. He is a jealous man who wants nothing more than power.

"He stole the orb from us when he stole my throne, during The Expunging. It was a gift from our grandfather to our father, so our father could always have a way to communicate with the home he left. That's one of the powers of the orb, being able to view far-off places and communicate with those who have an orb as well. When Magistrate Rufus stole it, he used the orb to attack our island relentlessly, hoping to get rid of me, his only true opponent. Through the orb, he learned of our plans, our fortifications. He saw how weak we truly are and exploited it by sending his Wardens. Do you know how difficult it is to plan a defense when the Magistrate can hear and see everything we do through that orb? It is the ultimate power. And now it appears that the orb is even more powerful than I thought." Joe can see the red rising in Jacob's cheeks as he becomes more impassioned in his speech.

"I don't know how you were able to attack us through the orb," Jacob addresses Joe. "If the orb does have this ability, then it is imperative to get it back at all costs. That's why we need a small party who can work quickly and efficiently to regain the orb. The elementals of Port Green are weak, too weak to defend the island on their own, much less stage an attack on Eastport in order for me to regain the throne. It's taken all of our power just to keep our people safe. And no, we cannot expect any help from Andulsae despite being the chief's grandsons."

Jacob sighs, the heavy burden of protecting his people evident in his defeated posture.

"After The Expunging, about three hundred or so elementals fled Eastport. We were packed tight on a ship, heading to Andulsae, but there was a storm at sea that wrecked us upon Port Green. The ship was beyond repair; we were stranded. The island is uninhabited for a reason. There's very little food. Not much grows. Over the years, our numbers have dwindled to just about one hundred souls. I've managed to secure trade with Lexington merchants, but even those supplies are meager at best. We've not got the means to leave the island, not enough aeromentals to transport everyone, no one who knows how to build a ship. Lexington isn't willing to send us a ship; they'd rather stay out of the Eastport politics. Even if we could leave Port Green, where would we go? I've even sent word to Andulsae, but they won't help in any way. No ships, no supplies, no place left to go."

Jordan steps over and, with a small smile, places a comforting hand on Jacob's arm. It's an endearing gesture, as if they've had this conversation before. Jacob takes a deep breath and stands up to his full height again, steeling his features so as not to convey one ounce of weakness. He holds Captain Merrill's gaze, daring him to speak. The captain doesn't bend under his stare.

"Why won't Andulsae help? They're your kin."

"Because," comes a quiet voice behind Jacob. Captain Merrill looks past Jacob's shoulder to see Jonathon speaking. "Our mother was human, so we aren't worthy in their eyes. Not all elementals agreed with the treaty between our two races. That's why our mother said we were important, that we were to be good examples of a better future of unity."

Jonathon rubs his bad knee, determined not to look at Jacob, so he doesn't have to see the blame for his mother's death there.

"Most people on Port Green," Jonathon continues, "are mixed. We don't belong anywhere. Our kin in Andulsae believe us weaker, too, just for being half-human. Our only hope was to stop our uncle's attacks. We get the orb away from him, then we have time to regroup. Lick our wounds. Maybe have a little bit of peace."

Jacob and Jordan share a look.

"I was able to get the orb out of the castle. I was supposed to take the orb straight to Jordan in Lexington, but I'm not very fond of sailing," he shrugs, eyes still downcast. "I happened to learn of a smuggler who was leaving for Lexington shortly, and once I saw Joe in the Black Goose…well, me coming back to Eastport and all those years spent searching for you finally paid off. I finally found my chance to reunite with you. I missed my little brother," he whispers, voice cracking just a bit.

Once again, Joe feels that protective pang in his heart. Jonathon seems so fragile that he wants to get up and hug him. Instead, he asks a question that's been bothering him.

"How did you find out about the orb? Why were you in Eastport if everyone else is in Port Green?"

"My powers allow me to hear many discussions on the wind," Jacob begins.

"I was the one who found out about the orb," Jonathon challenges his older brother, silencing him with a look. "Without me, you still wouldn't know how Uncle was able to decimate us. I work at the Siren Club," he offers to the cabin at large.

"You're the one who left us to become nothing more than a low-grade prostitute," Jacob snarls, pointing an accusatory finger at him. "You actually think you're useful?"

The entire room is stunned. Jonathon clenches his jaw, trying to resist the urge to rip open a hole to the center of the earth and watch his brother fall through.

"You whore yourself out and call it helping?" Jacob spits.

"Jacob, enough," Jordan warns.

Slowly, Jonathon straightens, trying to keep the weight off his bad leg, refusing to be cowed.

"It's all right, Jordan. Jacob's made his point."

With as much dignity as he can muster, Jonathon limps over to the door, determined to get as far away as possible before Jacob sees his anger boil over. As he opens the door, he almost runs straight into Matt, the stunned expression on his face matching Matt's own as he hurriedly backs away.

"I wasn't eavesdropping, I swear!" Matt holds his hands up in an innocent gesture. Pushing past him, Jonathon makes his way over to the fore railing, far across the deck from Merrill's cabin. Leaning heavily on his forearms, Jonathon watches the murky sea below as furious thoughts race through his mind.

This isn't my fault. Mother's death, Father's death, Joseph's adoptive parents. He sighs, not even believing himself.

Jacob's just jealous I'm becoming stronger than him. He fingers the slim case in his pocket. Hearing soft footsteps behind him, he quickly shoves it further down and tries to appear inconspicuous as Matt stops next to him.

What does he want?

Matt stares at him a moment.

"He's wrong, you know."

"What?"

"Your brother. He's wrong. About you." Matt reaches over and gently places his hand on Jonathon's.

Jonathon's brow furrows. Something about Matt's face, those green eyes staring out into a dark room, searching. Skin the color of burnt caramel, reminiscent of those tribes from the Wastes, hiding in the back corners of the Siren Club. Jonathon realizes it now. Matt's more than just the patron from that night who told him about the smuggler for hire. Matt was a regular at the Siren Club. He would always be off on his own, refusing advances from the men and women Jonathon worked with. Jonathon had actually found it odd that Matt was always by himself at the Club. What was the point in going if not to engage?

Jonathon looks down at Matt's hand on his, but doesn't shake him off just yet. "I'm trying," he starts again. "I'm trying to be a good brother, to be the son my parents would have been proud of. Lots of bad things happen when I'm around, but it doesn't mean that they're my fault. I mean, I loved Mother and Father, so why would I have wanted anything bad to happen to them? And I was trying to protect Joseph, like any brother would do. I just wanted him to be safe. Why doesn't Jacob see that? Why—"

Jonathon suddenly finds Matt's mouth pressed to his. Startled, he almost pulls away, but wills himself to remain still as he feels the tension slowly drain from his body.

All too soon, Matt steps back, a mischievous glint in his eyes.

"What was that for?" Jonathon asks breathlessly.

"Well, I had to do something to calm you down."

Dimly, below the frantic pounding of his heart, Jonathon feels a shudder subsiding through the ship. He had let his anger get the best of him. Jonathon drags a hand down his face, embarrassed.

Opening his eyes, he sees Matt still staring at him. Taking a step closer, Matt leans in and Jonathon catches a whiff of sea and pine.

"Also, I've always really wanted to kiss you," he whispers before he struts off.

Jonathon almost runs after him, but out of the corner of his eye, he sees Joe emerge from below deck. He closes his eyes and quickly relives the kiss, savoring the feeling of Matt's lips on his once more. For the moment, the case in Jonathon's pocket is forgotten.

14

acob is such an ass. It was so much easier being an only child. Joe sits on the wooden seat used as a toilet at the prow of the *Moro*. The head is the one place he can have semi-privacy to collect his thoughts. He wouldn't say that his first meeting with his older brothers went well exactly, but it could have been worse, he supposes. Crossing his elbows over his bare knees, Joe rests his head on his arms, watching the Eusgarian sea race by through the inch-wide gaps in the wooden slats beneath his feet. Ever since learning that he was one of the lost princes and had brothers, he'd been hoping that more memories from his past life would surface, but no such luck. The time before The Expunging is still a blank slate in his mind. Try as he might, he can't pull up any of his brothers' faces as they would have been fourteen years younger. Joe also tries to remember images he had seen of Queen Valencia, looking for some resemblance, but finds none. He'd have to look up illustrations in the Eastport library when this is all over.

Joe snorts to himself. This would never be over. He couldn't rightly go back to Eastport now and walk around as a free man. Sighing, he straightens up and places a hand out over the sea below to call forth a spray to clean his bottom. Leaving the head, he climbs the stairs back to the main deck. Stuffing his hands in his pocket, he begins to head back to Captain Merrill's cabin, as he doesn't know where else to go. Does he just resume his duties as normal? He really should find Nell, explain things to her. He changes directions, but notices someone walking toward him out of the corner of his eye. Jonathon slowly limps over, a sheepish look on his face.

"Well, that was a mess, huh?" he laughs softly, looking down at the wooden planks below his feet.

"Um, yeah, I suppose."

Jonathon's shoulders slump in defeat. Clearly, he thought Joe would be more excited. Maybe Jonathon forgot that he betrayed Joe to the Magistrate.

"I mean, it was surprising."

"Yeah." Jonathon quickly glances at Joe but returns his gaze to the deck. He wanted this moment for so long, to finally have his little brother back. So why is it so hard to speak?

The awkward silence stretches on. Around them, the crew bustles about, trying to look busy but anxiously eavesdropping on the odd pair. The sea rocks the ship, and the sharp tang of saltwater fills the air. The humidity is already relentless, despite the sun just beginning to rise, and Joe can feel his armpits becoming a sticky, sweaty mess.

"Why did you turn me in?" he blurts out.

Jonathon reels back as if slapped. The crack of the sails fills the void as Joe waits for a response. Jonathon's eyes dart around, momentarily resting on everything, anything, but his brother before him. He slumps, resigned. "I'm sorry. I wanted the pain to stop. He said he would stop if I told him. I failed you."

Joe shifts his weight from one foot to the other, subconsciously adjusting to the rolling of the ship. He doesn't understand this need of Jonathon's to protect him, why Jonathon seems to feel obligated to him. There was no debt to be repaid in Joe's mind before the betrayal. He wants to be mad at Jonathon, but he just looks so pathetic.

"Um," he begins, scratching the back of his neck.

"I've never really liked being at sea," Jonathon interrupts.

"Oh," Joe replies, taken slightly aback. "It's always felt like home to me."

Jonathon shrugs. "I just prefer solid ground beneath me. At sea, it's like I'm being pulled apart in too many directions, and I won't be able to put myself back together again. There's nothing out here for me to hold onto like there is on land. It's just not my medium, I guess."

That's the exact reason why Joe loves the sea. He loves the freedom of just following wherever the currents take him, with no one and nothing to tie him down.

"Maybe you just need to sail some more."

Jonathon gives a little laugh. "I don't think so. This is only my third time at sea. Usually I'm sick as a dog, vomiting everywhere."

"Well, there's still time for that."

Jonathon laughs for real this time, a full throaty laugh that shakes his body. It makes Joe smile. His laugh is infectious, and Joe wonders what happened to prevent this version of Jonathon from being the main version of Jonathon.

As quickly as it came, Jonathon's good humor swiftly leaves, replaced by a stony guilt.

"I'm truly sorry for what happened. I never meant for anyone to get hurt."

Jonathon can't meet Joe's eyes. Joe stares at him, willing him to look up, to be brave and to stand up for himself. But a part of Joe knows that he will always blame Jonathon for what happened, for his betrayal that ended in his parent's death, even if Jonathon never held the blade to Matilde's throat. He steels himself for the harsh truth that he must now deliver.

"Jonathon, I'm not the brother you lost. He hasn't existed for fourteen years. I know you had this dream that we would reunite and everything would go back to the way it was, but the fact is I don't know you, and you don't know me. I don't remember you outside of some nightmares I've had, and you turned me into the Wardens. And we both know how that ended up."

Jonathon cowers into himself, trying to hide the tears forming in his eyes.

Joe sighs. "Look. This relationship, between you and me, it's a lot to process. I'm going to need some time. Maybe we can start out as acquaintances and move on from there, okay?" He holds out his hand to Jonathon.

Slowly, almost reluctantly, Jonathon shakes it.

"Okay, great." Joe withdraws his hand, leaving a forlorn Jonathon behind. He feels a little bad for forcing the matter, but what he said is true. He is no more Jonathon's brother than he is a lost prince. Whoever he was fourteen years ago died in The Expunging. Now, he is Joe: smuggler, elemental, and a man who desperately needs to make amends with Nell.

Joe scans the deck, looking for her tell-tale braid. Sweeping his eyes up and down, he sees much of the crew but not the particular person he's after. To his right, he spies Matt, who points skyward, grinning. The crow's nest. Of course. Giving Matt a thumbs-up, he heads over to the mast and begins to climb.

"Mind if I join you?" he asks as he reaches the tiny enclosure on top. Nell focuses her gaze on the horizon, ignoring him as if he were no more than an annoying fly buzzing in her ear. But Joe sees the clench of her jaw and knows he has her undivided attention. He's careful not to brush against her as he joins her in silence.

The wind's stronger up here. It whips around the pair like a playful filly, drawing hair loose from Nell's braid to frame her face in a beautiful, wild dance. The immediate sky is clear, but clouds gather on the horizon, the rising sun painting them a fiery red. The image of sky and sea is one of perfect peace, and Joe can't wait to get home and describe it to his mother.

A sudden wave of sorrow crashes down on him as he remembers Matilde's blood pooling on the floor. His breath hitches in his chest, and his hands begin to tremble on the frame of the crow's nest. After a minute, he pushes the memory away, the need to move forward compelling him. It's easier to not remember.

"I'm sorry I didn't tell you," he begins. Nell doesn't acknowledge him.

Joe sighs but forges on. "There was a reason. You know what happens to elementals in Eastport. It's not that I don't trust you," Nell flicks her gray eyes toward him, "It's just that it was safer keeping it a secret."

Joe rubs his fingers along the wooden frame of the nest, trying to choose his next words carefully.

"I didn't tell you because I didn't want you to hate me. I know how your dad died, Nell. I know it was a hydromental. But I promise you, I'm different. I'm—"

"What, you think you're better? Better than all the other elementals, like the one who killed my dad? Well guess what," she whips around, pointing an unforgiving finger in his face. "You're worse, Joe. Because of you and your little secret, Captain Merrill lost a hand and the *Moro* is under the black flag. We are no longer free to sail wherever we want. We have to stay on schedule and check in with the Wardens or else. None of us can go back to our normal lives because you decided to have a little fun."

"I didn't realize that my parents being killed counted as fun," he snarled.

A blush hits Nell's face, competing in intensity with the almost-risen sun. Drawing a shaky breath, she replies in a dangerously low voice.

"Don't talk to me ever again. Better yet, get out of my life completely." Nell hurries down the rigging, leaving Joe fuming in the growing light.

* * * *

Jordan sits cross-legged on the seaman's trunk in the quiet captain's quarters, watching his older brother. Jacob had asked Captain Merrill for some privacy, and, surprisingly, he obliged. Jordan had expected more push back from the captain, but Captain Merrill seemed eager for some fresh air, with how quickly he raced from the cabin. Jordan snickers, knowing full well the captain is very uncomfortable having four elementals on board. Sure, he hides it well, but Jordan could detect the slight rise in body temperature, belying Captain Merrill's anxiety. Jacob frowns at Jordan's small interruption. Jordan huffs and resumes his silent musings. Reaching up, he pulls a lock of hair free from its ponytail and sets about picking off the dead ends. Queen Valencia didn't approve when Jordan started letting his hair grow out, but King Nils assured her it was traditional for men from Andulsae to have long hair. That wasn't true, but Jordan and his father kept up the ruse as an inside joke. In reality, he just enjoys playing with it. Keeps his hands busy.

Jordan straightens. Jonathon's hair is brown, he realizes, not its usual blond. Looking back, Jordan thinks he saw some blond peeking through at the roots. Jonathon surely has a reason for dying his hair. Jordan grunts, earning another frown from Jacob, and leans back against the wall. He examines the hard lines on his brother's still face. Those haven't changed. Jacob has been serious from the day he was born. Every memory Jordan has of his brother before The Expunging is one of Jacob in the library pouring over some book, or Jacob and their father together in the council room going over maps, or Jacob in their room late at night writing furiously by lantern light. Jordan learned long ago to stop encouraging his older brother to have some fun once in a while. Even now, Jacob sits stiffly in the captain's chair behind the desk, eyes closed in concentration. For once, Jordan is glad that his brother can only hear whispered conversations carried on the wind instead of actually reading minds.

Jacob slowly opens his eyes and his shoulders relax slightly.

"Well?" Jordan inquires, pulling his hair back into its ponytail.

"We're clear," Jacob responds.

"So, what's next?"

Jacob stares out the porthole behind him for a minute before answering. "We return to Port Green."

"What? Why? We're not far from Eastport. Let's stick to the plan, take over this ship, and turn it around. There's not that many crew; it'd be easy enough."

Tapping out an irritated rhythm on the desk, Jacob gives an unexpected answer.

"We go back to Port Green first. I want Joseph to see it. The destruction he caused."

"Isn't that a little cruel? He just saw his parents murdered."

"His *parents* died fourteen years ago," Jacob snaps.

Jordan sits back, eyeing his brother warily. The one thing Jacob will never let go: their parents' deaths. Jordan knows Jacob's masquerade with the orb, the plan to get it from the Magistrate to stop the attacks on Port Green. Jordan knows that what Jacob's really after is revenge. Revenge for his parents. Revenge for himself. The orb is just a small part of a grander plan.

"You wanted Jonathon to get caught," Jordan taps his chin. "To get him out of the way. With Jonathon arrested, we could sneak in and steal the orb for ourselves. He was a distraction. I get that." Jordan swings his feet down and gently kicks them against the trunk. "But you didn't plan on Jonathon actually getting the orb out of the castle, and you definitely didn't plan on Joseph coming back into the picture."

Jacob's tapping intensifies. "With Jonathon arrested, Uncle would have been occupied. I could have flown over, snuck in, and killed him in his sleep. Then the throne and Eastport would be mine, as it always should have been."

Jordan simply shakes his head.

"You don't agree?"

"It's been fourteen years, Jacob. Does it really matter all that much anymore? Nothing we do now will change the past. It won't bring Mom and Dad back, and life will never be what it was then."

"He killed our parents. He killed his own *sister*. He took my throne, the one I'd been preparing to claim for years. He hates elementals and has killed so many of us. We can't continue living on Port Green forever. Eastport is our home."

"We've made a good run of it so far on Port Green," Jordan shrugs.

"Are you blind?" Jacob scoffs. "We're barely surviving there. If I can reclaim Eastport, I could actually make a better life for our people. I could continue our mother's legacy. Make Eastport the city she always dreamed of."

"And killing our uncle will get you there?"

Jacob's fist slams down on the desk. "He deserves death! After everything he's done, everyone he's killed. He thinks he's more powerful than me because of that orb, but I'll show him. He'll never be more powerful than me."

"And what about the Wardens? What about the regular humans of Eastport? What would you do with them after you claim the throne? What if they don't accept you? Have you thought about any of this?"

"I'm the rightful king," Jacob reiterates through a clenched jaw.

"I don't think that matters to people anymore."

Jacob violently shoves the captain's chair back as he rises and strides out of the cabin.

20

onathon spies Matt further down deck coiling some rope and walks in that direction, a smile stretching on his face. Abruptly, he stops and chastises himself. He doesn't have any feelings for Matt. He can't afford to have feelings, he thinks as the sky above darkens with gathering clouds. If a storm is heading this way, it would be better to ride it out below deck. The queasiness he foretold is beginning to rise in his stomach.

As Jonathon heads across the deck to the sick bay, he runs into Jacob. A strained silence stretches between them as neither moves to admit passage to the other. Jonathon holds Jacob's gaze, refusing to back down this time. He is tired, sick, and sore, and he will not be bullied into submission by his older brother anymore. Jacob crosses his arms and squares his stance, ready for this battle of wills.

From behind, Jordan gives a small cough, gesturing to Jonathon. Sighing and inwardly rolling his eyes, Jonathon slowly steps aside, allowing Jacob to pass. Some battles just aren't worth it. Jacob strides past, triumphant, while Jordan places an apologetic hand on Jonathon's shoulder. Jonathon shakes him off and limps as fast as he can below deck to the sick bay, slamming the door behind him as he falls onto a cot. He looks longingly at the change of clothes still awaiting him on the workbench but is too tired to get up and put them on.

He instead turns onto his side, facing the wall, and tries to remember where it all went downhill between him and Jacob. There had always been a slight animosity between them, the way there is between an older brother who finds his younger brother annoying. But he first realized that Jacob truly hated him years ago, shortly after he turned fifteen.

*   *   *   *

Seven years ago on Port Green, Jonathon's fifteenth birthday had just passed, and being a year older and wiser, he found the courage to approach Jacob with a troubling confession.

"Jacob, do you have a minute?" Jonathon stood timidly in the doorway of the stone hut he shared with his brothers, leaning heavily on his cane. Even after all these years, he found the cane a nuisance, exclaiming for the world that he was disabled and fragile, but he just couldn't walk well without it.

"What?" Jacob didn't glance up from the maps and messages collected around him. A panoply of paper birds carrying written messages cluttered his workspace, which was a salvaged steamer trunk brought over by one of the refugees during The Expunging. It was one of few possessions that managed to survive the shipwreck. As Jonathon watched, Jacob finished his current message, folded the paper into a dove, and sent it on the wind to be carried to Andulsae, once again pleading for help from their father's kin.

Jonathon hobbled in and stood next to the trunk.

"I saw…I saw something," he stumbled over his words. "On that day."

Jacob lifted his head. He didn't have to ask what day. There was only one day that held weight. Slowly, he put down his pencil and removed his glasses, polishing them on his shirt. Replacing them, he asked in a measured voice, "What did you see?"

A sense of dread enveloped Jonathon. Jacob looked at him like a hungry shark, waiting to strike. Jonathon knew this wasn't a good idea. He tried to back away before Jacob could pull the truth from him.

In a flash, Jacob reached out and grabbed Jonathon's arm, holding him in place. "What did you see?" he repeated with a deadly calm. An image of Uncle Rufus' wicked grin plastered itself onto Jacob's face, and Jonathon began to tremble. Jacob's grip tightened like a snake.

"I saw Uncle poison Mother," Jonathon whispered in fear. The hand around his arm was a steel trap, and Jonathon struggled to get away, memories of his uncle in the dungeon zooming through his mind.

"And you did nothing," Jacob spat, his voice still quiet, but his cheeks turning redder by the moment. "You let her die, and you let our father die. Because you withheld the truth."

The words hit Jonathon like a slap. It was as he feared, that everything that happened that night was somehow his fault. He should have told someone, anyone, what he saw back then, but he had lacked the courage. It seemed that he still lacked the courage now.

Jacob inched closer to Jonathon's face, eyes magnified by glasses, not straying from Jonathon's. Jacob couldn't believe what he was hearing. Jonathon had known who had killed their mother and said nothing. Jacob remembered seeing Jonathon in the council room when Gregor marched in with news of Queen Valencia's death. He recalls Jonathon looking surprised to see their uncle in the council room as well, but he can't remember Jonathon ever speaking up to accuse him. Jacob's eyes narrowed as he searched Jonathon's face, looking for an answer to why he remained silent all these years. Jonathon trembled beneath his scrutiny. That was typical for Jonathon; he was always a scared, sniveling child, always clinging to their mother, never wanting to listen as Jacob shared the lessons from their father.

"I'm sorry, Jacob," Jonathon stammered. "I didn't know what to do, and then Uncle found me and he—"

"Excuses," Jacob interrupted, throwing Jonathon away. "Get out of here. I don't want to see you again. From this moment on, you are no longer my brother."

Horrified, Jonathon raced from the room as quickly as he could. He thought Jacob would be more understanding. He thought that he could finally unburden his guilt. But he was wrong. Jacob would never forgive him now, even though it had been seven years since their mother's death. Hurriedly swiping a sleeve across his face, Jonathon knew what he had to do. He would return to Eastport and find Joseph.

After The Expunging, Jacob refused to go back for Joseph, saying they didn't have the means. Jonathon needled his oldest brother relentlessly until Jacob finally admitted that Joseph was most likely dead, and it wasn't worth the risk to send elementals to verify. Jonathon always thought it was strange how quickly Jacob shut down any conversation about their youngest brother. Maybe Jacob thought Joseph was dead, but Jonathon didn't believe it. He would find Joseph and somehow make this all better. He would just have to find a ship.

Ships did not trade often with the elementals of Port Green, however. After they had shipwrecked on the island, Jacob took command, issuing orders to have land cleared, huts built, defenses made. Since he was the heir apparent and spoke with such authority, no one questioned him, and they willingly followed the twelve-year-old's demands. It took Jacob several months of negotiations, having to prove that the elementals of Port Green had something worthwhile to barter, before he secured a trade route with Lexington. One ship, once a month. That was all Lexington agreed to, as they knew Port Green was housing the refugees from Eastport and the free city of Lexington did not want to get involved in Eastport politics. The trading ship brought a meager supply of grain, fruit, and fabric. The elementals, in turn, offered their smithing services. While there was no ore to be found on Port Green, the trading ship from Lexington would bring ore to be made into not only weapons, but everyday items such as cooking utensils and farming equipment. Pyromental forges burned hotter, and the pyromentals excelled at their craft, creating weapons and plows with sharper blades and longer durability than those found in Lexington.

The next ship from Lexington was due in a week. Until then, Jonathon made himself scarce, hiding whenever Jacob or his other brother Jordan was in sight. Jonathon made a small bag of clothes for himself and hid out in the woods of Port Green among the hightower trees with their large fronds. At first, he only stayed in the woods during the day, not wanting to run into his brothers, but soon, he found himself sleeping the night under the trees, the warm air soothing him. He wondered if anyone noticed his absence, but since he didn't have a role in helping Jacob run the island, like

Jordan did, and he wasn't needed to help maintain the huts or fortifications, he doubted he was missed.

As one night turned into two, and two nights into three, Jonathon decided to spend his days exploring more of Port Green while waiting for the ship. The beach where the ship had wrecked seven years ago had been cleared to make way for various huts, two forges, a meeting hall, and a meager attempt at a brumbuck field. The soil was too sandy for the tuber to grow well, however, and their harvests were small. The terramentals were determined, though, and kept trying to grow the vegetable in the stubborn soil.

Jonathon ventured to the far side of the island, about half a day's walk through the woods, skirting the large central hill. He had his boots stowed in his bag and relied heavily on his cane as he moved over the uneven land. Barefoot, he trudged on, savoring the connectedness he felt to the island. Through this connection, he could tell the central hill was once a volcano, now centuries dormant. He could feel the landslides that had occurred, causing the volcano's cone to become filled in, allowing sparse grass to grow on its now sandy top.

Bushwacking through some dense overgrowth of wadlow vines, he emerged onto a very narrow strip of beach, the black rocks that made up its shore sharp on his bare feet. Jonathon pulled out his boots and put them back on before carefully picking his way down to the water. Using the cane as a guide, Jonathon slowly sat on the shoreline and stared out at the wide sea before him. Port Green was too small. He felt useless there. Even more so after confessing to Jacob. Eastport offered better opportunities, as long as he remained hidden from his uncle and didn't use his powers. Surely, the assault on elementals in Eastport had stopped by now. He would go to Eastport, find Joseph, and start over. How he would accomplish this, Jonathon wasn't sure. But at least he had the start of a plan.

It had been seven years since he'd last seen Joseph, though. Would he recognize his little brother? Would Joseph even remember him? What if he couldn't find Joseph? Or worse, what if his uncle found him first? He couldn't think of that now. It was more important to focus on the task at hand. The trading ship from Lexington would come in another three days. He had to find a way to get on and back off that ship without being seen.

After another two nights on the far beach, Jonathon hiked back to the village and waited for the ship in the woods lining the shore. Near dawn, the ship dropped anchor, and a longboat was sent out to bring goods and ore to Jacob and the waiting villagers. Jonathon evaluated his options. He wasn't a good swimmer, and sneaking onto the longboat seemed too exposed. In the end, he settled for calling the ocean floor up to meet him, and walked out to the ship in the gray dawn light. Poking his head over the railing, he saw the coast was clear and scrambled aboard as gracefully as his bad knee would allow, dropping his cane in the ocean as he felt it would be too large to conceal. Scurrying below deck, he made it to the cargo hold without being seen.

He hunkered down behind some barrels of coffee, sugar, and flour, heading for ports elsewhere, compacting his lithe frame into a small bundle and scrunching up his bad knee in an awful position that he would pay for later. He couldn't risk being found. He had to make it to Eastport and find Joseph. Thinking back on the conversation he had with Jacob a week ago, where Jacob made it very clear that he no longer wanted Jonathon around, Jonathon knew he was making the right decision. There was nothing left for him on Port Green. Sure, Jordan did his best to include Jonathon, but Jordan was always closer to Jacob. And in these years after The Expunging, the two became even closer, trying to figure out their next move. Jordan wanted to stay on Port Green and start fresh with this new refugee community. Jacob wanted the throne. Jonathon didn't belong with his brothers on Port Green. That's why he needed to find Joseph. To restore the balance. Before long, he felt the ship rattle and begin to move. Jonathon closed his eyes and waited for the journey to be over, hoping he wouldn't get too seasick.

Some time later, Jonathon heard shouts and moving feet coming from the deck above. The queasiness in his stomach subsided considerably, indicating to him that they must have docked. He waited for the voices to retreat, then sprang up from his hiding place and immediately fell back down. His bad leg had fallen asleep, and pinpricks of pain shot up and down his shin as the leg awoke. Time was running out. Gritting his teeth, he pushed himself upright, ignoring the pain in his knee, and sprinted up the stairs out of the cargo hold as fast as he could, forgetting his bag among the wares.

"Hey!" a crewman shouted as Jonathon shoved past him to the deck, down the gangplank, and into the city. Sparing a brief moment to look around, Jonathon was relieved to find that the ship had indeed docked in Eastport, as he hoped, instead of returning to Lexington.

Night fell like a curtain about him as he ran along the wharf, keeping his head down to hide from the Wardens and doing his best to hide his limp. Out of habit, he headed toward the castle before realizing his mistake. Seven years later and some part of him still called the castle home. Quickly, he ducked down an alley, silently cursing himself. What if he had made it to the castle and ran straight into his uncle? He shoved the thought to the back of his mind. It was not something he needed to dwell on.

He leaned back against the brick wall and transferred his weight to his good leg. Across the alley was a dim doorway under an even dimmer sign. Straining his eyes to make out the words, he quickly gave up. The alley was too dark and the sign too dirty. Breathing deeply, he took in the sounds of the city and relished his newfound freedom. Oh, how much he missed this city. Even the smell of fish from the market on the wharf was oddly comforting.

"Lost, kid?"

Jonathon's eyes sprang open at the sound of the gravelly voice before him. A large man across the alley was hurling the contents of a chamber pot into the gutter. After emptying the pot, he wiped his hands on his apron and started to make his way over. Jonathon made to run, but a beefy hand latched onto his collar.

"Hey now, what's your hurry?" The man smelled vaguely of piss and smiled a nearly toothless smile at him.

"Please," Jonathon stumbled. "I don't have any money." Unable to stop himself, Jonathon began to tremble. The vibrations ran down his legs, and the ground below started to buckle in response.

"You're an elemental!" the beefy man exclaimed.

"No, I swear I'm not," he quickly denied, even though he knew it was too late to backtrack.

The beefy man pulled him close, his foul breath biting Jonathon's nose.

"You in trouble, kid?" he gently asks. "I think you're in trouble. Madame Barnaby always helps the troubled."

"Please, let me go. I'll do anything!" Jonathon tried to stop the tremors, lest anyone else traced them back to him, but he couldn't keep the fear from his voice.

"No need to be scared, lad! We'll take care of you now." The beefy man dragged Jonathon through the door across the alley, allowing him to finally read the sign above: The Siren Club. The doorway opened onto a red-lit great room, filled with smoky tables and curtained booths. Several men and women were scattered throughout, burying their faces into necks and bosoms of the scantily clad workers, some of which then pulled the patrons to their feet and into dark curtained alcoves ringing the room. Jonathon felt a heat rising in his cheeks at the sights before him. Jordan had told him stories of what men and women do in the dark, providing examples of his own dabblings, but Jonathon had no desire to see such things for himself right then.

The beefy man pulled Jonathon over to a bar at the back of the room where a hefty woman with ample breasts spilling out of her dress stood behind the counter, sorting bottles of spirits.

"Evening, Madame Barnaby."

"Sully! When did you get in?" Setting down a bottle, she reached over the counter to hug the man, who hadn't yet let go of Jonathon's collar, squishing Jonathon awkwardly in their embrace.

"And who do we have here?" Madame Barnaby pulled away and coolly appraised Jonathon.

"I found him lurking outside. Seems like he could use a job," Sully widened his eyes at Madame Barnaby. Jonathon wished he would be less obvious.

"Oh?" Madame Barnaby raised an eyebrow at Jonathon. He shrunk under her gaze, wanting to say that he was just passing through, but the words stuck in his throat like molasses. She leaned over the counter toward him, giving him an uncomfortable view down her dress.

"You seem a little young," she squinted at him. "How old are you?"

Jonathon stared at his feet, willing the ground to open up and swallow him. How did he get here? If he tried to run away, would the man, Sully, turn him over to the Wardens? Then what would his uncle do to him? He was back in Eastport; that's want he wanted, but aside from stowing away on the trading ship, he had no further plan. He just assumed that Joseph would be there, right there waiting, and once they were reunited, they would figure something out.

He looked around the room, at the workers, gently laughing, or sitting on laps, or pulling patrons away for unknown acts behind drawn curtains. He didn't want this.

He quickly filed through his options. He could cause an earthquake and make a break for it in the melee that would follow, risking his luck on the streets. Or he could stay here, with only two people knowing what he was. He could still find Joseph. It just might take a little bit longer. But the price of staying here at The Siren Club: was it a price worth paying?

A weight like a stone settled in his stomach as he looked up at Madame Barnaby.

"I'm fifteen," he replied in a dead voice.

"Oh, dear one!" she laughed as she came out from behind the counter and squashed him in a bone-crushing hug. "I wouldn't have you work the floor, catering to the patrons! That kind of work is not for minors. What kind of monster do you think I am?"

"You wouldn't?" came Jonathon's muffled reply from Madame Barnaby's chest.

"Goodness, no! You can clear and clean tables, sweep the floor, help Sully in the kitchen if you'd like. I'm not in the habit of forcing people into doing things they'd rather not. Or you could leave. Up to you."

"He's a special case, Madame," Sully pointed at Jonathon with his chin, thinking he was being discreet.

Madame Barnaby gave him a long, appraising look. "Is that so? Well now, dear," she placed both hands on Jonathon shoulders and looked him straight in the eye. "You will be safe here, should you choose to stay. I know you're frightened and should hardly trust us, but I promise that no Wardens will arrest you as long as you're in my care. We don't hold those prejudices here." Jonathon earnestly studied the floor, not wanting to meet Madame Barnaby's eyes.

"Look," she continued. "We have spare rooms up in the attic, nothing extravagant, but a straw mattress and chamber pots, and you're welcome to a plate from the kitchen every day. Even if you decide that you'd rather not work here, that's fine. I've had *special cases* spend a night or two and be on their way. But if you'd like a job, we could always use extra help with those mundane tasks. All right?" Jonathon chanced a look around the room once more, peeking at the workers and patrons, but also noticing the ale mugs and plates scattered at empty tables. He gave her a small nod.

"All right then," Madame Barnaby beamed. "Sully, want to show him the ropes?"

"My pleasure," Sully bowed to Jonathon, gesturing toward the kitchen behind the bar. Jonathon stared unblinkingly, unsure how to process this strange turn of events. But he found himself placing one foot in front of the other as he walked into the kitchen. Sully began explaining what delicious smelling slop was boiling on the stove, where plates and mugs were stored, and the random workings of a kitchen, but Jonathon quickly tuned it all out and allowed himself a small smile.

Until he found Joseph, maybe he could be safe here after all.

21

A clanging bell reverberates throughout the *Moro*. Jonathon closes his eyes to block it out, but the insistent pealing burrows into his brain, refusing to grant peace. Moaning, he slowly pushes himself up to the edge of the cot, where he sits rubbing his eyes.

He wishes the bell would shut up. Whatever it's summoning, he doesn't want to be a part of it. He wants to hide in his cave of misery and avoid his brothers, especially Jacob.

The tolling bell grows louder, like a giant bird squawking in his ear. He feels the onset of a headache drilling its way into his brain.

"Just shut up!" he yells, flinging out his power from the sick bay and throttling the metal bell. Silence falls upon the ship, and Jonathon's shoulders slump. The noise stops, but his headache only intensifies into a mind-numbing fury, as if a million knives are being thrust through his skull.

Almost falling off the cot in pain, Jonathon catches himself on the edge and flops onto his side, trying to block out the world. An annoying lump presses against his thigh. Sighing in frustration, he wrenches himself upright and digs the offending lump from his pocket.

Straightening, Jonathon freezes. He forgot about the case with the vial and syringe. The headache still building, he frantically fills the syringe and shoots some Ink into his arm. Releasing an elated groan, he falls back on the cot, relishing the immediate bliss the drug brings. His contentment is short-lived as the door opens, causing him to jump up and quickly stuff the contraband back into his pocket.

"What are you doing?" Matt asks from the doorway.

"Nothing," Jonathon guiltily replies, rolling down his sleeve, but not before Matt sees the tracks on his arm. Frowning, Matt comes in, closing the door behind him. Jonathon looks at Matt warily, trying to appear nonchalant, but sweat breaks out at his hairline. Jonathon desperately hopes that Matt didn't see what he knows Matt already has. He mentally scolds himself. Why should he care what Matt thinks?

"Why are you always lurking?" Jonathon grumps.

Matt ignores his barb and reaches for Jonathon's arm. Jonathon tries to pull away, but Matt is quicker, grabbing his wrist and forcing the sleeve up. Matt's eyes widen as he sees the marks like angry bee stings covering the inside of Jonathon's arm. Jonathon tries again to pull away, but Matt's grip remains firm as he gently traces the constellation of pricks. Jonathon's breath catches as Matt's fingers play across his skin.

Jonathon smothers the staccato of his heart and compels himself not to look into Matt's questioning gaze. Matt releases his arm, but Jonathon lets it rest in his open palm a moment before pulling it back, remembering that he's angry at Matt for intruding.

Matt opens his mouth, but Jonathon cuts him off.

"Don't."

Matt snaps his mouth closed, watching Jonathon for an uncomfortably long minute before gesturing behind him.

"Captain Merrill's called a meeting. That's what the bell was for before you broke it."

"I didn't."

Matt silences him with a grin. "I'm beginning to recognize your pattern."

Jonathon stares ashamedly at the floor but reminds himself that he doesn't owe Matt anything. But then why does he feel like he needs to prove himself to Matt? It's as if Matt is atop the highest peak, and Jonathon is at the bottom, struggling to climb to him, just to show that he can, that he is worthy of that peak as well.

"Also, you might want to change out of your old clothes. They're covered in dirt and kind of smell. I brought an extra set for you," Matt gestures to the fresh clothes still sitting on the workbench. Jonathon looks longingly at the clothes and starts to unbutton his shirt, but stops when he realizes that Matt isn't leaving the room. Matt blushes from his neck to his ears as he quickly stands up.

"I'll just, uh, just wait outside for you then."

Jonathon ensures that the door is closed and hurriedly changes into the new clothes, concealing the case with the Ink in his pants pocket before heading out of the sick bay.

"Well, you clean up nice," Matt appraises him with a smile. "Except for your hair. Your roots are showing."

"I dyed my hair to hide from my uncle," Jonathon shrugs.

Matt gives him a dubious stare. "You really thought that just changing your hair color would prevent your uncle from figuring out who you were?"

Jonathon grunts in reply and follows Matt topside.

The entire crew gathers before Captain Merrill in the afternoon gray. It's drizzling, a wet soppy mixture of annoyance spattering the waiting crowd.

Joe huddles by himself off to the side, hunched into his jacket collar and cursing everything. Nell truly isn't speaking to him; he hates the cold, assessing glare of Jacob and the meek, placating smile of Jordan; and now the blasted rain is getting on his nerves.

He's tempted to divert the rain away from the ship, but he has a miserable, pissed-off image he wants to maintain, and the rain greatly improves the look. Plus, he doesn't want to freak the crew out with his powers any more than he already has.

Across the deck, Joe sees Matt leading a limping Jonathon to a spot in the amassed crew. Jonathon looks as bad as Joe feels, with dark circles under his eyes and skin reminiscent of a washed-out white daydrone. He steadies himself on Matt's arm, narrow eyes darting about like minnows. He trips, and Matt places a hand on the small of his back to brace him. After regaining his feet, Joe notices that Matt's hand lingers just a little too long before Jonathon awkwardly shrugs it off.

Captain Merrill fiddles with the sleeve dangling near his missing hand before coughing nervously. He straightens, consciously not looking at the invading brothers, before addressing his crew.

"All right, lads and ladies. As you may have guessed, our visitors," he nods to Jacob, Jordan, and Jonathon, "are elementals." He pauses as murmurs slide through the crew like an eel.

"Thank you, Captain, I'll take it from here." Jacob steps forward to address the crew.

"I think it would be better—"

"I'll take it from here," Jacob reiterates as he glares at the captain. Captain Merrill's jaw snaps shut, and he steps back with a grimace.

Jacob turns to face the crew. "This ship will be diverting course and will sail to Port Green. We will stay there for two days to gather my best men and women. Then, we will sail back to Eastport."

Angry whispers course about the mob.

"You're just gonna let these elementals take over?"

"Turn them in to Magistrate Rufus!"

"Have you forgotten that this is all *his* fault?"

Accusatory fingers turn toward Joe, who shrinks back like a turtle slipping into its shell.

"Enough!" Captain Merrill bellows. The crew quiets like well-trained cattle.

"Jacob," Captain Merrill addresses the eldest brother in a whisper. "We have to dock in Lexington in two days, else the Eastport Navy will be after us. We are under orders from Magistrate Rufus, and I cannot risk my crew by breaking those orders."

Jacob turns his granite visage on the captain.

Captain Merrill suppresses his torrent of exasperation and turns his face to the sky as if the sun above could give him strength. Except it's still cloudy and rainy, and he knows he's lost control of this situation.

Jacob faces the crew once more, arms clasped behind his back, and observes the crew before him with a cold, calculating gaze. Joe is struck with how Jacob presents himself exactly like the Magistrate.

"This ship will continue to Port Green," Jacob states with a deadly calm. "From there, it seems as if you have two options. You can remain on Port Green, marooned, or you can join our cause."

"Which is?" a crew member yells.

"To regain the throne from my uncle. By any means necessary."

22

att grunts as he pulls himself up the last bit of rigging and into the crow's nest, where Nell is sitting huddled against the rain.

"I thought I'd find you here. Hiding from Joe still?"

"I'd like to be alone, Matt. Shouldn't you be with the other one? I saw you all over him at the meeting."

Matt flops down next to her, pulling his own jacket tighter for warmth. "I walked him back to the sick bay. He doesn't do well with sailing. Puking and such."

Nell wipes away some wet hair plastered to her face and scooches closer to Matt until their knees touch. Matt bumps his shoulder into hers.

"I'm cold and wet. That's the only reason, Matt."

"Oh, I know. We could always head below deck, you know, get out of the rain."

"I'd rather not."

The two sit in companionable silence, listening to the soft patter of rain on the furled sails above.

"I can't believe Captain Merrill is just letting them take over the *Moro* like that. What happens to us when we don't arrive in Lexington on time?" Nell hugs her knees to her chest and looks expectantly at Matt.

"I don't know. Maybe we can hide out on Port Green."

"With all those elementals? Seriously? Aren't you pissed that Joe lied to us?"

Matt stands up and offers a hand to Nell. "Not really."

Nell almost smacks Matt's hand away but relents and lets him pull her up.

"Looks like we're here." Matt points to a smear of land on the horizon. Nell makes a noise in the back of her throat as she climbs down the rigging.

*   *   *   *

Joe joins the captain at the prow of the ship, absorbing the sight of Port Green as it comes into view. The terrible weight of familiarity rests on his shoulders as the island looms ahead. The rain does little to hide the destruction he caused. What were once bright, vibrant hightower trees now lie in tangled heaps like broken matchsticks littering the ground. Their roots stick up like hands in surrender, praying for mercy. The ground itself is ripped asunder, as if giant subterranean creatures burst forth, leaving frothy hollows in their wake. Amidst all the destruction are huts, dozens of them smashed to bits by the monstrous tidal wave. No building is left unscathed, the stone blocks scattered like discarded children's toys.

Joe traces the swirling path of debris up a now-barren hill to the sandy top. His eyes catch on the unblemished crown of the hill, and his knees almost buckle at the memory of Jacob, sinking in quicksand, the mother and her young daughter running into harm's way to help.

"I did this," he whispers, clinging to the railing. A burning shame consumes him. He was so willing to destroy this island to save Ian and Matilde, so willing to let all these people perish. Now that the *Moro* draws near, Joe sees what a mistake it was to give in to the Ink and follow Magistrate Rufus' orders. These people did nothing to him. He obliterated the home of innocents and failed to save his adoptive parents in the end. Captain Merrill places a comforting hand on his shoulder. The sharp click of boot heels sound behind him as Jacob strides up.

"Welcome to Port Green," he announces. He turns directly to Joe, who refuses to meet his gaze. "Or should I say welcome back." His words snarl through Joe's conscience.

"The Magistrate made me," he gulps. "I thought it would save my parents."

"Tell that to them." Jacob points to the flurry of activity from people who look like worker ants, trying to clear debris and rebuild.

Jacob grunts and summons a gust of wind to carry him the few yards from the ship to the awaiting island. He'll let the others figure out how to disembark when the only dock has been washed away.

*   *   *   *

Jonathon wearily rubs his hands across his face as the crew pre-
pares a longboat to go ashore. Not everyone will accompany the
landing crew, but he is expected to join. He desperately wants to
get off the ship and be on solid ground, but he can't bring himself
to set foot on Port Green. He thought he had escaped his brother's
realm when he left seven years ago to live once more in Eastport.

"Ready?" Matt leans his arms against the railing next to Jonathon. Jonathon rolls his eyes to find that, yet again, Matt is right at
his side. Matt may cling to him like a lamprey, but it annoys Jonathon even more that he's starting to enjoy having him around.

"If I'm being honest, no," Jonathon sighs. "I never wanted to
return here."

Matt just nods, clasping Jonathon's shoulder. "Well, come on.
We'll do it together." They board the longboat heading to shore,
and after a quick trip, land on a beach filled with flotsam.

Unexpectedly, the sight of the destroyed island hits Jonathon
like a blow to the stomach. He hates the place but can't stand to
see it in shambles. It's the only home these people have. The cold
fact is that Jacob will never take the throne from their uncle. These
people need a leader here on Port Green, to maintain some sort of
semblance of a normal life. If only Jacob could put aside his fantasies and focus on reality, maybe Jonathon could have found a
home here, or at least felt like he belonged.

Jonathon sighs. Who is he kidding? Wasn't he, not barely two
days ago, trying to make his own fantasy a reality? *We're both
deluded.* He grimaces. *At least we have that in common.*

Squaring his shoulders, he summons a core of stone from the
ground below and fashions a cane. He begins forward but is

stopped by a long whistle followed by a few short bursts of clapping. Turning, he sees Matt grinning idiotically at him.

"What?"

"Impressive," is all Matt replies, catching up to him.

"It's just a cane."

"Yeah, but it's nice to see you use your abilities for a purpose other than anger," Matt winks.

"I don't—" Jonathon feels a flush creeping up his neck. "Never mind." He turns quickly and follows the others down the soggy path to what used to be the village meeting hall.

*   *   *   *

Even though he's walking through it, Joe can't quite believe the utter annihilation of the island. He couldn't have caused this. Not willingly. But a part of him, buried deep down in the dark recesses of his soul, the part that bared its teeth, hungrily devouring the thrill of almost drowning the Warden, is proud. Proud, and a bit ecstatic, that he could do this, all of this, with his powers. He could be unstoppable if he wanted to. With his mighty powers he could…what? Rule the world? Force everyone to bend to his will? He shakes his head. That's exactly what the Magistrate does now, rule with fear. That's not what he wants. He just wants the Magistrate to be gone and to be able to use his powers without fear of ostracism. If he can create this much destruction, surely he could do just as much good, if given the chance.

Joe follows the others up a path from the beach to an area recently cleared of debris, and spies a half-erected wooden shelter, some planks assembled in a rough square with a partial hightower-frond roof to block the rain. An enormous pile of wreckage stands off to the side, the remnants of the old meeting hall. He stops before the shelter and turns, taking in the island aside from the damage. All around, men and women work to rebuild. No, he realizes, *elementals* work to rebuild.

Aeromentals create whirlwinds to remove heavy beams and tree trunks while pyromentals work to forge new structural supports in a makeshift smithy's stall. Hydromentals divert the standing water left from the flood back to the sea. Terramentals are rebuilding an earthen seawall around the village in anticipation of the next attack. Joe takes a shaky breath. The seawall may be a precaution, but Joe isn't going to attack Port Green anymore. Yet, Magistrate Rufus still has the orb, and he could find another elemental to inject with Ink and attack. Cold fingers creep up his spine as Joe realizes that the elementals of Port Green will never feel safe again, now that they saw firsthand how easily their defenses could be broken.

Jonathon stops beside Joe, Matt at his shoulder. Joe notices black veins on the back of Jonathon's right hand as it grips his cane. His eyes are an empty void looking out at Port Green.

"I hate this place," Jonathon hisses. Joe stares at him in surprise while Matt's brow furrows. "It will never be home," Jonathon growls as he brushes past them both and trudges inside.

Joe follows and sits on one of the many overturned crates, stumps, and rocks scattered throughout the shelter as benches. Jacob and Jordan hold court at the front, a battered steamer trunk filled with paper birds rising before them. Joe finds the paper birds out of place amidst the rubble and wonders why something so delicate would be here. He notices Jacob unfold a paper bird, read it, and crumple it in his fist. It must be a response from Andulsae; Jacob mentioned that his requests to them for help have always been rejected. Jordan grabs the message from Jacob and uncrumples it. His eyes quickly scan the response, shoulders slumping in defeat. What help is Jacob hoping to receive from the elementals up north? Does he just want to protect Port Green, or is he after something bigger?

Hearing a slight wheeze, Joe turns to find Captain Merrill moving to sit with him, his eyes roving uncomfortably around the space, taking in the haphazard seating under a mostly open roof. The few hightower fronds overlapping near the front of the hall provide minor shelter from the drizzle. Captain Merrill hugs his missing hand to his chest as he squeezes onto a stump next to Joe. Joe looks around to see who else from the *Moro* is present, scanning for Nell even though he knows she wants nothing to do with him now. Only seeing Captain Merrill and Matt in the meeting hall, Joe spins back toward the front, crestfallen that Nell seems to be absent.

Jacob's agitated movements catch Joe's eye. Joe is too far away to hear what is being said, but he can only guess it has to do with the message Jacob received, for he is gesturing angrily while Jordan tries to rein him in. More than once, Jordan puts his finger to his lips, reminding Jacob to keep their conversation as private as they can in the increasingly crowded meeting hall. It seems that every elemental on the island stopped what they were doing and congregated in the meeting hall as soon as they saw Jacob return to the island.

Craning his neck about, Joe watches even more people file in and claim the quickly disappearing seats. He recognizes the woman with her small child, reminiscent of his cousins Sara and Meg, push their way through the entry and up toward the front, standing along the wall.

At the front, Jordan notices the meeting hall filling up. He gives a curt word to Jacob, who frowns before facing the crowd. Jordan then raises his hand and calls for silence, which falls almost immediately. Not a voice can be heard, just the fidgeting of restless children, as the gathered elementals lift their solemn faces, waiting for Jacob to speak.

Joe shifts anxiously in his seat and glances at Matt to his right, sitting in between him and Jonathon. Matt frowns, his knuckles clenching as he takes in the acolytes. He reaches down and fidgets with the cuff of his boot, where Joe knows Matt keeps his knife. Joe doesn't usually see Matt so nervous. Generally, Matt's the easygoing one, always looking on the bright side of things. But now, his brows are pinched as he alternates reaching for his knife and reaching for Jonathon's hand, never committing to either.

Jacob stares out at the room, still as a statue, assessing before he takes a deep breath and begins.

"Thank you all for gathering with me today. I'd like to begin by taking a moment to acknowledge those who lost their lives during the most recent attack by Eastport." Jacob bows his head, and Joe's heart drops to his stomach as he watches the gathered elementals follow suit.

"Today," Jacob begins, his voice reverent as it carries out over the crowd, "we honor Eugene, aeromental, Kerrie, terramental, and Stewart, pyromental, all of whom gave their lives defending ours. They will be greatly missed. And as with those who have passed before them, they will not have died in vain. We give them up to the four elements, air, fire, earth, water, and keep their names forever in our hearts." Jacob pounds his fist against his chest four times, and the elementals respond in kind.

Joe shares a bewildered look with Matt as bile forms in the back of his throat. Three elementals died during his attack. He killed them? No, that couldn't be. Something else must have happened. It had felt so good to have almost killed that Warden, but this was different. These three elementals were innocent. Joe swallows rapidly, trying not to puke, but quickly doubles over as the bile threatens to explode from his mouth. Captain Merrill gives him a sharp thump on his back, and Joe swallows the bile, gagging at the taste, and manages to sit back up. Matt gives him a concerned look, but Joe just shakes his head as he wipes his mouth. A moist breeze careens through the partial roof and cools Joe's skin, alleviating some of his queasiness.

Back at the front of the meeting hall, Jacob straightens up and resumes his address. "The mission to retrieve the orb and stop the Magistrate's attacks proved unsuccessful," he states bluntly, hands clasped behind his back. He directs the words at Jonathon, his face solemn, a gesture to reassure the gathered crowd that despite his best efforts, things completely out of his control led to the mission's failure.

Several heads swivel, following Jacob's gaze to stare at Jonathon, who immediately drops his head and focuses on the dirt below his feet. A pang of annoyance hits Joe at the thought of Jonathon hiding in shame again. If only he would stand up to Jacob instead of taking all the blame like a kicked puppy.

"We need to do everything we can now to prepare for the next attack. Our distance from Eastport is no longer a guarantee of safety. It seems that Magistrate Rufus is able to use elementals on Eastport to attack us here, through the orb. The sooner we get that orb out of his possession, the better off we'll be.

"You may have noticed a ship other than the Lexington merchant moored off our shores. Jordan and I will take this ship to Eastport with a small group of our best men and women to steal the orb, by force if necessary."

Captain Merrill stiffens beside Joe. This is news to him. Agreeing to divert course to Port Green at the threat of being caught by the Eastport Navy for not turning up in Lexington on time is one thing, but allowing these elementals to take command of his ship and use it to launch their own attack on Eastport is out of the question. Captain Merrill grits his teeth, planning on what to say the next moment he can get Jacob alone.

"This new mission will need to be fast and stealthy," Jacob continues. "We don't want to attract attention at this point. There are tunnels we can use to get into the castle. From there, we can use Jonathon's intel to locate the orb and retreat back to the safety of Port Green. After that, we will use the orb to launch our own attack on Eastport."

A few murmurs echo through the crowd. Joe wonders how reasonable a full-blown attack on Eastport would be. If Jacob is successful in stealing the orb, then the Magistrate can no longer hurt the elementals of Port Green. An attack might not be necessary.

"What of Andulsae?" The question comes from the woman at the front, the one who reminds Joe of his cousin, Sara.

Jacob leans over heavily on the steamer trunk. "As usual, they will not help. We are on our own. But," he stands tall once more, "I know that once we have the orb, we can fight, and defeat, the Magistrate. We can reclaim Eastport for our own, and once we do, I can assure you that I will lead Eastport into prosperity as your king."

"It won't work," Joe says to himself. Jacob's head immediately snaps his direction.

"What was that?"

The crowd goes silent as Joe shrinks into his jacket.

"No, please, Little Brother, explain to me how this won't work."

Joe clears his throat and says as loudly as he can, "It won't work because Magistrate Rufus has weapons that can defeat elemental powers."

"Eusgare is not a hindrance—" Jacob begins.

"I'm not talking about eusgare." All eyes are now on Joe, and he feels heat rise in his neck. He wishes the breeze would return, no matter how damp and uncomfortable it is. "They have gwarem."

"Gwarem?" Jacob scoffs. "I've sat and listened to our uncle for years, and I've not heard of that before. If it were real, my father would have told me. I would have studied it when we still lived at the castle."

"No, it's real. The Wardens' cloaks have it woven in. They have swords and bullets and darts made from it. It inhibits power."

"All the times Uncle has sent his men to attack us, we've always been able to turn them away. There was no substance impeding us, aside from lack of defenses, people, and weapons." Jacob's brows furrow in confusion as he remembers past battles.

"Well, Magistrate Rufus has it now. I've seen it firsthand." Joe reaches up to where Bernard's gwarem dart pierced his shoulder during his arrest.

Jacob looks to Jordan, searching for confirmation, but Jordan just shrugs.

"Until I have proof of such a thing, we will continue as planned. Now as to those who will join me and Jordan…"

Jacob's voice trails off as Joe stares down at his feet. He tried to warn them, but after all the destruction he caused, he's not surprised that Jacob would be unwilling to listen. A shuffling sound like flies buzzing catches his ear, and Joe's attention is drawn to the ground at his brother's feet, where mini mounds of dirt begin to ball up and zoom around. Surprised, Joe looks up and finds Jonathon practically vibrating. Sweat breaks out at Jonathon's hairline. His jaw and fists clench while Jacob continues to drone on.

Upon closer inspection, Joe notices the black veins creeping up Jonathon's wrist where his sleeve has ridden up. They almost resemble tattoos, inky black lines tracing his forearm. Squinting, Joe can see that the black veins are moving ever so slowly up Jonathon's arm, like squid tentacles reeling in prey. Abruptly, the ground beneath Jonathon's feet splits open with a thunderous crack, creating a shallow fissure about a foot long. Joe almost jumps off his seat, and Matt hurriedly clamps his hand atop Jonathon's, squeezing while scanning the crowd to see if anyone's noticed. Jonathon closes his eyes as he takes a deep breath. He forcibly shakes off Matt's hand and angles slightly away from him on the bench.

Several of the elementals look about them, some glancing above to see if thunderclouds have gathered, each trying to pinpoint the source of the noise. Jordan beelines to Jonathon's side, stopping when he sees the rendered ground at Jonathon's feet. Jonathon begins shaking uncontrollably, clutching at his sides. Jordan reaches out, but Matt beats him to it. Matt pulls Jonathon close and rubs his back.

"Jonathon?" Matt tries to get a response.

A second crack like a cannon shot shakes the meeting hall as a rift opens the ground down the middle, causing elementals to jump out of the way and scurry to the door. The rift expands, swallowing stumps and debris into its abyss. Joe quickly grabs Captain Merrill's arm and pulls him back as his seat tumbles into the dark crevasse.

Jonathon collapses at the edge of the rift, his bad knee yelling out in protest. A rush like angry hornets fills his head, clouding his vision. He reaches out blindly for the vial of Ink in his pocket but closes on Matt's hand first. Jonathon breathes a sigh of relief upon grasping it, clenching it for dear life as his innards burn like fire. His core calls out for more Ink, knowing that is the only way to make the pain stop. Jordan frowns at his second youngest brother, the creases on his forehead protruding like a rock face. Jacob begins to issue some sort of scathing reprimand when a boy of about twelve bursts through the entrance.

"Jacob!" he shouts. "We're under attack! There are three ships just offshore!"

23

acob springs over the fissure in the ground and rushes out of the meeting hall, Jordan on his tail. As Jonathon watches them race past, he realizes that this is the first time in a long time that he's seen Jacob scared. Jacob didn't plan for this so soon after the last attack.

Using Matt for support, Jonathon grits his teeth and pulls himself up from the ground. Limping his way outside, Matt at his elbow, Jonathon grimaces against the pain in his knee. Three Eastport naval ships sit offshore, each turned broadside. The *Moro* remains anchored offshore as well, caught in the middle ground between the Port Green beach and the navy ships. The ships are huge, bulky affairs with two gun decks each. These are warships, sturdy and meant for a sea battle, not to attack a small island settlement. The rain remains steady, but Jonathon can see the flash of cannons igniting before hearing the roar of the cannonball as it flies through the air and crashes into the beach. The seawall that the terramentals had been rebuilding takes a hit and crumbles back to sand in the middle.

The cannon fire is relentless. The warships don't seem to have quite the range to reach the meeting hall, thankfully. Jacob quickly assesses the situation before calling out orders.

"Tula!" he points to an older woman nearby. "Gather the children and retreat to the far side of the island. Hide in the woods until the fighting is over. Those unfit to fight, follow her." Tula and several older elementals corral the children off to the woods behind the meeting hall.

"Jordan! You take the pyromentals and terramentals and work on getting those walls back up. We need some cover."

Jordan and his group of twenty or so elementals sprint off to the right, hugging the tree line as they race closer to the beach. Using the ruined huts as cover, they duck while another volley of cannonballs whistles overhead, blasting apart hightower trees and causing sprays of sand and rock to rise into the air. At the end of the tree line, Jordan gestures to his group, pointing at the battered seawall. The elementals immediately jump into action. They are prepared for this, having dealt with attacks from the Magistrate before. Terramentals lined up in a row collectively raise their hands, forcing the sand of the beach into a seven-foot-high barrier. The pyromentals crouch up behind the terramentals and take aim over their shoulders. Jets of fire shoot out from the pyromentals' palms, heating the sand wall with a blast of white-hot flames. The sand begins morphing into a sheet of glass, several inches thick. Cannonballs continue to strike at the newly created glass wall, but the terramentals and pyromentals work together under Jordan's direction to continuously patch the wall as it shatters.

"Aeromentals and hydromentals with me," Jacob calls out to the remaining elementals gathered around the meeting hall, ready to battle.

"Wait!" Joe shouts from beside Jonathon. "I can help. Where do you want me to go?"

Jacob spares him the briefest of glances. "Take shelter in the woods with the others. You'll only get in the way."

Jacob leads the charge down to the beach, with the aeromentals and hydromentals following close behind, dodging shrapnel from the cannonballs. The glass wall shatters once more as they near the sand, but Jacob gathers the glistening pieces of glass in a gust of wind and hurls them out over the sea toward the warships. Several shards pierce the ships' sails and embed themselves within the wooden hulls. The other aeromentals follow suit, sending gusts to redirect cannonballs back out to sea or to throw debris from the beach—shattered glass, hightower trunks, and rocks—out at the ships. The hydromentals work to haul the ships nearer to shore, giving the aeromentals closer targets.

Joe stands uncertainly in the rain outside the meeting hall. He's never been in a fight, much less a battle before, but he's an elemental, just like the rest of them. He can be useful. If Jacob didn't notice, he took on the entire island of Port Green on his own! Well, with the help of Ink. Regardless, Joe knows, even though he grew up with humans and never truly had to test his limits until a few days ago, that he can help defend this island. It's the least he can do.

A cannonball flies overhead and smashes into the meeting hall, tearing the half-rebuilt shelter asunder. Hightower fronds rain down upon Joe, Jonathon, and Matt, who are still nearby. Joe rips a fallen frond from atop his head and races down toward the water. If Jacob won't give him a role, he'll take matters into his own hands.

"Are you coming with me?" Joe pauses his descent. Jonathon seems to not have heard him, trembling as he stands in the rain, skin even more translucent.

Matt simply shakes his head. "What can I do in an elemental battle?" He shouts over the roar of the cannons. "I think it's better if Jonathon and I take cover in the woods." He grabs Jonathon's arm to pull him away, but Jonathon wrenches it free.

"I'm not weak. I can handle myself," he snarls, summoning a new stone cane from the ground, his old one lost somewhere in the meeting hall. Jonathon hobbles determinedly down to the beach where the cacophonous melee blooms before him like a painter's frantic brush strokes.

The warships are relentless, firing volley after volley, round after round. Smoke quickly fills the air, mingling with the rain to create a rancid fog. Jonathon reaches for the case in his pocket, his gut already burning in anticipation of the surge of power to come.

"Jonathon, no." A hand clamps down on his arm. "No more." Jonathon sneers as he meets Matt's gaze. Matt doesn't back down, his steely green eyes sharp and unforgiving. His grip tightens as he shakes his head, throwing a glance in Joe's direction, who is close behind, eager to find a way to help.

Jonathon flinches and tries to act normal, hoping Joe will simply pass him by without a second thought. Then he shakes his head angrily. Why should he care if Joe knows? Why should he hide his newfound strength? He's been hiding all his life, cowering in the corner while people walked all over him, used him. Everyone he's ever loved has been taken from him, and he's been too eager to stand idly by. To be weak. Enough is enough.

Turning his back to Joe, Jonathon throws off Matt's hand, takes out the vial, and fills the syringe. Holding it with his teeth, he shoves up his sleeve. Matt gasps at the black veins steadily crawling up the inside of Jonathon's arm. The veins are higher and thicker than they were before, rising almost to Jonathon's shoulder. At this rate, they will be up to his neck soon, where everyone can see. Ignoring Matt, Jonathon pricks his battle-weary skin and slams the plunger home. Immediately, his senses sharpen as power tingles from his toes to the top of his head. A contented sigh escapes his lips as he drinks in the now-familiar taste of enhanced strength.

Throwing aside his cane, Jonathon runs down to the shore, the pain in his knee vanished. He's dimly aware of Matt and Joe following close behind. He focuses on how best to attack the invading ships but sees that his brothers have beaten him to it. Jacob and Jordan are fighting and directing like a well-oiled machine, commanding their elementals to send fiery vortexes and tidal waves at the Magistrate's ships. Fire dances on the sea, catching sails, masts, and decking with flaming embers. Sailors anxiously rush about, trying to keep the fire at bay. It seems that the elementals are actually winning.

Jonathon looks around at the worn faces of the men and women surrounding him, exhausted from being attacked twice and having to rebuild in the span of a few days. There's grit here. These elementals are not going to give up. Cannon fire continues to rain down upon them, quicker than they can retaliate, but yet, they remain steadfast. They stay out of range and return fire with what they have available. When shrapnel hits the man beside them, they pull him to safety behind the seawall and keep fighting.

These are the people Jonathon left seven years ago, the people he was so willing to give up for the promise of something better in Eastport, for the promise of his little brother who doesn't even remember him. These elementals fought against the Magistrate every year. They strived to turn this volcanic rock of an island into a home when they had nowhere else to go. These elementals deserved so much better than what the hand of fate had dealt them.

A burning sensation crawls up Jonathon's gut, and with it, he feels his power searching, reaching out like roots. Thanks to the Ink, he can feel the ground beneath his feet, the connection to the earth that he has come to crave, even with his boots on. He stretches out his power, swelling with the might of the island beneath him. Oh, if he could only pair up with a pyromental and set this whole island on fire, wake the dormant volcano within once more. His uncle's Wardens wouldn't stand a chance. The ground beneath him begins to rumble, a low moan gathering in the bedrock. Jonathon directs the building earthquake out to sea and watches with satisfaction as the waves begin to grow in response to the quaking seafloor.

The warships bob like apples in a river. Smiling, Jonathon moves his hands in an undulating motion, churning the seafloor under the ships, encouraging the quake to build faster. He dimly hears someone shout next to him, followed by a tug on his sleeve. Sparing a brief glance, Jonathon sees the beach in a roiling turmoil, Matt and Joe both falling to the sand as they try to find purchase on the heaving ground. Jonathon clenches his jaw and carries on. His brother and Matt are simply collateral damage. Nothing will deviate him from sinking the Magistrate's ships.

The warships list wildly from side to side as the seaquake builds. Most of the cannon fire has stopped, the Wardens unable to lock onto a target, but one cannonball veers off to the left as its cannon slams loose from its mooring, succumbing to the quake.

The cannonball heads directly at the *Moro*. Without thinking, Joe leaps up and raises his hand to thrust a massive wave at the

Moro, causing it to tilt just enough for the cannonball to miss the mainmast. He quickly sends a counter-wave toward its starboard side to prevent a total capsize.

"Jonathon, what the hell are you thinking?" Joe yells at Jonathon's back. "My crew is still out there!" Joe comes around and pulls Jonathon's shoulder.

"Jonathon!"

Jonathon lowers his arms slightly, not relenting in his onslaught. Joe stands in front of Jonathon, trying to break his concentration but is instead greeted by Jonathon's sinister smile below unfocused eyes.

"Jonathon, stop!" Joe shakes his brother hard, and Jonathon snaps out of his stupor. Jonathon growls at Joe for a second before stalking off.

Worriedly wiping rain from his face, Joe spins back to the beach, the drizzle now a downpour. He could use this to his advantage, create a wall of rain so thick the Magistrate's Wardens couldn't see through it. Yet, the commotion on the beach has stopped. Joe no longer hears the boom of cannons over the rain. Out at sea, two warships limp away, half their sails torn asunder, gashes running through their hulls. The third ship is on its port side, charred and slowly sinking, its sails white shrouds on the waves. Elementals on the beach throw up a cheer, while others slump to the ground like wilted veralillies, glad to have spared their home from the worst of it. Joe scans the dirty faces and finds his eldest brother at the water's edge. Jacob stands menacingly, an air of victory hovering around him like a cape as he surveys the scene. Jacob crosses his arms and smirks at the ships limping away. Joe realizes that he's posturing for their uncle, for he is surely watching through the orb.

Joe shakes his head. Every day, Jacob reminds him more of the Magistrate, and every day, he likes Jacob a little less. Assessing the *Moro* once more, he's satisfied there's no lasting damage. Besides, there's not much Joe can do for the *Moro* from shore. Turning back inland, he trudges up to the remnants of the meeting hall, searching for Captain Merrill, whom he hadn't seen since the battle began, and hopes no more injuries befell him.

The rain falls in sheets, leaving no part of Joe dry. His socks squelch in his boots like soggy bread, and he sighs at the thought of the blisters he'll have later. His mind drifts back to a different day, when he was caught out in the gardens in a downpour just like this and tracked mud all over the hall rug. The Queen's maids were furious with him.

I've been in the castle gardens before? But why was I covered in mud? Shrugging at that odd recollection, he puzzles at the ground as he makes his way back to the hall, the only building he knows here on Port Green, even though it's missing most of its roof and walls.

The Magistrate sent only three ships. The elementals were able to damage the ships, so they couldn't have been lined with gwarem. Of the elementals who were injured, they seem to be relatively okay, so Joe assumes that the warships didn't have gwarem rounds. And if Magistrate Rufus is indeed watching through the orb, why did he send so few men, with no gwarem, ensuring defeat? Joe's seen his uncle's work firsthand. He's lived in Eastport his whole life, a city where he can't remember a time when the obelisks weren't guarding the place like death maidens, keeping elementals at bay. The Magistrate thrives on eusgare, and now gwarem, reveling in the power it gives him over elementals, especially since Gregor and his chemists invented Ink. Joe remembers the latest hanging, how Felix looked crazed, with black veins webbing his skin. The Magistrate had been experimenting for a long time then; it didn't make sense to Joe why he would send his Wardens to attack now without either eusgare or gwarem.

Joe slips in the mud as he continues to climb the rise back to the meeting hall, a pinch of a headache beginning to brew behind his eyes. He shakes his head to clear it when he notices a smudge of movement in the woods before him. It appears that Matt and Jonathon are heading to the meeting hall to regroup as well. Which is odd, since he left them back on the beach. Looking behind him, Joe sees that the beach is mostly empty, save for a few elementals gathering the injured. Matt and Jonathon are not in sight. Joe squints as he turns back to the woods and swipes his hand through the air, parting the rain like a curtain.

A column of Wardens stalk through the forest, rifles at the ready, aiming to bear down on the unsuspecting village.

Joe drops to the ground, looking for a place to hide. The path to the meeting hall is barren, however, leaving him exposed. He quickly thinks through his options. With all the rain and the ocean so near, his way forward seems obvious. But what about the island? What about all the lives he's already sidetracked? He can't put them in harm's way again. Joe frantically looks around for Jacob or Jordan, someone to alert, but he sees no one through the downpour. The elementals on the beach are too far away to hear him over the rain. Joe squares his stance. He wanted to fight; looks like he'll get that chance.

The column of Wardens comes to a halt as a brown-haired man in front signals. The man looks down at an object in his hand. The urgent need to act soon consumes Joe. He can't let these Wardens get to the villagers. If he has to fight them alone, he will. The memory of him attacking the Warden in the throne room barrels through his brain. It was so easy to slowly drown that Warden. Now, through the pounding rain and roaring ocean, he can feel the tug of two dozen bodies, little streams within waiting to do his bidding. It would be too easy. He can almost taste the salty blood that flows through their veins.

Joe raises his arm and smiles wide, ready to deliver a killing, redeeming blow, when a scream pierces his brain. All at once, his resolve shatters like broken glass, and Nell's face surfaces in his mind. Killing these men makes him no better than the hydromental that killed her father. If he does this, he would only be proving her right. She would never see elementals as anything other than killers. And she would never see Joe as anything other than a killer, either.

The weight of what he is about to do crushes him. He doubles over, gulping air, struggling to remember how to breathe. He is not a killer. He will not be like the hydromental who took Nell's father from her. He can be better.

"Ugh!" Heaving himself upright, he raises his hands to divert the rain toward the attacking men, hoping to create a massive deluge and buy the elementals some time. Having shifted his focus, he is bewildered to find himself suddenly thrown into the air before being slammed back down onto the churning earth, the ground eddying below him like a hungry maw. Joe's head crunches against the dirt, and bile fills his throat. A sickening sense of familiarity worms its way into his psyche. The action calls to mind another time, another place, where he was thrown into the air and violently crashed down.

Struggling through the dizziness to his knees, Joe sees Jonathon stalk pass him, eyes pure white as he throws his power at the men. The black veins are inching up Jonathon's neck in an unrelenting stampede. The Wardens regain their feet and aim their rifles at Jonathon. Dozens of wet, gleaming barrels all point at one man. Joe wants to yell at him to run, but his voice freezes in his throat as the guns burst.

24

aniacal laughter surrounds Jonathon as the Wardens open fire. He throws up an earthen wall, blocking most of the bullets, and realizes the laugh is coming from himself. He laughs because he's been here before. He laughs because this time he knows he can win. His brother won't be lost to him this time.

Jonathon hears the shuffle of rifles being reloaded in the rain. The Ink has sharpened his senses. He feels truly invincible now. He releases the wall, watching in glee as it tumbles to the ground. How he hopes his uncle is out there somewhere, watching through the orb. He won't want to miss what comes next.

Some Wardens struggle to reload while others are already taking aim again at Jonathon. Sneering, Jonathon raises both arms high above his head, letting his power build, filling him to the brim. He holds back until he is just about to overflow and almost attacks, but then he sees the Warden in front. Brown hair plastered to his forehead, almost obscuring deep brown eyes. His uniform bears a crest. The Captain of the Wardens: Bernard.

Blind rage consuming him, Jonathon slams down his arms with a guttural yell, sending calamity directly at his former boyfriend.

The ground heaves, bucking upwards and crashing down, shattering trees like broken glass. The earth, rumbling like an upset stomach, convulses, with pulse waves radiating outward in a spiral. The Wardens find themselves helpless, unable to remain standing, and crash to their knees in an attempt to crawl away. But Jonathon's had enough. Enough of his uncle and his uncle's Wardens. Enough of hiding. Enough of Bernard. Enough of all the people who told him he is worthless and weak. These Wardens have fired their last shots. No one escapes tonight.

A silent glee fills him as he twitches his fingers in a macabre dance, opening the ground beneath the Wardens. The dirt and stone crumble away, the Wardens falling into the earth one by one. A few try to cling to tree roots and pull themselves up to solid ground, but Jonathon widens his reach, toppling trees into the hole as well. Fear fills the air as the Wardens claw at the dirt, scrabbling for purchase. Their terrified screams are cut short as Jonathon closes the ground over them, leaving a barren plain where once was forest. His muscles relax in a much-welcomed peace.

Jonathon's dimly aware of Joe and Matt standing near him, frozen in shock, but they will understand soon enough. He just saved Port Green and took out dozens of the Magistrate's men. This victory will ensure future victories for the elementals. But most importantly, this victory is his.

A sharp intake of breath whistles in his ear, and the smell of gunpowder assaults his nose. He turns to his right and blinks several times to make sense of what he sees. Matt's face, contorted in pain as he clutches a bloody hand to his arm. Staring, Jonathon tries to understand why Matt's shirt sleeve is turning red. He slowly swivels back to the destroyed forest, denuded of trees and mounded like a recently filled grave. There, at the edge of the freshly consecrated ground is Bernard, safe where Jonathon left him in a circle of ruin. Kneeling, Bernard lowers the pistol, smoke still rising from the barrel. In a flash, Jonathon runs to Bernard, the earth coiling in his wake. Jonathon grabs his uniform collar and slams him against the ground.

Joe shakes himself from his shock and hurries to Matt.

"I'm fine," Matt grunts. "It just grazed me. Go stop Jonathon," he urges Joe forward with a nod of his head.

"Put some pressure on it," Joe advises as he runs toward his brother. Slowing as he approaches, he sees Jonathon's trembling back and hears venomous words spraying from his mouth.

"You vile creature! After everything you've done to me? I should kill you right now. I should take this and drive it through your heart! I can't believe I ever loved you, you worthless scum." Reaching a hand out over the earth, Jonathon calls forth a shaft of black volcanic rock, sharpened to a spearpoint. He holds it against Bernard's chest, pressing just enough to cause Bernard's uniform to dimple.

Joe pulls up short, panting in fear. He doesn't recognize this Jonathon, with hatred pouring off him in a dark cloud. He killed all those men as easily as swatting a fly. Gone is the sad, meek person Joe had begun to take for granted. In his place is this terrifying beast, and Joe's every instinct is to back away slowly before that rage turns on him.

Hearing rustling behind him, Joe spins to find that Matt has quietly joined him, a strip of torn shirt tied around his bleeding arm. Matt's grave look hardens Joe's resolve as he dares to approach his venting brother.

"Madame's first rule: Never fall in love with a client. I wish I had never met you at the Siren Club." Joe hears Jonathon sneer at the cowering figure of Bernard, flat on his back, gun still raised.

"But, then again, the ones we love always betray us, don't they?" Jonathon scoffs. "You hate dirty elementals, huh? You hate me? Fine. Being stabbed in the heart is too good of a death for you." Jonathon throws away his rock spearpoint. Gathering some dirt from the ground in his fist, he holds it in front of Bernard's face. Jonathon lets go, the dirt hovering in the air like a swarm of wasps, where Bernard eyes it warily.

"Jonathon," Joe warns.

But Jonathon doesn't listen. The dirt remains, inches from Bernard's nose. Joe notices tendrils of black running toward Jonathon's right eye.

"Jonathon," Joe approaches slowly, hands up in what he hopes is a non-threatening way. "Jonathon, come on. Let's go. He's not worth it."

"No. He really isn't, is he?" With a snarl, Jonathon's eyes go white as he sends the dirt straight into Bernard's nose and mouth. Coughing, Bernard tries to dislodge the dirt caught in his throat, but Jonathon clenches his hand into a ball, driving the dirt further into Bernard's lungs. Dropping the pistol, Bernard clutches his throat, gasping for air.

"Jonathon, stop!" Joe tackles his brother, pinning his arms to his side. "You're better than this!" Joe wrestles Jonathon away from the chaos he's caused. Bernard remains on the ground, clawing for air like a fish out of water.

"Dammit, Jonathon!" Joe struggles, dragging a straining Jonathon away from Bernard. The brothers roll on the ground as Jonathon throws out his hands, seeking to drive more dirt into Bernard's mouth. Joe latches onto Jonathon's wrists, trying to pull him away, but Jonathon's elbow connects with his chin, and Joe swears softly under his breath.

"Matt!" Joe shouts as Jonathon runs once more at Bernard, who still gasps for air. Matt jumps onto Jonathon's back and knocks him to the ground. Using his knees to pin Jonathon's arms to his side, Matt holds on as Jonathon quakes the ground beneath them, trying to break free.

"A little help here, Joe!"

Creating a disc of rainwater, Joe jumps to his feet and fires the water disc at Jonathon's face. Jonathon stills in surprise at the rush of water filling his eyes and nose. The earth rapidly calms as two more water discs strike him in the face.

Joe hesitates to throw his next water disc, waiting for Jonathon to send an earthen disc back at him, like they did when they were younger. The water disc dissolves into hundreds of tiny droplets as that thought enters Joe's mind. He played this game with Jonathon when they were kids. And Jonathon always let him win. *That's what I was doing that day. I was playing in the mud with my brother.*

Shaking off the memory, Joe runs over to help Matt pull a deflated Jonathon up from the ground. Between the two of them, they slowly manage to drag Jonathon back toward the ruin of Port Green. The distance seems to lessen Jonathon's anger, and his eyes return to their normal blue as he goes slack, all the fight draining out of him.

"What has gotten into you?" Joe hisses at him.

"I loved him. And I thought he loved me." Jonathon falls against his brother, eyes rolling back in his head as the black veins spread across his face.

25

Jacob watches his brothers leave the woods, Jonathon slumped between Joe and Matt. The black veins cover Jonathon's face like seaweed. After the victory on the beach, Jacob heard the far-off squelch of boots in mud. He had motioned to Jordan to look after the recovery efforts and slunk off toward the woods to locate the noise. Jacob arrived just in time to witness Jonathon bury a large group of Wardens and had quickly ducked behind a hightower trunk lest his brothers see him. Now, his eyes narrow as he crouches deeper into the trees' shadows, letting the group pass, Matt and Joe struggling under Jonathon's weight.

Typical, Jacob thinks. Jonathon never knows when to stop. With a frown, he steps out of the shadows and walks over the newly hallowed ground filled with dead Wardens to where Bernard sits gasping. Boots stopping just short of the quivering captain, Jacob sneers at Bernard's pathetic form. Using his toe, Jacob pushes Bernard onto his back. He tilts his head and stares at Bernard's red face for several moments, a frown spreading across his cheeks.

"Disgusting," he spits before shoving Bernard and turning away. But something shiny catches his eye and Jacob hurriedly spins back around. There, stamped into the ground slightly under Bernard's waist, is the orb. It sits innocently in the dirt and detritus of hightower fronds. Jacob leans over as he notices a swirling mist within the orb. The mist sends a shiver down his spine. It beckons like a finger, drawing him into its unknown dangers. He greedily reaches for it, pushing Bernard further away. Before he can pull it close for examination, a hand latches onto his wrist, holding him fast.

"Magistrate Rufus entrusted that to me. I will not let you have it," Bernard's raspy voice comes up from where he lies on his back.

"You're not in much of a position to negotiate." Jacob wrenches his hand free and holds the orb up to his face. This is it: the solution to stopping his uncle. It is such a small thing for it to be so powerful. Jacob twists the orb this way and that, wondering how his uncle was able to use it to attack. He remembers his father telling him that the orb could be used to communicate with their kin in Andulsae as long as someone there had its counterpart. His father tried to show him once, but Gregor burst in with news of the queen's death, and Jacob never got to see the orb in action.

For young Jacob, he was enthralled with this magical potential. Sure, he himself could hear across great distances, but to be able to see and converse with someone else? Especially with his grandfather, whom he had never met before. It was better than the pastries from the kitchens that he and Jordan often snuck.

Jacob frowns at the memory, as his grandfather has refused all communication with him since The Expunging. Perhaps now that he has the orb, his grandfather will have a change of heart. He could summon him on the orb, show him that he has made gains for the refugee elementals, that he can be a leader.

"Chief Markas Andulssan, Andulsae," Jacob declares to the orb as he brings it to his mouth. The orb remains silent, still showing the mist within. Jacob waits a moment longer and then shakes the orb, hoping to clear out the mist clouding its surface, and tries again.

"Chief Markas Andulssan, Andulsae," Jacob asserts once again. Yet the orb doesn't change. "Argh!" Jacob growls in frustration.

"See? It won't work for those who are unworthy." Bernard's coughing less, the dirt mostly expelled from his lungs now.

Jacob hauls Bernard off the ground by his collar.

"How come you have this? Why did the Magistrate give it to you?" Jacob demands of Bernard, baring his teeth. "Make it work for me!"

Bernard cackles. "You're going to lose. The gods don't favor inhuman things. And the world will be free of you one day, you'll see."

Jacob throws Bernard back onto the ground and closes his free hand into a fist. Bernard immediately reaches for his own throat, struggling to hold onto the air he just regained. Jacob stalks over, boots crunching on the fallen hightower fronds, to loom over Bernard.

"You will show me how this works," he says with a deadly calm and pushes the orb at Bernard, maintaining a grip on Bernard's air. Bernard shakes his head, so Jacob tightens his fist. Bernard scrabbles at his throat, digging his nails in as if to dislodge the blockage to his airway. His face begins to turn purple, eyes bulging in their sockets. Desperate, Bernard gives the smallest nod he can manage, and Jacob releases his grip enough for Bernard to siphon some air into his lungs.

Bernard's breath comes hard and fast, his chest heaving like a drowning man. He motions to his neck, begging Jacob to give him more air. Jacob doesn't relent, regarding his prey with contempt. After a minute of listening to the wet gasps, Jacob unclenches his fist a little more, allowing Bernard to suck in air as if he would never breathe again. And he still might not. Jacob hasn't made his mind up yet.

Jacob crouches down and pushes the orb under Bernard's nose. "Show me."

Bernard rubs his throat and pulls out a bronze knife from his waistband. Immediately, Jacob tightens his fist, restricting Bernard's air once more.

"Orb. Needs. Blood," Bernard squeaks.

The last piece of the puzzle falls into place. Jacob vaguely remembers his father telling him long ago that the user must give blood for the orb to work, but only once. Once the orb had your blood, you could use it at any time.

A searing pain explodes on Jacob's arm, causing him to drop the orb. Blood streams from a deep cut on his wrist, splashing upon the dirt. The skin around the cut steams and begins to flake as the pain crawls up his forearm like a spider.

"What the?" Jacob rubs his arm, trying to quell the pain that seizes him. His muscles spasm and then leave his arm numb. Below him, Bernard reaches to strike again, knife aimed at Jacob's chest. Jacob quickly shoves his other arm out, sending a burst of wind that picks Bernard up off the ground and slams him into a hightower tree. Bernard's back bends around the trunk with a sickening crack, and he falls to the ground.

Jacob strides over to where Bernard lies motionless at the base of the trunk, nearly folded in half from the force of Jacob's attack. His eyes are open, but his chest does not rise. The woods around them are silent, the rain just a soft patter on the leaves above. Jacob closes his eyes and inhales deeply, letting the cold, damp air sear his throat and chest. Backing up, he scans the ground for the orb.

It glistens just a foot ahead of him, the rain and his blood mixing with the dirt below it. Picking it up, Jacob runs his bloody forearm over the orb, ignoring the sting of pain as dirt worms its way into the cut. He'll have to ask Jordan for a poultice later, something that will make the numbness go away. Jordan is better with herbs and medicine and such.

Jacob brings the orb back to his mouth, thinking to summon his grandfather again. But why did Bernard have the orb? Jacob weighs the marble in his hand before demanding it: "Show me what you showed Bernard."

The orb pulses and begins to glow, expanding to fill Jacob's hand until it is the size of a brumbuck tuber. Squinting, Jacob can make out an image in the orb. It dissolves slowly into focus. He sees the black rock beach on the other side of the island, a lone ship anchored offshore. This must be where Bernard and his Wardens landed. Scanning the beach, he watches three men emerge from the woods, beelining for the longboat on the shoreline. Three Wardens, all alone.

"Show me what those three Wardens are doing," he requests of the orb. The image in the orb turns away from the beach and advances through the trees. It goes inland for about half a mile to a thicket of wadlow vines. Within the thicket, Jacob spies three open barrels. They appear to be ordinary wine barrels, save for a fine bronze mist emanating from them. The mysterious mist flows over the top and down the sides of the barrels, stretching through the air. It bends through the woods, heading toward where Jacob ordered Tula to take the children. It's thick, like fog; the rain doesn't seem to be dissipating it, and the trees seem unaffected.

Jacob frowns. Bernard had the orb and a column of Wardens at his back. He could have been watching the battle at the beach through the orb, planning the opportune moment to strike from behind. Instead, he was watching his Wardens place these barrels.

Suddenly, a scream shoots through the woods, high pitched and shaky. Another follows it, and then a whole pack of screams resound through the air. Jacob spins, trying to pinpoint which direction the screams are coming from. He looks at the orb and sees Tula and the children engulfed in the bronze mist. Several children run from the mist, terror etched on their faces. One young boy trips on a root and lands face first, the mist enveloping him. As it touches his skin, Jacob hears his shriek of pain.

The orb shrinks back to a marble as Jacob closes his fist around it and runs.

26

"You're injured. Let me carry him," Joe implores Matt, who props up Jonathon with his good arm, dragging him like a piece of driftwood alongside Joe.

"I'm fine," Matt replies, making his way down the path to the beach. Joe assesses him. Physically, aside from a grimace or two of pain, he does seem fine. The blood on his arm is more dry than fresh, and he doesn't appear to be hurt anywhere else. But Joe's known Matt a long time. He recognizes the creases of worry between his eyes and his tight-lipped frown.

Joe sees how Matt protectively grips Jonathon about his waist, senses Matt's fear that if he lets go, if only for a minute, Jonathon will be lost to him. Joe's own forehead wrinkles in an imitation of Matt's.

"He'll be okay," Joe puffs as he grabs under Jonathon's other arm. They trudge a few more steps before Matt answers.

"I'm not so sure."

Joe jerks in surprise.

"What makes you say that?"

They reach the beach, sand cratered with cannonballs from the recent battle, and place Jonathon gently against the longboat, which somehow survived the onslaught. Matt quickly looks around them, making sure they're unnoticed, before kneeling beside Jonathon and rolling up his sleeve. Joe's eyes widen at the angry red holes sprinkled among the black veins twisting up the inside of Jonathon's arm.

"I don't know what drug it is," Matt whispers, "but it's killing him."

From out of nowhere, Jordan appears next to them, silent as a shadow. He has a smudge of ash on his face, smoke still rising from his hands. Wearily, he swipes some loose hair out of his eyes, trying and failing to recollect it in his ponytail.

"What happened to him?" he asks, looking at each of them in turn.

Joe stutters, unsure how to respond. How is he supposed to explain that Jonathon so easily killed those men? Jonathon must have Ink somewhere in order to have done what he did. A clawing echoes in Joe's gut, a slight yearning to taste the power of Ink once more.

Joe places a hand on Jonathon's forehead and quickly withdraws it from the burning skin. Jonathon's being consumed by the drug, and Joe wants more Ink? Yet, Joe understands how Jonathon felt when he killed the Wardens, understands the seductiveness of committing an act so grand with barely any effort.

"He killed a bunch of Wardens," Joe mutters.

"He saved your people from being slaughtered," Matt retorts. "If he hadn't done something, you'd be facing an ambush, and you'd probably have lost. I'm taking him back to the ship. I'll figure out how to help him there." Matt busies himself inching Jonathon into the longboat.

Joe shakes himself into action. "I'll help." They nestle Jonathon between the benches and push the longboat out into the water. Almost forgetting, Joe turns back to Jordan, who worries the sand with his boot, stuck between needing to stay and wanting to make sure Jonathon's okay.

"He didn't kill them all," Joe confesses to Jordan. "The Captain of the Wardens, Bernard. He's still back there. You might be able to get some answers from him."

"Oh. Um yeah, okay. Once I find Jacob, I'll let him know." Jordan shakes his hands, heat still radiating from them. He glances at Jonathon's limp form in the longboat.

"Just take care of him, okay?" Jordan gives Joe a long look and goes to find Jacob.

In the longboat, Matt huddles over Jonathon, trying to ignore the pain in his arm and the dried blood sticky on his sleeve. Jonathon is still and pale, like a reflection of the moon in calm waters. Matt almost believes him dead. He pulls his knife from his boot and holds the blade up to Jonathon's nose. A faint fog finally obscures the metal. Matt breathes a sigh of relief as Joe pulls himself into the longboat and crouches beside him.

Joe's exhausted and wants nothing more than a bed to sleep in, but Matt's pleading eyes make him shift focus.

"We need to bring him to Nell."

Joe almost falls back at the suggestion.

"What? Why?"

"She's our best healer. I don't care if she's mad at you. You both can stop being mad at each other for five minutes to help him." Matt grabs the oars and settles them into the locks. Joe shakes his head and instead puts a hand out over the water. The waves crashing on the shore change direction and bunch up behind the longboat, propelling it the short distance to the anchored *Moro*. Smiling gratefully at Joe, Matt closes his eyes in relief, letting the rocking longboat calm his mind for a brief moment. In the span of a minute, they arrive. Joe and Matt throw up the ropes to awaiting crew members who haul the longboat up. At the railing, they unceremoniously drop Jonathon and themselves onto the deck.

A shadow falls over them, and Joe squints up to find Shorty anxiously wringing his shirt hem. The crew gathers around him, nervously watching the sea, expecting the warships to return.

"How bad's the damage, Shorty? Anyone hurt?" Joe inquires.

Shorty vigorously shakes his head. "Nothing we can't handle. The *Moro's* weathered the storm and the crew're mostly afflicted by nerves. Have you seen the captain?"

Joe wearily rubs his face. "No, I haven't. But I'm sure he's fine. We'll send a longboat back out for him."

"We thought he'd be fine before," Shorty replies, still shaking his head.

Joe flinches, remembering the empty sleeve where the captain's hand used to be.

"Shorty, he's fine," Matt snaps. "Go find Nell, and have her meet us in the sick bay. Once we take care of things, Joe and I'll go back out for the captain. Then we're all leaving." He directs the last part at Joe.

Joe returns his stare, not daring to blink. "Agreed."

Matt nods to Shorty, who bounds off after Nell, and he and Joe drag Jonathon down to the sick bay.

*　　　*　　　*　　　*

In the sick bay yet again, Matt hovers over Jonathon lying in bed and wipes some sweat from his brow with his sleeve. The black veins thicken across Jonathon's face, and the cool night air seems to be doing little to lower his fever.

"He's getting worse," Matt whispers to himself.

"I don't see how that's my problem," a voice snarls from the doorway. Joe blushes as he turns to face Nell.

"Hi," he offers.

She scoffs as she looks back down the hallway.

"Please, Nell. You're the best we've got," Matt implores.

Nell crosses her arms and gives Matt a hard stare. "And why would I help him? Or you?" she throws at Joe.

Matt's eyes flick from Jonathon's still form back to Nell's face, his teeth worrying his bottom lip. Matt turns to Joe, pleading. Joe sighs inwardly. Jonathon's getting worse. Nell really is their only option. Joe shrinks into his jacket.

"Nell, please," Joe begs her.

Nell pauses briefly on Joe before risking a glance at Matt, who kneels anxiously at Jonathon's side. Her face softens as she shakes her head.

"You really like him, don't you. Why?"

"It's not something I chose, Nell," Matt whispers. "It's something I know, with my entire being. I need him to be okay." Matt rests his forehead against Jonathon's, willing him to get better, that maybe some of Matt's own strength can pass into Jonathon simply by being near.

Nell toys with the end of her braid as she looks out the port-hole at the dark ocean. She finally turns back and addresses Joe.

"Fine. I'll see what I can do. But I'm doing this for him," she points to Matt, "not you."

Joe holds his hands up in surrender. "Thank you."

A sudden gasp emits from the cot. Three heads turn simultaneously as Jonathon arches his back, gripped in pain. His eyes snap open. They are pure white. Jonathon's hand shoots out and grips Joe's arm like a drowning man trying to pull himself into a boat. Joe tries to twist free from Jonathon's grasp, but his nails dig in like claws. His body shudders as he gives one last gasp, then falls back down, motionless.

Joe quickly reaches for a pulse at Jonathon's neck, hesitating for the briefest moment as his fingers near the black veins. He sucks in a breath and forges on while Matt rips open Jonathon's shirt, revealing black veins crowding his heart.

"His pulse is very weak," Joe says gravely.

"Nell!" Matt yells, but she just shakes her head, mouth agape.

"Nell!" Matt shouts again, desperation filling the small cabin. Coming back to herself, Nell pushes loose strands of hair behind her ears, grabs a cloth from the cabinet on the back wall, and dunks it in a bucket of water under the worktable. Keeping her back to Joe, Nell kneels beside the bed. She takes the damp cloth and stares down at Jonathon's sweaty body. Matt has removed and thrown Jonathon's shirt across the other cot. A nagging voice in the back of Nell's mind reprimands her for not hanging the shirt up and instead leaving it in a damp ball, never to dry. She shakes her head, shushing the voice, and runs the cool cloth over Jonathon's forehead and chest.

Jonathon's fever rages, and the black veins cross his body like paths in a forest. Occasionally, he gains brief consciousness, mumbling nonsense while his stark white eyes stare blankly ahead. He's deteriorating. Nell knows it. Joe knows it. Matt knows it. And yet, they all seem powerless to stop it.

Not for the first time, Nell blames Joe for this mess. If he had been honest with her in the first place, or better yet had never come to the *Moro,* they wouldn't be in such a predicament. She has a pang of pity for Matt, though, despite his attachment to an elemental. Matt looks so distraught, Jonathon's hand grasped in his, whispering mantras of good health in hopes that some deity hears. The worry lines on his forehead are permanently etched there, as if stone. Nell resists the urge to smooth them out with her finger.

Matt abruptly stands and pulls Joe after him. Joe staggers to a stop by the door, questions scrawled across his face.

"We need to ask your brothers for help."

"Matt, it's only been like fifteen minutes. Let Nell at least try. I don't think—"

"Look, they have to know something!" Matt pleads. "Please."

It's against Joe's better judgement, but Matt's determined, and Joe longs to hold onto this friendship, especially after losing Nell. Joe follows Matt above deck. Matt launches the longboat, and Joe propels them both to shore.

*   *   *   *

All appears quiet on Port Green, but, from the longboat, Joe can make out shadows of activity, elementals moving the injured off the beach, clearing debris from the meeting hall, trying to reattach hightower fronds for the roof. These people are exhausted. Joe can see it in the slump of their shoulders, the grim faces as they bustle about. The little progress they had made after Joe's attack has been wiped out, and few seem to be willing to rebuild again.

Joe moves the longboat closer to shore and spots a silhouette of a figure on the beach. With a start, he realizes it's the captain. Captain Merrill is bedraggled, clutching his missing hand to his chest. His pants are torn, and his normally tucked shirt is flying out behind him. Shame floods Joe. He has forgotten about Captain Merrill. The captain stomps hurriedly through the water and awkwardly climbs aboard.

"Take 'er back, Joe."

"Captain? Where were you? Are you okay?"

"Take us back to the ship. Now!" The captain stares down the ship, as if he can urge them there by will alone. Captain Merrill frantically glances back at the island, eyes roving the beach and woods beyond. "The devil is coming," he whispers shakily.

Matt stands, causing the longboat to wobble, and confronts Captain Merrill. "I'm afraid we can't do that, sir."

"Matt…" Captain Merrill threatens.

"We need their help." Matt juts his chin at the shore.

Captain Merrill sighs, but Matt doesn't wait for a response. He jumps from the longboat into knee-high water and slogs to shore. Joe shrugs his shoulders at the captain, grounds the longboat, and follows. Captain Merrill looks back at the *Moro* longingly before calling out to Joe in a hushed whisper. "I'll wait for you here. Be quick. I feel death is near."

Joe squints at him in confusion, but shakes it off and runs to join Matt, who is already halfway to the meeting hall. Matt doesn't acknowledge Joe as he matches his stride, but plods on determinedly. Everything happened too fast. First the dungeon, then the escape, the attack, and now this. Joe barely has a minute to wrap his mind around anything before the next disaster strikes. And if his brothers don't know how to heal Jonathon, then what? How would Matt cope? How would *he* cope? Joe has seen so much death the past few days. He's not sure he can handle one more.

Hushed voices greet them on the trail, a tinge of fear that quickly descends into chaos. From out of nowhere, a cacophony of fright fills the surrounding air. Matt looks at Joe, who just shakes his head. Elementals burst onto the trail in front of them, fleeing.

"Run!" a man shouts as he rushes past.

"What's going on?" Joe tries to ask a woman sprinting at him.

"Help us!" she shouts. "Help me, please!" She falls to the ground, coughing, struggling to expel death from her lungs as more elementals rush around them to the beach. Joe reaches to help her up but is stopped short when he spots blood on her lips. Bronze tendrils of what looks like smoke emanate from her mouth. An acrid taste hits his tongue, and he drops the woman back to the ground in fright. She convulses twice before going still, her eyes blank as the smoke drifts into the air. Looking up, Joe sees a cloud of it parading from the surrounding forest, hunting for victims. He quickly covers his nose and mouth with his shirt as his throat begins to seize. Grabbing Matt's arm, Joe drags him back to the shore.

"What is that?" Matt asks in horror as more elementals race them to the beach, while others succumb to the onslaught. They pass a dozen bodies, bronze smoke issuing from their mouths. Joe tries not to look, but he notices one of the bodies is smaller than the rest, and he recognizes it as the child Jacob saved on the hilltop as Joe attacked Port Green. Chest constricting, Joe feels Matt pull him along. There's nothing they can do for her.

Looking up, Joe sees Captain Merrill has taken the longboat back to the *Moro* and is already shouting orders to shove off. Around him, pandemonium is exacerbated as the elementals realize their only hope of getting off island is slowly sailing away. Disbelief fills Joe from the thought that Captain Merrill would willingly leave all these people behind, people who clearly need his help.

"No! Come back! Jonathon!" Matt shouts are full of anguish. His voice turns hoarse as he curses the captain.

Coughing, Joe raises a hand to draw the ship back toward shore, but he's hit with a wall of weakness. Lungs on fire, he falls to his knees, trying to expel the gas that he feels filling his body. He scans the beach, seeing the thick bronze cloud envelop the woods and village, gently rolling downhill toward them. A few more feet and even the beach will be covered. Elementals all around him, his people, are falling to the ground in fits, coughing, convulsing, some succumbing and lying still. Matt is at his shoulder, trying to pull him up and to the water, as if that could help.

Abruptly, the bronze mass halts, as if hitting a wall. It condenses, rising higher into the air. The poison cloud collects just above the tree line, swirling against the invisible force surrounding it. Joe watches in amazement as the cloud slowly forms a giant bubble, encompassing both woods and sky. With Matt's help, he stands and sees Jacob straining to contain the cloud in an air bubble, preventing it from further encroaching on the beach. The village has already been drowned in the gas, but the beach still provides a modicum of safety. Joe stumbles to Jacob's side, Jordan already there.

"Where is Jonathon?" Jacob spits through gritted teeth. "I need him to open the earth so I can bury this thing."

"He's unavailable right now," Joe gasps.

A silent conversation passes between Jordan and Jacob. Jordan shakes his head, helpless.

"Get everyone you can onto that ship. Leave those who have fallen. Be quick about it." Jacob's arms shake from the effort of containing the poison cloud.

"The *Moro*," Joe begins but is interrupted by Matt grabbing his arm. "Look!" he shouts, pointing out to sea. The *Moro* stops and launches its remaining longboats, crew rowing as fast as they can to shore.

Jordan nods at Joe. "Let get going, then."

Quickly, Jordan, Joe, and Matt help as many elementals into the longboats as can fit, struggling to drag those unable to walk to safety. Joe fumbles in the sand under the weight of a fallen man. The man's eyes are closed, but Joe can see that he's breathing by the bits of gas wafting from his open mouth. Joe's chest constricts as he tries to hold his breath, lugging the man swiftly toward the longboats. Joe stumbles in the sand, sinking to one knee, before heaving the man further up his chest and plodding onto the waiting longboats.

Suddenly, Jacob is at Joe's side, face red and straining as he maintains the gas bubble above. "Leave him," he says through gritted teeth.

"But we can help him," Joe gasps.

"Leave him. It's too late for him anyway."

Joe glances at Jacob, then back at the man in his arms. The man's face is slack, and there is no sign of life save for the bronze gas emanating from his lips. Jacob gives him a stern look, and Joe regretfully drops the man back onto the sand. Instead, Joe grabs Jacob by the back of his jacket and hauls him to the longboats. They clumsily board, and sailors from the *Moro* hurriedly row them back to the ship.

The longboats are unloaded one by one, poisoned elementals dropped on deck and rolled out of the way to make room for more. Joe's boat is the last to be hauled up. He falls to the deck as he disembarks, looking around him in bewilderment. Elementals are scattered on the planks like fish caught in a net, some gasping for air, others lying still. Joe feels as if his lungs have shriveled and that every breath he draws is swallowing an ember. Over his shoulder, he sees Jacob at the railing, straining to keep the gas trapped in its bubble over Port Green, the veins on his neck ready to burst from the tension. Jordan kneels next to him, peering out at the island, struggling to breathe just like Joe.

"Captain!" Jacob yells. "Get us away from here, quick!"

But the *Moro* is already moving, and it isn't Captain Merrill at the helm. Instead, Joe spots Shorty barking orders, moving the ship out into deeper water and away from the cursed island. Joe pulls himself to his feet and staggers to the railing, intending to provide a little push to speed them on their way. He barely raises his hand before collapsing against the gunwale. Matt grabs Joe's elbow and helps him stand upright as he descends into a coughing fit.

"Easy, mate. I think you best let us humans take care of this one." Joe sags against Matt, who helps him slide down to the deck and leans him back on the railing.

"It doesn't affect you?" he huffs at Matt.

"Doesn't seem so. Shorty's got everything under control. We'll get into fresh air soon," Matt clasps Joe's shoulder reassuringly.

"We need to get as far away as possible, as soon as possible. I can only hold back the gas for a little longer," Jacob strains.

It seems to take forever, but the *Moro* makes its way out to sea, leaving Port Green a smaller and smaller patch of land behind them. Jacob's knees buckle, and he falls to the deck, releasing the air bubble and setting the gas free. He remains on his hands and knees, shaking uncontrollably from the effort.

"It's not over yet," Jacob whispers as he looks around at the elementals dying before him. With great effort, he lifts his head and calls down a whirlwind to the deck. The sails whip fiercely, and the masts groan from the onslaught. The vortex disperses the remaining poison that lingers, and when he finally sends it away, there is a collective intake of breath. Jacob sinks to the deck, exhausted.

27

Silence descends upon the *Moro* as she drifts further out to sea. Port Green bobs on the horizon behind them, the cloud of poison sinking among the ruined trees, beckoning with menacing fingers for its residents to return. Soon, Port Green sinks out of sight completely, as does Joe's last hope. He remembers the hanging just before his arrest, how Felix had a crazed look in his eye, and he wonders once more just how long the Magistrate had been experimenting on his people. How many elementals has the Magistrate killed trying to create this gas? The thought infuriates him.

Joe has never before thought of the elementals as his people, but helplessly watching as so many were cut down stirred something in him. So many innocent lives snuffed out in one fell swoop. And if the Magistrate could do that to Port Green, what's stopping him from unleashing the gas on Eastport? Has he already? But who is Joe to stop him? Should he even try? Every move he's made has ended in disaster. But what other choice does he have? He can't sit back and do nothing. Not like he did with Felix.

Around him, he sees maybe three dozen elementals passed out or sucking in clean air. The crew stands silently by, unsure if they should lend a hand or continue going about their duties as if nothing happened. Shorty remains at the helm, and Captain Merrill is nowhere in sight.

A heavy sigh startles Joe as Jacob collects himself before pushing unsteadily to his feet. Jacob looks at his people trembling on the deck and turns to Jordan, almost helpless and searching for guidance. Jordan hauls himself upright with the help of the railing and slowly stumbles toward his brother. Placing a hand on Jacob's shoulder, Jordan nods once, offering a reassuring smile.

"You did the best you could."

Jacob simply shakes his head, and Joe is startled to see tears in Jacob's eyes, magnified by his glasses.

"You're only one man. You can't save everyone," Jordan continues. Jacob closes his eyes and inhales deeply, holding his breath for a long minute before releasing. He straightens his back and turns to face the remaining elementals.

"Recover as best you can. We have to be prepared for the possibility of more attacks." Without waiting for a response or even acknowledgment, Jacob marches below deck. Jordan hastily follows, as do Joe and Matt, curious to see where Jacob may be going. Jacob rushes down the hallway, thrusting each door open as he goes.

The last door on the left bursts open, and Jacob stops, freezing for a moment in the doorway. Rushing past Jacob, Matt pushes to Jonathon's side in the sick bay. Jonathon's chest barely moves as he breathes shallowly. Matt places a hand on Jonathon's forehead, worry crinkling his face. If anything, Jonathon has gotten worse. He's on the verge of death, and Matt is running out of hope.

Joe stands behind Jacob in the doorway, feeling shattered for both his friend and his brother. With a grimace, Joe recognizes that his uncle has claimed yet one more life. From his spot on the ground next to Jonathon's cot, Matt leaps at Jacob with a sudden fury, causing both Joe and Jordan to flinch back.

"You have to help him!" Matt screams, face red with anger. "He's your brother, and he's dying. Fix him."

Jordan blanches, but Jacob slowly shakes his head.

"He made his choice," Jacob responds.

"You can't be serious!" Matt gets in Jacob's face and grabs his collar. "He's your brother. I know you must have a heart somewhere in that callous body of yours."

Quick as a viper, Jacob grabs Matt's wound and squeezes. Matt winces in pain, refusing to let go of his grip on Jacob's collar, but he eventually twists out of Jacob's hold, gasping. A tense silence fills the room, Jordan looking back and forth at Jacob and Matt, holding his breath with the hope that Jacob, for once in his life, lets this go.

Matt examines his arm, the wound reopened and bleeding freshly onto his previously stained jacket sleeve, and he launches a punch right at Jacob's face. It connects with Jacob's jaw and sends him stumbling into the doorframe, the orb falling out of his coat pocket and onto the floor, rolling to a stop at Matt's feet.

"You little piece of shit!" Jacob throws himself at Matt, but Jordan quickly latches onto Jacob, holding him back while Joe jumps in-between his eldest brother and Matt.

"You're a poor excuse for a brother. You don't deserve him," Matt spits, chest heaving.

Jacob thrusts his hand out, and a sudden burst of wind knocks everyone off their feet, the shelves of the sick bay rattling their wares. Jordan recovers first, surrounding Jacob with a ring of fire, separating him from Matt and Joe.

"Jacob. Leave." Jordan propels Jacob out of the door with his ring of fire before extinguishing the flame and following, closing the door behind him. As soon as the door slams shut, Joe rounds on Matt.

"What were you thinking? He could've killed you," Joe exclaims, heart pounding in his throat.

"Someone has to care about him, Joe!" Matt retorts as he bends down to pick something up from the floor.

Joe slumps. "I care about him too, Matt."

"Do you?" Matt's question pierces him. It's a question Joe can't answer. He wants to say yes, yet he hesitates. Does he really care about any of his brothers? Can he, after not knowing them for so long?

Matt sighs. "We'll figure out how to help him ourselves, okay?" He holds out his hand to reveal the orb.

Joe's eyes widen. "How did you get that?"

"It was just sitting here, on the floor. It's magic, right? It's the thing that Jacob's been after? And you're an elemental. Maybe it will show you what we need to do."

Joe shakes his head. "Maybe."

The door springs open, and Jordan steps back inside, wearing a defeated frown. Matt shoves the orb back into his pocket before Jordan can see.

Jordan holds out a hand, palm up, in a gesture of peace. "I'm sorry. For what happened just now."

Joe crosses his arms as Matt grunts.

"Look," Jordan scratches the back of his neck. "I know that Jacob can come off as an ass, but's he's under a lot of pressure."

"That's not an excuse," Matt fires back.

"I know," Jordan replies. He looks out the sick bay porthole at the stars gathering in the night sky. "I truly wish we could help. You may not believe it, but I want Jonathon to be okay."

Jordan sighs, torn between his two brothers. "Can I at least fix your arm for you?" he gestures to Matt.

Matt regards Jordan warily but gingerly removes his jacket and rolls up his sleeve. The wound is an angry red frown across his upper arm, blood oozing from the gash. In his hand, Jordan holds a small flame that encompasses his entire palm. He gently approaches Matt, who gives a tight nod, before wrapping his hand around the wound. Matt gasps and closes his eyes against the pain. Gripping his arm tightly for a minute more, Jordan finally lets go, leaving behind a burned palm imprint. The wound leaves an ugly cauterized line, but the bleeding has stopped.

"There. The handprint will disappear after a while, and your arm should feel better soon."

"Thanks," Matt says stiffly. Jordan gives them both a sad smile and quietly leaves the room.

28

ordan finds Jacob at the stern of the ship, sitting down against the railing while examining his arm. The rain has finally let up, and night has fallen. The *Moro's* sails are drawn, and the ship gently flows with the current. They have no destination, as far as Jordan is aware. He sighs and cranes his neck back to look at the stars peaking their heads into the blackening sky. Behind him, the *Moro's* crew bustles about, lighting lanterns, coiling rope, trying to stay busy and avoid looking at the group of huddled elementals still gathered in the middle of the deck. The elementals cling to each other, eyes darting nervously about at the crew, a few coughs sounding here and there.

So many lost. Jordan can still feel a tickle in the back of his throat from the gas. A hundred souls, decimated to less than half that size. He wants his people to feel safe, but at this point, he's not sure that's a feeling they will ever have again. They've been run out of their home; where are they supposed to go now? Jordan knows that the group will be waiting for Jacob to make a decision, to guide them. He's counting on his brother to do that as well, once Jacob calms down.

He raises an eyebrow as he approaches Jacob, who is poking at his left arm.

"What's going on?"

Jacob flicks his eyes up at his brother, before resuming his investigation, prodding at the skin of his forearm. In the growing dark, Jordan can't see what he's looking at, so he fires up his palm and crouches to hold the flame close.

There's a deep slash on Jacob's forearm, the skin surrounding it dry and cracked like the deserts of the Wastes. An angry red webbing snakes up Jacob's forearm to his elbow, emanating from the cut.

"What is that?"

"That Warden cut me with a knife," Jacob grunts.

"Warden? What Warden? And I've never seen a knife wound do that before."

"At least my arm's no longer numb. Do you think you can fix it?" Jacob holds his arm out to Jordan.

Jordan whistles low. "I don't even know what it is. Was the blade poisoned or something? Again, what Warden?"

Jacob frowns and bows his chin to his chest. "The one I got the orb off of. I think this is that gwarem stuff Joe mentioned at the town hall," he admits. "He said that Uncle had weapons that could inhibit our power. I think the poison gas was made from it too."

"You got the orb?" This whole mission, all they've worked for, could finally come to fruition. If what Jacob says is true, maybe they can stop fighting now. "If you have the orb, then Uncle can't get to us. We can just leave. Start over someplace new."

"We're not leaving," Jacob says aggressively. "I've worked too hard for this." A crazed look paints his face as he starts rambling. "We can't go back to Port Green, not with the gas still there. We'll take this ship closer to Eastport and launch an attack from the ship. I don't know the range of the orb...maybe I can ask Joseph. Once we take out Uncle's Wardens, I'll go up to the castle and kill Uncle myself. I'm not like him. I won't fight my battles cowering behind others." His cold stare challenges Jordan.

"Jacob, look around us," Jordan gestures to the small group of scared elementals down on the main deck. "There's nothing left. Is claiming the throne and ruling a kingdom of people who might not want you as king really worth losing the only people we have left? You are their leader. Lead them to something better. They deserve that much."

"I've worked too hard for this," Jacob reiterates. "Mother and Father are both dead because of him. My birthright, my legacy, was destroyed because of him. I have a right to that throne. It's mine, and I will take it back. And once I do, I'll make Eastport the vision of peace Mother and Father always hoped it could be. I have to do this. I have to do this for them, so their deaths were not in vain." Jacob's words drip with bitterness.

"Do you really think killing our uncle is what Mother would have wanted?" Jordan asks softly. Silence descends upon the pair, thick as the humid night falling about them.

"Can you fix this or not?" Jacob huffs as he thrusts his arm into Jordan's face.

Jordan brings his flame back around to examine the cut, swallowing down his frustration. "I've never seen a wound do this before. I'd have to see what medicines they have in the sick bay and experiment some."

Jacob pulls down his shirt sleeve and pushes himself upright. "Never mind. It'll be fine. Come on," he motions Jordan to follow him. "If our uncle wants a fight, then he's getting one." Jacob strides across the deck to the grouped elementals, the planks echoing under his boots. Crew members scurry out of his way like rabbits fleeing into a bush. Jordan simply shakes his head and follows.

The elementals raise their heads as Jacob stops before them, their eyes full of hope. Here is their leader, who's seen them through the worst storms, who's reveled in their successes. Jacob, who watched them build up Port Green from an uninhabitable island to a semi-autonomous village. They've been dealt a great blow, but now their leader is here to guide them to safety and maybe, finally, to peace.

The lanterns throw menacing shadows on Jacob's face, causing more than one elemental to shrink away. Hiding his injured arm behind his back, Jacob gathers himself up to his full height and addresses those assembled before him.

"Take what rest you can. In the morning, we attack Eastport." There is no preamble, no lead-up to this decision. Jacob studies the faces of his people, sees the exhaustion, the fear, but he knows this is the only way to achieve peace.

"Jacob," Tula implores, hugging two children to her side, "look around you. We are in no shape to fight. So many of us have been lost already. Half of those who remain are old, injured, or children. You don't have many fighters left. Are you to sacrifice them by starting a war we cannot win?"

Several elementals nod their heads in agreement. Jacob notices the crew of the *Moro* inching closer, curious as to what he will do next. The problem is, he knows Tula is right. They have maybe twenty good fighters left, many of whom are still recovering from the gas attack, coughing to clear their lungs of the poison. But Jacob can't back down from his goal. He vowed to protect his people from harm, and he promised himself to reclaim the throne from his uncle. He knows his uncle will stop at nothing to kill every last elemental he can find, and Jacob's group is the easiest to start with, since they are small and weakened. Magistrate Rufus can experiment and enhance his weapons in a trial run against these refugees before he takes the fight to the elementals of the Mersae Mountains. And if his own people weren't the guinea pigs, Jacob might have let his uncle wage such a war with Andulsae. Serves them right for not sending help.

"I know you are tired, and hurt, and broken." Jacob takes a deep breath, making eye contact with as many elementals as he can. "But we have suffered long enough. This last attack just proves that the Magistrate will never stop trying to kill us. If we settle somewhere else, he will find us. We cannot stand by and wait for the next attack. We must take the fight to him. Hit him before he hits us again."

No one responds; the only sound is the lapping of the water against the *Moro's* hull. Jacob feels his hope slip away but betrays no emotion. If they won't help, he will do this himself.

"Can you guarantee that we will win? Or will you lead us all to our deaths?" The gravelly voice comes from a bearded elemental in front. He had to leave his sister, who succumbed to the gas on the beach in Port Green.

"I can guarantee that we have the advantage this time. The Magistrate won't catch us unprepared. I now have the orb." Jacob surreptitiously reaches into his jacket pocket, but his fingers close on nothing but air. Face still as stone, he furiously thinks back to all that's happened in the past few hours, trying to remember where he might have lost the orb. It was in his pocket during the gas attack, and now it's not. It must be on the ship somewhere. Jacob's fingers curl into a fist in his pocket.

A murmur rushes through the elementals. The orb has been the object of their leader's desire for years now. If he truly has it, maybe this wouldn't be a suicide mission.

"If you have it, then show it to us," the bearded elemental demands.

"When the time is right," Jacob retorts. "For now, rest and prepare yourselves. I'm going to see to it that our course is set. In the morning, we attack with everything we've got."

24

An hour since Jordan left the sick bay, Joe is at a standstill with Matt, not wanting to touch the orb again after his past experiences with it. Tired of Joe's hesitance, Matt shoves Joe toward the cot and pushes the orb into his hands. Joe cringes at the unbottled hope in Matt's eyes. Matt stares at him like an innocent child, expectant, as if Joe now holds all the answers. Joe almost drops the orb and runs out, not wanting the responsibility of having to put Matt back together when the orb doesn't work. Because, deep down, Joe doesn't believe the orb will work. He's only ever seen it be used to view and attack faraway places; why would it have the power to heal? But Matt is so insistent that Joe finally gives in.

They huddle over the orb, Jonathon still as a corpse on the cot, condition unchanged. Joe would much rather be back in Eastport, relaxing in his home on leave. There, with Ian and Matilde, he could have a few minutes of calm and normalcy to sort all this out.

He pinches himself. No use in wasting energy wishing for things that can never be. He's done very well so far to avoid thinking about how he'll never see his parents again. He doesn't need to break that streak now.

The door flies open as Nell shuffles in, breathless.

"Matt! There you are. Jacob's planning something with the elementals. The captain locked himself in his cabin, and Jacob's been pounding on his door, threatening to blow it down if the captain doesn't come out and change course back to Eastport. We need everyone up on deck, now!"

"We're busy here, Nell." Matt shoos her away with a flick of his wrist, intent on the task at hand.

Nell stops, noticing the tension in the sick bay and the orb in Joe's hand. "What is that?" She points at the orb, shutting the door behind her and approaching the cot. "Matt, nothing's worked so far. I don't think you should put all your hope into this thing." She places a gentle hand on Matt's shoulder, but he violently shakes her off.

"It's the last chance we've got," he growls, not meeting her eyes. Instead, he turns to Joe. "How did it work, when you were with the Magistrate?" Matt grabs the orb from Joe and thrusts it under his nose.

"When I was arrested and made into a weapon, you mean?" Joe glances at Nell, but she studiously stares at the planking below.

"Bigger picture, Joe."

Joe glares at Matt and sighs. Some fights just aren't worth it. "I don't know," he pushes his hair from his forehead. "He told it what he wanted to see, then I was able to work through it. He did prick my finger before and dripped some of my blood onto it though. He called it imprinting?" Joe shrugs.

"That's it? Just give it some blood, and talk to it?" Matt holds the orb up to the light of a lantern set into the wall.

"I guess?" Joe shrugs again and leans back against the cabinet, eyeing Matt warily. Matt's becoming a little manic. Joe's never seen him this invested in anything before, and his intensity is starting to unnerve him.

"Here," Matt shoves the orb back at Joe and grabs his wrist. Matt pulls his knife from his boot, and before either Joe or Nell can react, Matt slashes Joe's fingertip and smears the blood across the orb. "Ask it for a cure," he demands Joe.

"Ow, geez, Matt." Joe sucks on his finger to quell the bleeding.

"Just ask it!"

Sighing, Joe straightens and cups the orb in his hand. The orb expands to fill his palms. Feeling a little silly, he concentrates hard on the orb, as if it were water and he could control it. There's a slight tugging in his gut, his power rising in anticipation. Quickly, before he loses the feeling, he poses a query to the orb.

"Show us the cure for Ink. Show us how to make Jonathon better," he says to it, just like he saw the Magistrate do.

The orb pulses twice and begins to glow. Joe and Matt hover over it, eager. Nell, unable to hide her curiosity, edges closer. The orb brightens like a sun, becoming so hot that Joe almost drops it. He juggles it between his hands, trying not to get burned. Then, just as quickly as it began, the orb cools and dims, turning back into a small, hard marble.

All three stare at the orb, waiting for the answer, but nothing happens. Joe shakes it, as if to bring it back to life, but the orb stays silent.

"Damn it!" Matt snatches the orb. "Why won't you work?" he yells at it. He kneels before Jonathon, snot running from his nose, and places the orb on Jonathon's chest. Grabbing his knife once more, he pricks his own finger and drips a few drops of bright red blood onto the orb.

"Please," he pleads with the object. "I need you to heal him." Tears flow down his cheeks as he stares at the orb, imploring it to show them something, anything. Just like before, the orb pulses twice and begins to glow. Except this time, the orb expands to the width of Jonathon's chest, and the glow extends downward into his skin, tracing the black veins blue. Startled, Matt falls back, crashing into Nell's legs as she stands behind him.

"Joe! What's happening?" Matt asks, bewildered.

"I don't know," Joe hesitantly replies. All three crowd around the cot, watching in awe as the pulsing light from the orb wraps itself throughout Jonathon's body, like streams filling with water after a heavy rain, erasing the poison. They all scuttle back as Jonathon gives a violent arch, his back almost bending in two as he lifts off the cot, the orb glued to his chest. The orb flares like a dying star, then extinguishes, Jonathon's body drifting gently back down as the orb rolls off his chest and onto the floor, just a small, cold marble once more.

Matt gingerly inches forward and places a hand against Jonathon's cheek.

"Jonathon? Can you hear me?"

A rattle emanates from Jonathon's lungs, followed by a grating cough. His chest starts expanding like a bellows, and his eyes fly open. They zoom around the room, trying to understand what he's seeing, when they land on Matt, inches from his own face. Jonathon gives a tired smile, the cloud finally lifted from his mind.

"Have I been sleeping?" Jonathon's voice is hoarse, as if from screaming. A sob escapes Matt, overjoyed to see that Jonathon is not only alive, but that his eyes have returned to their normal shade of brilliant blue.

Jonathon looks from Matt to Joe to Nell. He feels lighter somehow, and a little empty. "Everything tingles," he tells the room.

Nell, ever-pragmatic, crosses to the cabinet and pulls out a bottle of Murky Bottom. "That's the withdrawal. Here," she thrusts the bottle at him. "A bit of this will help."

"What happened?" Jonathon tries to sit up but is too groggy to do it on his own. Matt helps him up and surrounds him with a hug.

"Nothing you need to worry about," he says into Jonathon's neck. "The important thing is that you're safe now."

30

Tiptoeing upstairs to the deck, Joe silently walks to the bow railing and breathes in the night air. It hangs humid and limp like a wet shroud about his shoulders. Reaching into his pocket, he closes his fingers around the orb. He's a little perturbed that the orb didn't work for him, instead seemingly working for Matt. He's more surprised that the orb worked at all, as he didn't see how anything was going to make Jonathon better. Turning, he leans back on his elbows and winces as he bumps his cut finger. He and Matt both bandaged their fingers with supplies from the sick bay after Jonathon woke up, but for such a small cut, it still stings.

Joe shakes off the pain and examines the deck. The elementals are still gathered in the middle, but someone has given them blankets, and many are now sleeping. Nell said that Captain Merrill had locked himself in his cabin and that Jacob was trying to break in, yet all seems quiet topside.

Scanning, Joe notices that none of the crew is present, only the elementals. Straining a little harder in the dim lantern light, he spies Jacob at the helm on the quarter deck, Jordan hovering near-by. Joe frowns. What is Jacob doing there, and where is the rest of the crew? The longboats are all accounted for. He straightens and begins to head to Captain Merrill's cabin when an angry shadow jumps out before him.

"So, what now?" Nell's cross glare slides into his field of view.

"I thought you weren't talking to me," Joe counters.

Nell crosses her arms, her eyes never leaving his face.

"I'm not."

"Nell, I'm sorry about what happened to your father, but you can't keep blaming me for that. I didn't kill him, and not all elementals are the same."

"Is that why you attacked Port Green? Or are you just a junkie like the other one?"

Joe's shoulders slump. It's no use fighting this. Nell has made up her mind about him, and all those years together aboard the *Moro* can't erase her hatred of elementals. Of him. He looks up, trying to think of something to say to her, and is surprised to see a silver sheen of tears tracing her cheeks.

"I trusted you," she spits, making no attempt to wipe away her tears. "I even liked you. But now? Now I don't know what to think. Who are you, Joe?" she implores him. "What other secrets are you hiding? How can I ever trust you again?"

She finally turns away, hugging herself. For the first time since he's known her, Nell looks frail, like a dead sand dollar. He reaches out, intending to lay a comforting hand on her shoulder, but stops short. They aren't friends anymore. Nell has made that perfectly clear. His heart plummets to see her so broken.

"I'm sorry," he whispers and immediately regrets because sorry is so inadequate. He shuffles his feet on the deck, watching the woodgrain dance with the swaying of the ship in the lantern light, hoping Nell will say something, but also hoping she doesn't. If this is the last conversation they will ever have, he doesn't want to add more. He already hurts enough.

"Just don't." She shoves past him, leaving him alone under the stars.

*   *   *   *

"Why did you stay with me?" Jonathon hesitantly asks, shifting on the cot as he tries to alleviate the pain in his bad knee. His body aches something fierce, but his mind is free from its haze. Matt explained that the orb had somehow healed him, had drawn out the poison, but Jonathon fears it has taken something else with it. He has his suspicions about the empty lightness that consumes him now, leaving him hollow.

"I couldn't leave you," Matt replies.

Jonathon shakes his head. "But why?" he repeats, unsure he wants to hear the answer. It would be a mistake for Matt to fall in love with him, and an even bigger mistake for Jonathon to fall right back. He doesn't have the best track record for keeping those he loves safe from harm.

Matt stares at him imploringly. He shakes his head and gives a sad smile. "I think you know why."

A blush begins to creep up Jonathon's neck as warmth fills his chest. Maybe he should let Matt in. Maybe he won't get hurt this time.

"Can I tell you something?" Jonathon scooches to the edge of the cot and stares at the floor. Matt sits down next to him and envelopes him in a blanket.

"Sure, I guess."

Taking a deep breath, Jonathon clasps his hands together between his knees.

"I was there when my mother was killed. I saw my uncle do it."

Matt stills. "Magistrate Rufus killed Queen Valencia?"

Jonathon tries to meet Matt's gaze, but he can't. A slight tremor begins to creep up his core. "I tried to tell my father. I just wasn't fast enough." A soggy hiccup bursts from his throat, and the words begin pouring out like melted wax.

"Father was trying to make sense of what happened. I never had a chance to tell him that first day. And every time I passed my uncle, he'd give me a look. He knew I saw. I was scared. I went to the dungeon. It was my safe place then, quiet and empty. But Uncle Rufus found me. He cornered me and told me not to scream."

The tremor consumes Jonathon's entire body now, until he is shaking like a tree in a windstorm. "I tried to get away, but I was just so scared. He followed me around everywhere after that, him, and the Head Chemist, Gregor. I knew they would hurt me again if I said anything. Seven years after The Expunging, I tried to tell Jacob. Tried to make him understand, but he wouldn't listen. He couldn't see past the fact that I never told our father."

Wiping his face, Jonathon recedes into himself, trying to disappear. "I never meant for any of this to happen," he whispers.

Matt gently places a hand on his shoulder. "It's okay. You're safe now."

"I'm a failure."

Matt wraps his arms around Jonathon as he collapses into Matt's chest, softly crying. "You're safe now," Matt repeats. "You're safe. And you're not a failure. You're one of the bravest people I've ever met."

"My power's gone."

Matt gapes at Jonathon. Surely that's not possible. Elementals are born with their power. It can't just disappear. Jonathon just recovered from an intense ordeal, Matt reminds himself. Once he's had some proper rest, he'll see that he's the same as he was before, powers and all. But Matt doesn't say this, feeling deep down that somehow it would be a false statement. What if Jonathon is right?

Standing, Matt walks over to the cabinet and pulls out the skeleton key.

"Here," he holds out the stone key to Jonathon. "Try turning this back into a pestle."

Jonathon shakes his head. "It's not going to work."

"Humor me."

Sighing, Jonathon reaches out from the cocoon of his blanket and grabs the skeleton key from Matt. He prods at the teeth with his finger, willing the key to reform back into a pestle. But the usual tingle in his gut is missing. Instead of the quiver of anticipation at using his powers, Jonathon feels nothing but emptiness. There's no connection between him and the stone in his hand. Resigned, he gives the skeleton key back to Matt.

"Told you," says Jonathon dejectedly. Matt replaces the key in the cabinet and returns to the cot. He surrounds Jonathon in a hug once more.

"It'll be okay. We'll figure it out together," he murmurs into Jonathon's hair.

Matt pulls Jonathon in tighter, wishing he could do more to ease his pain, wishing he could make Jonathon understand how much he cares for him, to let him know that he no longer has to go through anything alone. For now, though, Matt cradles Jonathon close, and waits for the tremors to stop.

31

J oe climbs up to the quarter deck above Captain Merrill's cabin to where Jacob is stationed at the helm. His oldest brother doesn't acknowledge Joe as he approaches, instead staring stonily out to sea. Jordan raises a hand in greeting, though.

"What's going on? Where're all the crew?" Joe dives right into it.

Jordan looks over at Jacob, waiting for him to reply. When he doesn't, Jordan sighs and runs a hand through his hair.

"We're heading back to Eastport. Jacob tried discussing it with Captain Merrill, but the captain refused to hold an audience. The crew all went below deck, to the galley? The hold? I'm not sure. Basically, if Merrill wasn't going to listen to Jacob, they weren't either. So, I guess we hijacked the ship?"

Joe stands there, mouth agape, trying to wrap his mind around what Jordan just said.

"You just took over the *Moro*? And none of the crew tried to stop you? Captain Merrill just let you? Why are we going back to Eastport? Isn't that a place you should avoid?"

The *Moro* creaks as if in agreement. Joe notices that the sails above are still furled.

"Do you even know how to steer a ship? Who's pushing us along?"

Jacob spares him the briefest of glances, the lantern light glinting off his glasses.

"We have a few hydromentals at the stern propelling us westward to Eastport. And I've led a village. Steering a ship is not a problem."

Joe rolls his eyes. Spinning around, he finally spots three hydromentals at the back of the quarterdeck, hands held out over the water, speeding them along. With the one lone lantern, it is hard to pick them out, but, from what he can tell, the hydromentals don't appear as eager to be heading back to Eastport as Jacob is. Not that Joe would call Jacob eager, exactly, more like determined. These hyrdromentals, however, seem resigned to forces beyond their control.

Jacob notices Joe watching. "You could join us."

"Join you in what?"

"We're taking the fight to Magistrate Rufus," Jacob replies grimly. "We're going to strike at dawn, use the orb to take them by surprise and ensure that once and for all Uncle is stopped. I'll reclaim the throne and bring Eastport back into prosperity."

"You just lost half of your people. Those who remain aren't up for another fight," Joe says, flabbergasted. "Why would you do this to them? You can't possibly think you can win."

"This is the plan, Joseph. You're either with me or against me." And for Jacob it's as simple as that. This is the course he has plotted, and he will not deviate now.

Joe looks to Jordan, who just shrugs. "You can't be serious. This is a suicide mission. Magistrate Rufus and his Wardens have gwarem. They might have more of that gas. Jacob, think first." Swallowing, Joe backs up a step. Jacob doesn't have the orb; he does. Jacob's going to attack Eastport betting on that orb. He's going to attack Eastport, with all of its innocent people, people who are not part of this war on elementals. And what happens when Jacob discovers the orb missing?

"We have a plan, Joe," Jordan reassures him. "With the orb, we can attack from a distance, like you did when you attacked Port Green. Our people will be safe, and once we've taken down the Wardens, we can march to the castle to claim the throne."

Joe simply nods. "I'm going to check on Jonathon," he says, backing away.

Jordan perks up at Jonathon's name. "How's he doing? Does he seem to be getting any better?"

"Uh-huh," Joe hurriedly offers as he heads down the stairs and knocks rapidly on Captain Merrill's door. There's no response. Joe knocks again, furtively glancing over his shoulder as he quietly calls out: "Captain, it's me. Joe."

A grunt issues from inside, followed by the sounds of a chair scrapping against the floor and quick footsteps approaching. The door swings open wildly as Captain Merrill pulls Joe inside, looking to the left and the right of his door as he closes it. Captain Merrill immediately slides the deadbolt home and shuffles back to his desk. The cabin is dark, no lantern illuminating the space. The only light is that from the stars in the night sky outside the porthole. Joe steps forward and almost yelps as his foot comes down on something squishy. Hesitantly reaching for the object, he sighs in relief to discover it's just the wool blanket from Captain Merrill's bed. Joe tosses it aside and slowly approaches the captain's desk, picking up the overturned armless chair and sitting down.

Captain Merrill stares intently down at a mess of charts spread out on his desk, absently fiddling with the sleeve of his missing hand. The captain's nose is almost touching the charts, bent over to see in the dim light. He's muttering to himself, nonsense words that Joe can barely make out. "Lunatic" and "escape" are two that he hears over and over.

Joe clears his throat. Captain Merrill startles, noticing Joe before him.

"Captain?" Joe prods.

"That lunatic has ahold of my ship. Sailing back to Eastport. With furled sails! They just move us along with but a hand over the water! Not natural. Need to get away before the navy finds us and arrests us and takes more than hands." Captain Merrill's eyes frantically run over the charts once more.

"Captain?" Joe tries again, wary of the crazed look on Captain Merrill's face.

"He's going to attack Eastport, with wind and fire and floods and quakes. None of us will be safe." Captain Merrill lunges across the desk and grabs Joe's shirtfront. "Joe! My family's there! What about my family? How do I get them and escape?" The captain continues to mutter to himself as he releases Joe and returns to the charts on his desk.

Captain Merrill rubs his stubbly chin in agitation. Joe stares at the empty space where Merrill's hand should have been and hangs his head. The ocean is near motionless outside the cabin's porthole, as if waiting to exhale. It stirs up a strange sense of exciting antici-pation and dread in the muggy night air. Closing his eyes, Joe tries to find the peace that nights like this used to bring him, when he felt limitless and the world was full of possibilities. Now, he opens his eyes, and all he sees is his one-handed captain in a messed-up situation that he helped put in motion.

"We need to escape, quickly," Captain Merrill says again.

"Captain, we need to rally the crew and change course. We can't head to Eastport. The Magistrate is looking for you since you didn't dock in Lexington, not your family. They will be safe." Joe swallows down the lump in his throat as he says this, knowing that none of the crew's families are safe since Magistrate Rufus has marked them as criminals.

"No, no, we head to Eastport. We never checked in at Lexing-ton, so as soon as the Wardens see us, they'll be coming. Yes, that's good. That's good." Captain Merrill picks up a quill and scratches something on the map in front of him. "My family, Joe!" he exclaims, causing Joe to jump. "Yes, we'll dock while it's still dark, before sunrise. The crew can disembark before the Wardens come. I'll get my family and escape all of this, go to Lexington, perhaps further south. They won't find us here on the *Moro*."

"But Captain, what about the elementals? If they're still ship-board when the Wardens come—"

The captain looks up from his mutterings and gives Joe an unfathomable stare. "They can fend for themselves." Captain Mer-rill turns back to his maps without another word.

*   *   *   *

Captain Merrill looks up and finds himself alone in his cabin as the *Moro* races toward Eastport, that elemental at the helm. He knows that this will be the end of his seafaring career. He can't find it in his heart to continue.

Once they get to Eastport, he's rushing straight to his wife and daughter and hustling them away to anywhere else. He'll have to think of some lie to explain it all, plus his lack of a right hand. Twenty years of this life, twenty years on this ship, the ship he bought and crewed and sailed, and he never expected it to end like this.

He falls back into his chair, leans his head in his remaining hand, and cries.

32

After his conversation with Captain Merrill, Joe hurries down to the sick bay, tripping in his haste. He hopes that Matt and Jonathon are still there. Jacob's going to realize soon enough that the orb is missing, and they need to be long gone when he does. Throwing open the door, Joe is relieved to see that not only are Matt and Jonathon still there, but Nell is there also, mixing up some concoction from the cabinet for Jonathon to regain his strength. Joe shuts the door and motions for them to be quiet.

"Jacob's heading for Eastport. He's going to attack the city through the orb. We need to get out of here."

"But Jacob doesn't have the orb. You do," Matt says, confused.

"Shh!" Jonathon whispers. "Don't say that too loudly. Jacob might hear you." Jonathon glances nervously at the ceiling above them.

"That's why we need to leave. Before Jacob finds out that he doesn't have the orb. If we're sneaky enough, we can launch a longboat and be well on our way before he notices. Jonathon, can you tell how far from shore we are?"

Jonathon grimaces and worries the edge of the blanket about his shoulders. "Well—"

"Why do you care if Jacob attacks Eastport?" Nell interrupts.

"Because, Nell," Joe replies, exasperated. "The people in Eastport are innocent just like the people in Port Green. Jacob isn't going to care who gets caught in the crossfire, so let's ensure there won't be any crossfire. He doesn't have enough elementals who are well enough to launch a full-on battle. That's why he wants to use the orb and attack from the safety of the *Moro*. If we take that away from him, he won't attack. He won't endanger his people's lives anymore."

Matt nods. "I do think it would be better if Jacob didn't attack Eastport. I've seen enough death these past few days to last me a lifetime."

"And why do you think we'll help you?" Nell crosses her arms as she leans back against the cabinet.

"Well, I thought, you know," Joe stumbles. "We all helped heal Jonathon, and we're friends, and I care about you guys." Joe stuffs his hands into his pockets. Why is Nell making such a big deal about this? Jacob's going to attack Eastport with the orb. Joe would've thought that Nell would jump at the opportunity to prevent that.

"Nell," Matt starts calmly. "Eastport's our home. As Joe said, there are innocent people there. They should at least get the chance that your father didn't."

There's a shushing sound as Jonathon shifts on the straw mattress. Joe tries to look at anything else but Nell, instead focusing on a slim case resting on the bed next to Jonathon. Matt holds Nell's stare though, unafraid of any wrath she might unleash. Nell just slumps against the cabinet, hugging her arms close to her sides.

"I hate when you make good points."

"I know," Matt smiles.

"Fine." Nell straightens and addresses Jonathon. "How about you? Can you walk?"

Just then, the sick bay door slams open, causing all four of them to jump.

"Give me the orb!" Jacob yells at Joe, a gale of wind accompanying him as he thunders into the small room. Jacob grabs Joe by the collar and pins him against the worktable.

"Jacob, enough!" Jordan pulls him away in a bear hug as Jacob sends bottles, bandages, and medical instruments flying about the cabin.

"I said enough!" Flames burst up and down Jordan's arms, singeing Jacob's jacket and eliciting a small yelp from his older brother. The wind stops, and Jacob stills. Jordan extinguishes the flames as he lets go.

"Sit," he commands Jacob, who begrudgingly sits on the cot opposite of Jonathon. Jonathon huddles on his own cot under a blanket. Joe slides down the worktable to a crouch, rubbing his neck.

"What the hell?" he shouts at Jacob.

"You have the orb! You stole it from me!"

"What? I have no idea what you're talking about," Joe feigns innocence.

"I heard you talking with Merrill. And I heard you talking down here about how you plan to keep the orb from me. I would not advise that," Jacob menaces.

"I'm not going to let you use it to attack Eastport." Joe slowly stands from his spot on the floor, making eye contact with Matt and then flicking his eyes to the door, hoping he understands. Matt gives the smallest nod, tightening his grip on Jonathon's hand as he tries to get Nell's attention.

Jacob's eyes narrow to slits. "That orb is our only chance of defeating the Magistrate and putting an end to elemental persecution." He then grimaces, as if swallowing a ball of nails. "It's the only way to ensure our victory in our current state."

"Jacob, I can't let you have the orb. I can't let you attack Eastport. It's my home." Joe takes a step toward the door, where Jordan, arms smoldering like wasted coal, is blocking the exit. Nell inches toward Jonathon and grabs his upper arm while Matt tenses on the cot, ready to spring.

Jacob notices the movement and raises his hand to send a gust of wind through the tiny room. But just at that moment, a loud screech, as if from a flock of invading seagulls, resounds throughout the cabin, followed by an even louder crunch of impact. Nell crashes into Jonathon, knocking both him and Matt to the floor. Joe falls to his knees while Jordan is thrown into the hallway and lands on his back. Jacob is tossed from the cot into the wall.

Joe recovers quickly and seizes the moment, springing up from the floor.

"Come on!" he shouts to Jonathon and Matt as he pulls Nell up, dragging her to the door.

"Jordan!" Jacob shouts from the cot, trying to untangle himself from a blanket. Still on his back in the hallway, Jordan sends up a wall of flame, blocking the sick bay's only exit. Joe and Nell rear back from the heat, bumping into Matt and a wobbly Jonathon. Without thinking, Joe swings back to the porthole and summons a column of water, shooting it directly at the flames barricading the door, extinguishing them and raising a cloud of steam. He then guides another geyser of water at Jordan, slamming him back down onto the planks of the hallway, leaving no inch of him dry.

Joe grabs Nell once more and hops over Jordan in a dash for the stairs. Matt and Jonathon stumble out close behind. Matt stops just outside the sick bay.

"What are you doing? We have to go!" Jonathon exclaims.

Matt pulls the sick bay door shut on an irate Jacob and wedges the slim case of Ink paraphernalia under the door.

"It will hold for a little bit!" Matt explains, slinging Jonathon's arm around his shoulders as they hobble-run up the stairs to the deck.

"Here!" Nell waves the boys over to where Joe is lowering the gangplank. Matt hurries Jonathon across the dark deck and past the startled elementals hiding under blankets. Upon reaching the railing, Matt sees that the *Moro* rammed into a wharf at the Eastport harbor. The figurehead of Captain Merrill's wife took the brunt of the damage, her wooden left arm breaking off and her face split in two. Peering over the railing, Matt can see a long gash in the hull where the *Moro* scraped against the pylons of the dock.

Joe finishes setting the gangplank, and the four race across it to the dock. Lamplight surrounds them as they follow Joe into the shadows of the wharf. The group arrives at the fish market, ducking down behind the stalls. Pausing a moment to catch his breath, Joe peers over the table of the oyster seller's stall to see if Jacob is following. Hearing wheezing behind him, he turns to see Jonathon leaning heavily on Matt, panting while standing on one leg. Joe shares a concerned look with Nell, wondering how they will be able to move fast enough to evade Jacob.

A clamor sounds from the *Moro* as Jacob and a still-soaking-wet Jordan burst onto the deck. There are no other options. Joe knows they need to move while they still have a slight lead on Jacob. He grabs Nell's hand and urges her, Jonathon, and Matt forward through the remaining stalls toward the business district, just as vendors are beginning to haul in their wares to the market.

33

The pre-dawn gray dances above Eastport in a waltz with the slowly vanishing stars. The lamplighters still have thirty minutes before true dawn and needing to snuff out the lamps strewn about the city. A pair of sailors stumble, happy and drunk, out of the Siren Club and head back to their berth in the harbor. The smell of the just-opening fish market competes with the delightful scents from the bakery, cod mixing with cinnamon buns. The pair swerve into one another, laughing as they lurch down to the docks. The staccato clacking of boot heels greets them, interrupting their gaiety. Not wanting to be reprimanded for public intoxication, the sailors scurry off into the shadows of the nearby buildings as a patrol of Wardens pass by.

Clinging to each other, the pair of sailors sees the Wardens march in formation, two columns of six, their bronze-colored cloaks gliding behind them and bronze-colored breastplates glinting in the starlight. Each one now carries either a rifle or a crossbow, added measures the Magistrate instated once only three Wardens of his contingent sent to Port Green came back. They are grim-faced and silent as they make their rounds, ever vigilant for suspicious activity.

The two sailors slink deeper into the shadows, turning down an alley and skirting behind buildings as they make their way to the docks, wishing to avoid any more patrols. Coming out of the alley, they run into an obelisk, the etching of the Magistrate's face stern as ever. The two men recoil, the shadows from the fading dark making the obelisk loom even taller over them. Shivering, they rush on, eager to be back on their ship.

A breeze rises up from the ocean, cooling their tired bodies. The sailors sigh at the welcome intrusion but look curiously about them as the breeze swiftly becomes a gust. It picks up discarded newspapers and leaf litter, tossing the refuse about the stone buildings nearby. The sailors struggle to move forward against the wind, which only increases in intensity with each step.

In addition to the wind, a dull, thundering echo charges at the pair. The sailors stop in the middle of the street, straining against the glare of the streetlamp to see what's causing such noise. Squinting, they can make out four bodies running in their direction, a vortex at their backs.

*   *   *   *

"Come on, he's gaining on us!" Joe pants.

They have run about three blocks inland but are moving too slowly. A sleepy lamplighter jumps out of the way as Nell bursts past, Jonathon and Matt tottering along behind. Joe chances a look back to see Jacob, in the middle of a windstorm, quickly bearing down on them. Focusing on his irate older brother, Joe almost bowls over the confused lamplighter. Mumbling an apology, Joe glances behind him once more then pushes himself faster up the cobblestone street. A cloud of newspaper, pastry wrappers, and dirt envelops Jacob as he draws nearer.

With how fast he's moving, Jacob will be on the group in a matter of minutes. Joe frantically searches for a way to slow him down as they run to the city square. The small fork of the Plebeum River is to his right. Joe throws out his arm and calls forth a jet of water, directing it backward toward Jacob's vortex. With dismay, he sees Jacob snatch the water up and spin it away into the gutter.

In front of him, Joe spies Jonathon urging Matt down an alley that connects to a residential area.

"No, stay in the business district! Away from people's houses!" Nell barks at them.

Smart. Bringing Jacob's wrath down on sleeping citizens is not the outcome Joe wants. They race past the bookstore, the wine makers, and the clothiers, getting closer with each step to the city square. Joe can feel Jacob's wind tugging at his jacket, reaching to pull him down. They need to go faster, but Jonathon is already limping worse than he was on the *Moro*. As they pass the inn, Joe double-takes as he spots the innkeeper throwing a bevy of chamber pots into the gutter. Immediately, Joe reaches out his hand and directs all the wastewater straight at Jacob, not caring that the innkeeper will see him.

The wastewater hits Jacob in the face and he falters, losing control of his vortex and tumbling to the ground as the winds peter out. Joe gives a silent whoop and puts on a burst of speed, catching up to the others in front of the Black Goose.

"Jonny," Joe pants as he comes alongside his brother. "Can you cause an earthquake or a rockslide, something to slow Jacob down?"

Jonathon leans heavily on Matt's shoulder, the two of them doing an odd three-legged shamble as they try to continue moving forward. Matt's doing his best to pull Jonathon along the cobbled road, but Jonathon is still pale and weak from his recovery.

"You. Haven't. Called me. That in. Ages," Jonathon gasps. Sweat is pouring from his every orifice, and his knee is screaming in pain, as if it had been shot again. He wants to tell the others to drop him and continue on, but he also doesn't want to be left behind.

"It just slipped out," Joe ducks under Jonathon's other arm, and with Matt, lifts him completely off his feet as they follow Nell past the Black Goose, its sign squeaking in the wind. "Can you be a terramental and help me out now, though? Throw rocks at him or something?"

"My powers are gone," Jonathon squeaks as he tries to keep his feet clear of the ground, hopping along between Matt and Joe like some kind of odd stork.

"What?" Joe almost stops dead in his tracks.

"There's no time, guys!" Nell shouts as she points behind her. The trio looks back to see that Jordan has helped Jacob recover from his chamber pot facial, and the brothers are right on their tail. Jonathon finally clenches his core, lifting both legs fully off the ground, and the group starts dashing toward the Agate Bridge. They pass a startled newspaper vendor making his rounds and dodge around a laundry woman hauling clothes down to the Plebeum.

Night is lifted enough that the first rays of sunrise begin to illuminate the stone monstrosity before them. At each end of the bridge, Magistrate Rufus has installed mammoth gwarem statues, much bigger than the obelisks found in Low and Mid Tide. They stand as light-consuming giants, still carved in the complete bodily likeness of the Magistrate. The statues have their right hands raised, palms out, as if to say "stop." A creeping sensation crawls up Jonathon's spine as they pass the statues and continue onto the bridge.

"Out of the way, you idiots!"

Matt hauls Jonathon out of the path of a cart laden with cabbages as the driver yells at them. Even though it's early, the bridge is starting to fill with vendors making their way to the business district.

"Joe, there're too many people," Matt strains to be heard over the roar of Jacob's tornado. Joe glances about, seeing the cabbage cart reach the end of the bridge behind them. Two more laundry women start across on the far side, gossiping among themselves, oblivious to their surroundings. This is a mistake. Joe has lead Jacob straight into the heart of Eastport. He has brought doom on these unsuspecting people.

"Get off the bridge!" Joe yells to the laundry women, hoping they can hear him, or at least see the whirlwind bearing down. The women look up from their conversation. One of them shouts in surprise and drops her basket. Her companion quickly shoves her back off the bridge and they hurry away. Sighing in relief, Joe forges on, still needing to put distance between himself and his enraged brother.

A few steps ahead of him, Nell cries out, flinging an arm over her face as a wall of fire spreads across the bridge in front of her. She backs up into the trio, and as a group, they turn to see Jacob and Jordan at the entrance to the Agate Bridge. Jordan rotates his hand, and the wall of flame surrounds the group, trapping them.

34

agistrate Rufus stands alone in front of the tapestry behind his throne, studying it for the thousandth time. No matter how many times he ponders the weaving, it always reveals something new. The woven strands are quite a marvel themselves, shot through with streaks of gwarem. He finds their hidden shimmer soothing. Considering the stress he has been under, soothing is what he currently seeks.

He sent Bernard Lowain, wholly qualified Captain of the Wardens, to Port Green with the mission of setting the poison gas upon the elementals, killing them once and for all. It should have been foolproof. Gregor and his chemists had perfected the formula; it was tested on select elementals arrested previously and yielded outstanding results. Magistrate Rufus even gave Bernard the orb to ensure the plan could be enacted without any surprises. That was two days ago. Bernard should have returned, with Rufus' orb, by now. Instead, only a handful of Wardens came back from Port Green. If Captain Lowain was still alive, Rufus is certain he would have found a way to sail back to Eastport with the orb. Since there has been no word or sign of Bernard, Magistrate Rufus can only assume that he is dead, and that the orb is in Jacob's hands.

As he contemplates how best to proceed from this disadvantage, Gregor throws open the door to the throne room, coming to a stop by Rufus' side. Gregor stands at attention, waiting to be acknowledged.

"What now, Gregor?" Magistrate Rufus waves his hand lazily, indicating that Gregor should speak.

"Sir, there is trouble on the Agate Bridge."

"What kind of trouble?" the Magistrate asks, interest piqued.

Gregor nods at the window. "See for yourself."

In two steps, Magistrate Rufus is before the window, squinting out against the rising sun. Shading his eyes with his hand, he can make out several figures, and smoke? Yes, there is the dancing orange of fire in the middle of the bridge. And within that fire is Jacob.

"Gregor, ready my armor," the Magistrate demands through clenched teeth. "Seems that if I want something done right, I'll have to do it myself."

*　　　*　　　*　　　*

"Give me the orb, Joe." Jacob holds out his hand and motions for Jordan to cinch the fire closer to the group. Jordan hesitates, the fire already only three feet away from his brothers, but he eventually complies. Joe releases Jonathon and takes a small step backward. With a thrust of his arm, Joe sweeps up water from the swirling greenish mass of the Plebeum River below and douses Jordan's flames.

"Enough!" shouts Jacob as he flattens them all to the bridge, compressing the air above the group until they are thoroughly pinned down. Nell's on her back, eyes full of terror as she tries to lift her head. Stuck on his stomach, Matt's arm is pinned under Jonathon. Joe attempts to wiggle his fingers, anything to call forth more water from the river. But even the slightest movement is un-attainable with the weight of a ton of rocks pressing them into the stone of the Agate Bridge.

"I'm done playing games." Jacob confidently approaches, hand out, keeping them all pinned down. He towers over Joe, blocking out the peach-hued glare from the rising sun. With a sneer, Jacob bends down and retrieves the orb from Joe's pocket.

"Look out!" Jordan cries as a blast shatters the ground in front of Jacob.

Jacob looks up to find the mountainous Head Chemist training a pistol on all six of them. Jordan immediately raises his hand to throw a jet of fire, but another bullet ricochets off the bridge rail-ing, stopping him.

"I wouldn't if I were you." Cocking the hammer, Gregor, cov-ered in gwarem armor from the chest down, takes aim once more at Jacob. "Hands up where I can see them. Bring the orb to me. I won't miss again."

Jacob grimaces as he notices the Magistrate several yards be-hind Gregor at the foot of the Agate Bridge, decked out in similar gwarem armor. It's the first time Jacob has seen his uncle since The Expunging. He seems shorter than Jacob remembered. Less intimidating for a man who has caused so much harm to Jacob's people. How could it be that Jacob hasn't dethroned him yet? Teeth grinding, a wind subconsciously rises at Jacob's back. Final-ly, Jacob is face-to-face with his uncle, the man who killed his parents and stole his throne. All Jacob has to do is suction out all the air from Magistrate Rufus' lungs, or use a gale to slam him against the ground repeatedly, or send a gust to knock Gregor's pistol from his hands and use that to shoot his uncle, killing him without powers. Magistrate Rufus has most likely planned for an elemental attack, but would he be prepared for something as mundane as a bullet?

Jacob deliberates his options as he stares down his uncle, and slowly realizes that the Magistrate is not alone. Surrounding the Magistrate are three gaunt figures, black veins webbing their faces. From this distance, Jacob can just make out two men and one woman in tattered clothes, arm and leg bones poking against taut skin. The people aren't in uniform, so they mustn't be Wardens. The men and woman stare at Jacob with haunted white eyes and sunken cheeks under the black veins. They remind Jacob of the story his father told him once of the madaenko, a cannibalistic creature that prowled the forests of the Mersae Mountains.

"No time for heroics, dear Nephew," Magistrate Rufus calls out. "Hand the orb over to Gregor."

Quickly taking stock, Jacob notices that his uncle and Gregor are unguarded, save for the three odd people. There's not a Warden in sight, no gwarem weapons except for what Gregor himself is carrying. Puzzling for only a moment, Jacob strains his ears to pick up any indications of Wardens approaching. He catches a smattering of conversation coming from near the castle. It sounds like the Wardens on duty heard the pistol shots and are rousing to investigate. Time is running out.

Jacob sweeps his arm in front of him, creating a chokehold of wind around Gregor's head, the only part of his body unguarded by gwarem. Jacob then lifts Gregor into the air but is hit in the chest by a swirling disc of fire. Dropping Gregor, Jacob surrounds himself in a column of wind to extinguish the flames.

"Jordan!" Jacob accuses. But Jordan simply shakes his head.

"It wasn't me." He points at the three people next to Magistrate Rufus. The three pale figures raise their hands in unison, calling up discs of fire, wind, and stone from the Agate Bridge. The elementals launch their discs at Jacob and immediately call up more.

Jacob throws up a wall of solid air as Joe simultaneously draws a geyser from the Plebeum to meet the attack. Jonathon drags Matt and Nell down to the bridge as the stone disc crumbles against Jacob's wall. Joe manages to douse the fire disc while the wind disc repels harmlessly off of Gregor's gwarem armor and is lost. Jacob barely has time to process the sight before him, elementals attacking for Magistrate Rufus, before the next barrage is upon him.

Stone and fire rain down on the group, and wind blasts from the aeromental, sending the brothers stumbling. Gregor moves off to the railing, pistol dangling at his side as he watches his experiments with glee. They are performing much better than he expected. The hunger for another dose of Ink shines in the elementals eyes, and Gregor knows that this success is just the beginning. He spots a group of Wardens surging up from the castle, just yards away from the Magistrate, but Gregor holds up his hand, ordering them to halt. He wants to see how his elementals do first.

Jacob, Jordan, and Joe struggle to fight back. It's three on three, but their opponents don't seem to tire. Occasionally, one of Joe's water discs slams into the pyromental, but it barely seems to slow him down. The pyromental's flames douse and sputter out, but he merely shrugs it off and launches another attack. As quickly as Joe can counter, another fire disc flings his way. Meanwhile, Jordan focuses on the aeromental, trying to pen her in a cage of fire. Yet, the aeromental suffocates Jordan's flames as soon as he can make them. Jordan has never had to call up his powers this fast in all his life. Jacob attacks the terramental, blasting his stone discs out of the sky as soon as they are made. Sending gust after gust, Jacob tries to knock the terramental off his feet, but can't zero in on his attacker before needing to defend against a stone disc.

Jacob can feel his strength waning. The attacks are too frequent, and he can't maintain the upper hand. He sees Joe stumble, momentarily losing sight of the fire disc heading for him, and Jacob sends a gust of wind to flatten his youngest brother to the bridge, the fire disc narrowly avoiding Joe's head. Jordan's tiring fast as well, his flames reigniting a bit slower each time, the aeromental's wind discs pushing him closer to the bridge's edge. How long before he and his brothers falter?

No. Jacob hardens his resolve. *I didn't wait all these years and come all this way to be defeated.* With a roar, Jacob calls forth all the power within his core and throws his fiercest gale down the bridge at the Magistrate's elementals. They fly backward in the air sixty yards over the waiting Wardens' heads and crash hard against road beyond the bridge. The elementals land in a broken, unmoving heap.

Jacob immediately turns to Gregor and, with both hands, grabs him by the throat. He remembers the day that Gregor stormed into the council room with news of his mother's death fourteen years ago. He wished he had known back then the role both Gregor and his uncle had played in Queen Valencia's poisoning. It also dawns on Jacob that, being the Head Chemist, Gregor must have created the gas that killed half of the elementals on Port Green. It didn't matter that the Head Chemist had been acting on Magistrate Rufus' orders, and it no longer mattered to Jacob who he killed. If anyone was conspiring with his uncle, they deserved to die. Fingers tightening on Gregor's neck, Jacob longs to dig his nails in and rip out Gregor's throat. With a rage that's been building for years, Jacob instead slams Gregor against the bridge railing, once, twice. Gregor's pistol flies from his hand and lands at Nell's feet. Jacob slams Gregor against the railing once more before upending him into the Plebeum fifty feet below. Silence descends on the Agate Bridge.

Jonathon and Matt slowly raise their heads, surveying the damage. The bridge is pitted with holes, scorched stones steaming like early morning fog. Jonathon watches Jacob panting at the railing, awed that even without using his powers, Jacob is still a force to be reckoned with. Jordan sinks to his knees, trying to catch his breath.

Jonathon swivels and sees that Magistrate Rufus is alone and unguarded at the foot of the bridge, slowly making his way toward his nephews, armor ringing with each step. The Wardens are still some yards behind him, too stunned yet to move. An involuntary shudder arcs down Jonathon's spine at the sight of his uncle. He wishes he hadn't lost his powers, but Jonathon was never able to call them forth when his uncle hurt him. He had always been too afraid to act. Now, Jonathon wonders if Ink, if he had any, would help him feel brave and strong, even without his powers. Shrugging off the thought, Jonathon knows the Wardens will be on them soon. He, Joe, Matt, and Nell need to make haste.

A clicking sound draws Jonathon's attention. Nell holds Gregor's pistol and is training it on Jacob.

"Yes, good job, girl. Now shoot him!" Magistrate Rufus shouts as he advances further onto the bridge, a hungry gleam in his eyes with the orb so close to being in his possession once more.

Jacob immediately raises his hand again, ready to knock Nell over the bridge as well.

"No!" Joe yells, jumping in front of Nell. Matt and Jonathon also rush to her side, surrounding her in a semicircle with the railing at their backs, keeping an eye on both Jacob and the Magistrate.

"Stop, please!" Joe pleads with Jacob. "Here, just take it." He hands the orb over to his eldest brother.

Jacob hurriedly grabs the orb. He stares at this odd group before him, seeing how Joe guards Nell, how Jonathon clings to Matt's arm protectively. Here are his younger brothers, protecting humans. Humans were the reason Jacob had to flee Eastport. Humans were the reason he never got to ascend the throne. Humans were the reason that his mother and father were dead. And yet, Joe and Jonathon stand with these two humans. More so, these two humans stand with Joe and Jonathon. Maybe Jacob's mother was right, that humans and elementals can live peacefully with one another. It's a fleeting thought that Jacob finds he has no time to ponder. He looks up to see Magistrate Rufus only a yard away. The Wardens, now shaken from their stupor, start advancing from the foot of the bridge.

"Come on already, shoot him! By order of your Magistrate!" Spittle flies from Magistrate Rufus' mouth in anticipation of finally being rid of Jacob and touching the orb again.

Nell swivels the gun at the Magistrate, who stops a mere foot away from Jonathon. "You don't get to tell me what to do. And you," she swings back around to train the pistol on Jacob once more, hand shaking ever so slightly, "Don't even think about using your wind powers on me."

"Now, everyone, stay calm. We can talk this out," Jordan says softly, not wanting to startle any trigger fingers.

But the Magistrate is tired of waiting. His fingers twitch, itching to grab the orb from Jacob's palm. It is finally close to being in his possession once more. With the sun fully risen now, he can tell that the group before him is exhausted, dark circles under their eyes, standing upright only due to adrenaline. This is a moment Magistrate Rufus had never dreamed would come, the chance to take out all of his nephews at once.

"You think you're so special, don't you, Jacob." Magistrate Rufus pulls his nephew's attention while deftly reaching for the belt at his waist. Which one would be the best to target first? Killing Jacob now would be ideal, as he has always been Rufus' primary threat. But Joe, Jonathon, and those two sailors stand in between Rufus and Jacob. Jonathon is the closest of his nephews, and the weakest. He sags against the railing, panting. Jonathon was always so afraid, Rufus remembers. He would be easy to take out.

"You think you're owed this castle, this kingdom, this land, just because you are an elemental. That being an elemental makes all of this your birthright. But that's where you're wrong." Rufus takes another step forward, holding his hand behind his back. "You're owed nothing. Humans defeated your kind decades ago. This land is no longer yours. Elementals were too weak to hold it. Having powers does not make you the most powerful. In those regards, you're just like your father."

Jacob's brow furrows. "What do you mean by that?"

Magistrate Rufus advances another step, his Wardens striding ever closer to the group at the center of the bridge.

"Your father thought he was owed this land too. He thought that just because he was an elemental he was better than me. Oh, how he loved to torment me with his aeromental powers. I was so dismayed when your aeromental powers manifested, knowing you would turn out just like him. I was not wrong." Rufus' arm tenses as he takes one more step closer to Jonathon. "But in the end, it was your father who was weak. His aeromental powers didn't help him as I strung him up on the gallows, and they won't help you now!"

"Look out!" Nell shouts as Magistrate Rufus pulls a bronze-colored dagger from behind his back and advances on Jonathon's unsuspecting form.

Jacob flies over to his brother, pushing him to the ground as he greets his uncle's dagger with his gut. Grunting in surprise, Jacob watches with amazement as a crimson tide spreads across the front of his shirt. With a violent twist, the Magistrate rips the dagger from his stomach, letting Jacob crumple to the ground.

The screams come from everywhere at once, a cacophony of pain lifting into the wind.

"Jacob!"

A shot rings out, and the Magistrate falls to the ground, a perfect circle appearing on his forehead. Jacob, vision blurring, cranes his neck to see Nell, feet firmly planted, lowering Gregor's pistol. Jacob feels Jordan's fiery palms on his midriff trying to staunch the bleeding, but Jacob knows it's too late. Joe gapes, unable to comprehend what's just happened, while Matt gestures frantically at the Wardens running toward them.

"Why did you do that?" Jonathon whispers as he crawls to Jacob. Or maybe he shouted. Jacob can't really tell anymore. He reaches out and grips Jonathon's hand, pressing the orb into it.

Jacob tries to smile, hoping to convey to Jonathon the words that have always failed him.

A warmth spreads up from Jacob's middle as the world turns fuzzy and, finally, black. Muffled as if coming from underground, Jacob can hear voices, murmurs, but perhaps these are only sounds his mind is creating as they soon give way to a silent void. The warmth in his abdomen is painful now, like being stabbed by an angry crow. He tries to lift his hand to brush it away but realizes he can't feel his hand. Something was happening, something big. He did something, but he can't remember if it was to help or to harm. He can't remember anything anymore, but he's not sure he really cares as he feels himself begin to float. Ahead of him, he sees a pinprick of light. It grows larger and brighter as it comes closer. An imperceptible form reaches out from within, beckoning to Jacob. A soft voice, close to his ear, his father gathering him in his safe embrace.

"Welcome home."

35

oe sends a jet of frothy river water at the approaching Wardens, knocking them down onto the Agate Bridge. Trapping the Wardens in a bubble of water, Joe looks helplessly at Jacob, Jordan at his side trying desperately to close the visceral hole in Jacob's stomach. Joe has to do something to help, but if he releases his hold on the river, the Wardens will shoot them. Frantically spinning back to the Wardens, Joe realizes that the longer he holds them in the water bubble, the sooner they will drown. Does he want to add even more bodies to the list of those he's killed?

Jordan kneels at Jacob's side, the stone of the bridge grating against his knees as he tries to stop the blood seeping from his brother's gut. Jonathon sits next to him, dumbfounded, fiddling with an object in his hand. Grabbing Jonathon's shoulder, Matt nervously glances behind him. He catches Joe's eye. Despite what just happened, they need to get off this bridge. Joe can't hold the Wardens off forever, and more are sure to come.

"We have to leave now!" Nell says urgently, snapping every-one back to reality. She points to the far end of the bridge, down the road, and to the castle, where additional Wardens are advancing, drawing and aiming rifles at the group. The Magistrate was killed in front of the entire guard, and she's holding the smoking gun. Nell quickly shoves the pistol into her waistband and starts ushering the brothers and Matt onward.

Joe takes the hint. "Over the bridge. It's our quickest option," he commands as he grabs Jordan with one hand to pull him away from Jacob's body, straining under the effort of maintaining the water bubble around the Wardens. "Come on, we need to go."

"He...he can't just be dead," Jordan sniffs. Small flames still run over his palms, as if his powers are unsure whether he wants to explode in rage or silently smolder in sorrow. Jordan extinguishes his palms, wipes an arm across his face, and stands.

"Are you crazy?" Nell shouts. "We'd never survive that fall."

"Never say never. Trust me, I have a plan." Joe shoves Jordan toward the railing.

"We need to get Jacob." Jordan jerks away and stoops to pick up his fallen brother. "I won't leave him." He lugs Jacob over his shoulder, staggering under the weight, and turns to Joe.

Joe nods, then urges the group once more. "Jump over the railing. I'll make sure we make it down okay to the river."

Matt just shrugs and helps a frightened Jonathon to the railing. Jonathon locks his hands around Matt's waist as he contemplates the drop to the Plebeum below. He was in this same spot fourteen years ago, screaming for his little brother. The same brother Jonathon had accidentally thrown over this railing now wants him to willingly jump fifty feet to his death. Jonathon shakes his head. Joe said he had a plan. Jonathon has to trust him.

Nell looks nervously from the railing to the Wardens quickly gaining ground, then back to Joe. A week ago, she didn't even know Joe was an elemental. He was just some love-struck loony she took extreme pleasure in teasing. Now, Nell has no other option but to place her trust in an elemental, a hydromental no less. She just killed the Magistrate. What else is she to do? Gulping, Nell grips Joe's free hand in hers.

Nodding at his brothers and friends, Joe releases the water bubble, and the trapped Wardens splash onto the stones, gasping as their limbs twitch at the onslaught of oxygen. Joe hauls himself and Nell up onto the railing, balancing precariously on the edge as the rest of the Wardens bear down on them with rifles and cross-bows drawn. The wind plays about him, pulling at his jacket. Joe takes it as a sign from Jacob, and squeezing Nell's hand, steps off. He twists around to see Matt tumbling over the edge with Jonathon and Jordan leaning backward over the railing with Jacob's body until gravity takes them both.

All five of them rush the fifty feet to the river below just as the first rifle shots shatter the stone above them.

Joe flings out his hand, calling the Plebeum up to meet them. They fall a few feet before splashing down into a column of water as large as a longboat, sparkling in the sun. Jonathon's stomach flies to his throat at the sudden descent. He grips his fist tighter around the orb, not willing to lose this parting gift from Jacob. Tangled up with Matt, Jonathon struggles to find the surface of the water column, memories of drowning in the ocean as he escaped Eastport with Joe taking over his rational senses. Jonathon begins to sink, gulping for air but finding only water. Something grips his shoulders, and Jonathon can blearily make out Matt hauling him up to the surface as Joe rapidly lowers them to the river proper.

Jonathon's scream is cut short as the group slams into the Plebeum in a spray of blue-green water. Joe strains to bend the currents and gather his companions. Nell manages to grab Matt and Joe's own jacket as the river attempts to pry them apart. Joe hangs onto Jordan with his free hand, using the other to gather water to the group, keeping them together. Jordan is dazed, but clings to Jacob's body, red blood eddying against his back. With his brothers and friends bobbing next to him, Joe propels them rapidly downstream, away from the barrage of bullets raining down from the Wardens gathered at the bridge railing above.

They race along at an alarming pace, the swift-moving Plebeum not needing Joe's powers to push the group quickly downriver toward the Eusgarian Sea. Joe focuses all his efforts on holding everyone's heads above water and not crashing into boulders that spring up from the depths. He almost loses his concentration as they hit an eddy near the left bank. Circling his fingers, he draws the water tighter about the group, bringing them closer to himself. Abruptly, Joe then propels the group to the right in order to avoid a riverboat heading upstream, its paddlewheel churning determinedly against the current.

This odd human-made barge passes several startled fishermen lining the shore. Joe attempts an innocuous smile but refocuses on steering. He almost crashes everyone into a small pier extending out into the river, surprising a gaggle of boys playing marbles. The buildings on either side of the Plebeum grow denser as the group floats closer to the ocean. On the rocky bank ahead, Joe is blinded by a gleam reflecting off something metal on the shore. He thinks it might be a discarded pot, but as they pass by, Joe recognizes it as the gwarem armor of Gregor. He lies half out of the water, a deep gash oozing blood from his hairline. Sparing a peek at Jordan, Joe sees that his second oldest brother has latched onto Jacob's body like a squid. Jordan spits out river water as his lips move in what appears to be a silent prayer, unaware of the prone man lying on the shore. Joe gulps as they float past Gregor and are greeted by a downed tree spanning half of the Plebeum. He quickly shifts their course, the branches scrapping his shoulder as they spin away from the tree.

"You need to pay attention, Joe." Nell glares at him over the frothy water, struggling to keep her head clear of the river. "If you get us hung up on a tree or boulder and the Wardens catch us, we're done for." Joe nods his understanding. They were all fugitives now, standing there as Nell shot Magistrate Rufus. They needed to get out of Eastport. Joe had already been arrested once; he didn't want to be arrested again.

The buildings continue to rush by, citizens staring in wonder at the odd procession floating in their river. Several Wardens stop and stare, unaware that this group just killed the Magistrate, the news slower to flow than the currents of the Plebeum. The river widens as it comes to the mouth, the docks looming to the right. Squinting against the blinding sun bouncing off the waves, Joe makes out the *Moro*, still crashed against the wharf. Several ships down, he spies a patrol of Wardens making their daily rounds of the harbor. They'll notice the wrecked *Moro* and come to investigate soon enough. Joe and his brothers need to be gone before the Wardens get there. He angles their route to the ship, trying to figure out how he can use his powers to get the *Moro* seaworthy again.

"Joe," Nell sputters to get his attention. "Two of the longboats are gone." She jerks her head at the *Moro*, swallowing a gulp of seawater as she does. Joe scans the deck and sees that she's right.

The *Moro* itself is broken at the bow, and the hull is starting to sink beneath the waves. They won't be sailing the *Moro* anywhere. But there is one longboat left. Joe could work with that.

"Just get us close enough for me to scale the side to the remaining longboat. I'll lower it down," Nell offers, reading Joe's mind.

Joe brings them to a sloshy stop against the side of the *Moro*, hoping that the patrol of Wardens doesn't walk past just then. Nell scurries up the hull, finding handholds and toeholds in the barnacles studding the side. She works the ropes and lowers the remaining longboat to Joe eagerly awaiting below. Joe motions for Matt to climb in first.

Matt slithers aboard and reaches down to heave Jonathon over the side. Holding out his hand, Matt helps drag Jacob's body aboard. Jordan follows, sliding to the bottom of the longboat and clutching his knees to his chest as he stares blankly at his brother's body. Jonathon shivers from the swim, his fist cold from clenching the orb so tight. Jordan notices and calls forth a small flame to his palm that he holds out to Jonathon, who hovers over it gratefully. Joe clambers in and looks above for Nell.

He searches the deck as far as he can see, but Nell isn't there.

"Nell?" He calls out tentatively.

Matt gestures to him to be quiet, nervously looking at the wharf as the patrol of Wardens edge ever closer.

"Nell!" Joe whisper-shouts.

"Keep it down!" Matt shushes him. "If she's not here then she's not here. We need to go."

Joe looks up once more, hoping Nell is making her way down, but sees nothing. Dejected, he holds his hand out over the water, ready to call a wave to push them out to sea, as he knows Matt is right. A thud lands beside him, and he startles to see Nell removing and tossing a rucksack into the bottom of the longboat.

"What are you waiting for? Let's go!"

Joe needs no further prodding. The wave comes at his command, and they jet away into the Eusgarian Sea just as the patrol reaches the *Moro*.

36

The longboat bobs in the middle of the wide Eusgarian Sea. It is but a pinprick against the fathomless depths below, teeming with unknown life. Joe is exhausted, having sailed them from the harbor miles south toward Lexington. Flopping back, he closes his eyes and takes a few deep breaths.

Nell sways on the bench seat of the longboat as they bounce on the waves. She's thankful that the sea is calm for now, but worries that the clouds on the horizon could spell disaster should they gather into a storm. It's possible, she begrudgingly admits, that Joe could divert the worst of the rain around them and maybe still the seas should a storm break, but she doesn't want to place too much trust in his elemental powers just yet. Besides, Nell's not sure how much help he would be right now. His face is drenched in sweat from pushing them far away from Eastport, and it's all he can do to keep from sinking down into the bottom of the longboat and falling asleep.

Taking a look at the others, Nell realizes that none of the elementals are in any shape to think of a clear way out of this situation. Jonathon has squeezed himself next to Matt, who places a protective arm around him. Jordan stares unblinkingly at his brother's body, gripping Jacob's hands in his own, unwilling to let go. Their brother just died. They need time to grieve. But they aren't out of the woods yet. With the Magistrate dead, surely someone will be coming after them. They are sitting ducks out here in nothing but a longboat.

"I grabbed what I could from the *Moro*," Nell says to none of them in particular. "The elementals are all gone. I'm guessing it was them that took the other longboats. The captain and crew are gone as well. No clue what happened to them."

Matt nods in response, as if this was the only expected outcome. Jonathon cradles his hand to his chest, huddling next to Matt.

Nell reaches out to Jordan, who has Jacob's head propped up in his lap. With a damp torn-off shirt sleeve, Jordan is wiping the dirt and blood off of his brother. The dried blood is gummy and hard to remove, but Jordan is determined to wipe away the marker of death from Jacob's stomach. Jacob's skin has gone pale, and his limbs have begun to stiffen, but the creases on his forehead have relaxed, giving the appearance that Jacob is finally at peace.

"I brought some repair sailcloth." Nell pulls out the bolt of fabric to show Jordan. "I'm not sure of elemental customs, but I've helped with more than a few sea burials. If you want."

Jordan studies Nell's face and then looks at the sailcloth in her hands. Tears well up in his eyes as he reaches over to gather Nell in a hug. Startled, Nell almost pulls away, but she relents and hugs Jordan tightly in return. He sits back, wiping his nose on his sleeve, and nods. It's all too quick. Jacob's body lying there with a gaping hole in his stomach, blood and intestines and life flowing out. All that he could have been, just gone.

"Thank you," Jordan manages.

They clean him up as best they can in the small longboat and swaddle Jacob's body, awkwardly maneuvering about one another in the cramped space. Gently lowering Jacob to the sea, Joe pushes his body out a few yards and Jordan sets him ablaze as they send Jacob off. Standing wobblily in the longboat, Jordan gulps down his sorrow as he says Jacob's last rites.

"Today we honor Jacob Montavalo, aeromental," Jordan commences shakily. "He gave up his life to protect his family. He struggled endlessly to create a home for the elemental refugees on Port Green. He had dreams of a bright future for elementals in Eastport, our home that was lost. He strived to keep his promise of one day returning to Eastport, of making it a better place for all."

Jacob's body drifts further away, slowly sinking below the sea as the fire continues to reach toward the sky, setting Jacob's spirit free.

Jordan wipes away the tears that drip down his cheeks. "We give Jacob up to the four elements, air, fire, earth, water, and keep his name forever in our hearts." Jordan finishes by pounding his fist against his chest four times. Matt and Nell look at each other, unsure if they should partake in this custom. Matt turns to Joe, but he shrugs, eyes red. Joe has only seen this custom once before, after learning that his forced attack on Port Green killed three elementals. He didn't grow up with elementals; to partake seems almost an insult. But Jacob was his brother. That is a truth Joe can finally accept. This is his family. So he closes his eyes and pounds his fist to his chest four times as well, hoping he is doing right by his people.

Jonathon tremulously raises his fist and does the same as a sob escapes his chest. He begins to heave, trying to breathe. Matt places a comforting arm about his shoulders. Jacob took that dagger for him. And left him the orb. After all these years of hating his brother, Jonathon will never get a chance to make things right. Opening his palm, Jonathon gazes at the orb, tears dripping down his nose and landing on the opalescent surface, wishing that Jacob was still here. As his tears splash onto the orb, it pulses once and briefly flashes an image of what resembles Jacob's face. Jonathon cries out and drops the orb in the bottom of the longboat.

"What is it?" Joe asks.

"I swear I just saw Jacob looking at me through the orb," Jonathon points to the bottom of the boat.

Jordan crouches and grabs the orb, holding it up to the sky. He squints, turning it this way and that. Another pulse and the face resembling Jacob appears once more. Jordan's eyes widen, and he stuffs the orb into his pocket.

"Jordan? Who was that?" Joe questions.

Jordan sighs and runs a hand down his face, looking haggard with hairs coming loose from his ponytail. This is a position he never wanted to be in. Jacob was always in charge, always had the plan. Jordan was happy to simply follow along.

"That was our grandfather. Looks like we're going to Andulsae."

Epilogue

The old man slowly unfolds himself to his full height, taking time to first push up from the ground, pausing to stretch his back as he bends forward, hearing all the creaks and pops, before finally working his muscles loose enough to fully straighten. He shuffles his weight from his right foot to his left as he shakes feeling back into his legs, having sat cross-legged on top of this mountain for quite some time listening to the goings-on further south. The rich earth beneath his feet depresses as he stands.

He lifts his wizened face to the sky, the skin deeply tanned from so many days out in the high sun that never seems to sleep this far north. Surrounding him are the rocky tops of the Mersae Mountains, jagged teeth that give way to abundant valleys below the tree line. Taking a deep breath, he ponders over what he's just heard and decides the time is right to bring this news to the chief. Holding his hand out over the earth, he calls forth a cane made of stone and slowly hobbles down the rocky mountain path toward the village. The path is lined with monuments to the ancestors, each carved with a different elemental symbol. He bows his head at each he passes until the path levels out, and the surrounding terrain becomes green with life.

Closer to the village, he passes elementals harvesting bangerines from an orchard, all stopping to stare as the old man passes, for he has only come down from the top of the mountain once before in their memories, and that was when Queen Valencia and King Nils of Eastport died all those many years ago. The elementals put down their baskets and follow him, the strange procession picking up more people as they make their way through the village to the meeting hall.

Once there, the doors of the hall are held open for the old man to enter. He nods his thanks to those who have accompanied him and shuffles his way to the chief sitting on a stone throne at the back of the hall. The chief lifts his head from the orb in his hand. The old man bows low before his chief.

"Eastport has fallen. And they are coming."

Acknowledgements

Writing a book is no easy matter. This novel would not have come to fruition if not for the help and support of many people. Many thanks to my primary editor, Christian Loeffler, for taking a chance on this story and pushing me to make it the best it can be. Many thanks to Ben Fraley for his unwavering support and encouragement throughout the entire process. Thanks also to my parents, family, and friends, both near and far. And thanks to Feek, and thanks to The Dreiks; I owe you both a shout out!

ABBY LATTANZIO hails from central Illinois and has been writing since junior high, when she learned the stories in her head could become something more. She graduated from Northland College with a degree in writing and is a cellist in her local orchestra.

Abby has work published in Underwood Press, as well as several short stories published in Northland College's literary magazine. She is often found hiking, reading, watching *New Girl*, or crafting. She is also owned by two cats who barely tolerate each other.